A Gangster's Girl Saga

ALSO
BY
CHUNICHI

A Gangster's Girl

Married to the Game

The Naked Truth

A Gangster's Girl Saga

Chunichi

www.urbanbooks.net

Urban Books
1199 Straight Path
West Babylon, NY 11704

ISBN-13: 978-1-60162-024-8
ISBN-10: 1-60162-024-1

First Printing November 2007
Printed in the United States of America

10   9   8   7   6   5   4   3   2

Submit Wholesale Orders to:
Kensington Publishing Corp.
C/O Penguin Group (USA) Inc.
Attention: Order Processing
405 Murray Hill Parkway
East Rutherford, NJ 07073-2316
Phone: 1-800-526-0275
Fax: 1-800-227-9604

Dedication

This book is dedicated to everyone who has walked along my side during this long journey.

Acknowledgments

By now you all should know the routine; so here we go. First, I would like to thank God for brining me so far. In the beginning, I had had no idea God had such a huge blessing waiting for me. I was so appreciative and humble just for the opportunity to write one book; now look what He has done!

Thank you to my fans. Without you all there is no me. I appreciate all of the continuous support.

Shouts out to my literary family, Carl Weber, and Roy Glenn, The super agent, Marc Gerald, and my big sis, Nikki Turner. I am overjoyed with the idea of combining this series into one fantabulous book!

Thanks to my extended family and friends. All my girls back in the A, and the Nanston Naughty girls. Even though I'm gone, you guys are still showing support. Now that is real! NeNe and the Major Creations crew, thanks for keeping the head tight and books in rotation. You know it's that beauty salon gossip that really gets the word out! To my friends for life, Kicia, Tracey, Chele, Melanie, Sara, Toya, and Meisha thanks for being not only friends, but sisters. To my brother by another mother, Dante' Davis, thanks for being there no matter how bad I treat you. You know it's just the *girl* in me. Can't forget Stephanie, Tasha, and Sophie;

you girls are definitely one of a kind. To all my Jamaican massive, back home and in the U.S., Big up!

To my family, I give never ending thanks. I love you guys! Mom you're always by my side standing proud and telling everyone you know about the books. You still show the same excitement now as you showed with my very first release. Don't worry there will soon be a book you can tell your "church folk" to buy. ☺ Dad, thanks for making me the firecracker I am. To my baby bro, Vincent, forget those tacky hoes; your sister's the Urban Diva! Tell them to read The Saga. To my loving husband, Aron, I know I pluck the hell out of your nerves, yet you're always so patient and understanding. It takes a special man to deal with such a spoiled, divalicious chick such as myself. A girl couldn't ask for anything more. Smooches!

Ain't nothing changed, so finally the middle finger to all the haters!

Prologue

My name is Ceazia, pronounced *see-asia*, Devereaux. It's 12:15 a.m. and I've spent the entire day in bed crying. I'm only twenty-five, but I have experienced as much as a 40-year-old woman.

At age twenty-one, I was unstoppable. At five-feet-five inches tall, 125 pounds, measurements 36-26-40, size six shoes and the caramel skin of a newborn baby, I lived care-free in a three-bedroom condo overlooking Waterside in downtown Norfolk, Virginia. I felt on top of the world as I drove around town in my Lex coupe, labeled down in the latest Iceberg or Versace prints. Needless to say, I was hated by many and loved by few. But, that was my motivation. The more they hated, the more I flaunted.

My girls and I were the hottest chicks in the Tidewater area. Many knew of us, but not many actually knew us. They knew our names and faces, but that was about it. We were all "breeded beach girls." That's right, born and raised in Virginia Beach. We had the best of everything and never wanted for anything. Living with our parents, we were only expected to do well in school during the week and attend church on Sunday. As long as we followed those rules, the rest was whatever we wanted.

My dad was so furious about my decision to move out that he cut me off completely. He had plans for me to live at home until I got married, but the excitement of independence was just too much to bear. I had to move out.

I was quickly hit with a dose of reality when I decided to move out. Of course, I had a job and a comfortable savings, but that just wasn't enough to pay the price of being the shit! We had an image to maintain, and by all means, we were determined to do so and thus we began our female hustle.

We decided to start a little side business of our own. With the help of our close associate, Cash, we were on and popping in a matter of days. Who had any idea that one could work only two days a week and bring in two grand?

Chapter 1

Ceazia

The Beginning of the Hustle

It was my first day on the job, and I was nervous as shit. Although I wasn't sure if I would actually have the guts to go through with the date, I'd prepared very carefully for this day. I chose to wear my hair long and straight in order to accent the creep neckline of my black Versace dress. The dress was cute, yet classy, and my matching black sandals would add just the touch needed to emphasize my long, sexy legs. Of course, you know I had to splash on just enough Hypnotic Poison, my signature fragrance, to tickle the nose of those who passed by. I wasn't quite sure if I would have to drive, but in case that I did, I got my car detailed and pulled out my wide selection of CDs instead of the typical reggae selection that usually blasted from the Alpine system. I was planning to make an impression—a big impression.

As I entered the lobby, I straightened my dress and adjusted my cleavage. I took a deep breath to calm my nerves as I pressed the number eight on the elevator panel. *I can't do this. I just can't,* I thought as I contemplated turning around and returning home. There was no other option; either go on the date or be evicted. The more that realization set in, the more I hated my dad for cutting me off. I stepped off the elevator and walked into the very busy law office of Shaw, Glenn and Goldstein with my head high and breasts out. These were the best defense attorneys in town. They were notorious for defending all the big time drug dealers.

"Hello, my name is Ceazia Devereaux. I have a two o'clock appointment with Mr. Glenn," I said with a smile as I approached the receptionist's desk.

She advised me it would be a few moments, so I took a seat and glanced through the latest issue of *Vogue*.

After about five minutes, a nice-looking young man came in and sat next to me. "How ya doin'? I'm Vegas," he said, extending his hand and speaking in an arrogant, yet sexy tone.

He was cute, but just a little too confident, so I responded by saying, "Is that Vegas as in Las Vegas or Garcia Vegas?"

"What you know about Garcia Vegas?" he asked while laughing.

"More than you, I'm sure," I replied.

"Is that so?"

Somehow, one word led to another, and we found ourselves still conversing five minutes later when he was called into his lawyer's office. I watched as he walked away, sporting his Coogi jogging set and fresh, wheat-colored Tims. His hair was cut close and had enough waves to make you seasick. He must have felt my eyes on him, because right before entering the office he turned around.

"Yo, shortie, that phone on the table is for you. We're going out this evening. I'll hit cha later with the details." He winked, then hit me with the most mesmerizing smile.

Before I could come to my senses and give him one of my sarcastic responses that I'm known for, the door was closing behind him.

"Ms. Devereaux. Excuse me, Ms. Devereaux!"

I was so taken by Vegas that I didn't even hear the receptionist.

"Mr. Glenn will see you now."

I rose from where I had been sitting and advanced toward Mr. Glenn's office, but not before picking up my link to that fine, but cocky-ass specimen who had sparked my curiosity.

As I placed the phone inside my purse and walked toward his office, my stomach bubbled with fear. I entered the room and stood motionless, watching as he talked on his cell phone. The man before me was quite attractive in his navy Armani suit. He seemed to be in his mid-thirties. His skin was pale, hair was dark, and his eyes were green. He quickly wrapped up his phone call and gestured for me to have a seat. He suggested we stay in his office instead of going out for lunch.

I have to admit I was a little disappointed, especially since I hadn't had anything to eat all day. Just then, I noticed him closing the blinds, and I became even more nervous.

"Would you like a rum and Coke?" he asked.

I let out a thankful sigh. I could definitely use a drink. "Yes, please."

After two drinks and thirty minutes of idle chit chat, he was ready to get down to business. To be honest with you, so was I. His request was that I role-play as the wife of one of his clients. He wanted me to pretend we were discussing my husband's case and that he was threatening to quit in the middle of trial because he hadn't been paid. In what would be a desperate plea for him to stay on the case and clear my husband's name, I was to knock everything off his desk, climb on top, and start to masturbate, seducing him to the point that he would do what I wanted him to do.

After he finished explaining his fantasy, I stared at him with an incredulous look. *I can't do this,* I thought. *This is not me. I don't care how much I need the money. I just can't do this.*

As you may have already realized, I'm an escort, or at least I'm attempting to be an escort. This was my first assignment, and well, to be honest, I thought it would be easier.

Mr. Glenn must have noticed the hesitation on my face. He attempted to ease my fears by bringing up the subject of money. "Look, why don't I pay you first? How does a thousand dollars sound?"

"A thousand dollars?" I replied. The agency said I'd only get two hundred fifty and that I was going to have to split that with them. Needless to say, one thousand dollars in cash was a great motivator. With that incentive, I knocked all the shit off his desk and slowly climbed on top of it, spreading my legs and lifting my dress. I moved my hand slowly down my stomach and toward my panties. I threw my head back and closed my eyes, moving my fingers in tune with the slow rotation of my pelvis. The whole time, thoughts of that sexy-ass Vegas helped to get me in the mood. All I could picture was his waves and his pretty smile. As I moved my hand across my vagina, I imagined him caressing my body and kissing me softly.

After a while, it was as if Mr. Glenn wasn't even there. I moaned as my hand became moist with my juices. I continued to envision Vegas slowly kissing my thighs as I ran my fingers across the ocean of waves he had for hair. I could feel his moist tongue enter my poonani and him sucking my clit until I moaned with pleasure.

Just then, something jarred me from my private interlude with Vegas and back into reality. It was the sound of Mr. Glenn moaning along with me. My eyes opened wide with surprise. I have to admit, I was shocked beyond belief at the sight of him tugging and pulling on his little-ass penis until his load shot out and dripped on my stomach, signaling the end of our date.

I left in a hurry, feeling disgusted.

Once home, I adjusted the shower setting to steaming hot and scrubbed my body, trying to wash all the defilement down the drain. When I finished, I lay in my bed and cried myself to sleep. I'd never felt so dirty in my entire life. The shower may have cleansed my body, but it sure as hell hadn't cleansed my soul.

Chapter 2

The Life of Mr. Vegas

I was dreaming. Dreaming about that fine-ass Vegas I'd met earlier in the day. He was wining and dining me, taking away all the pain from the gruesome encounter with the lawyer.

Unfortunately, just when my dream was getting good, I was awakened by the shrill sound of my phone. I picked up, but only a dial tone greeted me. Then I heard it again, only the phone couldn't be ringing, because I was already holding it up to my ear. Now I was baffled.

What in the hell is going on? Am I still dreaming? I scratched my head, and then I realized what it was. It was the cell phone Vegas had given me at the lawyer's office. I scrambled over to my pocketbook and desperately emptied out my purse until I was holding the ringing phone.

"Hello, hello!" Damn! No answer.

However, that wasn't necessarily a bad thing. Although Vegas was cute and I desperately wanted to see him again, I didn't wanna seem pressed. And after looking at the mess on my bed, I realized that I had been a little too anxious to answer his call.

I decided to call my girl, Meikell, and tell her about my first day at the service. I didn't really wanna relive what happened, but she was probably gonna call me soon anyway.

"Hello," Meikell's tired voice said.

"What's up, Mickie?"

"Nothin'. Just chillin'. How'd everything go?"

"Horrible, but lucrative."

I told her every detail of my encounter, from the thousand-dollar decision I had to make to the degrading joint masturbation experience with the attorney. Just the thought of his sperm flying in the air made my stomach turn.

"Damn, girl, so now you officially a high-class ho."

Just as I began to respond to her, Vegas's cell phone rang again. This time I was determined to answer, so I ended my conversation with Meikell without as much as a goodbye.

"Hellllooo," I sang into the phone.

"Yo, *C!*"

This time I was on point with the sarcasm and responded with, "This is Ceazia. There's no *C* here. Who is this anyway?"

"Come on, now, you know who this is. That's why you sounding all sexy and shit, ma."

I don't know what it was about this nigga, but just the sound of his voice made me quiver. Give me a thug over a square any day.

"Look, I'm at the barbershop right now, but I'll be done 'bout seven o'clock. Why don't you pick me up at Granby and Twenty-Seventh around then?"

"You're joking, right?"

"What, you ain't got no car?"

"I was just about to ask you the same damn thing."

"This ain't about what I got. This is about if you gonna

pick me up or not. So, what up, ma? You gonna pick me up or what?"

"Okay," I said without resistance, and he hung up.

I thought to myself, *Okay? Okay? You couldn't have thought of a better response than okay? You could have at least played a little hard to get.* Any other nigga would have been shot down at the snap of a finger, but this wasn't just any ol' nigga. He was so damn thugged out, it was turning me on.

Sticking to my belief that first impressions make lasting impressions; I walked to my closet and pulled out the best. This time, I chose the newest Iceberg Snoopy print pants that were tight to perfection, and a matching fitted T-shirt. Like always, I wore matching boots with a Coach belt and bag.

It was a little breezy, so I grabbed a jean jacket to complete the ensemble. As I walked to the garage, I patted myself on the back for having gotten the car detailed earlier.

It was about quarter after seven when I arrived at Granby and Twenty-Seventh, located in one of the roughest neighborhoods of Norfolk. I parked directly in front of the barbershop, which was one of the six storefront shops of the mini-shopping complex. Like every shopping center in the hood, it consisted of a corner store, Chinese restaurant, barbershop, pager store, nail shop, and beauty supply store. Of course, fifty percent of the shops were owned by Asians.

There was much activity going on in the small shopping strip. Cars were playing loud music, an audience circled guys who were battling above the beats, and some guys just looked like they were up to no good, pacing and looking nervously back and forth.

I noticed an obviously young girl who looked terrible for her age asking a number of people for a dollar. After about five minutes of begging, I saw her approach one of the nervous guys, make an exchange, and scurry off like a little mouse. Call me naive, but it took a moment before it finally registered in my mind. The nervous men were drug dealers, and the young girl was a fiend.

Suddenly there was a knock on the door, and I almost jumped out of my seat. My hand went straight to my chest, as if to keep my heart from leaping out. When I nervously turned toward the knocking, I was relieved to see Vegas staring at me.

"What's up? You gonna open the door or what?"

"Oh my God, you scared me."

I unlocked the car and Vegas jumped in. Once inside, he directed me to an old house a couple of blocks away. The house was huge and looked as though it had at least five bedrooms. A long driveway led to a gated backyard. Parked in the driveway was a black Honda Accord with dark tinted windows and an older-modeled Maxima. I was silently praying that the Honda was his.

He quickly ran inside and emerged with a Neiman Marcus bag. "You's 'bout a size six, right?"

"Yeah."

"And a European shirt forty-two?"

"Uh-huh."

He tossed the bag on my lap nonchalantly. "Well, this is for you."

I opened it, peeking inside, and then smiled a smile so broad that it showed all thirty-two of my pearly whites. It was my favorite—Versace! He was definitely on the right track now.

I leaned over and kissed his cheek. "Thanks. You didn't have to do this."

"You right, I don't gotta do shit. I just wanted to." He smiled. "You hungry?"

"Yeah, I could eat something."

"Then why are we still sitting here? Drive." With a huge smile, he reached down and reclined his seat.

Dinner was great. We ate at a nice little low-key seafood restaurant down by the ocean front. We ate a candlelit dinner on the deck while admiring the stars and listening to the waves and the seagulls. It was so romantic, something I was not very accustomed to. After eating, he suggested we take a stroll along the beach, talk a little, and get to know each other better.

It seemed like he only got to know me, because I did most of the talking. I was surprised that he was truly interested in things that were important to me, like my goals, school, and work. I told him I graduated from high school as an honor student with an advanced studies diploma and that I attended Hampton University, where I received my degree in dental hygiene. He was pleased to learn that I had no kids and worked full time as a dental hygienist in a large dental clinic.

When it was his turn to share, he told me that he was the youngest of three boys. He also had no kids but wanted some eventually. He was born and raised in the streets of Norfolk, repping Park Place to the fullest.

"How did you get the name Vegas?"

"I used to be a big gambler," he explained. "After a few big wins, my friends started calling me Vegas. Plus, I was living the lifestyle like those flamboyant niggas from Las Vegas."

As we continued to talk, he said my chestnut eyes originally mesmerized him. Then, when he saw how snappy my attitude was and how curvaceous my body was, he knew he just had to have me by his side.

After about an hour on the beach, he asked if I wanted to stay at the ocean front for the night. At first I was hesitant, then I thought, *What the hell?* I didn't want to fuck up what may be a good thing by acting like Ms. Goody-Two-Shoes. Shit, I had done far worse before with people I didn't even like, so I agreed.

He chose the best hotel on the strip. He paid for the room and valet with no hesitation. Don't call him cheap.

Once inside the room, I took a seat in the small sitting area and flicked on the television while he showered. Emerging from the bathroom, he walked over to the Jacuzzi in the corner of the room, drew the water, and lowered his buck-naked ass inside.

I can't believe this guy, I thought as I admired his body through the mirrors surrounding the Jacuzzi. He had the build of a god! His ass and thighs were as firm as an NFL ballplayer's, his abs were rippled, and his man parts, well, let's just say, *Daaaaammmmn! It has got to be a crime!*

"Want to join me?" he asked. "You can wear your panties if you're uncomfortable about getting undressed."

With a dick like that, nigga, I'm getting in ass naked, I thought. "Okay, I'll be right in. You got to try to control yourself, though."

I undressed slowly as Vegas watched my every move in the mirrors. I was precise with each movement as I lifted my shirt and pulled down my pants. As I tempted Vegas with my tantalizing striptease, I could tell by the way he was licking his lips that he was enjoying the show. My breasts popped out with ease as I unsnapped my front closure bra. Because of the way his eyes were dilating, I was certain that Vegas was quite pleased with my physique. Lastly, I slowly removed my butterfly thong and began to walk toward the Jacuzzi. I could see Vegas's dick rise as I stepped into the water. Little did he know I was just as pleased as he was.

Chapter 3

Girls' Night Out

The next morning, I was awakened by the shining of the sun through the crack in the hotel curtains. I jumped up. "Oh shit! I'm gonna be late for work! Goddamn it! Vegas, wake up! Wake your ass up!"

He didn't budge, but that was his problem. I was the one driving, and if he didn't leave when I did, that was just too damn bad.

I searched frantically for my clothes as he slept like a log. Not able to locate my panties, I grabbed his underwear and threw them on along with my pants and shirt. Shit, guys had been stealing my panties for years.

Now, I know I was wrong for doing what I'm about to tell you, but I couldn't resist. Since he was sleeping so soundly, and since I was already going to be late for work, I decided to go through his pockets. A sistah's gotta know what she's dealing with, right?

Like most of the thugs I'd dealt with, Vegas didn't carry a wallet. I was able to locate his money rather quickly simply by digging deep. He had exactly thirty-five hundred dollars in one pocket and a little over a thousand in the other. As I continued my search, I came across a few phone numbers. One read *Kim*, then *Steeze*, and one was surrounded by little hearts and read *Jalisa*. I got a good laugh at that one as I ripped it up. I figured that he was pretty popular with the ladies, from the way his pager was blowing up every five minutes the night before. It eventually got to the point where he had to turn it off. My biggest concern was that he might have been married.

I came across his ID, which listed his name as Laymont Jackson, and Virginia Beach, Virginia as his place of residence. Now that was strange. I thought he was from Norfolk. Still, none of that was as confusing as his date of birth, which read September 17, 1980. At first I didn't pay it any mind, but then I realized he was younger than I was. That's when I started to do the math and counted the years in my head. *Oh, my God, this nigga is only eighteen years old.*

Just then, Vegas started to stir, so I quickly replaced the card inside his pants' pocket. Part of me wanted to confront him about his age, while the other part just wanted to have a good time, which was exactly what he had shown me.

"Yo, why you up so early?" he grumbled.

"Because some of us have jobs. I'm gonna be late for work."

"Fuck that shit. You wit' me. Chill out, lie back down, and get some rest." He rolled over, trying to get comfortable.

"Look, Vegas, I'm the only dental hygienist at a very busy dental clinic. I can't just stay home."

He rolled back over and stared at me. "How much do you make in a week, ma?"

"Not that it's any of your business, but I bring home about a thousand dollars a week," I lied.

"A'ight, I got you. Hand me my pants."

I did as he asked and was surprised when he pulled out the smaller roll of money, counted off ten hundred-dollar bills, and handed it to me like it was ten dollars. "Now come back to bed, a'ight?"

If I had known that was going to be the outcome, I would have told him I made twice as much. I called the office and used the excuse of a family emergency to get me out of a day of work. Then I returned to bed and to the comfort of Vegas's arms.

Two hours later, we were up and on our way to Norfolk. It was the day of the Rap Concert '99, so I was happy that I had decided to take the day off. That way I would have plenty of time to prepare for the show. During the entire ride to Norfolk, Vegas was on his cell phone.

As a subtle hint, I sang softly with Aaliyah, "Your loooove is a one in a million. It goes oooon and oooon and oooon."

The way he laid it on me the previous night was definitely what I would call some one-in-a-million loving. I must say, that was the best sex I'd ever had. And who would have ever imagined it would have come from an eighteen-year-old? He had all the characteristics of a grown-ass man, including dick, body, and mind. He actually had me screaming his name.

As I listened in on his cell phone conversation, I came to the conclusion that he was planning to have a meeting with this guy he referred to as Red. He also mentioned someone by the name of Martinez, but not a word was mentioned about going to the show that evening. I did wonder what all this "business meeting" stuff had to do with.

I drove Vegas to the same house we had stopped by the previous night.

Before getting out of the car, he gave me the number to

the cell phone he had given me at the attorney's office and told me it was mine to keep.

He also slapped another thousand dollars cash in my hand. "I know you're going to that show tonight and may need a little extra pocket change."

I gave him a small peck on the lips before he got out. I watched him walk toward the house. "Damn! That's a fine-ass nigga."

When I pulled off, I immediately called my girl, Dee Dee, and made a hair appointment. I knew she would be booked up because she was the hottest stylist in the Tide-water area. She even did cornrows for all the niggas around town. Somehow she managed to squeeze me in.

Then I called my girls to find out what the plans were for the night. I started with Tionna and then called Mickie and Carmin. The four of us always rolled together, though at times our clique could get as deep as eight girls. We all agreed to meet at Carmin's house at seven. That would give me enough time to get my hair done and purchase an out-fit.

After my do was done, I hit the mall. I was able to find an outfit and get my nails done in record-breaking time.

I rushed to Carmin's house. Although Carmin was pure Italian, she was the blackest chick I knew. Her name should've been Tameka. She was knowledgeable in all the latest fash-ion and had majored in international design. She did free-lance design for a number of artists and lived the life that many only dreamed of having. She knew all the hottest stars, went to all the celebrity parties, and even screwed a few of them too.

During her ideal life, Carmin had fallen hard for a new artist on the charts. The only problem was, he was in a relationship and had no intentions of leaving his girl. He claimed he loved her, but at the same time, he just couldn't stay away from Carmin. When he would go on tour to places like Europe, he would take her along. He kept her laced in the finest fashions and even purchased her a Lexus SUV. Still, he stressed to her that he was not her man. That's the kind of shit that makes you wonder. You give a man your all—sex, head, and love—and he can't give you any type of commitment in return. And to make matters worse, he has the nerve to be possessive. If he even thought Carmin was letting another nigga hit that, he would snap. But if Carmin saw him with his girl, she had better not even think about cutting her eyes wrong, or there would be problems.

Carmin was one of the wildest, coolest, funniest people you could meet. She had a gorgeous body with a waist and hips like Beyoncé Knowles. She didn't have to put up with being second if she didn't want to. Not to mention, she was voted MVP of the group when it came to giving head. With those qualifications, she could've had any man on the entire East Coast.

Her two-bedroom apartment screamed her name. To most people, it would resemble a *Trading Spaces* project gone bad, but I thought it was the shit. She had a twist between eclectic and vintage furniture. Against the wall sat an old leather couch. It was a rust color with metal button accents around the arm. On her mantle were blown glass vases in cobalt blue and orange that held huge sunflowers. Her walls were bordered with pages from the latest fashion magazines. And my most favorite decorative piece of all was the portrait of Marilyn Monroe that hung on her living room wall.

Soon, everyone had arrived and we decided to have a couple of drinks, put on some Lil' Kim, the Queen Bitch, for some girl power, and spark one. The mixture of apple martinis, hydro, and the lyrics of No Time put us in the mindset we needed for the night to come.

Tionna, the title holder for doggie style, was the comedian of the group. Our friends could always count on me to come in and form a comical tag team with Tionna. She drove a cute little bubble Camry that we often joked with her about. Not that anything was wrong with it, because her shit was paid for, but it was just so funny when the rest of us had such elaborate cars. To understand the car, you must understand Tionna. Born and raised in New York, she never learned how to drive. We had just recently taught her to drive, and the Camry was her first choice for a car. Tionna was also the penny pincher of the group. Now don't get me wrong, she had just as much loot as any of us, if not more, but the bitch was just so damn cheap.

After our drinks, we were ready to get dressed. We all put on our best because we knew the world would be watching. For some reason, all eyes of the area were always on us. It was four of us total, so we had to decide which cars to drive. We pretty much knew we could rule out Tionna's ride. We decided that Carmin would drive her Lex, that way we all could roll together.

Once we hit the coliseum, it was on! Niggas were everywhere, and every single one of them was flaunting their jewels, cars, clothes, and women.

"You have to be careful," Tionna quickly reminded me, "because if you don't, you could be fooled by the once-a-year show outfit."

She was referring to the girls who didn't really have it the way that they would like to have you believe, but instead spent their whole welfare check on an outfit and accessories so they could be jiggie for the show. But catch them the next week and they were straight up "Reebok broads."

Once we found a space, Carmin parked the truck and we headed for the doors. It seemed like we would never get there. We walked briskly as the wind whipped through our little outfits.

Standing in line was out of the question, so we did like always did and politely said, "Excuse me," to each person until we reached the front. We acted as though we were shareholders of the establishment.

It's amazing how each person stepped aside without hesitation. After three minutes of waiting, we were in and headed straight to the bathroom. Afterward, we headed to the arena floor to check out the scene.

At every show there were your chickens, whores and hood rats, all trying to get backstage. There was no question we would get back there, though. Carmin already had things on lock.

We headed directly to the back and Carmin whispered in the security guard's ear. "Scratch my back and I'll scratch yours."

Instantly, we were in. It's crazy how one simple phrase and a little sex appeal can go so far with men. As we watched the show from backstage, a couple of the artists started conversing with us. After a few minutes of chatting, they were ready to chill.

"Yo, y'all mad cool. Wanna smoke one?" one of the guys asked.

Wanting to be social, but at the same time not trusting any nigga, I responded by saying, "Yeah, we can spark one, but we'll roll our own shit."

They thought my response was real funny but decided to smoke with us anyway. We meditated on the herb for a while then decided to leave.

Before we left, though, I noticed Mickie and one of the guys exchanging numbers. I wondered why she would even waste her time, like there was any chance of them actually hooking up.

After a while, we made our exit. The spot to hang after the club was always Fat Danny's Soul Food Restaurant, so that's where we headed. Again, we walked right in and sat down, bypassing the line. This time things didn't go as smoothly, though.

We were only sitting for forty-five seconds before this terrible looking hood rat came over and said, "Hey, we've been waiting here for thirty minutes and y'all just walked in and took our seat!"

We all just looked at her and busted out laughing.

"I bet your ass won't be laughing if I smack the shit out one of y'all bitches!"

Mickie stood up face to face with the girl. "If you see a bitch, smack a bitch!"

The girl wasn't about to back down. "Cross this line, bitch." She drew an imaginary line with her foot.

Mickie and I both looked at each other from the corner of our eyes to give a silent signal for attack.

We both launched on her ass simultaneously.

Immediately, her girls ran over to her rescue, but they got the same beatdown as she did. Out of nowhere Tionna produced a blade.

After a minute, blood was everywhere and we were out.

We headed straight to Carmin's.

Once in the car, Mickie counted off, "One . . . two . . . three!"

"Friends are forever!" we all shouted together.

On the ride to Carmin's, Mickie received a phone call from Cash, the manager of the escort agency we worked for.

"I need you for a job. Where you at, yo?" I could hear him yelling through the phone.

"I'm coming through the tunnel. Meet me at Ocean View."

We agreed we would never do spur-of-the-moment jobs, but for some reason, Mickie agreed. I didn't know about anyone else, but I found that quite shady. Still, we dropped her off and continued on to Carmin's. Later, we found out she was so eager because Cash had arranged a date for her with the rapper from the show.

When we got to Carmin's house, my cell phone rang. It was Vegas. I was surprised to hear from him so late.

"How was your night?" he asked.

"It was all right."

"That's it, just all right? From what I hear you had a pretty exciting night."

"What are you talking about, Vegas?" I asked, annoyed at the little game he was playing.

That's when he went on to tell me all about my night. I mean, he knew everything from what I had on, to us smoking with the rappers, to us fighting. I couldn't figure out how in the hell he knew this shit.

I know this nigga ain't psycho enough to follow me. Not wanting to get into it with him while my girls were within earshot, and much too tired to argue, I decided it would be best just to end the call and deal with him later. "We're at Carmin's, and I'm really tired. I'll holla at you in the morning."

"A'ight," he said, leaving me to stare at the phone in wonderment.

Chapter 4

Mickie's Hustle

A couple of months passed, and things between Vegas and me grew. Things were moving really fast. Vegas moved in with me and we planned to purchase a house the following year. We had plenty of room in my crib, but he still wanted a house. Really, the only thing he could complain about was the garage. He had two cars of his own, plus my car, and my garage was only equipped for two. Not that it mattered, because his brothers were always driving one of his cars anyway. Speaking of cars, I was happy to learn that neither of those cars parked in the driveway of that big old house in Norfolk belonged to him. Vegas drove an Acura coupe for daily activities and his big boy Escalade for night excursions. Damn, that truck was tight! It turned me on from the first time I saw it. It was pearl white with mirror tint and twenty-two-inch rims. The inside was equipped with five TVs, one in the deck, one in each visor, and one in each headrest. Of course, there was also a DVD player and PlayStation attached. The interior had upholstery made of beige leather. I swear, if that truck had a dick, I would have fucked it. Needless to say, that truck was his pride and joy.

Since it had been declared that I was officially Vegas's girl, a lot of things had to change. The first and most major was the escort job was out the door. There was no way his girl would be doing something like that. I had no problem giving that degrading experience up, though. Vegas had the best of everything, so he made sure I had it too. But the closer we became, the more Meikell and I separated.

Meikell seemed to think all the luxuries went to my head, and that's what eventually forced us apart. On the other hand, I thought she had become too involved with the side job and had changed herself. To her, it was no longer a side job, but her way of life. In fact, she quit her job as a director at a franchise daycare to escort full time. She talked, walked, looked and acted like a cheap whore. She wore wigs of every color, talked with ebonics slang, and dressed very distastefully. Cash was no longer just providing protection and setting up dates. He was now playing the role of her pimp. He had her fucking anything, including women, for little or nothing. The thought crossed my mind that she may have even been strung out. Word on the street was when she wasn't hooking, she was at the strip club trying to make a dollar.

I decided to have a heart-to-heart talk with her. She was my friend, and I wasn't going to idly stand by and watch her destroy herself.

"Yes, Mrs. Vegas," Mickie answered.

"Mickie, I know things have been rough between us the last couple of weeks, but I'm calling to speak to you about the situation."

"Okay, so speak."

I knew Meikell was not going to make this easy for me, but I wasn't going to give up yet.

"Mickie, you really need to stop doing the side job."

"And why is that, Mrs. Vegas? Just because your life is so perfect now and you have all the things you want, you think you're better than me? Did you forget you were doing the exact same thing not so long ago? I'm sorry, *C*, but I'm not as fortunate as you are. I have to work for mine. Besides, it's not much different from what you're doing. I mean, you fuck Vegas, don't you?"

"You know what? I was actually trying to help your ass out, but you're obviously jealous of me. So do you. And just so that you know, niggas on the streets are saying you're hooking and stripping and all for small change."

"So what? Fuck those niggas and fuck you too." *Click.*

I couldn't understand Mickie. Hooking and stripping? And where was the money going? She had the same crib, same car and same clothes. At least I cared enough to say something. Everyone else was just disassociating themselves from her. But after that last note, I was joining the disassociation group my damn self.

One day me and Vegas were in the mall and out of nowhere this ghetto-ass park chick comes behind us yelling, "Your son here! I know you hear me. Yo' son here!"

Vegas just kept walking, looking straight ahead as if he didn't even hear her. I had to see who the fuck this chick was just in case I was out one day and something jumped off. You just never know with those park bitches.

The more he ignored her, the more ghetto and louder she got. Vegas wasn't the type that liked drama, so he decided we should just leave.

Of course, she followed right behind us. When we got to the car, she got in his face and said it again.

"I ain't got a damn son," he said back to her calmly.

Then he stepped around her and closed the door to the truck.

She stood there yelling in the middle of the mall parking lot, looking like a damn fool.

I folded my arms, rolled my eyes, and grinned in her face as we pulled off. But by no means was that the end of it. I had a thousand and one questions that I needed answers.

"Your son? Your son? What the fuck was that about?"

"She's a chick I was screwing while I was with my ex-girlfriend," he explained. "When I tried to cut things off, the bitch cried pregnant. So, to shut her up, I gave her five hundred dollars to get an abortion. More than likely, she used the money to buy a new outfit. Mainly, those park bitches are only after the money. Now, months later, she's hollering some shit 'bout the baby being here. I haven't even spoken to her since the day I gave her the money."

"Yeah, well, time will definitely tell. Just as time told that your ass lied about having no kids. When we first met, you told me you didn't have any children. The next thing I know, you got three."

Vegas just glanced over at me with that dumb-ass blank expression.

"And now it's turned to three and a fucking possible!"

He stared at the street and shook his head as he exhaled heavily.

When I'd first found out about the other three kids, he said he didn't tell me about his oldest because he didn't think the kid was his. He never had a blood test. He just took the responsibility. And the other two lived in DC, so he thought I would never find out. He said that his reason for not telling me that he had kids was because I didn't have any and that I seemed like the type who wasn't trying to be bothered with no baby-momma bullshit. And his ass was right!

"And why do you have a Virginia Beach address listed on your ID?"

Finally, he opened his mouth. "I lived there with my kids' mother and when I left her, she packed up and moved to DC with her family," he said, with a pitiful-ass look on his face.

Chapter 5

A Sister's Deceit

It was September 17 and Vegas's birthday. I swung by to pick up Tionna and her little sister, Tonya, and then we headed to the mall. I purchased Vegas a Versace sweater, Versace jeans and some Durangos. It didn't take me long to figure out what he liked when it came to style. His taste was similar to mine. I guess that was just another reason why we were such a good match.

While out, Tionna bought her sister a few things.

Tonya had been living with Tionna for a few months now. Tionna decided to take her in after their abusive aunt damn near beat Tonya to death. One night, she came in pissy drunk and accused Tonya of sleeping with her husband. Tonya responded, "Maybe if you weren't drunk all the damn time, you'd be fucking your man and wouldn't be worried about me fucking him."

The aunt beat Tonya until she was delirious. She beat Tonya with anything she could get her hands on, not to mention all the punches and kicks that were included in that beating as well.

By the time the police arrived, Tonya was unconscious and literally near death.

Of course, after that incident Tonya had to move out of her aunt's home, but there was no place else for her to go. Their mother was serving a life sentence for murder, and their father was nowhere to be found. Their grandmother was already raising their younger sister and brother, so there really was no room for Tonya in her home, either.

Tionna and her boyfriend, Shawn, were the happiest couple I knew. They had their ups and downs, but that's what made their relationship so strong. When Tionna met Shawn, he was in the Marine Corps and quite demanding. After a night out with the fellas, he would come home drunk and start drama. He never hit Tionna, but he would do much damage around the house. Although he didn't physically hurt her, he would verbally abuse her by calling her all sorts of names. His acts of rage got so bad that Tionna began to question if he was on drugs. After investigating, she found it to be true.

Tionna was furious when she learned that Shawn was occasionally sniffing heroin. She immediately kicked him out. Afraid of losing her, Shawn begged for forgiveness and asked her to help him. Not wanting to ignore his cry for help, Tionna got him into an inpatient rehabilitation center. While in rehab, he began to explore the Muslim faith. It was as if he became a completely different person. He was much calmer and more sincere. His whole demeanor changed. He was just a humble man overall. Witnessing the change, Tionna decided to stick by him, and they made it through that difficult time together.

After shopping, Tonya seemed to be in a rush to get home, so we dropped her off, and then Tionna and I headed to the twins' house.

* * *

India and Asia were new to the circle of friends, but no one would have ever known. They were both account executives at major banks in the area, and they both screwed their way up the corporate ladder to get those positions. Contrary to the way they were now living, they were raised as perfect Christian girls. Their father was a pastor, and they had attended Christian schools. They still lived at home, but were no longer those perfect twins that Daddy raised.

Asia had twins out of wedlock and was currently dating a married man. India was a player in the cash exchange for all the major drug imports into the East Coast of the U.S. Her fiancé was a kingpin out of Kingston, Jamaica. This guy was honestly the craziest muthafucker I ever met. He had a tall, fragile frame, with dark skin, and eyes as cold as ice. He spoke with a deep voice and strong accent. Each time I saw him, I froze up with fear. He had India under some sort of trance, but no one realized it except me. With my Creole background, I noticed the power of voodoo very quickly. At times, it was as though India wasn't even herself.

India was planning to move and join her fiancé in Jamaica the following year. He told her that by then he would have reached his $2.5 million mark and would be ready to retire.

The drug ring that her fiancé operated had been passed on in his family from generation to generation. However, with that title came a lot of other shit that I didn't think India even knew about.

I'd learned from firsthand experience. The guy Red, who Vegas dealt with, was part of the Dominican drug ring. I'd seen this guy fly to the States just to kill a nigga. He even had a little ninety-pound chick that he would send at times to do the job for him. The shit was wild, and I definitely didn't want any parts of it.

* * *

As we sat and tripped out with the twins, Tionna's phone rang. It was her sister's boyfriend. I could hear him yelling into the phone, "Tonya had an accident! Get to the house quick!"

We dropped everything and drove to her apartment in record time.

"Toooonyaaaaa!" Tionna screamed as she burst through the door, but there was no answer.

Tonya's clothes were strewn all over the living room floor and loud music was coming from the direction of her bedroom.

Tionna twisted the doorknob, but the bedroom door was locked. Out of panic, she busted the door down and there was Tonya, completely naked, and she wasn't alone. Tionna's man was in there with her.

It was terrible. Tionna's face was filled with hurt and anger. She stood motionless, screaming as I rushed over to hold her. She resisted my hold and began to fight frantically as a half-naked Shawn approached her.

I immediately pulled her from the house and into the car. This was truly a sad day for both of us.

Once Tionna calmed down, I took her back to my condo. I tried everything to make her feel better, but after such a traumatic experience, I knew it would be a long time before she healed. She had lost two people that meant the world to her. As we were talking about the situation, Tionna received another call from Tonya's boyfriend.

"Is Tonya okay?"

Tionna wasn't sure how to break the news to him. "Exactly what happened to make you think Tonya was hurt?"

"I got a call, but when I answered, no one spoke," he explained. "I heard a lot of commotion in the background, though. I recognized Tonya's number, so I kept listening.

There was a lot of tussling and moaning, like some kind of struggle. I started calling Tonya's name to see if she could answer me, but there was no response. I hung up and called back from my cell phone, but I just got a busy signal. I was afraid Tonya was hurt and just couldn't get to the phone. That's when I called you. I knew you could get there faster than me."

Tionna probed further to see if there was anything else Tonya's boyfriend could add to make the situation clearer. Unfortunately, there was not. She would never know what really happened.

As Tionna and I resumed talking, Vegas walked in. "What's up, baby?" he said as he kissed me on the lips.

"Nothing, honey. Just comforting Tionna."

"What's the deal, *T*? No jokes today?"

"Nah, not today. I'm not in the mood, Vegas," Tionna responded in a daze.

"Damn, we can't have that. Why don't you ladies come with me? I'm gonna take y'all out. We can go to this spot on the oceanfront. I got one quick stop to make on the way, though. Is that cool?"

"I don't know. I'm not really in the mood to be social," Tionna said.

"Aw, come on, you need to get out," I said. "Not to sound insensitive, but sitting around harping on the situation is not gonna make it any better. I know how hard it must be to cope with something like this, but putting yourself in an upbeat environment may be just what you need. If you don't feel any better once we get to where we're going, I'll have Vegas drop us back off."

After I finally got her to agree to come along, we all hopped in the truck and headed toward the downtown tunnel.

"Where we headed, baby?" It looked like we were going

to Portsmouth, but Vegas hated Portsmouth. He would always warn me to stay out of Portsmouth because that's where the grimiest niggas lay.

"I gotta meet my man real quick at the . . . umm . . . strip joint," Vegas said hesitantly.

"The strip joint?"

"Yeah, baby, don't trip. It'll only be a minute," he said as we pulled in the parking lot.

"Whatever! And your ass got exactly one minute too," I yelled as he was shutting the door.

After ten minutes, Vegas still wasn't back. I decided to go in after him. "I'm going to get his ass, *T.* You comin'?"

"I guess I better go, just in case you start wildin' on a bitch."

We climbed out of the truck and headed in. The club was dark and smoky and sounds of Luke came blasting from the speakers. The DJ announced each girl as she entered the center stage. The girls danced, crawled, and climbed the pole, while guys threw dollar after dollar on the stage. I searched and searched, but I didn't see Vegas anywhere.

Since he was so popular, though, I knew all I had to do was ask just one person in the establishment and they would tell me where he was. "Excuse me, do you know Vegas?" I asked the bartender as I approached the bar.

"Yeah, he was just with Martinez. Hold on, I'll get Martinez to take you to him."

Martinez? I remembered hearing Vegas refer to a friend of his by the name of Martinez quite often, but I never met him. I was pretty certain this was the same guy, though.

The bartender finished serving a drink, and then shouted to a guy in the corner who was speaking to a nicely built female. "Yo, Martinez!"

The guy walked over to the end of the bar, and they

began to exchange words. As they were speaking, Tionna and I walked toward them. The closer we got, the more familiar the guy looked.

"Oh, shit. What the hell y'all doing here?" Cash asked nervously.

"I'm looking for Vegas. So you're the infamous Martinez, huh? I had no idea. You do know that Vegas is my man, right? So, Cash, why does everyone else call you Martinez?"

"It's a long story, ma. Follow me. He's right in here speaking with my man."

We followed Cash to a room labeled VIP. In no way was I ready for the sight before me when he opened the door and we stepped inside.

"What the hell are you doing?" I yelled.

Tionna's mouth dropped to the floor as we watched this trick suck dick in front of a group of men. She was oblivious to our presence as she continued to suck and stroke this guy. As she was going down on the one guy, another was smacking her ass from behind.

I couldn't stand there and watch any longer, so I walked over and snatched her by her head. "What the fuck are you doing, Mickie? Get the fuck up!"

"What the fuck you doin', shortie? We paid for this shit. What the deal? Are you trying to take over?"

One guy actually had the audacity to grab my ass.

At that point, Tionna and I both lost it, but before we could react, I heard a sound that resembled the cocking of a gun.

Click, click!

The sound was enough to make everyone freeze. It was Vegas, and he had his gun to the guy's head.

"You got a problem with your hands, man?"

The guy pleaded with Vegas, "Nah, Vegas. Man, I ain't

know that was your girl, man. I'm sorry, man. You know I wouldn't disrespect you like that."

"Not only did you disrespect me, but you disrespected my girl. I think you owe her an apology," Vegas calmly responded.

The guy turned toward me with tears in his eyes. "I'm sorry, miss. I'm sorry. Please forgive me."

"His life is in your hands, baby," Vegas turned to me and said. "Do you forgive him? If not, he got to go. So, what's it going to be?"

I couldn't just stand there and let Vegas kill the guy simply because he touched my ass. I mean, what he had done was disrespectful, no doubt, but I would live.

I eyed the nigga up and down as if he wasn't even worth the bullet. "I forgive him, Vegas. Let him go."

Vegas lowered the gun.

As the guy ran for his life, the front of his pants clearly showed how frightened he was. I looked over at Mickie as she grabbed her clothes and ran to the dressing room. Tionna and I followed closely behind.

"Mickie, why are you doing this? You are too good for this. You don't have to stoop to this level," I said.

"Yes, I do." Meikell began to cry. "I don't have it as easy as you, *C.* I have to do this to maintain. I wish I didn't, but I do."

Tionna and I both hugged her as she continued to cry. There was no need to say anything more.

"You ladies ready?" Vegas yelled from the dressing room door.

"Yes, baby, we'll be right out."

We told Mickie we loved her and that we were sorry for isolating her. We hoped she would forgive us and that we would hear from her soon.

The ride home was rough. Once again, I had a thousand questions for Vegas.

"Why didn't you tell me you knew Cash?"

"You never asked."

"So why haven't I ever met him? I mean, you always talk about him, but you never bring him around.

"You know I don't bring business to the house, Ceazia."

I could tell by his tone that my many questions were starting to annoy him, but that didn't stop me.

"So why did you have to meet at the strip club? Do you meet him there all the time?

"No, I don't. I meet him wherever he's at when I call."

"So why when I came in there you weren't with him? If y'all were doing business, shouldn't y'all have been together?"

"Ceazia, if I was up to some shit, I would not have even brought y'all along. Damn, I was talking to Red about some shit that didn't involve Martinez, so we asked the nigga to step out. You don't know anything about the game, so please stop questioning me about how I run my shit."

"He's got a point, *C.* Cut him a break. Like he said, he was just handling his business," Tionna said from the back seat.

If I had been smart, I would have taken the advice of my friend and ended the conversation there, but I just couldn't. I needed more answers. "Well, why didn't you tell me Mickie be up there doin' shit like that? I'm sure you knew, since you're so close to Cash.

Vegas's nose flared as took a deep breath. "*C,* you're getting on my fucking nerves with all these damn questions. I can't know that man's hustle. That'll be like him trying to tell me who to sell my shit to. Shit, Meikell is a grown-ass woman. Maybe if you would mind your damn business y'all wouldn't be beefin' now."

Smack! "Who the fuck you talkin' to?" I yelled at him.

Skuuuuuuuurrrrrrrr! The screeching of the truck's brakes was the last thing I heard before Vegas grabbed me by the back of my neck. "Bitch, I don't put my fucking hands on you, and I expect the same respect from your ass!"

"Okay, Vegas, I think you made your point. Let her go." Tionna pulled on his arm, trying to loosen his grip.

When he released his hold, I began to cry hysterically. I couldn't believe he put his hands on me. Needless to say, we didn't go out that night, and the rest of the ride home was silent.

A few minutes later we arrived at Tionna's apartment. Still a bit shaken, I stepped out of the truck to give her a hug. "I love you, girl. Keep your head up," I told her before kissing her cheek.

"I love you, too, and you do the same. From the looks of things, we're gonna need a 'waiting to exhale' party," Tionna said with a small grin.

I gave her a slight smile in return as I climbed back into the truck.

When I got home I received a call from Tionna. She briefed me on the events that occurred after we'd dropped her off.

When she entered her apartment, she immediately noticed that Tonya's things were cleared out and her room was vacant. However, Shawn was not gone. He met Tionna at the door, his eyes red and filled with tears.

"Could you please leave? Take all your clothes and just leave!" she shouted, and then stood looking at him coldly.

Shawn could see how angry she was, so he did as she asked. He grabbed what he could carry and made a quick exit.

After he left, Tionna cleaned the house and threw out anything left behind that was affiliated with Shawn or

Tonya. After all she had done for the both of them, she couldn't believe they would actually do something like that. She took her little sister in because she had no place else to go, and this was the repayment she got.

Not wanting to face all the hurt and betrayal that she was feeling, Tionna took two Vicodin and cried herself to sleep as she thought about all the events of the day.

Chapter 6

Tionna Faces Death

It had been almost a year since the incident with Tonya and Shawn, and Tionna was gradually getting better. She was seeing our therapist and making good progress. Charlotte was the therapist we had all consulted at some point in our lives. She was a young, white girl who knew her shit. It was unfortunate, but divas need therapy too.

Tionna was looking great. She had gone shopping and purchased new clothes. She got her hair done and her nails and toes done, too. She even sported a new style. It was sort of funky, with a video chick swing. It was like old times. I had really missed her during her deep depression. I was glad that my girl was back in the swing of things. That situation had really taken a toll on all of us.

One evening, we all gathered at her house to celebrate and have a girls' night out, which we referred to as "therapy outside of therapy." We laughed and joked as we thought about old times. Meikell brought her friend Linda and Linda's daughter, Shykema. Immediately, everyone noticed how Shykema resembled Asia's twins. Asia's daughters were named Shameah and Shakeya, and they were beautiful. They had gray eyes, long legs, and French vanilla skin, just like their father. We found it quite peculiar that Linda's daughter, whose name was quite similar, had green eyes, long legs, and caramel skin.

The curiosity was killing us all, so someone had to say something.

India, the feistiest of the twins, spoke up. "Your daughter surely resembles my nieces," she said in a sarcastic tone.

"Oh, really? Well, Shykema's father named her. She looks just like him."

"Oh, that's interesting," India said. "My nieces were also named by their father. So where is their father from?"

As Linda spoke, things fell into place and just as we all thought, Asia's twins and Shykema were sisters. Linda seemed undisturbed by the whole revelation.

Asia had the look of death on her face. "Where were his standards?" She looked at Linda with disgust. "I mean, look at you and look at me. I'm a part of corporate America, and you are just simply a disgrace to America."

To everyone's surprise, Linda responded very calmly. "I understand you're upset, but you shouldn't be. My daughter is two years older than your twins are, and besides, I have no contact with her father whatsoever. We didn't have much of a relationship. I met him at the strip club one night and we ended up having sex. Unfortunately, the condom broke, and I had Shykema. He ended up leaving right after her birth. We had some major conflicts of interest, if you know what I mean."

Asia said, "No, I don't know what you mean. Why don't you elaborate?"

"Not that it's any of your business," Linda said calmly, "but I am no longer interested in men, so you really shouldn't worry."

We were glad Linda responded the way she did, because anything else would have been detrimental to her health. We all exhaled as the tension slowly left the room, and we continued to drink and trip out as before.

Asia wasn't worried that her twins' father would get with Linda. She was just upset that she didn't have any idea about his other child. Even though she hadn't known the twins' father during the time he conceived this other child, it still made her mad. It shouldn't have, though, because now he was doing ten years in federal prison. Asia was getting all his money and had a man on the side.

Just as we were leaving to go out, there was a knock at the door, which was quite surprising since all of us were already there. Tionna opened the door and there stood Shawn, looking just as pitiful as the day he left. In his hand he held a folded piece of paper. He handed Tionna the paper and left without saying a word.

Tionna quickly unfolded the paper and stood silently as she read.

"Nooooo! Oh God, no!" Tionna burst into tears.

As we crowded around and read over her shoulder, we all cried with her.

Dear sir/madam:

We have reason to believe you have come in contact with someone who might be infected with the HIV virus. Please report to your city public health department as soon as possible for testing.

We couldn't believe this was happening. Things were so perfect, and now this. How could this happen to someone we loved so dearly? It wasn't fair. Tionna had only been with Shawn. They weren't using protection because they supposedly had a monogamous relationship. She never worried about getting pregnant because her doctors said she would never have children.

The next day, Tionna headed for the health department. With her head down, she walked in and handed the letter to the receptionist then looked around for a place to sit. The place was crowded and noisy, with babies crying, mothers yelling, and nurses calling names every five minutes. She was afraid to get too close to anyone or touch anything because everyone, even the children, looked as though they were infected with some deadly disease.

After a few minutes, the nurse called out, "Tionna Davis, exam room three."

Tionna walked into the exam room and the nurse advised her to get undressed. Once the nurse left the room, Tionna pulled off her clothes and put on the paper robe. A few minutes later, the doctor walked in. What Tionna did not want to happen, did happen. The doctor was a man and he was gorgeous. Not exactly the type of person she wanted to see as she was getting checked for HIV.

He explained that he would be doing an exam for STDs as well as taking blood to test for HIV. Tionna hated the pelvic exam. The feeling of that cold metal instrument was so uncomfortable. She tightened her muscles as the doctor inserted the cold speculum.

"Relax, honey," the doctor said while patting her knee. "Take some deep breaths and spread your legs."

She cringed. "Ugh!" She did what the doctor instructed and relaxed.

"All done," the doctor announced three minutes later. "I didn't see any signs of an STD. You will be contacted, though, once the blood results are back. I think I should also explain that just because you received the letter doesn't mean you are definitely infected."

Tionna sighed with relief. He actually made her feel a

lot better. "Hey, doc, if the test comes back negative, let's have dinner," she said and giggled to herself as she disappeared behind the curtain to get dressed.

A couple of days later, Tionna received another knock at the door. This time it was two detectives. She knew the day would come when they would catch up with India and come knocking at her door in search of answers. Tionna often broke into cold sweats as she played over and over again in her mind the answers she would give to those questions regarding India and her involvement in the drug ring.

Nervously, she opened the door. As she looked the detectives in their faces, she wasn't sure what to say or what not to say.

"How can I assist you today, detectives?" Tionna asked, her voice shaking.

"Ms. Davis?" one of the detectives asked.

"Yes, I'm Ms. Davis."

"May we come in?"

"Sure. How can I help you?"

To her surprise, they wanted to speak to her about her sister, Tonya. She hadn't heard from Tonya or even spoken her name since the day of the incident.

"When was the last time you saw Tonya?"

"I haven't seen her for some time now."

"Do you know the names of some of her friends? What about some other family members who may have seen her?"

"What is this investigation about?" she asked, wondering if Tonya had gotten into trouble again or if she was missing or something.

Before they could answer, there was another knock on the door. This time it was a social worker.

"This is Mrs. White from Virginia Beach's Department of

Social Services," one detective explained. "She will be speaking with you as well."

"Exactly what the hell is going on?"

After suggesting that Tionna have a seat, the detective told her, "Tonya was recently murdered. We suspect her boyfriend and plan to charge him with the murder."

"Ahhhhhhh!" Tionna screamed out in pain.

Over the wail of her cry, the detectives continued to tell her the story of Tonya's death. "Once Tonya's boyfriend found out she was unfaithful he was infuriated. He called her constantly demanding answers, and your sister eventually changed her number. Our reports show at that point he began to stalk her."

"No!"

"There are numerous police reports filed by Tonya. There are also reports about him following her from her friend's house, sitting outside the laundromat as she washed clothes, and even him sleeping in his car as she spent the night at her girlfriend's house. Things became more violent as Tonya's stomach grew and she became afraid for her life. She knew once her boyfriend found out she was pregnant by another man he would kill her."

"Oh, God! Nooo!"

"She eventually filed a restraining order with the Virginia Beach magistrate. Unfortunately, that didn't stop the harassment. We learned from witnesses that a man named Shawn picked her up from her doctor's appointment and they headed to his house. After a few hours, Tonya decided to go for a walk. As she closed the door behind her and turned around, her boyfriend stood there staring her in the face. He grabbed her by the arm, put a 9mm to her back and instructed her to get into his car. They drove off, and approximately three hours later, her body was found."

"Why?"

"He tied her to a park bench, molested her, and then shot her in the head. She didn't die instantly. She died slowly as she struggled for her life."

As Tionna listened to the gruesome details of her sister's death, she felt like someone had just stabbed her in her heart. Her little sister was dead. She couldn't help but think that if she hadn't told Tonya's boyfriend what had happened that night, she'd still be alive.

The social worker wanted to speak to Tionna about taking custody of the baby.

"We were able to save the baby, but there are a few problems," Mrs. White said. "The father has disappeared, and the baby may be infected with HIV."

This was when Tionna knew for sure that the baby was Shawn's. They must have continued sleeping together even after she'd caught them and kicked Tonya out.

"There are currently no traces of the virus in the baby," Mrs. White continued, "but Tonya was diagnosed with the virus during her pregnancy. We would like to know if you would be willing to care for the child since you are the next of kin."

With all the things that were going on, Tionna asked for time to think things over.

Honoring her wishes, they agreed to leave her alone and give her time to think through her decision.

Tionna drifted into another deep depression. She was not eating, sleeping, bathing or talking. She just laid in bed and wept. It was as if her whole world caved in on her. After three days of showing no improvement, we decided it was time to have her admitted to the hospital. She had lost five pounds during those few days. Her eyes had huge, dark rings around them, and her body was fragile. Her hair fell out strand by strand as we combed it. This was the worst we had ever seen her.

When we arrived at the hospital emergency room, they asked her a series of questions regarding her health. When they reached the question concerning HIV or AIDS, Tionna began to go crazy. She started yelling weird things, throwing things, and became very combative.

Right when the doctors rushed in to control her, she began to have a seizure. They rushed her off through the double doors labeled "trauma" and left us standing there in total disbelief.

We later found out Tionna had a nervous breakdown. The events in her life had finally taken a toll on her body. It was a struggle for her from the beginning. Her parents were absent during her entire life, and she had to take on adult responsibilities at a very young age. Then, the two people that she had invested so much love and time in betrayed her. A combination of those events, plus her fear of the possibility that she may have contracted HIV, her sister's death, and the guilt she felt for telling Tonya's boyfriend of her infidelity, was just too much for her body to handle.

After a few weeks in the hospital, it was time for her to come home. We went to her house and cleaned it from top to bottom. We brought in fresh flowers, opened the windows, and made it bright and refreshing. We even purchased her a new bathroom and bedroom set. We turned her room and connecting bathroom into a tropical paradise. There were palm tree prints, plenty of plants, a relaxation fountain, and aromatherapy candles everywhere. It was beautiful. We felt that was just the atmosphere she needed.

As we gathered her mail, we noticed a letter from the

health department. We weren't sure if she needed to see it right away, especially since she was just recovering from her breakdown. We didn't open it because we were afraid that if the results were bad it would be hard to keep the secret from her. Therefore, we decided it would be best to hide the letter and give it to her when we felt she was capable of handling what could possibly be bad news. There was a letter from social services as well. We figured we would encourage her to read that letter just in case she decided to take custody of the baby.

Tionna was glad to get home. She was happy to see the house in such great condition. We all ate and laughed and enjoyed each other's company. Tionna was happier, but she still wasn't quite herself. After we ate dinner, she inquired about the mail. We handed it to her, and she glanced at each envelope quickly.

"Is this all the mail?" she asked.

"What? That's not enough bills for you?" I joked.

We all laughed—all except Tionna.

"Yeah, I was just expecting my test results from the health department."

"We hid it, girl. We thought that maybe you shouldn't read it right away." India went to retrieve the envelope and handed it to her.

Tionna hesitantly opened the letter and began to cry. But this wasn't her ordinary cry.

"What does it say? What does it say?" Carmin asked.

"Well, it says that, that all my tests, well, they were negative."

For the first time in a long time, we were all happy. This situation brought us all together as one. It even brought Meikell back into the group.

"Guys, after all that we have been through, I've realized

life is too short and that I need to make some changes. I'm going to give up escorting and dancing," Meikell vowed.

I smiled. "You're making the right decision, Mickie. If you need anything, let me know. We're here for you."

We all began to hug and cry. At that moment, we all realized anything could happen to any of us at any time.

Chapter 7

What Goes On in Cancun Stays in Cancun

Two years had passed since Vegas and I first got together, so we decided to celebrate by taking a trip for two to Cancun, Mexico. The flight there was great. It was Vegas's first time flying, and he was terrified. It was funny to watch the terror in his face as we loaded the plane and took off. I never saw him so afraid.

"Will you be having dinner and drinks?" the airline attendant asked, once we were in the air.

Vegas shook his head. "No dinner for me. I don't think I can hold it. But I will take a Remy and Baileys." After his first drink, we began to drink shots of Cuervo 1800. Before I knew it, Vegas was tore up and began yelling, "Shots for everyone."

His ass ended up buying the whole plane shots of 1800. Once we landed at the airport, things were chaotic. People were everywhere, yelling and reaching for our bags. We allowed one of the overly zealous guys to take our bags and lead us to the loading area. There were cabs, vans and limos waiting for passengers. We decided to go with the limo. On the way to the hotel, Vegas drank a Corona. The Coronas there were huge! They were all black and the size of champagne bottles.

Once at the hotel, we checked in and headed directly to our room. The room resembled a small apartment. There was a separate area for the living room and kitchen, and through the French doors was the bedroom. Attached to the bedroom was an enormous balcony that overlooked the ocean. We could see everything on the beach. The balcony was equipped with a table, two chairs and even a blind we could pull down to block out the sun and add privacy. The bathroom had a standing shower and a whirlpool tub. There was even a telephone on the wall beside the toilet.

As soon as we finished a tour of the room, we stripped naked and got into the Jacuzzi. We relaxed and sipped on the complimentary bottle of Dom *P* that was placed in the room prior to our arrival.

Thirty minutes later, we heard a knock. It was room service with our order. We indulged in a seafood feast. The dinner consisted of everything from mussels to octopus. It was delicious.

By nightfall, we were at the pool. As we sat at the bar, I noticed a young woman dropping her bikini top and teasing a few men. When Vegas looked over, she began to lick her lips and jiggle her breasts at him. I became infuriated! Oh no the hell this bitch ain't! I guess she could tell by the look on my face that I was not pleased with her actions.

"*Perdon.* I did not know he was *su hombre*," she said in broken English while looking at me.

I just rolled my eyes at the hussy as I turned my attention back to Vegas and we downed the shot that sat before us. After another, we both became quite frisky. We were in a hurry to finish our drinks so we could return to our room for some passionate lovemaking.

Right before we drank what we said would be our final drink, "Miss Titty Jiggler" came strutting over. "May I join in your next shot? The next one will be on me."

Of course we accepted the free round, and we all drank up. After the shots, we all became more relaxed and began to chat. We learned that the young lady's name was Arizelli and she was from Brazil. Her skin was like a rich, creamy caramel, and her hair was long, black, and silky. She had a tall, slim build. The Cuervo must have gotten her frisky as well because she began to get very friendly with Vegas and me. She was constantly playing in my hair and rubbing my back as we talked. She eventually directed us to a secluded area next to the pool.

"Your breasts are so beautiful." She untied my bikini top as well as hers.

The alcohol must have been having a bigger effect on me than I realized, because no way under normal circumstances would I have allowed another woman so much control over my body, not to mention my man.

She motioned to Vegas. "Go ahead, touch them. What do you think?"

He touched them and compared firmness. "They're both nice and firm," he said.

"Well, don't you want to compare taste?"

Vegas took her up on the invitation and began to caress and lick our nipples. He massaged our nipples until they rose and then licked each one until they were covered in the wetness of his tongue.

"Do you guys smoke ganja?" she asked.

We both nodded our heads in the affirmative.

"Well then, let's go through the waterfall to the cave and smoke a blunt," Arizelli suggested.

We followed her in there, and sat and smoked until we were super nice. The weed and tequila mix had us horny as hell. Vegas and I began to kiss and undress, forgetting Arizelli was even there.

She helped undress us both and caressed our bodies as we kissed. As Vegas went down on me, she licked and caressed my nipples tenderly.

When Vegas lay down and I began sucking him madly, she grabbed my waist and started grinding against me gently. Next, she got on her knees and licked my womanhood from behind.

After a while of this, I yearned to feel Vegas's manhood deep inside me, so I mounted him slowly. The whole time, Arizelli was right behind me, squeezing and moving along with me as I rode him into ecstasy. He moaned and grabbed Arizelli's ass as we exploded together.

The next morning, we woke up bright and early and headed for the booze cruise. It was a small cruise ship with an all-you-can-eat buffet and an open bar. The ship was to take us to a private island, which had more food and drinks. Everyone was wilding out! It was so wild that they didn't allow cameras or camcorders on the boat. As we passed an area on the way to the private island, the tour guide told everyone to throw money into the water and make a wish and it would come true.

Many of the people were throwing coins, and a few people threw dollars, but Vegas was so drunk that he started throwing fives, then tens, and then twenties. Soon, he was throwing fifties and people began to jump off the boat after the money. We were weak with laughter watching those crazy ass drunks. The captain stopped the boat, fished out the dummies, and then asked that no one else throw money.

Once we got to the island, Vegas and I decided to partake in some of the available activities. We rode Jet Skis, went horseback riding and parasailing.

Parasailing was the worst! Vegas threw up everywhere. After we took a moment for him to compose himself, we went snorkeling. I hated it. In fact, I didn't even want to get in the water. There were fish all over. I hated the feeling of them flapping on my skin.

After a few minutes of panicking, I finally got it together. We followed as the guide pointed out all sorts of colorful fish and coral.

"Don't get too close to the coral," he warned.

"Oh shit! I'm cut!" I had gotten a little too close and ended up with a number of cuts and scrapes. I was bleeding everywhere. Then I heard someone yell something about a shark. I almost shit in my thong. "Vegas! Help! There's a shark and I'm bleeding. Don't let me die," I cried hysterically as I swam toward him. I could see the shark at the bottom of the ocean. I thought for sure that I was going to die.

"Calm down, everyone," the guide shouted. "There is no need to panic. This type of shark only eats from the bottom of the ocean."

Vegas looked at me. "I know this nigga don't think we buyin' that shit. That's why their asses always the first ones to be eaten. Come on, baby, let's go."

Vegas and I hauled ass back to the Jet Ski so we could head toward shore.

Beating Vegas, I said, "I want to drive, baby."

"Girl, you know damn well you don't know how to drive a Jet Ski."

"But I never tried. Please, baby?"

"Go ahead, but be careful."

We climbed on the Jet Ski and I started it up. I decided I would ride around a little while before going to shore. I didn't do well at first. I was afraid to go too fast.

"Give it some gas!" Vegas yelled. "Go!"

Pissed at all his damn yelling, I ended up giving it too

much gas, and we shot off toward the ocean going at least fifty miles per hour.

"Slow the fuck down, girl!" Vegas yelled as water splashed in our faces from the waves.

I was just starting to get the hang of things when I hit a wave.

"Ooohhhhh shiiiiiiit!" is all I heard as Vegas went flying off the back of the Jet Ski.

The engine was smoking, and I couldn't start it back up. I sat there laughing as he floated in the middle of the ocean with a terrible grimace on his face. He didn't find a damn thing funny at all.

Within a few minutes, the guide came over and pulled Vegas out of the water. Then they came to get me, and took us back to the shore.

The next morning, a little Mexican lady awakened us. "*Buenos dias, senorita*! Housekeeping!" she yelled from behind the door.

I sat up and my head was spinning. There was no way I could make it to the door, so I just yelled back. "No, thank you! No housekeeping!"

After a few more hours of sleep and a morning's dose of Alka-Seltzer, I was able to get up. I got the tray from the door. It consisted of a newspaper, towels, fresh flowers, and a breakfast menu. We ordered brunch and ate on the balcony as we watched the various activities on the beach. There was volleyball, and a beach party thrown by the hotel. We decided to go and check out the beach party. I wore a gorgeous, tropical print string bikini. As the finishing touch, I wore a small wrap around my waist. Vegas wore Versace swimming trunks and black, Italian leather Versace flip-flops.

On our way to the party, we ran into Red. Now, wasn't

that a coincidence? To say that I was surprised to see him would be an understatement.

Vegas didn't seem the least bit surprised. They walked over to the beach bar together and chatted as I sat at a nearby table.

A few moments later, Vegas approached me. "You mind if I step out for a few hours, baby?"

Although I was irritated at Red's presence, I agreed. I wasn't sure what it was about Red, but I just did not trust him. For some odd reason, I would sometimes have thoughts that he might try some shady shit and I'd have to kill him.

Not wanting to attend the party solo, I returned to the hotel room to get some much needed rest. A few hours later, Vegas returned, loaded down with bags. He bought me Prada and Gucci sneakers, a Dolce & Gabbana swimsuit, a Louis Vuitton bag, and two pair of Pradas for himself. I was so thrilled with the gifts.

"Thanks, baby! You are the sweetest person ever," I cried with joy. I was already overwhelmed by the trip, and the gifts just made it all that much better.

He must really love me, I thought. As a way of showing my appreciation, I pleasured him with an hour of passionate sex.

After making love, we made another attempt at heading to the beach party, which was still in progress. We arrived just as they were having the Shake-What-Cha-Momma-Gave-Ya dance contest. Women crowded the stage as the DJ played "Lap Dance" by the Nerds.

"Ooh, baby, you want me?" The girls on stage yelled as they danced provocatively.

The way they were shaking, gyrating and degrading themselves, you would have thought the prize was more than just an off-brand bikini and a bottle of Cristal.

The men went crazy as the girls began to take their clothes off.

I noticed Vegas inching his way toward the stage. He glanced back at me for approval.

"Go ahead, baby. Do you," I said, smiling.

He was surprised at my response but didn't hesitate to head straight for the stage. One by one the judges began to eliminate girls. The closer they got to the final girl, the wilder the show became. Pretty soon, the girls were all butt naked. When they got down to the last two, it was downright terrible. They were doing anything in a desperate attempt to win.

One girl pulled Red on stage, laid him down, massaged his penis, put her breasts in his face and bounced on his dick to no end. All this while naked! Her butt jiggled like Jell-O, and her boobs bounced liked balloons as she went up and down.

When it was time for her competitor to perform, she was determined to win. All morals and values were out the door. Butt naked, she grabbed a girl wearing a string bikini out of the audience. She lay on her back with knees bent, and pulled the girl on top of her in the same position. The girl from the audience lay, back to breast, with her legs straddled outside of the competitor's.

The competitor massaged the girl's breasts with one hand, while caressing the clit with the other, all the while their bodies moved together. Then out of nowhere, Red's drunken ass jumped in front of the girls, dropped to his knees, threw their legs up, and began to pump them wildly.

Needless to say, the competition was over. By a unanimous vote, the "liberal lesbian" won. The bottle of Cristal was popped and poured all over her. The crowd went crazy as the women bathed in champagne and licked it from each other's breasts. *What a waste of some good-ass champagne.* After their show, they both ran into the beach water, and the party moved there.

Vegas quickly made his way back over to me.

Looking at each other in disbelief, we laughed and said in unison, "What goes on in Cancun stays in Cancun!"

The next day, it was time to head home. I had a great time, but I was ready to go. Believe it or not, I had started to get homesick.

We arrived in Norfolk about seven p.m. and were home in no time.

As we approached the door, Vegas noticed that it was cracked. "Shhhh, be quiet," he whispered. "Hold on. Don't go in."

He pushed the door open a little, and I managed to catch a glimpse. My condo was trashed! Furniture was turned over, and stuff was everywhere.

The anger must have been written all over my face, because Vegas immediately put his hand over my mouth. "Shhhhh. Don't say shit."

It took all I had to keep from screaming.

He rushed to the car and retrieved his gun from the trunk. Just as Vegas entered the house, the burglar stopped in his tracks, standing right before him. Vegas held fire as he looked the young guy in his eyes. He recognized the teen as one of the young runners from out the way. He knew the kid was working for someone else, so he decided to spare the kid's life. He had a better plan for payback in store.

In a matter of seconds, the kid ran out through the French doors. We looked around but found nothing missing. A lot of my furniture and expensive paintings were destroyed, though. I never thought I would need my homeowner's insurance, but that incident certainly made me thankful I had it.

After examining the condo we went to the garage, and that's when I lost it. I certainly wasn't keeping quiet then. "My car! My fucking car!" I yelled at the top of my lungs as tears welled up in my eyes. My pride and joy had been vandalized! They stole my rims, my TV from the dash, my system, and destroyed my interior.

"I'm calling the police!" I searched though my bags frantically for my cell phone.

"No!" Vegas snatched the phone from my hands. "Look at this house. It's obvious this was a drug burglary. If we contact the cops, all it will do is make our spot hot. Don't worry, baby. I'll handle this shit."

After Vegas convinced me not to contact the police and assured me he would take care of things, I calmed down somewhat.

Then I noticed a very worried look on his face. "Baby, what's wrong?" I asked.

"I feel responsible. I should have never brought this shit around you."

Even though none of Vegas's associates ever came to our home, he still felt like the break-in happened because someone thought he had money or drugs in there. He pointed out how the burglar searched in odd places like the toilet, washer and dryer, under the mattress, and in the closet paneling. All were places people would normally hide drugs or money. Not to mention there were plenty of things in the house worth stealing that weren't even touched.

We called the insurance company, locked up, and headed to a hotel at Waterside. Once we were checked in and settled in our room, I questioned Vegas.

"Baby, why didn't you shoot when you saw the burglar?"

I was certain my man was thugged out, so I knew it couldn't be because he was scared.

"Well, I recognized that lil' nigga who broke in our crib," Vegas explained. "He's too young for me to bust up, so I got another plan. Now get dressed. Dress comfortably and wear dark colors. You're coming with me."

I did as Vegas instructed and followed him out to the truck. We drove to one of his boy's houses and traded off the truck for one of his cars.

Vegas mounted a pair of thirty-day tags on the car. "You ready, baby?"

"Yes, I am," I responded eagerly, showing my man I could be his down-ass bitch.

"Well, jump in the driver seat." Vegas handed me the keys. He lay on the floor in the back seat and directed me to the location of the guy's hangout.

Once I reached the area, Vegas pointed him out.

I drove up to the group of guys and said, "Excuse me, do any of you guys know where Berkley is?"

The young kid who had robbed us was the first to respond.

This was working out perfectly.

"Yeah, it's about five miles away." He started giving me detailed directions.

Pretending to be confused, I used my sex appeal to persuade him to get into the car. "That's a lot for me to remember. Do you think you can ride with me out there? I'll pay for a cab to get you back, or you can just stay at my crib if you like."

Hearing that, he jumped right in with no hesitation. He had no idea what was in store for him. When he got in, I immediately hit the lock.

Vegas sat up quietly and put the gun to the back of the guy's head.

"Look straight ahead. If you turn your head in either direction, I will blow your fucking brains out, got it?"

"I got it, man, I got it," the terrified little boy said.

"Who in the fuck sent you to my house? I know yo' punk ass don't have the balls or the brains to come up with that shit on your own."

"Man I'll tell you everything. Please, just don't kill me. Niggas on the streets is hating, man. They mad 'cause you got all the parks on lock. Bear paid me to break in and steal yo' stash and money and shit. I wasn't trying to do it, man, but I had to do it to clear an old debt I had with him. Come on, Vegas, it's part of the game."

"What, bitch?" *Pop! Splat!* Vegas pistol-whipped the young boy in the head, and blood splattered against the car window.

"What the fuck you know about the game? Lil' nigga, you don't know shit. Have you moved any keys? As a matter of fact, have you even seen a key? What about raw? Have you even had any raw? You been on this corner for years, man, pushing nick, dimes, and caps. You ain't shit, nigga. You haven't even entered the game, bitch."

After a little more terrorizing and spitting in his face, Vegas let the guy go.

Chapter 8

Holiday Celebrations

After the break-in, Vega s didn't waste any time buying a new house. We paid off the balance owed on my condo and quickly moved into our new five-bedroom house in Church Point. We lived near all the stars, from entertainers to athletes. The house was gorgeous. It was on the water and surrounded by a huge wrought iron gate. There was a three-car garage and a huge backyard. In the backyard was a deck with a gazebo, a boat ramp with his and hers Jet Skis, and a large pool.

The inside of the house was like a small palace. Our bedroom was separated into two sections. The first room had a huge bay window with a beautiful view of the water and was equipped with a Jacuzzi in front of a fireplace. The other section of the bedroom consisted of our bed, closet and bathroom. Our TV rose from the foot of the bed at the push of a button, and our walk-in closet was the size of a small bedroom. The closet had a rotating rack and compartments for shoes, hats and bags. The bathroom had a standing shower separate from the tub. The tub had a built-in whirlpool. There were also his and hers toilets and sinks. The living room had a huge, vaulted ceiling with skylights, a marble floor, and a beautiful fireplace.

The entrance of the house opened to a winding staircase on each side that led to a loft overlooking the living room. We even had a theater room with a wall projector and surround sound, a weight room where I could practice my shadow boxing, and laundry chutes in each upstairs bathroom that led directly to the laundry room.

Before we knew it, summer was over and it was my birthday. We were spending so much time working on the house that we hadn't had time for anything else. So when Vegas suggested that I should take the day off on my birthday, I agreed.

By noon, we were out of the house. We jumped in the truck, and he blindfolded me.

He drove for about fifteen minutes before stopping. Then, he helped me out of the truck. After helping me take a few steps, he removed the blindfold.

"Oh my God! Oh my God! I can't believe it!" I screamed. "Thank you! I love you so much!" I jumped up and down for joy like a kid on Christmas day. I couldn't believe it. It was my dream car.

When I'd originally mentioned it to Vegas, he told me it was out of our price range.

How did he do it? I wondered. In front of me sat a red Lexus SC 430 with a huge bow around it. I had been in love with that car since the first time I saw it.

Immediately, I jumped in. The interior was all white leather. There was a single TV in the dash, twenty-inch Sprewell rims, light tint and a fully customized system.

"Follow me to the Lexus dealership," Vegas said as I adored my new car.

When we arrived there, Vegas walked off and talked with an older white guy for a few minutes before handing him an envelope. Then, the white guy handed him an extra key and the title.

There is no way Vegas purchased this car in cash, I thought. But I wasn't about to ask any questions.

The more I adored my car, the more my conscience would eat at me. I loved my car, but I still wondered how Vegas was able to afford it. So, I did a little research of my own.

It turned out the white guy at the dealership made a little business transaction with Vegas, and that's how he was able to get the car for me. At that point, I knew there wasn't anything Vegas wouldn't do for me.

Christmas followed my birthday. I purchased Vegas a two-way pager, an X-Box game system and an earring so big, it could have made him part of the Cash Money Millionaires. It was platinum and covered in princess cut diamonds.

He bought me a red mink and some matching red alligator boots, which he special ordered from the Mauri catalog. They were knee-high with pointed toes and graphite stiletto heels.

But the best gift of all was my puppy! He bought me the cutest tan cocker spaniel. "Oh, my goodness!" I said as I burst into tears.

"Her name is *Prissy.* She reminds me a lot of you. I hope you like her."

"I think that name suits her perfectly," I said as I picked her up. She wore a diamond collar with the name *Prissy* around it.

Later that night, it was time for the Annual Baller Christmas Gala. This was like the Players' Ball, but with a gangsta twist. This was the time for all the area ballers to show off their girls, jewels, clothes, and rides.

Vegas wore a deep royal blue mink, matching gator boots and belt, and a mushroom-colored suit underneath. I wore a dress of the same blue that dipped in the back to just above my butt crack. The front was sheer, and my private parts were covered only by a small rhinestone design. It was gorgeous.

We pulled up to the red carpet that lay in front of the hotel and stepped out of the stretch Mercedes. I must say, we were the hottest couple there. The party was off the hook.

Throughout the night, I noticed a number of the local hustlers whispering in Vegas's ear. "Look, man, give me a call so we can do some business," they would say.

Among them was a hustler who went by the name of Bear. Bear had no idea that Vegas knew he paid the young punk to break into our place.

"Vegas! What's up, baby?" he said as he dapped him up. "How you doin', miss lady?" He gave me a seductive smile.

I didn't speak, just smiled slightly.

Bear turned his attention back to Vegas. "Shit is rolling on the streets, man. What 'cha gon' do? I'm trying to get you on my team, nigga."

Vegas arranged to do business with him.

"Baby, why are you talking to him like everything is cool?" I asked after Bear walked away.

"It's all part of the game, baby. It's safer that way. I prefer to keep my enemies close."

After a night of socializing and showing off, we headed home, pissy drunk. Vegas couldn't keep his hands off me during the ride home.

The slightest touch was turning me on. My head was spinning as I lay back with my legs cocked open.

Vegas buried his head between my legs, making me moist with every kiss. He pleased me exactly as I imagined he would when I masturbated in the lawyer's office on my first escort assignment.

In fact, it was even better. His tongue was wet and warm inside me.

I grabbed the back of his head as I came in his mouth.

By the time we reached home, we were both drained beyond belief.

Vegas had become quite annoyed over the past few days. It had been months since he had heard from Red. We were straight living off the stash, and he was worried about what the future would bring.

"I think you should get your mind off money for a while, baby. Let's go to DC to celebrate the New Year," I suggested.

He agreed, and we headed to the club. We arrived at about eleven o'clock New Year's Eve. The club was packed. The line was wrapped around the corner. In front of the club was an entourage of nice cars lined up for valet parking provided only for a selected few. I'm not sure what made us so special, but I guess our abundance of cash flow had a lot to do with it.

As we approached the entrance, a huge, dark guy said, "A hundred dollars starting here."

Vegas paid the man, and we headed straight to the VIP room. Once we entered the VIP room, we sat at a table.

The waitress ran over. "Hey, Vegas. What are we having tonight?" The bony little waitress smacked on her bubble gum.

Vegas ordered a bottle of Cristal to pop after the countdown and a few drinks for us to sip on until then.

With only seconds until the start of a new year, we all began the countdown.

"5, 4, 3, 2, 1 . . . Happy New Year!"

Bottles began to pop everywhere. We clanked our glasses together in a toast and followed it with a long, passionate kiss. Confetti dropped as the DJ played "Auld Lang Syne" and everyone sang along.

"I love you, baby. And as long as I walk this green earth, you'll never have to worry about anything."

"I know, baby. I love you too."

While everyone celebrated, Red walked up. Was it me, or did it seem that he always popped up at the wrong time?

"I gotta holla at you, man," he said in Vegas's ear. "Take down my new number and hit me up."

Vegas took out his phone and entered Red's number, then Red left.

We partied for another hour before heading for the hotel. We were extremely drunk as we waited for our car. We were damn near to the point of having to hold each other up as we waited for the valet to bring our car around.

We heard a woman yell from behind, "What the fuck is this?"

We turned around and there stood Vegas's baby momma, all in his face, yelling and screaming. "You all the way up here and you can't even call or try to come see your kids?"

I grabbed Vegas's arm. "Come on, honey, our car is here."

That must have really upset her, because she turned to me and pulled out a blade.

Before I could react, Vegas grabbed her and slammed her against the hood of the car. "Bitch, you done lost yo' damn mind!" He strangled her and continuously banged her head against the hood of the car. He was choking her so terribly that her eyes began to roll to the back of her head. I could hear her gasping for air. Vegas wasn't himself. His eyes were cold and still.

"Vegas, baby, please let her go! You're going to kill her, baby! Let her go!" I begged him to stop as the police rushed over.

They immediately tackled him to the ground face first. I cried hysterically as they cuffed him and placed him under arrest. I followed them to the police station so I could immediately post bail.

I waited hours in the cold jail before they informed me he would not be released.

The next day, I headed home alone. The ride was long and horrible. I was tired and worried. I arrived home around four in the afternoon. As soon as I walked in the doors of our big, lonely house, the phone was ringing. I rushed to answer it. "Hello? Hello?"

"You have a collect call from—" the operator began to say.

I immediately accepted the call. It was Vegas. "What's up, baby?"

"The charges were dropped, but I'm being transported back there for probation violation because I was out of state. I spoke to Bear, and we came up with a way to continue business. I'm going to need your help, baby."

"I got you. Just tell me what to do."

"Just keep a lookout for the mail."

In a couple of days, I received a letter from Vegas with instructions. I was to be the backbone of the plan. It was my job to get the product and give it to his brothers. Once a week, I would meet Bear and pick up the raw heroin. I would spend hours in the basement mixing the product to form a missile that would blow the fiends' brains. I had to be sure to add just enough cut so that the dope wouldn't be weak. Once my mixture was right, I would fill the caps one by one.

Normally, Vegas would have someone else do the capping for him, but he didn't trust them enough to send me to them alone. Once the package was complete, his brothers would sell them by the bundle and give me the money as they pumped it.

Vegas was expedited to Norfolk jail a few days after I received the letter. He was convicted of the violation and sentenced to sixty days.

Just as he'd instructed, I picked up the product once a week.

After a while of this, I began to notice Bear coming at me incorrectly. One day when I went over to his home, he had the lights dimmed, music on and drinks out.

"Why don't you stay and have dinner with me?" he suggested as he grabbed the package.

"No, thanks. I'm in a hurry."

"Okay, but you're missing out. You look really nice today. That outfit really complements your body."

"Thanks, but I have to go."

Eventually, I couldn't take it anymore. I had to tell Vegas, and planned to do so when he called later that night.

"Hi, baby."

"What's up, ma? You sound stressed."

"Baby, Bear has really been saying some slick things out his mouth. When I go over, he procrastinates and does all sorts of things to try to make me stay."

"Did he touch you?"

"No, baby, but I'm starting to feel a little uncomfortable."

"I'm sorry you have to go through this, baby girl. l told you I would never let anything happen to you, and now this nigga is violating. Don't worry, ma, I got this. I get out in two weeks. I owe that nigga anyway. Make the pickups as usual."

Click!

In two weeks, my baby was finally home.

I took him to the basement and lifted the cement block to expose his money all wrapped and stacked. $300,000 dollars exactly, and not a penny off.

His face lit up. "Damn, girl. You handlin' shit, huh? Charlie B ain't got nuttin' on you. You that down-ass bitch that niggas dream about."

He gave me a bear hug, lifting me off my feet, and followed it with a big, wet kiss.

After dinner, he said, "Baby, I can't let shit ride. Bear has crossed me for the last time. I got something for that nigga, but I need to ask for your help."

Vegas had that cold stare on his face once again. I knew it could only mean one thing—death. Still, I loved my man, so I agreed to help him.

No one knew Vegas was home, so I made arrangements for the next pickup as if nothing had changed. I met Bear at his house about eight p.m.

Once again, he had set the mood for lovemaking. "Why don't you come in?" he asked. "I cooked seafood, your favorite."

This time, I played along. "Sure. What did you cook?" I walked in.

"I cooked boiled snow crab legs, shrimp, lobster, broiled fish, and linguini."

We ate dinner and drank champagne at a candlelit table.

After dinner, he dimmed the lights, and we moved to the couch to watch a movie.

Suddenly, Bear felt very sleepy.

I sipped on some Moet as he laid his head on my lap.

Bear had one of those huge remotes that controlled nearly everything throughout the house. I pressed a switch and instantly the lights were off. Within minutes, he was asleep.

Zzzzip! Smack!

Bear woke up unable to move. "What the fuck is going on?"

"You had your head in the place I lay my dick at night," Vegas replied calmly. "If you don't want dick in your face, don't block my spot."

I could have died from laughter. Vegas had actually unzipped his pants and smacked Bear in the face with his big, black dick.

Bear's head was spinning, and within a few minutes he was out cold again. Those pills I had slipped in his drink really had him delirious.

I knew he was out of it, but I was still concerned that he might remember bits and pieces of the night once he came to.

"Baby, what if remembers it was us that did this to him? He'll kill me, Vegas."

"He won't remember anything, *C.* Come on, don't be getting all scared on me now. I got you, ma, I got you."

We robbed him of all his stashed dope and at least fifty thousand in cash. Then we took a few other things to make it appear like an actual break-in had taken place.

Before we left, we placed him in the tub, hog-tied with tape.

The next day, word on the street was that someone had broken into Bear's house. It was amazing how the story changed. The word was Bear had taken some bad Ecstasy and was robbed by some chick he was dealing with. Bear thought one of his close friends was suspect.

No one had any idea it was Vegas and me.

Vegas laid low for a few weeks then finally announced that he was home. Shortly thereafter, he received a call from Bear.

"What's up, man? You know some bitch set me up. You hear anything about it while you were in 811?" That was the name everyone used when referring to Norfolk City Jail, because the building's street address was 811.

Vegas kept it short and gave him some bogus story.

"Man, that shit really got me fucked up. I'll probably be out for a minute. I'm gonna hook you up with my man so y'all can keep shit flowing."

A few weeks later, Vegas hooked up with Bear's connect, and he was back in business.

"Baby, you aren't dealing with Red anymore?" I asked, realizing that I hadn't heard Vegas mention him in a while.

"Red told me he'd been out of the country taking care of business for the past few months. I'm skeptical about that though, ma. I think I'm just gonna cut that nigga off."

Chapter 9

Anniversary Perks

It was March and our third anniversary. Vegas had planned a wonderful night out for us.

"Hello."

"Hey, baby, dress nice and be ready by seven. I'm taking you out."

I didn't waste any time preparing because I knew Vegas would have something special planned. I wore a black dress with the front open down to my belly button. It was long, with a single split to my upper thigh. I wore my hair up with large, dangling diamonds, a wide diamond bracelet, and a small belt with a rhinestone buckle. To finish off the outfit, I had a small clutch bag with rhinestones.

"Happy anniversary, baby," he said, coming in the house dressed to impress and handing me a dozen red roses. He followed the words with a small kiss on the lips, being careful not to smear my MAC lipglass.

Vegas wore a light green suit, a green mock-neck shirt and dark green gators with a matching belt.

My secret spot began to get moist just from his appearance. *Damn, he looks so good,* I thought as I got a whiff of his Versace Blue Jeans cologne. I loved it when my man dressed up, and it must have been clearly written on my face.

"Get your mind off sex, baby. We got a long night ahead of us. You've got plenty of time to get this dick." He smacked my ass.

I placed the flowers in a vase on the living room mantle, and we headed out.

He took me to a downtown upscale restaurant. He had reserved the basement room for us. The setup was gorgeous.

The cook came in and offered suggestions from some of the selections that were on the menu. He gave me so many options that I couldn't make up my mind. He then decided to bring me a healthy sample of all the seafood entrees.

We ended up having a four-course meal. We started with a Caesar salad, spiced onion soup, and garlic bread. Then, we ate oysters for an appetizer. The main course was wonderful. It was the best seafood I've ever eaten. It consisted of clams, lobster, shrimp, and calamari.

After we finished, Vegas excused himself for a few minutes. When he returned, he was followed by what seemed like the entire restaurant staff and patrons.

He walked up to me and got down on one knee. "You have been there through the ups and downs, you had faith in me when no one else did, and you have proven to me that you are down with me no matter what the situation. So I have to ask you with all the love in my heart, Ceazia Devereaux, will you do me the honor of being my wife?"

"Yes, yes, Vegas, I will," I replied as I burst into tears.

The whole room erupted with applause as he placed the ring on my finger. It was a platinum ring, with a 3-carat princess cut diamond and baguettes in a cathedral setting. It was a perfect fit.

"Thank you, baby. From this day forth, I send my love,

and it's up to you to receive my heart," Vegas said in the most sincere way.

"I will, baby. I will," I said through the tears.

After dinner, we boarded a yacht Vegas had chartered for a little cruise. The cruise was romantic. The music was soft, and the night was cool. We walked to the top level outside the boat and danced slowly to the music.

Vegas held me tightly as he whispered in my ear. "I love you so much, girl. I'm ready to spend the rest of my life with you."

We kissed passionately.

Vegas bent me over slowly and I clutched the rails of the boat as he ran his hands up the split of my skirt. The feel of his hands running up my thighs was instant stimulation. Vegas lifted my skirt slowly and slid my panties to the side.

I moaned as he gently inserted his penis into my vagina, which was now dripping wet.

When the cruise ended, we went home. In the bedroom I had placed rose petals, and candles all around the Jacuzzi. There were strawberries with melted chocolate and a bottle of Cristal in an ice-filled bucket beside the Jacuzzi. I figured there were only a few things you could give a man who already had everything, so I had to get creative.

I gave him all the pleasures a man could desire. I started by giving him a full body massage, then I fed him strawberries and let the warm chocolate drip over his body. I licked the chocolate from his chest and stomach.

Next, I performed for him. I danced erotically and used toys as I performed. I covered a dildo with whipped cream and licked it up and down before inserting it into my vagina.

After my performance, Vegas was ready for the sex of his life. We made love in every position, including anal. After hours of lovemaking, I brought out his gift, a multicolored

Jacob watch. Each section was colored, with a matching diamond bezel. It was the hottest watch on the streets, and all the rappers were sporting it.

"Damn, baby! You're spoiling me. Where the hell you get money for this shit? You been digging in my stash?"

"Baby, you know I wouldn't touch your money." I playfully punched him in the chest.

I don't think he realized that I had been saving all my checks. Since we were living together, I didn't have to pay anything. He covered all the bills and bought me everything I needed. As a result, I ended up accumulating a huge savings.

The next day I immediately contacted the crew to tell them the news. Everyone responded with the same excitement I felt when Vegas proposed. Everyone except Meikell. Carmin and Tionna argued over who would be the maid of honor, while India demanded I choose bridesmaids dresses that complemented her boobs and play reggae at the reception so that she and her Jamaican mate could "wine" to the Caribbean tunes. Asia, on the other hand, was only concerned with the budget.

Meikell didn't seem enthused at all. Although we had squashed our differences a long time ago, she still seemed a bit jealous. Instead of congrats and best wishes, she gave me warnings and cautions. Nevertheless, I was happy and couldn't wait to spend the rest of my life with Vegas, and not even Mickie could ruin such a wonderful day.

The next couple of months were great. Business was wonderful with the new connect and Vegas was on a roll.

As I dressed for work, I stood naked in front of the mirror and asked, "Do you think I've gained weight, baby?"

Vegas walked behind me and looked in the mirror. "Yeah, that ass is getting kinda fat." He smacked my butt.

"I'm serious, baby. It looks like I've gained a lot of weight."

"Okay, okay, let's see." He paused while he took a closer look. "On the real, your ass and your titties are growing, babe, but it's cool. You look nice like that."

Vegas loved it because I had more butt and my breasts were huge, but I was concerned that I might be losing my hourglass figure.

When my period didn't come, I knew there was more to it. I went to the doctor and sure enough, I was pregnant. I was ten weeks along and carrying twins. I guess all that anniversary sex had planted something in the oven. I couldn't wait to tell Vegas the news.

"Baaaabyyyyyy!!!" I sang as I walked in the house.

"What's up?"

I walked into the bedroom, but he wasn't there. "Baby, where are you?"

"I'm in the weight room. What's up, ma?"

I quickly headed to the weight room and opened the door. The room reeked with the smell of sweat, but the sight of Vegas's perfect body laying horizontal on the weight bench instantly caused my juices to flow. I stood at the door motionless as I adored the sight. His legs were open and I could see the imprint of his penis through his 76ers shorts.

He wiped the sweat from his face. "What's up, baby?"

I was so turned on I had forgotten what I wanted to say. As he rose to a sitting position on the weight bench, I walked over to him and straddled my legs over his.

Vegas immediately lifted my lavender Coogi dress and ripped off my G-string. I guess all the lifting had him pumped.

I untied the string behind my neck so that my now huge breasts flopped out.

Vegas lifted them one by one and licked my nipples.

"What . . . did you . . . want to . . . tell me?" He asked between licks. He slipped his penis inside me in one swift motion.

I was so aroused, I could barely speak. Just as I felt an orgasm coming, I yelled it out. "Baaabyyy! We're having a baby!"

The room fell silent, and Vegas lifted me off his penis. "What did you say?"

"We're having a baby. I'm pregnant with twins."

"Damn, baby! When did this happen? How many months are you? Boys or girls?"

I immediately called all my friends and shared the news. Everyone was just as ecstatic as Vegas. Vegas and I were the first couple in the circle to have a child, which added even more excitement to the good news.

As the days passed, I couldn't wait for five months so that I could begin to shop. I had already chosen names—Anaya and Zanaya Serene Jackson. They would share the same middle name. I didn't bother choosing boy names, because I was sure I would have girls. Vegas didn't care either way. He was just happy that I was having his child or, should I say, children.

I spent each day watching *A Baby Story*, *Maternity Ward*, or reading parenting magazines. I often looked at interior design magazines for ideas for the twins' bedroom. It was a battle between Pooh and sleeping teddies for the theme. Of course, I couldn't even work on that until after five months. This self-imposed five-month rule was really killing me. There was so much that I wanted and needed to do.

I figured since Vegas and I were going to have a baby, there needed to be some changes. I wasn't sure how he would take it, but I wanted him out of the game. I figured we could start a business to keep the flow of money coming in. We had plenty of money on hand, as well as a whole lot invested.

Asia made sure we all invested our money as it came in. She was like the Suze Orman of the group. That's how she earned the title "Ms. Moneybags."

I decided it was time for me to discuss my decision with Vegas.

"What's up, baby?" Vegas said as he answered the phone.

"Vegas, we need to talk. Can you come home right away?"

"Yeah, ma. There's nothing wrong with the twins, is there?"

"No, everything is fine. We just need to talk."

"Okay. I'll be there in about twenty minutes. Catch my heart," he said before hanging up.

"I love you," I responded.

When Vegas proposed he said he'd always send his love and it would be up to me to receive it. So each time he said the phrase, "Catch my heart," I was sure to respond. It was just a simple reminder of the commitment we'd made. Vegas would say it after arguments, when leaving, when getting off the phone, or anytime he felt I needed a little reminder.

Vegas had been wonderful from the time I announced I was pregnant. He was very attentive to my needs. He would drop everything if I needed something or if I didn't feel well. Within thirty minutes he was home.

We sat down and I grabbed Vegas's hand, looked him in the eyes, and began to explain. "Vegas, it's very important that you are here for our twins. I'm afraid that with the life you're living there's only two destinations—jail or death."

"I've been thinking the same thing. To be honest, I was actually afraid to mention it to you because I thought you wouldn't agree. I shaped you to be high maintenance, and if we had to budget and couldn't do things like the trips, cars, jewelry and designer wear, I was afraid you wouldn't be happy."

I couldn't believe he thought I was so shallow. "Baby, I am the happiest woman in the world. There is nothing else I want except security. I want to know that my husband will be home every night."

"Like I've said many times before, I got you, and you don't ever have to worry. I always got cha back. Now catch my heart, girl."

I hugged him and gave him a passionate kiss.

After talking for nearly two hours, he agreed to get out of the game. We came up with a plan to keep our income pretty much the same.

Vegas didn't hesitate to call his connect. "Yo, *P*, this is Vegas, man. There's gonna be some changes. I'm out the game. I'm passing the baton to my brothers now."

Of course, the connect did everything he could to talk Vegas out of getting out, but there was no use.

Next, he called his clients to tell them the same.

Over the next couple of weeks, we purchased a few laundromats in the area and began remodeling them. We made them larger, cleaned them up, equipped them with a variety of machines, added a drop-off service, a few TVs, a nice bathroom, a microwave, a number of snack machines and video games. We also allowed 24-hour access.

Within a couple of months the laundromats were fully operational. They blew up very fast. We had all types of promotions to boost business. Things turned out better than we'd ever expected.

Life was better than I ever thought possible. I was now four and a half months and already huge. It had been confirmed that I was having girls. I had known it all along.

Vegas and I joined a church not far from our home. We became active members and began to arrange for the wedding as well as the twins' christening.

I was counting down the months as they passed. I couldn't wait until that fifth month so that I could start my shopping spree.

Vegas and I decided I would take leave from work during my pregnancy, so I had a lot of time on my hands to prepare for the twins' arrival. Even though I was no longer working, I was always doing things at the church, keeping everything up to par at the laundromats and constantly doing things around the house.

Vegas quickly noticed that I was pushing myself too hard. "Why don't you take a break and let me handle things for a while?" he suggested.

That night, he cooked dinner, and we ate in bed. Within a matter of minutes, we were both sound asleep.

Arf! Arf! Arf!

Bing! Bang! Boom!

We woke to the sound of Prissy barking nonstop and a noise that sounded like the house was caving in. The huge spotlight that flashed through the bay window blinded me. I didn't know what was going on.

Vegas turned to me and asked, "You trust me, right?"

"Yes," I responded.

"Well, I want you to listen to me and do exactly what I say. You know I would never let anyone hurt you or do anything to hurt you. I want you to lie down, close your eyes, and go back to sleep. When you wake up, everything will be okay."

I trusted Vegas. He never let me down before, so I did just that. I had no intentions of going to sleep until I knew Vegas was safe, but I did close my eyes as he had asked me to do. I began praying to God for our safety as all the commotion went on outside my bedroom doors.

"I love you," Vegas whispered and kissed me. Then, he walked out of the room, closing the door behind him.

I could hear people coming from every direction, stomping up the stairs, slamming doors, and tossing things everywhere.

After a few minutes, the house was silent.

I walked in the hall and watched as Vegas walked to the foyer with his hands up. He stood still and spread his legs. The men ran toward him and Vegas lay on the ground slowly. This was the moment I had been dreading our entire relationship. They were there and taking my husband-to-be away from me.

I cried silently as I helplessly watched.

"Keep your hands up! Don't move!" A dark, heavy man walked up and cuffed Vegas.

"Laymont Jackson, you have the right to remain silent . . ."

The rest of the words were a blur. I felt faint as I watched the men escort Vegas away.

Vegas looked back at me. "Catch my heart, baby. Catch my heart." A single tear rolled down his face.

The men pulled him, and eventually all I could see was the reflection of the letters *FBI* on the back of the men's jackets.

The next day, I sat by the phone and waited to hear Vegas's voice, but he never called.

A day later, he called right after breakfast. "What's up, baby girl?" he said in a low, dismal voice.

I couldn't respond. I just burst into tears.

"I'm sorry, *C.* I know I let you down."

"You said you would always take care of me, Vegas. You knew this was my worst nightmare, and you didn't prevent it from happening."

"I never meant to let you down, Ceazia. I did everything you asked of me. This was out of my control, baby. I would never do anything to hurt you."

"What about our twins being without their father and me without a husband? There is no way we can do it on our own."

"Baby, I need you to get it together. I need you to stand behind me. Everything will be okay. I need you to go downtown and speak with my lawyer. He'll know exactly what to do."

Vegas was charged with conspiracy to traffic and distribute a controlled substance with Leonardo Figueroa a.k.a. Red. I knew something was up with Red from the day I met him, but I couldn't understand what the authorities had against Vegas. He had been out of the game for months, and he hadn't spoken to Red in even longer.

The next day, I headed for the attorney's office. Once again, I was in the same elevator, pressing the button for the eighth floor. I never would have imagined I would be taking that trip again.

As I walked in, I gave the receptionist my name. It was like deja vu. "My name is Ceazia Devereaux. I have a two o'clock appointment."

Right away, I was called to the back.

Again, I stood at the door nervously as I avoided eye contact with the handsome, pale man before me.

"Have a seat, Ms. Devereaux."

It seemed like he didn't even recognize me, or at least he acted as if he didn't. He already knew why I was there, so he basically told me the game plan and the price.

"It seems like Mr. Jackson has gotten himself in a little bind. I'm sure it won't be a problem to get a deal for two years in a program. The Feds only have a few photographs of him with another dealer in Mexico and some other places, but no real hard evidence. They didn't recover any drugs or money from the home, and all the money in his accounts trace back to a legitimate source," the attorney explained.

"The only reason Laymont is being held is because narcotics had a big drug bust in Park Place and some of the small fish ratted on the big fish to shorten their time. With the help of those guys, they were able to build a tree of all the dealers in the area. Laymont, along with Red, Bear, and a few other guys, were at the top of the list. After they got all the small fish off the street, they forwarded the information to the Feds so they could get the big fish. You shouldn't worry, though," the attorney assured me. "Laymont will be home in no time."

"Sounds great. How much will all this cost me, sir?"

"Because this is a federal case, we're looking at ten thousand."

Without any hesitation, I wrote him a check in the amount of ten thousand dollars and left.

As soon as I walked into the house, the phone rang. "Hello," I answered.

"Hey, baby. What's the deal?" Vegas asked after I accepted the collect call.

"Everything sounds good, baby. Your lawyer says there's no need to worry. At the most, you're looking at a couple of years in a program."

"What?"

"Two years, baby. What's wrong with that?"

"That just won't do, baby. I can't settle for that. Who the fuck is going to be there for you and the girls?"

"We can manage, baby. Things could be worse."

I told Vegas about the bust they had out the way and their intentions to work out deals with the small hustlers so they could get to the big hustlers.

Vegas was well aware of the tree. The Feds actually showed him the list when he was in interrogation. He went on to tell me about his experience. "Yeah, they showed me all that shit during interrogation. They kept asking me about some guy out of Jamaica. They've been following this nigga and his family for years. They were on his ass, but that nigga got smart. The Feds are having problems tracing the money. Without an exchange in money and drugs, there's no way they can pin him. They did seize a ship once, but that led them to a dead-end."

As Vegas told me the details of what the Feds had said, my heart froze with fear. *Oh my God, they're talking about India's boyfriend, and if they find out about the money, she'll be on the list as well.* I probed to see how much Vegas knew about the Jamaican kingpin. "So are you going to work with them, baby?"

"Hell nah, ma. I don't even know this cat. They offered me a deal if I would give him up, but I can't fuck with that. I have too much on the line to become a snitch. And like I said, I don't even know him."

He expressed his worry about the safety of the twins and me. I told him not to worry and that he would be home soon. He felt a little better but was still upset that he would miss the growth of his twins. He would not be at their birth, and he would not witness their first steps, first tooth, or first word.

I cried as I thought of not having him with me to share in the milestones of our daughters' first year of life.

Chapter 10

A Lonely Battle

As the months passed, I became depressed and lonely. I turned to the one person who could offer me the support and comfort I needed without being judgmental.

"Hello," my mother answered with her warm voice.

"Mommy, I miss you. I'm so alone and depressed," I whined.

"Awww, baby. Why don't you come and visit me for a couple of weeks?"

Since I hadn't seen her or my close friend, Chastity, in at least a year, I agreed.

My mom had moved to Atlanta shortly after her divorce from my father. She felt like she needed a new beginning; Atlanta was the place for Chastity's new beginning as well. She'd moved there shortly after her father's death. Hell, if it worked for them, I figured it couldn't hurt me to visit for a couple of weeks, so I happily took my mom up on her offer.

Once I received my call from Vegas and told him of my plans, I quickly packed four weeks' worth of clothes, even though I only planned to stay for two.

I loaded the Louis Vuitton luggage in the truck and headed for the airport. Two hours later I was in Atlanta.

My mother was at work when I arrived, so Chastity was there waiting for my flight. I was so excited to see her. We had been friends since we were tots. I could see her chatting away on her cell. Her petite frame was outfitted in a power blue business suit, stiletto pumps, with a Gucci clutch bag in hand and Gucci frames.

Chastity was about business. Ever since we were young, she knew she would be an entrepreneur. She owned two businesses in the metro area, a strip club and a soul food restaurant, both upscale. She ran her strip club with strict rules. Her girls were top-of-the-line, and she took no shit. If they didn't follow her guidelines, they were out the door. Her restaurant, a quiet, after-work spot with a jazz band, served some of the best food in the area.

"Hey, Momma! I can't believe how big you've gotten," Chastity said, hugging me tight.

"I know. It's all stomach, girl," I said as I hugged her back.

On the drive to her house, I updated her on all the drama of our friends.

In no time, we were pulling up to her house in Buckhead. It was beautiful. I was so proud of Chastity's accomplishments.

After an hour or so, my mother arrived at Chastity's house.

I ran toward her like a small child. "Mommy, I missed you sooooo much!"

"I've missed you too, honey," she said as she kissed me on my forehead.

My mother was the happiest person I knew. No matter what hand she was dealt in life, she would pick herself up, dust herself off, and keep going. Because I had chosen to stay with my mother after her divorce, my dad decided to leave her with everything. That was a wonderful gesture, but the problem was that he left no means of maintaining them. My mother was left to foot the bill for a quarter-million-dollar home, three elaborate cars, and my college education. She barely had enough money from her nursing salary to pay our mortgage and was forced to stretch her check to maintain the lifestyle that we'd become accustomed to.

"God will provide," she would constantly say as she hummed the tune of "What a Friend We Have in Jesus."

I hated my father for making her suffer the way she did. She worked two jobs just to pay the bills and make sure I had the things I needed during college. I never went without, but I was angry that my mom had to work so hard to make sure of that.

After I graduated from college my mother felt comfortable enough to move to Atlanta. I, on the other hand, decided I'd made my imprint on Virginia, so it was here I had to stay.

My dad was furious at the idea, but there was no changing my decision. To sway me to change my mind, he eventually cut off my weekly deposits. I soon experienced the struggles my mom had once felt, but not even that could change my mind. I was in Virginia and there was not changing my mind.

My father was the VP of marketing for one of the largest record companies in New York. While in Virginia he held an executive position at a local record company and would often travel back and forth between Virginia and New York. This worked great until the time span between the visits began to get longer and longer. It eventually got to the point where we were only seeing him on holidays.

My mom suspected foul play. And like every woman, she

did her homework to find out. Needless to say, her suspicion was right. My dad was cheating with a young, southern white girl who was working as an intern with the company. He eventually left my mother for this white woman who was half his age.

When I think back, he was never a dad. He was so consumed by his job that he never had time for his family. He missed birthdays and even anniversaries. All my mother and I really had was each other, so when he left, I didn't feel alone. Actually, I saw little difference in life at home. There was a financial difference, but that's about it.

Not long after my mother arrived, we decided to head to the mall. Chastity stayed behind, saying she would give us some time alone to catch up.

"I am so excited about my first grandchild!" my mother expressed as we swung into the parking space.

Once we entered the mall, she went wild, wanting to purchase everything. I figured it was okay since I had finally reached my fifth month. She purchased everything from clothes to cribs. She even planned to turn one of her extra bedrooms into a room for the twins.

"I expect to see my grandbabies at least once a month. And when they come, they'll be comfortable in their own little room."

As the days passed, I started missing Vegas more and more. I cried myself to sleep each night, as I lay alone in my bed. My life seemed so empty without him.

One morning, I decided to take a long, hot bath to relieve some of the pain I was feeling from carrying the twins. I'd been having a lot of discomfort the last few days. I lit the aromatherapy candles surrounding the bathtub and immersed my body in the water.

After five minutes of soaking, I had a sudden urge to urinate. I struggled to lift my one hundred sixty five pound body out of the tub. I took the first step out, then a watery fluid gushed onto the floor. "Aaaaahhhhh! Mommyyyyyyyy!!!" I screamed in fear as I stood with my legs apart.

She rushed into the bathroom and looked down at the floor. "Your water has broken, baby. It's a little too early for that, but don't worry." She calmly dialed 911.

My stomach cramped so bad that I gently lowered myself to the bathroom floor and rolled on my side in a fetal position.

"Breathe, baby, breathe," my mother instructed.

Based on the closeness of my contractions, the 911 operator informed my mother that I was going to deliver soon. I positioned myself on my back and bent my knees. My body shook with pain as sweat rolled from my forehead. With every contraction, it felt natural for me to push. It seemed that was the only way to stop the pain. So, with each contraction I pushed.

After several pushes, my first twin was out, but there was no crying, only silence.

"Mommy, why isn't she crying? Why isn't she crying?" I began to panic. "Please, give her CPR, Mommy. Please, do something to help her breathe."

It was at that moment the emergency rescue team rushed into the bathroom. They immediately grabbed the first twin, cut the cord and began to deliver the next.

Once again, I pushed and the second twin was out. She came into the world with a small, broken cry.

Again, the emergency technician snatched the twin away. They hurried us all to the nearest hospital as I bled continuously.

When we got to the hospital, I was in terrible condition.

I felt like my life was slipping away. I became really cold, as everything went black and I fell into a deep sleep.

I opened my eyes slowly to the bright lights above my hospital bed. Beside me sat my mother. Her head rested on my leg as she rubbed my hand. She was so excited that I was awake. I could not speak and my body was very stiff. I looked around the room for my twins, but they were not there. I wanted to ask where they were, but I couldn't find the strength for words.

As the hours passed, the doctors ran a number of tests and removed many of the tubes that were attached to my body.

The next day, I felt much stronger and was able to speak. The only thing I wanted was to see my twins. Again, my mother was right beside me when I awoke.

"Mom, how are my twins, and where are they?" I had a heavy feeling in my heart as I awaited the answer. By the look on her face, I knew it couldn't be good.

"I'm sorry, honey. Your twins didn't make it. I already contacted the prison so they could relay the news to Vegas. I'm so sorry, honey," she said in a broken voice.

She explained to me that I had been in a coma for the past month. She went on to tell me the events that followed the delivery of my babies.

"After giving birth to the twins, your uterus didn't contract, so you kept bleeding. You lost so much blood that you became unconscious and eventually comatose. Once they got the babies and you to the hospital, they rushed you into surgery. The entire time you were in a coma, your twins struggled for their little lives. They were less than two pounds each and very underdeveloped. One struggled with lung problems, while the other struggled with fluid on her brain."

I cried as my mother told me the ups and downs of their

struggles. I felt so bad. My mom said the girls fought until I came out of my coma, at which time they died simultaneously. I didn't understand what I did to deserve such pain. I thought maybe that was the ultimate punishment for all the bad things Vegas and I had done.

I prayed for an answer, "God, we turned our lives around and attended church each Sunday. I gave continuous praise and worship for all my blessings. I just don't understand why You would allow something so terrible to happen."

A week later, I was discharged from the hospital.

"Honey, I think it's best you stay with me a little while longer. You seem a little depressed," my mom suggested.

I agreed to stay with her a couple of weeks longer.

During that time, I constantly questioned the Lord. "If all things of the Lord are good," I asked my mother, "then why does He allow tragedy?"

"The Lord doesn't allow anything to happen in vain. He allows us to go through things to bring us closer to Him."

Sad to say, I wasn't happy with the "God-works-in-mysterious-ways" or "it's-just-a-test-of-faith" or "the-Lord-has-a-plan-for-you" responses. I felt like God had played a cruel trick on me, and I definitely didn't find it funny. At that point, the Lord and I were on opposing teams.

My mother sensed my anger and felt there was only one way to save me from my despair. "Why don't you come to church with me this week?" she said. "We're having a healing convocation. I think it may help you feel better."

I refused with no explanation and shut myself off to all things. I just wanted to return home.

Chapter 11

Divas Need Therapy Too

By the time fall rolled around, I was back to wearing a size three. The laundromats were doing great, and Vegas was doing well, too. I traveled to Richmond each weekend to visit him. He had been sentenced to one year. The federal charge was dismissed, but he had to serve one year for violating his probation for being out of the state when we went to Cancun.

My body recovered well after my surgery, but emotionally, I was still in pretty bad shape. I decided to visit Charlotte in order to cope with the anger I was feeling over the twins' death. Our meetings were productive. Each week, she would give me a task to work on. One particular week she instructed me to take notes of the times when I was happy and not feeling frustrated at all. Before she gave me that task, I felt that I had little to no frustration, but once she gave me the task, my life became hell.

On the way from the session, a police officer pulled me over for a fake-ass violation, but I knew my only real crime was driving a nice car in the Great Neck area of Virginia Beach while young, black, and beautiful.

When the prick walked to the car, he didn't ask for a registration or license, but instead ordered me to step out of the car and put my hands on the hood.

Of course I refused.

"What exactly are you pulling me over for, sir? Would it be racial profiling, by chance?"

He got very angry and proceeded to pull me out of the car. Once he got me out, he held one arm behind my back and grabbed my neck with his free hand. Then he forced my face on the burning hood of the car and put the cuffs on me.

Needless to say, I went straight to jail with no get-out-of-jail-free card. He claimed he was pulling me over because my car fit the description of a stolen vehicle, even though I didn't fit the description of the suspect.

As soon as I was released on a personal release bond, I called my attorney. Then I contacted Asia. Asia was the bitch of all bitches when it came to things like this. As a bank executive, she rubbed elbows with all sorts of powerful people. There wasn't an issue she couldn't solve. She told me not to worry, she would take care of things. I didn't worry, because I knew that with my attorney and Asia's connections, plus her super-bitch attitude, the devil would run for cover.

It seemed like that incident was the beginning to an eternal hell. The few days after that were even worse. After working out one afternoon, I came home to a yellow bag from the Sheriff's Department. I wasn't happy seeing that damn bag on my gate. I snatched the bag off and began to read: *Virginia Beach Juvenile and Domestic Court in reference to Karen White versus Laymont Jackson.*

Now I was pissed. *What in the hell does he have a subpoena for? And who the hell is Karen White?*

I couldn't wait to get his call. I was prepared to fry his ass. *He's already put me through enough shit and now this*, I thought as I walked to the front door.

It wasn't long before I received the call that I had been anticipating.

As soon as he said, "Hello," I let him have it.

"What are you talking about, *C?* I never even heard of a Karen White."

I wasn't buying it. How could he not know her when she's got our address, his name, and his date of birth? I felt like I was going to have a nervous breakdown.

I screamed and slammed the phone down. I walked back and forth and let out a crazed cry. I was acting so crazy that Prissy ran under the bed and hid during my tantrum. I had to do something to calm down, so I made myself a drink. I had a Belvedere wth orange juice, and turned on "No Letting Go" by Wayne Wonder. I then sat in the Jacuzzi, and smoked some hydro. I was blazed as I sang with Wayne:

Got someboooooody,
Sheeee's a beauty,
Very speeeeeecial,
Really and truuuuuuuuly.
Takes good care of me,
Like it's her duuuuuty.
Walk riiiight by my side,
Niiight and daaaaay.

The truth in those words was amazing. The girl he spoke of in that song was me. I did all those things for Vegas and he deceived me. I went against everything that my parents **taught me** for the love of Vegas, and he stabbed me in the back. That brought so much pain to my heart that I just sat and cried.

A little while later, I found myself tipsy and decided to get some rest.

I awoke to the sound of the intercom. "Ceazia! Ceazia!"

It was Asia at the gate. I buzzed the gate open and met her at the door.

Asia stopped by to give me an update on everything she had done. "I contacted the officer's superior and filed a complaint for you. I also contacted the mayor's office and a local newscaster. I notified the NAACP and a local chapter of civil rights activists. Once we finish with his ass, he's gonna be willing to turn in his badge. I'm thinking you should even pursue a civil suit."

That's why I loved Asia so much. She was definitely a doer and not a talker. Her mission to make the officer's life a living hell was just about complete.

As we were talking, the phone rang. "Hello."

"Hey, girl," India said. "I need to talk to you."

"I swear you twins have some psychic connection. Asia just came over."

"Well, tell her to leave. We really need to talk."

I told Asia I would speak to her later since her sister was having a crisis. Asia left, and I went back to the phone.

India was so upset. She told me about a very disturbing call she'd received from her fiancé's brother. "Samuel has been apprehended by the Jamaican police. They tied him to a number of murders, and it doesn't look good. Samuel was set up by someone, but we have no idea who. He knows it had to be someone close, and from the way his brother speaks, I'm a suspect," India said, crying uncontrollably as she told me the story.

We all knew what that meant. Whoever Samuel felt had

the slightest possibility of being the snitch was surely on death row. He would kill every possible witness before he would serve time. We were surprised he didn't have a shootout with the police when they arrested him. Normally, all types of soldiers ready for war would have been surrounding him, but this time the authorities caught him alone. His brother didn't exactly say what Samuel was doing at the time he was apprehended, but the evidence pointed toward sex.

India didn't know what to think. Not only was her man in jail, he was cheating when he was arrested, and he might even have someone try to kill her. She wished that she had listened to me when I used to tell her about all the wicked things involved in that life.

We had to do something, not only for her safety, but also for her sanity. Our plan was to find out who set up Samuel and to find out if he really was cheating. The most important thing was to keep India alive while we were doing our research.

She decided she would stay at my old condo and take leave from work until things got a little safer.

The following weekend, I went to my next counseling session with Charlotte. When I walked in, she said, "Oh my, Ceazia, you look terrible. Why didn't you call for an emergency session?"

I cried as I told her all the events of the week. I didn't understand how so many terrible things could happen to one person. I just wondered what was in store for the next week.

"Well, let's see how we did on the assignment. Tell me a time when you felt relaxed," she said.

"Sadly, the only time during the entire week that I was

truly relaxed was after a ten-minute session with my dildo," I responded, truly embarrassed.

I would have told her about the time I sat in the Jacuzzi and drank Belvedere as I listened to reggae and smoked a blunt, but I didn't think that would draw a pretty self-portrait. I would be classified as a drunk and druggie, on top of having to discuss how I used artificial things to give me false happiness.

As we talked, she gave me a number of exercises to do when I found myself most stressed. They included breathing exercises, meditation, and muscle stretches. I thought it would be much easier if she would just prescribe Prozac, but at this point, I was willing to try anything.

Due to a call from my father as soon as I got home, I had the opportunity to try the stress relief exercise Charlotte taught me.

"I would like you to come to New York for Thanksgiving," he said.

"No way. I refuse to spend Thanksgiving with you and your dumb blonde wife. Besides, since you cut off my weekly deposits a long time ago, I can't afford a trip to New York," I lied to make him feel guilty. "Anyway, I'm sure you'll be busy working, so what's the point?"

He was so persistent that finally I just agreed to go.

Once I hung up, I did the exercise. I started with my toes and tightened each muscle then relaxed it. I did this for each muscle until I reached my neck. Amazingly, it worked. I actually felt relieved after I did the exercise.

That night, I called the girls and we decided to have dinner. We went to one of our favorite spots, a local soul food joint in downtown Norfolk. I was happy. It had been a long time since all of us were able to get together in one location.

Tionna was excited to tell us about her new man, Jonathan. He was the gynecologist who'd examined her at the health department. We all found that very funny. She told us how she ran into him a month later at the grocery store. He approached her and actually asked her out, and they had been dating ever since. She told us that they even talked about adopting Tonya's baby. They decided that since Tionna couldn't have children, they would adopt the little boy. They didn't have a decision from the adoption agency yet, but they were confident that everything would go through.

After we ate, we decided to go sit near the stage and listen to the poetry. As we listened, I noticed India kept looking over her shoulder.

"What are you doing?" I asked her, annoyed at her constant motion.

She pointed to a tall, slender, dark-skinned girl who sat at the bar. The girl was dressed plainly and wore a turban. India said the girl had been looking in our direction for the past thirty minutes.

I assumed she was just being paranoid, so I ordered her a Long Island Iced Tea to calm her nerves.

That dinner was just the atmosphere I needed. For the first time in a long time, I felt relieved. There was no stress at all. We all laughed, joked, and drank for the next hour. When it was time to go, we were all pretty toasted.

I decided to follow India to make sure she got home safely, since she was the most drunk. The condo was on the way to the Interstate, so it was on my route home. As she was pulling off toward the complex I saw her make a sudden stop.

I stopped behind her and headed toward the car door. As I approached, she opened the door and stuck her head out. Two seconds later, vomit was everywhere. Just the smell of it made my stomach turn, so I quickly turned and headed back to my car.

"Pull into the garage," I yelled. I followed her and helped her into the condo.

When we got inside, I filled the tub with aromatherapy bath pearls and warm water. I helped her undress and placed her inside the bathtub. While she was bathing, I went to the kitchen to make some cappuccino.

All of a sudden, I heard a loud thump. I figured she had probably fallen, so I headed to the bathroom to make sure she was okay. On the way, I felt a draft coming from the direction of the living room.

When I reached the living room, I noticed the French doors were cracked open. I opened the doors completely to inspect, and there was India standing on the balcony, butt naked and dripping wet, pointing a gold Glock with a pearl handle to her head. She had no idea I was standing right behind her.

She sobbed as she prayed in a soft whisper, "Lord, forgive me for the ultimate sin which I am about to commit." *Bam!*

At that moment, we both spun around at the sound of the French doors shutting. A tall, slender frame stood before us. In the person's hand was a long, silver machete that glistened in the dim light.

Instinctively, I jumped on the person and pushed the lanky body against the rail of the balcony. As we struggled, the towering person pushed the machete toward my neck. I became weaker and weaker as the struggle progressed. The person didn't seem to lose any strength as the machete was pressed against my neck.

It took every ounce of energy in my body to keep the force from cutting my throat. I could feel the pain as the knife began to slice my skin and the blood slowly trickled down my chest.

Bang! Bang! Bang! Bang! And the struggle was over.

The dark beast fell to the ground, stiff and lifeless.

I turned around to see India standing motionless with the gun pointing straight ahead, smoke rising from the barrel as she stood in the dark.

Chapter 12

Wonderful Closures

Things slowly came together as the months passed. I attended court with Vegas for the case he had in Virginia Beach Juvenile Domestic Court.

"Karen White versus Laymont Jackson," the court clerk announced.

As I walked in, I noticed a much older woman with a child who looked at least twelve years old. Now I knew Vegas was a male whore in his younger days, but this was ridiculous.

They brought Vegas from the holding cell in the back and stood him in front of the judge. Then the judge explained that they were there for child support.

Vegas looked back at me pitifully, and I glared at him with a look of death.

While the judge spoke, the woman looked at Vegas as if she was in a state of confusion.

"This in not my child's father," she said. "I'm here to collect back child support from Laymont Jackson."

"That is Laymont Jackson," the judge responded.

As it turned out, the courts had subpoenaed the wrong Laymont Jackson. Vegas was telling the truth. He didn't know the woman after all. I felt so bad that I had doubted him.

As the deputy took him away in shackles, he looked at me and gave me that same mesmerizing smile from the first day we met and whispered, "Catch my heart."

Tears rolled from my eyes as I blew him a kiss and mouthed the words, "I love you." For the first time in months, I felt like I loved Vegas and missed him. I had so much anger and frustration inside of me that I nearly forgot what it was like to love.

Things with India were continuously progressing. She returned to work, and with Charlotte's help, she got over Samuel as well.

After the shooting at the condo, everything came together. The masked person from that night was a female by the name of Chantelli, one of Samuel's soldiers. It was the same girl India had seen in the restaurant that night. We'd slipped while we were out enjoying ourselves. Samuel knew India would end up there eventually, so he had the girl stake out the place for weeks until we showed up.

We soon found out that Samuel's brother was the culprit behind all the hysteria. He was jealous of Samuel's success, so he set him up. He knew if Samuel was killed or jailed, the empire would be passed on to him. He'd contacted the authorities and gave them leads on a number of murders, then he gave them the cue for the arrest.

Because he was Samuel's brother, he knew there were only a few instances when Samuel would be alone. Usually Samuel was surrounded by his soldiers, and they were always ready for war. However, his brother knew Samuel had one thing he did alone, and that was sex. So, when Samuel was in the act, his brother gave the signal.

The police rushed in and caught him with his pants down, literally. He was standing ass naked, getting what seemed to be the head of a lifetime.

We were surprised to learn a "battie boy" was giving the head he was receiving. Who would have ever thought the "don dada" would be getting sucked off by a homo? He was so afraid of someone finding out about his secret life that he would risk his safety and send his soldiers away. Any good kingpin would have known that would be his downfall.

India was infuriated by Samuel's infidelity and wanted him to pay dearly for breaking her heart. She had put her career and her life in danger by doing the money exchange for him. She was even going to leave the States, move to Jamaica, and marry Samuel. And to think the entire time he had a secret life.

India asked that I lay an evil cloud above his head for the misery and pain she'd suffered. The evil spells of voodoo were not something I usually practiced, but I agreed. The smell of cinnamon was in the air as I did the wicked trickery. The empire of his family would surely fall, and his soul along with it.

Tionna and Jonathan decided to get married. They were planning a huge wedding at the Botanical Gardens in Norfolk. Tionna arranged for a wedding party of at least fifteen and invited five hundred guests. They would spend their honeymoon in Paris. I was so happy for Tionna. She deserved Jonathan, the wedding, and the honeymoon. Dealt bad hands her whole life, it was finally her turn to be blessed.

Although they were not granted the right to adopt Tonya's

little boy, she was still happy. The adoption agency felt the circumstances under which the child was conceived didn't make Tionna the best candidate for the adoption. They did grant the adoption to her uncle, though. We were all just happy the child was going to be raised by a family member.

Tionna and Jonathan had plans of their own to have a child. With Jonathan being a gynecologist, he did plenty of research on a number of studies about infertility. He arranged for Tionna to try infertility pills, injections, and if neither of those methods work, in vitro fertilization.

Once they got married, they were planning to move to Atlanta. Jonathan landed a job with the Centers for Disease Control, and Tionna wanted a new start. Her life was finally on the path we all dreamed of, and we wished her well.

As the days passed, I continued missing Vegas more and more. Each weekend I would travel one hundred miles to visit him. I hated the constant struggle with the deputies every weekend. First, all the visitors had to line up to be sniffed by a dog. Then the butch female deputies sexually harassed us. One particular female deputy always gave me a hard time. *I wouldn't be surprised if she was fucking Vegas*, I thought to myself.

One visit she had the audacity to say, "Excuse me, ma'am, do you have a thong on?"

I looked at her with a cold stare and said, "No, I do not." In fact, I had no panties on at all. It took all I had to keep from smacking the color off her face.

Even though I went through hell to see Vegas, I enjoyed each visit. I was always dressed for easy access.

Vegas had it worked out with the correctional officers to simply ignore us when we went into the broom closet during each visit. The closet was about the size of a bathroom—just the right size for a quickie. Vegas would unfold the chair that was conveniently placed in the closet, pull down his pants, and sit with his penis at attention.

That was my cue to pull up my skirt and hop right on it. It was amazing all the positions we could do in that chair. Vegas's favorite position was when I would sit on his penis facing away from him, grab my ankles, and bounce up and down. He loved to see my ass bounce while he watched his penis disappear deep inside my vagina.

After our quick session the visit was usually over. I would immediately run to the car to retrieve the wet wipes and panties that I had waiting. I would clean myself up, put on the fresh pair of panties, and hit the road.

Chapter 13

Reach for the Rasta

Thanksgiving finally rolled around and it was time for me to take that dreaded trip to New York to see my father. When I arrived at the airport, old blondie herself was waiting.

"Hel-lo," I greeted sarcastically.

"Darling, you look terrible. Was your flight here okay?"

Now what type of shit is that to say? What if I thought I looked great? "Yeah, the flight was kind of rough." I glared at her. "So what's your excuse?" Even though the flight was fine, I needed a comeback.

During the entire drive to the house, she quizzed me. "How are things back home? Did that boyfriend of yours get out of prison yet? How is your mother? Is she still caring for sick poor people at that city hospital?"

When she finally took a breath, I got my chance to fire back. "Life at home is great. The business is doing well, and Vegas will be home soon. And as far as my mother is concerned, that's none of your business. Now, if you would like to know how things were before you became my father's mistress, I can certainly tell you about that."

I would never tell that wench anything she could use to belittle me. She did everything she could to make me look bad and make herself look good. That was the only way she could lift herself up, because in reality she was nothing without my dad.

It was cold and windy as I walked to the front door of my father's house. The butler met me and quickly took my coat. The house was warm and I could smell the aroma of fresh brewed coffee.

I was shown to my "quarters," as the balding butler said in an English accent. The room was huge, but not very welcoming. I didn't know who my dad used as his interior decorator, but from the looks of things, I was sure the dumb blonde had a lot to do with it. I felt like I was walking into a barn. The theme of the room was antique country and it was disgusting. I felt like singing "Old Mac Donald," as I entered. There was definitely a *moo-moo* here and a *quack-quack* there. There were farm animals everywhere—the wallpaper border, linens, and even the pictures on the wall.

Once I was settled, I decided to give Carmin a call. She was in New York preparing for a Thanksgiving fashion show for the stars. I was glad she was close by to provide me relief from "the Addams family."

"Carmin's Creations," she said as she answered the phone.

"Hey, girl! Where's the party at tonight?"

"Ceazia Devereaux! What the hell is going on? You know the fashion show is on Thanksgiving, so I'm gonna be really busy. But I'll pick you up and we'll go to the show and then the after-party. I have someone I want you to meet."

Carmin knew damn well I wasn't trying to meet nobody. I told her, "Don't nobody want to meet no possessive-ass I-

want-you-and-my-girl-plus-my-man's-girl type nigga," I com-
plained.

"I'll be there at eight," Carmin said. "Dress to impress."

"Aight, girl."

Just then, the butler knocked at the door. "The man of
the house would like you in his presence."

I laughed and said in a mocking voice. "And where
might that man's presence be?"

He directed me down a long hall to my father's study,
where my father sat behind a huge maple wood desk in a
burgundy leather chair reading a newspaper.

When I entered, he looked over his glasses. "Hi, darling.
How are you?"

He seemed happy to see me, but I'll never know if it was
genuine. My father had changed so much. He acted like he
had a stick up his ass. He was such a stiff.

When he lived with my mother and me, he didn't speak
the way he did now. He didn't dress the way he did now and
he definitely didn't have the same taste in women. Who
said money doesn't change people?

I gave my father a big hug. I really did miss him even
though he did so much to hurt me. I told him about everything that was going on at home.

He gave me a long lecture about moving to New York so
that I could be closer to him. This way he could protect me.

The next day the maid knocked on my door. "Breakfast,
Ms. Devereaux."

I looked over at the clock and it read seven a.m. "Come
in," I said, still half-asleep.

The maid walked in with a tray that consisted of breakfast, a newspaper, and a carnation. It instantly brought back
memories of Cancun.

"Thank you," I said as she turned to leave. I barely touched the food as I cried. I thought of the wonderful times Vegas and I had in Mexico and how much I missed him.

Ring, ring! Ring, ring!

"Who in the hell is calling me so early?" I looked at the caller ID on my cell phone. "What the hell does Carmin want so early in the morning? Hello."

"*C*, wake up."

"I am awake. What do you want so early?" I plucked the crust from my eyes.

"I'm headed to a video shoot and I want you to meet the artist. I'm on my way to get you now. Get dressed!"

Knowing that putting up an argument would be useless, I dragged myself out of bed and got dressed.

Thirty minutes later, Carmin was out front and honking her horn. It didn't take long for us to arrive at the location of the shoot. It was just as I imagined. There were cameras, half-dressed chicks, make-up artists, and lots of wannabes everywhere.

"There's Cobra." Carmin grabbed my arm and pulled me along.

A dark-skinned, bald guy asked in a deep, scratchy voice, "What up, Carm? Who's that you got with you?"

I really wasn't interested in entertaining this guy or his entourage, but I spoke up for Carmin's sake. "I'm Ceazia, but you can call me *C*."

"Okay. Nice to meet you, *C*."

As he was speaking, I noticed one of his boys who stood apart from everyone else. He seemed to be in a deep phone conversation, but he was constantly giving me the eye. I pretended not to notice and walked over to the refreshment table for bottled water. That was the only escape from Cobra.

Carmin walked over soon after me. "So what do you think, girl?"

"I think I'm not interested. But his boy, the one with the dreads, Lakers throwback, and baby blue Pradas, he can get it."

"Damn, girl, you were watching him like that?"

"Don't front, Carmin. You know how we do. It doesn't take but five seconds to do a complete rundown and calculation of net worth, deductions already included."

"Okaaaaayyyyy!" We both shouted in our best "sista girl" voices as we gave each other a high-five.

The video shoot was long and tiring. I could have sworn they shot each scene at least ten times. It lasted until ten at night.

Afterwards, we all decided to meet at Club Inferno at midnight. The club was jumping. People were packed shoulder to shoulder, as we squeezed our way to the VIP section. We sat amongst Cobra and his crew.

I made it my business to sit as close as possible to the dread-wearing brotha from earlier.

The waitress brought over bottles of Cristal back to back. That's when he finally spoke. "Ya want a drink, gal?"

Oh my goodness, he has an accent. I think I'm in love.

"Aye, ya 'ear me, gyal? Ya want a drink?"

"Yes, I do. I would like a screwdriver," I said in my most seductive voice and gave him the eye.

It was as if he didn't even notice as he ordered the drink for me.

"I don't know what his problem is, but I am the hottest chick in here," I whispered to Carmin. "He can't front for too long. I *will* have him by the end of the night."

As the night went on, I did everything I could to get his attention without making it too obvious. I bent over the table to speak to Carmin so that my breasts would clearly be visible. I crossed my legs so that the split in my dress would show my thighs up to my hips, and I even started small talk with him first. Nevertheless, he still seemed unmoved.

I was finally fed up with this Rasta, so I decided to go find Carmin. In no time I found her at the bar talking with a few Spanish girls. I noticed one girl staring at me, so I decided to break in the conversation and get Carmin's attention. "Excuse me. Carmin, I need to speak to you for a second."

"Hey, girl! Let me introduce you to my girls. Everyone, this is my girl, Ceazia. *C*, this is Maritza, Chloe, Lachele, and Arizelli."

Arizelli, Arizelli? Why does that sound familiar? I looked at the girl and tried to put a face with the name.

My confusion must have been obvious, because Carmin began shaking my shoulder and shouting. "*C*, you all right? What the hell you been drinkin', girl?"

That's when it hit me. *Cancun. I know it's a small world, but how the hell did this happen?*

"Hellooooo, Ceazia?"

"Oh, I'm sorry, girl. My head is just spinning. I think it's from mixing those drinks. I just came over to tell you I'm giving up on Donovan. For some reason, he's just not feeling me."

"What? Nah, there has got to be something up. I'll be over there in a minute. You need to sit down and sober up a little."

As I walked away, I noticed Carmin grabbing Arizelli around the waist as they whispered in each other's ears.

I returned to a seat far from Donovan the Rasta. I made it a point not to notice him or acknowledge his presence at all. Then, just as the night was starting to get boring, the DJ began to play reggae, and the party was on.

"Come down, selecta!" I heard a voice yell.

Donovan was once again turning me on. Each time the DJ played a rhythm the crowd liked, Donovan would throw his fingers up and yell, "Buk, buk, buk, buk," and bang his Guinness bottle against the table.

I was feeling nice and having a ball. When the DJ played Sean Paul's "Gimme the Light," I jumped to my feet and started to wind. Everyone stared as I moved to the West Indian tunes.

Out of nowhere, someone came behind me and began to dance along. I turned around and smiled when I realized it was Donovan.

"Ya dance like a yard gyal," he whispered in my ear.

I did it. I finally did it. If I had known all I had to do was wind, he would have been mine a long time ago, I thought as I continued to dance even more seductively.

"Thanks, but no yardie taught me these moves," I said as I walked out of my wind and into the steps of Spragga Benz. Dancing was my drop, so if that's what he wanted, then that's what I was giving. I did every dance move I could think of.

By the end of the night, he was eating out of the palm of my hand.

"Dancehall princess, come 'ere. Mi want ta speak wit' ya," he said as I took a break to sip on my drink.

I sat beside him. "Dancehall princess?"

"True. Ya move dem crowd. It's like a wicked spell."

"Oh, that's what it is?"

"Mi na know the trickery of ya Creole gal. You wind up mi heart with that evil art."

Listening to Donovan was like interpreting Shakespeare, but I did well with my interpretations. "Are you insinuating that I used voodoo to put you in a trance through my dancing?"

"Ya, mon. I notice at first glance ya to be wed, so mi stand clear. But now, like a magnet, you're near."

I don't know if it was the drinks or what, but the more he talked, the more he sounded like a reggae song. I had to clear my head, so I excused myself. "I'm sorry, but I'm feeling a little sick. I'm going to get a bottled water."

"Take dis. Keep da change."

I walked away and headed back to the bar. As I got closer, I could see Carmin still chatting with Arizelli. She kissed her on her lips and began to walk in my direction.

Oh my goodness, Carmin is gay. What do I do? Does she know I just saw that? I don't know if I'm ready to have this conversation with Carmin. "Hey, girl. I thought you were going to come back over to VIP with me earlier," I said nervously.

"Well, reggae came on, so I knew you would be fine. How long you been standing here?"

"Not long. I mean, I just started walking this way."

"Ceazia," Carmin said as if she knew I was lying, "follow me. I need to introduce you to someone."

We headed back toward the bar with the same girls.

"Okay, Carm, I think you had too much to drink now. Ummmm, you introduced me to all these girls earlier," I said.

"l know, but I really need to explain some things about one girl in particular."

Once we reached the bar, she grabbed Arizelli by the hand, and we all went back to the VIP section. To my surprise, Cobra and his crew all knew Arizelli.

This is getting weirder by the minute.

We all sat down, and Carmin began to explain.

"Ceazia, Arizelli is more than just a friend to me. She is my lover."

"Lover? As in your gay lover? Or your I'm-just-curious-so-let's-try-this lover?" I asked.

"I'm not gay, *C*, nor am I just curious. I love Arizelli, and I am bisexual," Carmin said with confidence.

Now, how was I supposed to tell Carmin that both me and Vegas had sex with her lover? I pinched myself to see if I could wake from this nightmare.

"*C*, what's wrong? Do you have a problem with my sexuality?"

I guess I was thinking a little too long. "Nah, girl. Do you. You're my girl. I'm going to love you regardless of your sexuality, but just explain why."

"*C*, I could no longer continue being second. No matter how hard I tried or what I did, I was never going to be number one in my previous relationship. When Arizelli came along, I was number one. She loved me unconditionally, and she gives me all the attention and affection I could ever want or need."

I reached over and hugged her. "It's cool, Carm. I love you, girl."

As we hugged, Arizelli licked her lips and blew me a kiss.

"Thanks, *C*. I love you too. Let's keep this just between us for now, okay?"

"Okay."

A while later the club began to clear out, so we said our goodbyes and went our separate ways.

Chapter 14

Thanksgiving with the Addams Family

"Rise and shine," the maid said as she knocked on the door.

Again, I was greeted with breakfast in bed. I ate the fruit as I thought about the previous night. *Carmin's lover is Cancun Arizelli. Wait until I tell Vegas. Even worse, I think Arzelli still wants me. Or maybe she wants Vegas, because she never really got a taste of the dick. Do I tell Carmin or not? If I tell Carmin, then my secret is out, but if I don't, then it's like I'm betraying her.*

Knock, knock!

"Yes."

"Good morning, honey. Can I come in?"

"Sure, Dad. Come on in."

My dad came in and sat at the end of the bed. "We have a long day today. I want to start the day off with church service. Then we'll eat about three. How does that sound?"

"That's fine, Daddy. I promised Carmin I would go to the Thanksgiving celebrity fashion show with her tonight, though."

"Hey, I have tickets to that. Maybe your mother and I will go too."

"That's *stepmother*, and I think I'd rather go with Carmin."

With nothing left to say, my dad left and began to prepare for church.

Church service was long and boring. It was nothing like the down-home Baptist services that I was used to. I couldn't believe this woman changed everything about my dad, from his attire to his religion.

Dinner was served shortly after we returned from church. The table setting was beautiful. The room was dim with candles lighting the table. There was enough food to feed a village in Africa for at least a month. At the table were my father and I, the wicked witch, and a few of her family members. My dad and I were outnumbered even in his own home. A pianist played classical music as we ate dinner, and the butlers stood at each end of the table waiting to move on command. I found this all quite humorous.

"Darling, what is so funny?" the gold digger asked.

"Nothing. I was just thinking to myself."

"Why don't you tell the family about the little business you run in Virginia?"

Like always, she was trying to make me look like I was nothing.

"If you are referring to the chain of laundromats I own, I will be more than happy to share," I responded.

"Oh my, that is a wonderful success story. I'd love to hear about underprivileged black kids who grow up and make something of themselves, like you and your father."

My father must have seen the steam rise from my head because he quickly intervened. "Mother, you are out of line. My child has never been poor."

That's it! Dad was only offended by the suggestion that I was poor? What about the generalization of black people? I tried my best to bite my tongue. Only five seconds passed, but I could no longer do it. "I have had it with all of you! Dad, you are a poor excuse for a strong black man. You're the reason our black youth have no male role models. And to the wife and mother blondie, neither of you have ever accomplished anything in life. It's like you were raised to seek men who are well-off, so you can sit on your uneducated, Southern-belle asses. I'm out of here. Dad, you can have your so-called family!"

I stormed to my room and immediately called Carmin.

"Hello."

"Carmin, it's *C.* Come get me, girl."

"Okay. What's wrong?"

I told her all about the dinner conversation as I pulled out something to wear.

"Ceazia!" my dad shouted as he stood at the bedroom door.

"I don't want to talk. Leave me alone."

He entered the room anyway. He tried hopelessly to explain away the incident that had occurred during dinner.

I ignored his weak excuses for his so-called family and continued to prepare for the night.

"Do you hear me talking to you?" he asked angrily.

"Yes, father, I do hear you. I hear all the tired excuses you're giving for your family, for your actions, and for their actions. I'd rather know your reason for leaving me and mom. Or your reason for leaving me to fight on my own after college. You're quick to tell me that Vegas is not the guy for me, but he's the one that's been there for me for the last couple of years. He's been doing all the things that you used to do. I don't know what happened, dad, but you've truly changed, and I really wish I could have my daddy back." With that I grabbed my coat and headed toward the door.

Carmin was out front in no time.

I jumped in her truck, and we headed for the plaza where the fashion show was being held.

It was chaotic getting to the front row seat Carmin had reserved for me. I sat amongst Cobra and his crew once again. I was disappointed that Donovan was nowhere to be found.

Cobra looked up and down my body. "What up, *C?*"

"Chillin'. What about you?" I sat one seat away from him, refusing to be right underneath his annoying ass.

The music blasted as the first model walked out. Carmin had really outdone herself this time. The models' outfits were the shit! I was so into the show, I didn't even notice someone had taken the seat next to me.

"Whattem," I heard a pleasing voice in my ear.

"Donovan. What's up, baby?"

"Ya save da seat 'ere for mi, gyal?" He licked his sexy lips.

Just his presence was making me moist. "Not exactly, but if you would like to sit here, that's fine."

In no time the show was over and I headed to the back to meet Carmin. On the way, I stopped by the concession stand to purchase a dozen roses.

"You did great, girl!" I rushed over, gave her a hug, and handed her the roses. I had no idea Carmin was doing such great things with her career.

"Thanks, girl. I put a lot into this show. So you really enjoyed it?"

"Sure did," a voice said before I could respond. To my surprise, it was Arizelli.

"Hi, baby," Carmin said. They greeted each other with a small kiss.

Cobra walked over with his entourage. "What up, Carm? That shit was hot!"

I was really beginning to get irritated when Donovan caught my eye. I gave him my most seductive glance then turned to Carmin and finished our conversation. I was sure to give him just enough attention to turn him on, but not so much that I looked desperate.

It worked. He's on his way over, I thought as Donovan walked toward me.

"Whattem?"

"Hey, Donovan. What's the deal?"

"Not much. You goin' to the dancehall tonight?"

"I think so. I'll have to see what Carm is doing."

"Hope ta see ya dere," he said as he walked away.

Just as I expected, we headed to Club Inferno after the show. This time the club was twice as packed as the night before.

The bouncer unhooked the velvet rope so that Carmin, Arizelli, and I could enter. "Hello, ladies. Right this way."

As soon as we got in, Carmin excused herself to go to the restroom. "I'll be right back. Nature calls."

Not thirty seconds had passed before Arizelli was moving her hand up my thigh. I grabbed her hand tightly and whispered through my teeth, "I don't know what you're trying to prove, but I'm gonna let you know up front ain't nothing jumpin'."

"In due time, baby, in due time. Carmin said the same thing at first. Now look at her." Arizelli licked my earlobe and grinned.

I can't believe this bitch. It took all I had to keep from smacking the shit out of her. I immediately got up. I could no longer take it. I had to tell Carmin what was going on. I didn't care how she would respond.

I hadn't taken two steps before I was knocked off my feet. People were running frantically as I heard the gunshots ring out over my head. *Pop! Pop! Pop! Pop! Pop!*

I crawled under a nearby table to keep from being trampled. I sobbed softly as I waited for the chance to escape to safety.

"Come wit' me," I heard Donovan say as I was lifted into the air.

I didn't say a word as he carried me out through the side door. Outside the door, people were screaming, crying, bleeding, and searching for their loved ones. All the mass hysteria reminded me of 9-11. We rushed over to Donovan's car and jumped in.

"I have to find Carmin," I said in a panic.

"No fear, princess. She wit' dem man."

I assumed "dem" was Cobra. I decided to try calling her cell. The phone rang constantly, but there was no answer.

"Can you call Cobra? Carm isn't answering her phone, and I want to make sure she's okay."

Donovan called and got the same response. Now I really began to worry.

"Dere is much commotion. Dem can't 'ear dem phone. Come wit' me to dem hotel. Dem be dere shortly."

Once we got to the hotel, the valet came out and parked the car. It wasn't until that moment that I realized the model of car Donovan was driving. I could have fainted.

Oh, my fucking stars! This nigga drives a Mercedes CL6.

Again, my face must have been screaming my thoughts because Donovan gave me a devilish grin as he said, "Me princess like dem car, aye?"

"It's nice," I replied, trying not to seem too impressed.

Before heading to the room, we stopped in the hotel restaurant to grab a bite to eat. We called Cobra and Carm's phones constantly. Eventually, my phone went dead.

"Can we go to your room so I can use your phone?" I asked. I was beginning to get tired, but couldn't even think of sleeping until I was sure that Carmin was okay.

Upon entering his room, I immediately plugged my phone into the charger that I had luckily placed in my purse before leaving home. I called Carmin's phone again. This time her voicemail came on immediately. I didn't know what to think. We couldn't reach anyone. Cobra and Carm's phones must have both been dead.

All sorts of thoughts ran through my head. *Why didn't they call anyone? Wouldn't Carm want to know I'm okay?*

We tried calling Cobra's room, but there was no answer. Donovan even hit him on the two-way. Still there was no response.

"Why doncha take a hot bath? Relax yaself," Donovan suggested.

Before doing so, I left a message on every phone.

As Donovan filled the tub with hot water and bubbles, he called some of the other guys from their crew to see if anyone knew anything. He left the bathroom to give me some privacy while he continued to make some calls.

Once the bath was ready, I jumped in and turned on the jets for a more calming affect. It felt like a load was lifted off my shoulders as I soaked.

Donovan brought in a glass of champagne for me to sip as I relaxed. The only information he could get was that a female was shot. No one knew who she was or her condition, but they did say they saw Carmin and Cobra leaving the club during all the commotion.

After hearing that, I was able to relax.

Ring, ring! Ring, ring! Ring, ring!
I woke to the sound of the phone. My head was spinning as I sat up to answer. "Hello."

"*C?*"

Her voice sounded weak and sad. I could feel something was wrong. "Carmin, where are you?"

"I'm at Manhattan Hospital," she said. "I need you to come here right away."

"What's wrong? Where's Cobra? Didn't you get my messages? Are you all right?"

"*C*, please, just get here. I need you now, *C.*"

I immediately hung up the phone and jumped up. My body ached all over as I struggled to get out of the bed. Underneath the terry cloth robe, I was naked. I couldn't remember how it happened, but I really didn't have the time to figure it out. I just assumed that I must have fallen asleep in the tub and Donovan put me to bed.

"Donovan, wake up!" I shook him as he lay on the couch.

"Whattem?" he responded sleepily.

"We got to hurry. Something's wrong with Carmin. She's at Manhattan Hospital. She sounded really upset."

We quickly hit the streets and made it to the hospital in ten minutes.

As soon as I walked through the sliding doors, I saw Carmin. Cobra was holding her as she cried uncontrollably.

"Nooooo!" she screamed, her body trembling.

I walked over to her, and she hugged me tight.

"Why, *C?* Why?"

"Why what, honey? What's going on?"

"I can't live without her. I just can't."

That's when it hit me. "Is it Arizelli, Carm? What's wrong with her?"

"She's gone, *C*, she's gone."

Chapter 15

A Lover's Triangle— Who's to Blame?

When I returned home from New York, I had a continuous discomfort in my vagina. I thought it might be a yeast infection, but Monistat just wasn't giving me any relief. I called and made an emergency appointment with my gynecologist.

When I walked in the busy office, I was seen right away.

"Right this way, Ms. Devereaux," the nurse said. "Exam room four. Get undressed from the waist down, please. The doctor will be right in."

"It looks like you have gonorrhea," the doctor said offhand.

"I don't think that's possible, doctor. I'm in a monogamous relationship."

"I'm most certain it's gonorrhea, Ms. Devereaux."

Okay, maybe this bitch doesn't understand. "As I said before, I was recently examined, and there was no trace of an STD," I lied.

"Well, either way, you have gonorrhea, and it needs to be treated. You're more than welcome to have a second opinion if you prefer. Would you like to have an HIV test as well, ma'am?"

"No thank you." I jumped off the table and snatched the prescription out of her hand. "What I would like is to get dressed now." I glared at her.

She attempted to explain the course of treatment, but I quickly interrupted her and again requested she leave so I could get dressed. This time she left without hesitation.

How in the hell did this happen? I asked myself repeatedly on the way home. I tried to think of every possible scenario.

My cell phone rang as I was driving. It was Donovan. "What?" I yelled into the phone.

"Why princess raise 'er voice so?"

"Fuck you, Donovan. I know what you did, you filthy, nasty, walkin' STD!"

"Whattem?"

"You, you raped me! You preyed on me when I was weak. You put something in my drink when I was in the tub. That's why I couldn't remember how I ended up with the robe on. That's why I had such a headache, and that's why my body ached so badly the next morning. You raped me. I hate you, and I hope you die!"

"Ya fall asleep in da tub and me tek you out and wrap you in a robe. Me even sleep on da couch and leave da bed for da princess."

Donovan sounded sincere as he explained, but the suspicion was still there.

"Liar! You fuckin' liar! I hate you! Don't ever call me again!" I slammed the phone shut as I cried.

The days were cold as December rolled in, so the girls and I decided to go on a little winter shopping spree. We hit every mall in the area. We started at Lynnhaven and ended at Patrick Henry, hitting every one in-between.

Since we'd been together all day, we decided to go to the club later that night. We all rushed home to get dressed. The plan was to meet at the club around midnight.

I decided to wear one of my new outfits. I laid out my khaki cargo pants with the drawstring, my burgundy Gucci pumps with legwarmers, and a burgundy sweater that hung off one shoulder. I wore my hair in a side ponytail to with huge gold bamboo earrings and a tan Kangol hat.

I looked in the mirror once I was fully dressed and laughed to myself as I looked at my gear.

Ring, ring! Ring, ring!

"Hello."

"Whattem, princess."

Why in the hell is he calling me from a local number. "What do you want? I asked you to stop calling. What don't you understand about I hate you and I hope you die?"

"Mi come to get da princess back."

"Look, Donovan, I was never your girl, gal, or princess, so I would really appreciate it if you would leave me the hell alone, okay." *Click.*

Ring, ring! Ring, ring!

Oh no, this muthafucka is not calling back. "Hello!" I screamed at the top of my lungs.

"Why the hell are you yelling, *C?*"

"Oh sorry, girl. I thought you was someone else."

"Whatever. I'm ready, so come get me," Tionna demanded.

"And who the hell said I was picking you up?"

"No one. It's understood. I'll be waiting. Blow when you're out front."

"Goodbye," I said before hanging up.

Five minutes later, I was at Tionna's house.

She ran right out. "What's up, bitch?" she said as she jumped in. She turned up Sean Paul as we headed to reggae night at Club Cabana.

The parking lot was full when we arrived. That was of no concern to me, since I was utilizing the VIP parking.

"What's up, Mrs. Vegas? Pull right in there." The dark, heavyset bouncer pointed to a parking spot right in front of the club.

I could tell by the familiar rides that all of Vegas's boys were in the club. *Good thing I kept it classy tonight,* I thought as I parked the car. Vegas's boys were sure to tell if I had on my "fuck-'em-girl" dress.

We walked right in as the other girls stood in line shivering. Once inside, we headed straight to the bathroom, where we met Mickie, Carmin, India, and Asia. They were all touching up their hair and makeup.

Once we finished the final touches, we headed out of the bathroom.

"Yo, *C!* What up, baby?" Vegas's older brother yelled.

"Hey, Snake. What's been up?"

"Same shit. You all right? You need anything?" he asked.

Since Vegas's brothers had taken over the empire, things were lovely for them.

"I'm fine. Thanks for asking."

"Well, at least let me buy you and your girls a drink."

"Hell, yeah! I'll take a margarita. That's what I'm talking 'bout."

All my girls jumped at the opportunity for a free drink, shouting out their drink orders.

"Well, I see everyone is in agreement, so let's head to the bar," Snake said as he slithered over there.

"Girl, he is fine. Hook a sista up," Mickie whispered in my ear as we trotted to the bar in single file, like a group of kindergartners.

"Girl, we don't call him *Snake* for nothing," I said, trying to give her fair warning.

"Pssshhhh! Nothing I can't handle."

"Mickie, his name describes him perfectly. He charms women so well that they're blind to his venom. I've even heard stories of him screwing his girl, then while his girl slept, he went downstairs to screw her sister. If that's not the moves of a snake, I don't know what is."

"Well, I'll be the first to break him," Mickie said. "Are you gonna put me on or not?"

"Okay, but don't say I didn't warn you."

I walked over to Snake as he was handing out the drinks.

"My girl Mickie wants to know what's up with you."

"Oh yeah? Where she at?" He scanned all my friends with his shifty little eyes.

"She's the one with the big breasts, wearing red."

He quickly spotted her and landed his eyes on her breasts as she walked forward. "Daaammmnnn, baby. You're wearing that dress." Snake handed Mickie her drink.

"Oh, you like this?" she asked in her most seductive tone.

Just looking at them made me sick. "All right, y'all, I'm out. Do your thang."

As the other girls hit the dance floor, I stood near the floor as I sipped my drink. I refused to walk on the floor and be called out by the DJ.

"No drinks on the dance floor," the DJ yelled.

I laughed as I saw the culprits trying to play it off and dance their way off the floor.

"Whattem, princess?" I heard Donovan's voice as he squeezed my arm.

What the fuck is he doing here in VA? "Donovan, you're hurting me. Please let me go."

He pulled on my arm. "Come wit' me."

"Okay, just let me go. I don't want to make a scene."

I tried to make eye contact with Mickie and Snake as I was leaving the club, but they didn't even notice. I could see Snake's hand up Mickie's dress.

Just as I was hitting the door, Martinez was entering. With his big-ass mouth, he was sure to tell Snake I left the club. He was my only savior, so I had to get his attention.

"Martinez!" I yelled.

"What up, baby girl? You out already?" He looked from me to Donovan.

"Yeah, the girls are in there, though. I don't feel well. I just need some fresh air."

"Aight. Holla back, mami." He shrugged his shoulders and walked inside the club.

The cold winter air hit my body as I walked toward my car.

"Why dem act so angry to me?" Donovan asked.

"I know what you did, Donovan, and I hate you for it, so please just leave me the fuck alone."

Donovan's eyes became fiery. He grabbed me by my throat. "What da bloodclaat? Dem go nowhere, muddaskunt."

Tears rolled down my face. I spoke to him calmly as I unlocked the Mace on my key chain. "Please, Donovan, let me go. We can work this out." Then I emptied the can in his face.

"Aaaaaauuuuuuuuuuugh! Bitch!"

"I hate you, and for the last time, I hope you die, you Rasta bastard. Now who's the muddaskunk?" I jumped in my car and skidded off. I had never been so afraid in my life. I never thought I would need that Mace, but it certainly came in handy.

The next morning, Vegas called bright and early. "How you doin', baby?" he asked in a strange voice.

"I'm fine, boo. How are you?"

"I'm good. How was the club last night?"

I knew the word would get to him pretty quickly since all his boys were there.

"It was all right. Don't worry, baby. I represented well."

"Oh, I'm not worried about that. Anybody fuck with you? Any disrespect?"

Should I tell him or not? He may already know and is just testing me. I had to think quickly. "Why you ask that?"

"*C*, answer me. Did anyone fuck with you?"

"Yeah, baby, but I took care of it."

"What you mean, you took care of it? Is this nigga still breathing?"

"Of course. You know I didn't kill him."

"My point exactly. So you ain't take care of shit. Next time, don't let me have to ask you when some shit like that go down. That needs to be the first thing out your mouth. Now stay the fuck out of sight for a while." *Click!*

The next few days were quiet. I was surprised I hadn't received any harassing calls from Donovan.

Just as Vegas requested, I stayed out of sight. His brothers were handling things for me at the laundromats while I enjoyed the relaxation. Every day I would practice my shadow boxing then relax in the Jacuzzi.

My nights were spent reading in front of the fireplace or watching a movie in the theater room. This was the first time I actually had a chance to enjoy the amenities of our home.

"*C*, open the damn gate," Mickie yelled through the intercom. "It's cold as shit out here."

I buzzed her in.

"Giiiirrrrlllllll, that Snake is something else." She handed me the stack of newspapers that were collecting at my gate.

I began to go through them as she rambled on.

"He sexed me so good last night."

Must run in the family, I thought, as I reminisced about all the times Vegas made sweet love to me.

"Girl, I think I'm whipped. He kissed and caressed every inch of my body. He took his time and pleased me in every way. It was like he was truly in love with me. It felt like we were making love. My pussy is getting wet just thinking about it."

"Oh my God!"

"What girl? What's wrong?"

I couldn't speak. I just covered my mouth. My heart was pounding profusely.

"Ceazia, what the hell is going on, girl? Talk to me." Meikell tried to shake some sense into me.

I read the headline aloud "Body Found Hanging from Chesapeake Bay Bridge." I continued, "West Indian native identified as Donovan Daniels was brutally murdered. The body was found missing arms, and the genitals were also removed. This is one of the most brutal murders in this area in the past decade."

Mickie had no knowledge of the incident between Donovan and me, and I was glad that I hadn't shared our escapade with anyone.

"That's Carmin's friend, right?"

"Yeah, girl. It's crazy how you can be here one day and gone the next."

"I know. Well, on that note, I think I better run and try to get some more of Snake's dick, because who knows when it may be my time to go."

"Mickie! That's a horrible thing to say."

"Whatever, girl. I'm out." She gave me a big hug and left.

Ring, ring! Ring, ring!

The caller ID read *Carmin Sorano.*

"Hey, Carm."

"Did you read the paper?" she asked.

"Yeah. Isn't that sad?"

"Sad? This is terrible. You don't even seem worried."

"Why should I be worried?" I asked. I thought that maybe Carmin was insinuating the Jamaican mafia would be after me or something.

"*C*, how much of the article did you read?"

"I read the part about his death. Did I miss something?"

"Obviously, Ceazia. You're wanted."

"What?" I could feel the tears beginning to well up in my eyes.

"If you had read the whole thing you'd know it says he was last seen in front of a local nightclub with you. They described you from head to toe and even your car. They have a witness saying they heard you telling him you hated him and that he was going to die. You're the lead suspect. What are you going to do, girl?"

"I didn't do it. Carm, you know I'm not capable of doing such a thing. How did I get myself into this? I have to go."

I hung up the phone and began to pace back and forth. *What in the hell is going on? What did Vegas do? I can't go to jail, Lord.*

The words, *Lord, help me*, almost escaped my lips, but I quickly remembered the evil trick He'd played on me by taking my twins.

I knew I didn't have much time before the detectives showed up at my front door asking questions, or worse, to take me into custody. I thought about calling my mother, but I didn't want to worry her.

Why the fuck isn't Vegas calling? I wondered as I watched the seconds tick on the grandfather clock.

Not able to wait any longer, I got dressed and headed to
the state penitentiary.

"Visit for Laymont Jackson!" the butch yelled.

Once Vegas entered the visiting room, I walked right up
to him, firing questions. "What the hell is going on, Vegas?
I'm wanted for murder. I don't know what to do. I can't—"

Vegas put his finger to my mouth. "Shhhhhh," he said.
He took my hand and led me to the broom closet, where he
started to kiss me passionately.

My heart began to beat uncontrollably. *Oh shit, we can't
have sex. I may still be infected with gonorrhea.* As a distraction,
I began to cry.

"Sit down and listen to me," Vegas said, trying to offer
comfort. "You don't need to worry. Go ahead and speak
with them. You didn't do it, so you know nothing."

"But what if they don't believe me, Vegas?"

"Baby, didn't I say I will always protect you?"

"Yes."

"Well then listen to me and do as I say."

Vegas opened the door and kissed me on the lips before
walking away. "Catch my heart," he said before walking
through the prison door and back to his life behind the
prison walls.

"I love you."

I headed out the door and toward my car. *That visit was
really odd.*

"Bye," the deputy said, a smirk on her face.

That was also odd, because normally that same bitch
would have been giving me a harder time. Now more than
ever, I considered the possibility that her and Vegas were
fucking. It was just too much of a coincidence. Vegas didn't
push me to have sex, he cut the visit short, and then that
bitch says goodbye to me on my way out.

I began to think, *maybe Vegas did give me gonorrhea.* If Vegas gave me gonorrhea, then that meant Donovan was innocent. That would also mean he was killed for no reason. If I had never accused him of raping me, he would have never come to Virginia and would still be alive. I cried the entire way home as I thought about the terrible mistake I might have made.

As I approached the house, I could see police cars surrounding the block. I knew exactly why they were there. They had finally caught up with me. I was so exhausted and drained at this point that I didn't even run. Besides, where would I go? I had been struggling for the past few years and was finally tired of fighting, so just as Vegas did the night of his arrest, I surrendered peacefully.

I stepped out of the car, hands in the air and legs spread apart.

The officers quickly ran over and patted me down. Then they placed the cuffs on me as they read me my rights. Once they explained that I had been charged with the murder of Donovan Daniels, I was placed in a car and rushed off to the police station.

When we reached the station, I was immediately placed in an interrogation room. The process was long and draining. The detectives asked me the same questions repeatedly. "Where were you on the night of the murder of Donovan Daniels? How did you know Donovan Daniels? How long were you acquainted with Donovan Daniels? How were you all acquainted?"

They went on and on with question after question. They knew someone else must have been involved, so they offered me numerous plea bargains to give up that person. The detectives had evidence they wouldn't reveal that indicated I wasn't the actual killer, so they reduced my charge to accessory to murder. Because I didn't give them the name of the killer, they thought I was trying to protect someone, and that's how I was stuck with no bond.

My hearing followed shortly after my arrest. Things were going downhill fast.

Chapter 16

What Happened to "I'll Always Protect You"?

The court was silent as the twelve men and women walked in and seated themselves. I looked at my girls and gave a sigh.

This is it, I thought, as the reality sunk in. It had been two long weeks of court sessions, but it only took two hours for deliberation.

"Please stand for the verdict," the judge said in a cold voice.

The bailiff brought over a small piece of paper that held my destiny.

"We the people find Ceazia Devereaux guilty as an accessory to the murder of Donovan Daniels," the judge read aloud. "Sentencing is as follows. Ten years, two of which will be served in the state penitentiary, then released into the state's women's recovery program for the remainder of the sentence."

Bam! The judged banged his gavel, and the deputy walked over and slapped the handcuffs on my wrists. I ached with pain as the metal squeezed against my bones.

I looked back at all my family and friends who had come to support me.

"Noooooo, don't take my baby! Nooooooo!" my mother screamed. The guilt I felt was almost unbearable.

My father grabbed her as she collapsed to the ground.

I couldn't take it any longer. I stopped and looked at her. "I'm sorry, Momma. I'm sorry." Tears rolled from my eyes.

I kept asking myself over and over again as I was escorted from the courtroom, *Who's protecting me now? Where is Vegas?*

The Virginia State Penitentiary for Women was no place for a prissy little Virginia Beach girl like myself, and they made sure I was aware of it. Everyone hated me, from the deputies to the inmates. I had to stand my ground and make a name for myself, and I did just that. It's just unfortunate that it was a deputy who had to feel the pain of my pent-up aggression.

As I was in line getting breakfast, a deputy approached me. "Identify yourself, inmate!" she yelled in my ear, demanding I read off my inmate number.

Unfortunately, memorizing a six-digit identification number was not a priority of mine, so I didn't know it. "My name is Devereaux. Ceazia Devereaux," I responded, avoiding eye contact.

"Identify yourself, inmate!" she yelled again.

At that point, I knew she wasn't going to leave me alone until I gave her the response she wanted. I decided to look at my wristband and read the number off to her. Just as I lifted my wrist to read the numbers, she hit my arm with her baton.

Without thinking, I jumped in her face. "What the fuck are you thinking, bitch?"

That's when I recognized who she was. It was the deputy from the penitentiary where Vegas was being held.

"Sooo, I finally got a response out of you?" she said with a mischievous grin.

"Look, I don't know what it is you have against me, but I don't want any problems," I tried explaining.

"Yeah, once I heard Vegas's little princess was an inmate here, I put in a request to pay you a little visit. I intend on making your stay here a living hell."

"Okay, Deputy. May I continue to get my breakfast now?" I figured being passive was my best approach to the situation.

"Sure, you may leave, but before you go, I think I oughtta tell you something."

"And that is?"

"Vegas likes it when I bounce on his dick while he sits in the chair too. Now catch my heart, bitch."

Smack! I lifted my tray and hit her across her face. I completely blacked out as I continued to hit her over and over again with the metal tray.

Other deputies and correctional officers rushed over within seconds. They grabbed me and dragged me straight to solitary confinement.

The cell was lonely and cold. I sat in my new home, depressed.

Vegas did have sex with her. He actually fucked her. I repeated those words in my head. I never thought the day would come when Vegas would cheat on me. I always thought he loved me with all his heart. Now I knew he was the one who had given me gonorrhea. It was because of his deceit and lies that Donovan was dead and I was in prison.

For days, I sat without food or water, hoping that I would die without anyone even noticing. The New Year was two days away, and I planned to pass into a new life just as midnight rolled in. I figured that seven days of forced starvation would put me right at the dying point. I also had a suicide drink that one of the inmates slipped me, just in case.

I spent half an hour writing a letter to my loved ones as the final hours before midnight quickly approached.

To all I love and adore,

I have reached a point in my life that I am no longer a pleasure to you all, but a problem. When one thinks of me, it's no longer with love, but with sadness. Sadness that I am away, disappointment for the actions I've been accused of, and anger for such a sudden separation. I sat and wondered what I have done to deserve such a punishment. It's as though I have a curse upon my life. So, I've decided to free us all of the misery and lay down for an eternal rest. I love each and every one of you.

I didn't even bother to sign the bottom. There were five minutes left until midnight and I could feel the energy leaving my body. In five minutes, I would drink the suicide concoction. Even though I was tired of life, I still wanted to be welcomed at the gates of Heaven, so I decided to pray. "God, I ask for Your forgiveness as I leave this place. I ask that You have mercy on my soul and allow me to enter the eternal gates of Heaven. I can no longer live the curse I am living each day. I was torn from my children, I have been falsely accused, and I am alone, Lord. This is the bed I have made and I am prepared to sleep. If You are truly present, please help me."

I held the drink and prepared to take my final breath. Suddenly, my body became numb. I tried to lift my arms to swallow the suicide drink, but I was unable to move.

Boom! Boom! Boom!

I could faintly hear the sound of fireworks outside my

window. I opened my eyes and watched from my cell window. From a distance I watched. I knew that people were dancing, yelling, and hugging in the city streets afar. It was now 2003, and I was still here. I was still alive by the will of God. Vegas didn't protect me, my mother didn't protect me, and not even my friends could protect me.

My body was physically restrained, but my spirit was now free. "Thank you, Father, for rescuing me," I whispered softly as I shredded my suicide letter.

Chapter 17

Welcome Home

"See you soon, Jackson!" the deputy yelled through the gate.

"Fuck you, deputy. You'll never see me in this bitch again," Vegas responded as he walked toward his brother, who was waiting in the car.

It had been ten long months, and Vegas was happy to finally be released.

Snake hugged his younger brother. "What's up, nigga?"

"Happy to be home, man. Happy to be home."

"We got some shit planned for you, man. I'm gonna take you to the crib and let you get situated. We'll be there to pick you up around noon."

"I see everything is still intact here. You guys even kept up the landscaping and maintenance," Vegas said, surprised at how well his brothers had kept up the house.

"Yeah, man. We weren't trying to hear your fuckin' mouth," Snake joked.

Vegas jumped out of the car and headed to the house.

"I'll be back about twelve, man, so be ready," Snake yelled out the window as he pulled off.

Arf! Arf! Arf!

Vegas could hear Prissy barking as he put his key in the door.

"They even took good care of you, Prissy," Vegas patted her on the head.

When he entered the room, he paused. The full-size portrait of Ceazia really saddened him. "I'm sorry, *C.* I'm sorry. I was supposed to be there to protect you. Nothing was ever supposed to happen to you. I love you, baby, and I'm gonna get you home."

Vegas exited the shower, ready for a new beginning. He turned toward the closet, disappointed that he had to wear an outdated outfit. *Damn, I'm not trying to wear no old-ass shit. If my baby was here, I know she would have all the latest shit here waiting for me.*

"Daaaammmmmn!!!" Vegas yelled as he opened the closet door.

His brothers had looked out for him, big time. His closet was stocked with all the new Tims in every style and color, all the newest throwbacks, Prada sneakers, Evisu jeans, team jackets and even a few packs of fresh, white tees. They got him everything he could possibly need, including socks, boxers, toothbrush, his favorite toothpaste, deodorant, and lotion. All of his jewelry was freshly cleaned and buffed.

After dressing he decided to check out the rest of the house. Everything was exactly as he remembered. He then decided to make a few calls, since he still had some time to kill.

"Hello," a female voice answered.

"What's up, yo?"

"Who is this?"

"Come on, I don't have time for the games. Where my kids at?" Vegas asked.

"What kids? Oh, we've found another baby daddy," she said before hanging up in Vegas's ear.

Before he could pick up the phone to dial again, it rang. "Hello."

"You have a collect call from—" the recording began to say.

Vegas immediately accepted the charges.

"Hey, baby!" Ceazia said, excited to hear his voice.

Vegas had no idea the deputy had spilled the beans about his infidelity, and Ceazia decided not to bring it up, keeping in mind what Vegas had taught her in the beginning of their relationship—"Sometimes you just have to let shit ride and keep your enemies close."

"How are you, *C?* Everything okay? Are they treating you right in there?"

"I'm fine, baby, considering my state."

"Well, I'm gonna do everything I can to get you out of there. First thing tomorrow, I'm gonna holla at my lawyer about getting you an early release, okay."

As much as Ceazia loved Vegas, the deceit remained in her head. "Okay, baby. Do what you can."

"All right, baby. Call me tomorrow. I love you, baby girl."

"I love you too," Ceazia said before the call was disconnected.

Ring, ring! Ring, ring!

"Hello," Vegas answered again.

"Yo, nigga, come the fuck outside," Snake said. "You ready to roll?"

"Aight, nigga."

When Vegas opened the door, his other brother and Martinez were there to greet him with a bottle of Belvedere.

"What's up, nigga?" they both yelled before bombarding him with hugs.

"I hope you ready, nigga, because this is about to be a three-day party," Martinez said as they got in the car.

They both handed Vegas a thousand dollars in cash as a welcome home gift.

"Thanks, niggas. That's the least y'all muthafuckas could do since y'all been living in my shit rent-free."

They all laughed.

"I see you like the gear, too," Martinez added.

"Whatever. Y'all niggas did aight."

They continued to laugh as they made the first stop of the day, the barbershop.

By the time they left the shop, they had finished the bottle of Belvedere, so they headed to the liquor store to replenish their stock. They purchased a bottle of Hennessy and more Belvedere.

After a day of visiting and catching up, it was time for the welcome home bash. Martinez and Snake arranged for the party to be held at the local strip club. They had one section of the club reserved for his guests only. They had all types of food trays, including wings, seafood, cheeses, fruits, vegetables, and other finger foods. The section was decorated with a *Welcome Home* banner, and a huge throne awaited the king of the night.

"Welcome home!" everyone cheered as Vegas entered the club.

Strippers were coming at him from all directions and seemed to be more excited about the party than he was.

As soon as he sat in the chair, the party began. Snake and Martinez had paid the dancers in advance to give Vegas the show of a lifetime. They did everything except sex each other in front of everyone.

Chapter 18

Bring Home My Baby

After all the partying, it was time for Vegas to begin his mission to rescue Ceazia. Early Monday morning, he went to see his lawyer.

"Mr. Jackson, glad to see you." The lawyer extended his hand. "Back so soon?" He directed Vegas to be seated.

"It's not me this time, man. It's my girl. You handled her murder case for me. Her name is Ceazia Devereaux."

"Oh yes, Ms. Devereaux. That was a tough case. What can I do for you?"

"Well, I was hoping for a reconsideration on her time. She has no priors, and I think we can get her released into a program or probation or something. I just need to get her out of there."

"I understand, Mr. Jackson, but without the actual killer behind bars, it's hard to get her off. She's going to have to work with the detectives on this one. Murder cases aren't my specialty, but the Commonwealth attorney and detectives were willing to work something out if she would give them some leads. Unfortunately, she wasn't budging. You think you can get her to work with us?"

"She really doesn't know anything, man. She told you all she knew. Is there anything else I can do?"

"I really don't think so, Mr. Jackson, but I'll speak to the Commonwealth and see. How has her stay been so far? Any disciplinary actions?"

Vegas hesitated. "Well, she started off on the wrong foot. She was sent to solitary confinement for assaulting a deputy, but I think she was provoked."

"Okay, well, let me see what I can do. Maybe I can use that as grounds for reconsideration, if I can find mistreatment in the facility."

"Okay, man. Just do what you can, and keep me posted."

Vegas exited the building and headed to the mall. He went to every jewelry store in search of the perfect wedding band to match Ceazia's engagement ring. After looking in four jewelry stores, Vegas still hadn't found the ring he was looking for. One of the young ladies in the store suggested he get a woman's opinion.

He called Mickie. "Yo, Mickie."

"Yeah?"

"This is Vegas. Hey, I need you to help me pick out a ring for *C.*"

"Okay. When you tryin' to look?"

"Well, I started looking today, but I'm gonna look some more tomorrow. I'll give you a call."

"Aight, that's cool."

After the mall, Vegas made his rounds to all the laundromats and then headed home.

The phone was ringing just as he walked in the door. "Hello."

"This is a call from inmate—"

Vegas pressed one to accept the call.

"Hey, baby."

"What's up, ma? I spoke to the lawyer today, and we're gonna work on getting you outta there. I got big plans for you when you get home. We're gonna make some serious moves."

Ceazia wasn't excited. In fact, she wasn't even sure she wanted to go home to him at all. She still hadn't healed from his infidelity but made sure to play her cards right. "That sounds good, baby. I just can't wait to get out of here. So how's life on the streets?" she asked, certain he was living it up, probably with another woman.

"Shit is lovely, baby. Your house is just like you left it, the laundromats are doing very good, and Prissy is still healthy. All I need is you here to make things complete."

"Well, I'm gonna go now. I'll see you Saturday. This time I need you, baby. Catch my heart."

"I love you, momma."

Vegas planned a huge party at the crib for Snake's birthday. The hot May weather was perfect for a cookout. He pulled out the grill, jet skis, and patio furniture. Guests included all of Ceazia's friends, Vegas's boys, and his family. Vegas had two tents set up outside, one for the women to change into their swimsuits, the other for the men.

Vegas also had a special room set up for the birthday boy and did all he could to keep everyone outside. He really didn't want much traffic inside the house.

As Vegas was bringing the meat outside to put on the grill, he ran into Mickie.

"What's up, Vegas?"

"What's up, Mickie?" Vegas noticed the very attractive young lady beside Mickie staring at him seductively. "Who's that you got with you?"

"Oh, I'm sorry. This is Sonya."

"Hi, Sonya." Vegas extended his hand. "You ladies enjoyin' yourself?"

"We sure are. Where's your brother?" Mickie asked, unable to locate Snake.

She and Snake had continued their sexual escapade from the night that Ceazia had introduced them at the club. Now they were actually calling themselves a couple.

"He's around here somewhere. I'll tell him you're looking for him."

After eating, everyone began to do their own thing. Some people were in the pool, others rode Jet Skis or played cards, and some were dancing. Vegas decided it was time for Snake's grand finale, so he headed out to find him. He looked all over outside, but Snake was nowhere to be found.

He decided to head in the house to look for him. He noticed the bedroom door was open and entered the room slowly. The first section of the room with the Jacuzzi was empty, so he continued to the back, where the bed was located.

"Hi, sexy," a female voice sang as Vegas turned the corner.

Vegas stood in shock at the naked body that lay before him.

The young lady caressed her clit with one hand, and her breasts with the other. "You like what you see?"

"Nah, shortie, you got to get the hell out of here."

The female looked down at Vegas's erect penis. "Well, from the look of things, you like what you see." She crawled across the king-size bed toward Vegas, unzipped his pants slowly, and pulled out his dick.

Vegas tried to resist, but her lips were already around his penis, giving him crazy brain.

He grabbed the back of her head, gripping her long, black hair. "Aahhhhh," he moaned. He was so taken by the head he was getting, he didn't even notice Snake and Mickie standing behind him.

"Sonya!" Mickie yelled. "What the fuck are you doing? Vegas, I can't believe you." Mickie glared at him and shook her head in disbelief.

"Ah damn, Mickie. It ain't like that."

"Damn, lil' bro. You doin' your thang." Snake tried to dap his little brother up. "She gives some good-ass head, don't she, man?"

"You mean she sucked your dick too, man?"

"Yeah, man. That's our thing. She would have been in there with me and Mickie if you ain't come in and cock-block. Me and Mickie were in the bathroom getting our thing on while Sonya was out here getting herself prepared. I always have to get my first nut with my girl, but after that, Sonya comes in and joins us for the second round. She usually likes to listen and play with herself. Sometimes she watches too. All that shit turns her on," Snake explained.

"Man, I wasn't even tryin'a fuck with her. She just started sucking my shit. Damn, I fucked up. I fucked up, man." Vegas knew there was no way he could keep Mickie from telling Ceazia.

Chapter 19

A Turn in the Tables

As Vegas enjoyed life on the outside, I made do of my world behind bars. To utilize my time, I constantly studied law books. I was sure there was some loophole or something that could get me out of jail.

I was no longer in solitary confinement, and life in population was better. I didn't need to prove myself. In fact, I had a few chicks who were serving me. My cellmate, Brook, was one of them. She was serving time for embezzlement and had already been turned out in her short stay of only twelve months. She had a huge crush on me, and it was her personal mission to sex me. At times, it was pretty tempting. Brook had a gorgeous shape and a pretty face, unlike most of the females in there, with their million-dollar bodies and food stamp faces.

Brook was my partner in crime. We masterminded a scheme to get me out. With my knowledge in law, and her skill at scheming, we came up with the perfect plan. We just had a few final kinks to work out before executing it.

Saturday rolled around in the blink of an eye, and I was

anticipating Vegas's arrival. I had a huge surprise for him. Mickie had told me about his little dick-sucking incident. She told me not to mention it to him and tried to explain how Sonya had provoked him.

Of course none of that really mattered to me. I was able to keep my composure on our calls throughout the week, but I was going to make it my duty to show him a thing or two at visitation. Vegas had fucked me over once, and I'd be damned if he was gonna get away with it twice.

I loved Vegas with all my heart and tried with all I had to put things behind me. I knew if I just remained humble, the truth would prevail. I hoped the truth would have been that Vegas really loved me and would never betray me, but deep inside I knew he was as much of a snake as his older brother.

"Ceazia Devereaux, visitation!" the deputy called.

I took my time walking to the gate. I could see Vegas's nervous smile as I approached.

"Hey, baby," he said as he hugged me tight.

I returned a loose hug. "How was your week?" I asked with a mischievous smile.

"It was cool. What's up with you, *C?* Why you actin' all strange?"

Smack! I threw my hand across his face. "Fuck you, Vegas. You just can't seem to keep your dick in your pants, can you?"

"I'm sorry, Ceazia. It was a mistake. I understand if you don't want to be with me anymore, but please just give me a chance."

"The Vegas I loved protected me, was there for me, loved me, and damn sure never cheated on me. I hate you, and I never want to see you again." As a final touch, I spat in his face then walked away.

"You're making a mistake, Ceazia! You're making a big

mistake. Did Mickie also tell you that she accepted three grand to keep her mouth shut? She's jealous of you, *C*. She doesn't want us together because she knows how happy you'll be. The bitch is sheisty."

The pace of my life did a one hundred and eighty degree turn after that. The days began to move slowly. With Vegas out of my life, I was miserable, but I couldn't continue to be with someone who was unfaithful. He had cheated on me a second time and that was the final straw.

Weeks passed and I did not call Vegas, nor did he come to visit.

What if Vegas was telling the truth? The more I thought about things, the more I wanted Vegas back. My life was empty without him, and I wouldn't be whole again until I had my man back in my life. I could no longer bear the pain. Sure it hurt when I learned of the times he'd cheated, but the emptiness after we parted was consuming me.

I convinced myself that Vegas deserved another chance. I broke down and called him.

The phone rang, but there was no answer. I found that strange because it was ten in the morning, and Vegas didn't normally get up until after ten. I took that as a sign and left the situation alone. If it were meant to be, we would be reunited somehow.

"Ceazia Devereaux, please stand for the court's decision," the judge said.

My stomach turned. This was an all-too-familiar feeling as I waited for another judgment.

"I hereby release you into the probation program of Virginia Beach, Virginia."

I could have pissed in my pants. I burst into tears as the words registered. I left the courtroom on top of the world, even though there wasn't a friend or family member there.

I thought about how I could go about getting Vegas back as I rode home. The bus ride was long and rough, but nothing could stop my joy.

I planned to surprise Vegas. No one knew I was coming home, and that's just the way I wanted it. Sure, Vegas had really done some terrible things, but I had forgiven him. After days and days of soul-searching, I figured there were too many what-ifs and decided to give him the benefit of the doubt. I figured all the ups and downs throughout our relationship would only make us stronger. He had asked me to be his wife, and I had every intention on being just that.

From the bus station, I took a cab to my house. A huge smile came across my face as I pressed the digits of my birth date on the keypad and the gate opened. I walked to the door slowly. I didn't want Vegas to hear me enter.

I became more and more anxious, the closer I got to the bedroom. I could hear the jets blowing in the Jacuzzi. I figured Vegas was probably relaxing after a long workout. I cracked the door just enough to peep in.

The vision before me would never leave my mind. There were Vegas, Mickie, and Sonya all ass-naked in my Jacuzzi, sniffing cocaine. I stood frozen in my tracks. I didn't know what to do.

I managed to back away from the door without being noticed and proceeded to walk to the basement. When I got to the bottom step, I reached on top of the water heater and it was there, just as I had left it. I loaded the gun slowly as tears escaped the confines of my eyelids and rolled down my face.

I walked back to the bedroom and opened the door. They were so high, they didn't even notice my presence. I watched Vegas laying back in enjoyment as Sonya sucked his dick and Mickie rubbed all over his body. I couldn't believe she would stoop so low.

Bang! Bang! Bang! Bang!

The room fell silent. They had no idea what hit them. I watched as the Jacuzzi water quickly turned red. Vegas, however, wasn't dead yet.

"Ceazia, I'm sorry, baby," he whispered as blood streamed down the side of his face. "I'm sorry. I'll always love you. Catch my heart."

What have I done? I've killed the love of my life. My brain was racing. *How can I live without him?* "Vegas, wake up! Please, wake up!" I shook his body frantically, but he didn't move.

I'd been through every hustler in the Tidewater area of Virginia, and there wasn't one nigga that could hold shit down like Vegas. I even settled for that nigga Bear, but he couldn't even do half of what Vegas was doing. He also had the nerve to be talking 'bout love and "wifing" me up. Needless to say, it wasn't long before I had to let him go too.

"Karma is a muthafucker," I said aloud as I struggled to pull my Louis Vuitton pilot bag from the trunk of my brand new white 745LI. A year ago, Vegas would have been by my side pulling the luggage from the trunk as I grabbed the shopping bags from the back seat. Unfortunately this time I wasn't returning from a week's trip in Cancun, Mexico, but was headed to the ghetto-fab runway of the ho stroll.

The only purpose for my Louis Vuitton luggage was as a dance bag to carry my many multicolored striptease uniforms. No more Prada sneakers and Versace sets, it was straight stilettos and dance costumes now.

It was a damn shame I had to resort to this shit, but a bitch had to do whatever to stay on top. So if that meant I had to shake a leg or two for a minute, so be it. Like every top-notch chick I had a plan, and I was already executing. This time shit was a little more risky, but I loved the challenge. This was the true test. I was about to see just how far a bomb-ass chick could get with the power of booty and beauty.

Chapter 20

BJ

Who Says I Got to Stay in Your House?

Bam! I slammed the door behind me as I rushed outside. "I hate you!" I screamed upstairs to my aunt, who had custody of me for the past twelve years.

My mother was doing time in the Virginia Women's State Prison for child neglect. One night after a three-day stay at the crack house, the constant cry of my five-month-old brother seemed to be driving her insane. I was hiding under the table, which faced the bedroom my brother and I shared. She couldn't see me because it was extremely dark in the house. We only had a candle lighting our house because the electric company had turned off our services due to non-payment.

My mom yelled, "Shut up, boy! Shut up!" and shook my brother until he was silent. Once he was quiet she laid him on the mattress we had for a bed in the middle of the floor, and pulled out a cigarette.

I peered at her as she left the room to go lay on the couch. It wasn't until then I felt safe enough to come out. I crawled into the bedroom to lay beside my little brother. I cried silently as I touched his still hand.

"Wake up, little Jay, wake up," I whispered, but there was no response.

I wrapped my arm around his little body and fell asleep.

Beep! Beep! Beep!

I woke to see red, orange, and yellow flames all around me. It was amazing that I could still see the fire because the air was filled with thick smoke. I couldn't breathe and didn't know where to find my mom and little brother. I felt my way to the back door. "Mommy, Mommy!" I yelled.

I managed to get outside the house, where I saw all my neighbors looking on at the scene, but my mom and little brother weren't out there. It also seemed that no one knew there were people in the house, because they all seemed surprised when I came out.

As soon as the firemen pulled up, I begged them to save my brother and mother.

Within minutes they were out. They both lay still as the paramedics tried to resuscitate them. My mom came around shortly after, but my brother was covered with a white blanket, a sign that he was gone.

Everyone figured it was from smoke inhalation, but I knew the truth.

Until this day no one knew that my mommy really killed little Jay. My mom was arrested for child neglect. It didn't take long for the paramedics to realize she was high.

The neighbors had reported her to Child Protective Services a number of times, and this time when she fell asleep with the cigarette lit, it was the last straw. She was sentenced to the Women's State Prison, and that's where she'd been for the past twelve years.

In those years I'd blossomed from a timid five-year-old to

a rebellious teen. The constant bickering between my aunt and I let me know she was just about sick of my mess.

My aunt yelled after me, "If you hate it here so bad, then leave! Where you gonna go? Don't nobody else want you." She opened the screen door.

"I hate it here. I'd rather be dead than live here with you," I shouted back.

Smack! My aunt's huge hand swept across my face. "You better watch your damn mouth, little girl. You gettin' a little too hot for your damn pants."

I jumped up and smacked her right back.

In a matter of seconds, my aunt's two-hundred-fifty-pound frame was all over me.

I screamed, hoping my grandmother would come to my rescue. "Gggggrrrrraaaaaannnddddddmmmmmaaaaa! Help! She's trying to kill me."

My grandmother was out the door and pulling my aunt off me in no time. I was big for my size, but my one-hundred-fifty-pound frame was nothing compared to the strength of that beast.

I rushed upstairs to my room as soon as I was free. "I'm packing my bags!" I shouted as I ran up the stairs.

I pulled out my Polo backpack and stuffed it with toiletries, underclothes, a pair of "Daisy Duke" jean shorts, a white wife-beater, slouch socks, and a fresh pair of white Air Force Ones. I planned to stay at my girl Gina's house. Her mom worked the overnight shift from seven p.m. to seven a.m. at the hospital, so we would always have a ball at her house.

It was right around six o'clock, so I knew her mom would already be out the crib and on her way to work.

"I'm out," I yelled one last time as I ran back down the stairs.

My grandma yelled, "*BJ!*"

That was the nickname the family had given me. My name was actually Jasmine, and everyone called me Jay. But when my brother was born, he was named Javon, and we called him Jay too. So to distinguish who was who they began calling us big Jay and little Jay. Eventually big Jay turned into *BJ*.

"Yes, Grandma?" I stopped at the back door to hear her out.

"Don't go out there getting in trouble, ya hear?"

"Okay, Grandma. I'll call you."

I loved my grandmother, but I just had to do me for the time being.

Knock, knock, knock! I knocked on Gina's front door. I could hear the music blasting from her bedroom window. "Yo, Gina!" As I grabbed the doorknob, I noticed the door was open.

I grinned to myself as I slowly entered the house. Walking through the doorway, I noticed the door frame was broken. A huge knot formed in my stomach as I looked around. I wasn't sure if I should run up the stairs or out the door. "Gina!"

There was no response. I couldn't leave without checking to make sure Gina was okay first. I rushed to the kitchen and grabbed a butcher knife. *It's either do or die.* I crept up the stairs toward Gina's room, praying she was okay.

When I got to her door, I busted in, ready to stab the first thing moving.

"Aaaahhhhh!" We both screamed at the top of our lungs.

"Oh my God, Gina. What the hell are you doing?" I laughed at her and Duke as they both struggled to get dressed.

Gina jumped up and pulled the covers over her naked body. The smell of sex and weed filled the room.

Duke was a friend of ours since elementary school. He'd gotten into a little trouble and was sent off to South Carolina for a few years, but he began doing big things once he returned. Although he was nineteen before he managed to graduate from high school, no one could take away the fact that he made it through.

Duke and Gina always argued and fought with each other during school and even as kids. They had me convinced they hated each other. I had no idea they were actually doing the nasty.

I became kind of jealous myself. "Ah-ha! I knew something was up with y'all. Ain't no way in hell two people could hate each other as much or as long as y'all two."

"Why didn't you knock first? How the fuck you just gonna run up in my shit, BJ?"

"Actually I thought something was wrong with your ass, since the back door is damn near off the hinges. I was trying to come to your rescue, bitch!"

Duke took his time getting dressed. I noticed him eyeballing my breasts and massaging his nice-sized penis. I gave him a seductive grin. I'd never noticed just how sexy Duke was until then.

Duke stood a perfect six feet, with washboard abs and flawless chocolate skin. His body was decorated with ink, and every tattoo seemed to lay perfectly, complementing his thug sexuality to the tee.

Gina quickly interrupted our flirting session. "Duke, I think you should leave. I'll call you later."

"Aight, momma." Duke kissed her on the cheek and, before exiting the room, gave me one last glance and a nod.

"Bye, Duke," I said, grinning.

Now it was time for me to confront Gina. "I always thought we both were virgins and that when we decided to have sex we would let each other know. Why didn't you tell me, Gina? And why the hell is the door jacked up like that?"

"Why you all up in my grill, BJ? If you must know, Duke broke the door. We had a heated argument earlier in the day, and I'd been ignoring his calls. So he decided to come over, but I wouldn't let him in. And you know Duke and his temper. He told me one time if I didn't open the door he would kick it in. Although I know his ass is crazy, I didn't think he would actually kick the door in." Gina shook her head.

"That boy is a damn fool," I said aloud, although the thought actually turned me on. "So I guess that heated argument quickly turned into make-up sex, huh?"

Gina looked away. "I haven't been a virgin for a long time, BJ, but the first time was out of my control. I wish I could tell you more about it, but I can't."

I could see Gina wipe the tears from her eyes. I hugged her tightly. "You can tell me anything, Gina. I won't think any different of you. You're my girl."

Gina forced the words out between a huge cry. "It was Bubba, BJ. It was Bubba."

Bubba was Gina's mother's boyfriend. I couldn't believe what my ears were hearing.

"Bubba? You had sex with Bubba?"

"Yeah. One night he came home drunk from the club. Of course my mom was at work, so I was here alone. He came in my room and started to pull my pajamas off and forcing his hands inside me—"Gina stopped in the middle of her statement and began to cry.

"It's okay, Gina. You don't have to say any more." I hugged her.

"He raped me, BJ, he raped me. And my mother called me a liar when I told her about it. I don't know what hurt more, the rape or my mother's disbelief."

I had no idea Gina had so much pain and hurt inside. I just listened and consoled her as she released all the misery she held inside.

"It's okay, Gina, it's okay," I said softly, rubbing her back.

At that point I knew not only did I have to do something to get out my grandmother's home, but I had to get Gina out her mother's home as well. We were both alone. Gina's mother had deceived her and chose a man over her child, and my mother had deceived me in an equal way. I made a personal vow. No matter what it took, I would get us both out of this situation.

Chapter 21

Duke

Little Soldier in Training

Sex with Gina was always good, but I really wanted to hit BJ. I could tell she wanted me from the way she looked at me. She said she was still a virgin, so I knew her pussy was steaming for some sex. I was just the man to give it to her, too, but I wasn't going to rush it though.

I was a Jackson, and we were known for getting any female we wanted. My uncles, Vegas and Snake, ran all the ladies before Vegas was killed. In fact it was Vegas's womanizing that got him murdered. I planned to follow right in my uncles' footsteps, but I was gonna be much wiser with my shit.

Since I'd moved from South Carolina to Virginia, I'd received constant training from my Uncle Snake about the game, and for the past two years, he'd kept me tight in all the hottest gear and jewelry. Snake had been caught up in the game for a long time now, and his money was long enough to do things the average nigga couldn't.

Snake liked doing things for me because he always referred to me as his little soldier in training. He even bought me a car before I had a driver's license. I knew soon I'd have a piece of the empire and be doing big things just like him. I began to lay out all my plans, getting a dope-ass house like Snake, all the luxury vehicles, and the utmost respect from other ballers.

One night I called him to see what he was up to. He told me we needed to go out, so we could cover strip club etiquette. I arrived at his house around ten o'clock and was greeted at the door by his girl, Danielle.

Danielle Stevens was this fine-ass bourgeois chick my uncle met at Hampton University just before he was leaving the campus from serving some boys over there. Her mother was a doctor, and her father was a lawyer, just like some shit straight off *The Cosby Show*. She was never really exposed to the streets until hooking up with my uncle. She loved Snake's bad boy traits and the excitement of all the financial perks that came along with being a gangster's girl.

Danielle was definitely a dime piece. She had a butterscotch complexion, hair down her back, and a small waist with a big ass.

"What's up, Danielle?" I admired her phat-ass booty on the way in.

"Hey, Duke. What's going on?"

"I think we're going to hit the strip joint tonight."

Danielle darted her eyes in Snake's direction. "You goin' to the strip club tonight, Snake?"

"Nah, baby. I don't know why you always let lil' soldier get in your head. He knows you hate it when I go there, and that's why he said the shit. Lil' soldier, stop fucking with my woman's head." Snake took one last pull on his blunt filled with purple haze.

I tried to make Danielle feel like she couldn't take a joke.

"Damn, Danielle, I didn't know you let a young nigga like me get in your head like that. My uncle better watch out," I said, with a smirk on my face.

Danielle rolled her eyes and began to clean up the small mess my uncle left behind. "He thinks I'm fuckin' stupid. Yeah, keep taking my kindness for weakness. Just wait until I catch his ass. Y'all think I won't serve a nigga about playing with me, but try me and you'll find out that shit's going to really hit the fan!"

"You better watch your mouth, girl," I said in a seductive, yet teasing manner.

"We out, baby girl." Snake smacked Danielle's ass then kissed her on the lips.

"Whatever." She followed Snake to the door.

I could see the frame of her thong through her sheer robe as I followed close behind her. Looking at Danielle's ass shake through that robe made my dick hard. "We out, baby girl," I mocked. Then I smacked her on the ass, causing it to jiggle.

They both laughed.

I was planning to fuck that ass from the back one day soon. *It may take a while, but I'll get it.*

From the look in Danielle's eyes, she knew I wanted her. I winked at her and grabbed my dick, giving it a gentle massage before closing the door behind me.

We jumped in Snake's Denali and headed to the strip club. I was a little excited, but I knew I had to play it cool as we pulled up to the club. I followed Snake past the security inside. That was the first lesson. I made a mental note. *Get familiar with the security. Give them a nice amount of cash to avoid lines and searching.*

Once we were inside, the first stop was the bar to see who the bartenders were for the night. After determining everything was straight with who would be fixing his drinks, he led me to a spot in the corner near the exit door.

He beckoned for the waitress and handed her a generous amount of money. "Courvoisier, and keep 'em comin', " he told the skinny half-dressed woman.

That was several lessons in one. Snake walked right in without much noise and went over to the bar to make sure he was familiar with the bartenders just in case someone in the game might be trying to set him up by slipping a mickie in his drinks. Then he headed to a spot near the exit so he could watch everyone that entered and exited without them even noticing him, and also for an easy escape.

I also liked how he paid the bartender and waitress up front with a generous amount, to avoid having to constantly flag them down to place orders.

We chilled in the corner for about forty-five minutes.

At first that was cool, because I was checking out some of the amazing things those chicks could do on the pole, but after a while the entertainment was no longer holding my attention.

Females were coming over left and right asking for a dance, and Snake was turning them down just as fast as they were coming.

Now that part of the lesson I didn't grasp at all.

"Unc, why you dissin' all the honies?"

"Some of them are tricks, and we don't do tricks. You see the hot bitches, they used to gettin' any nigga they come at. If you're that one nigga that don't budge, then they're going to want you even more. You feel me, lil' nigga?"

"I feel you, unc, I feel ya."

Snake led me to the velvet room. Shit in there was set up like a little Egyptian paradise, and the women were nothing but top-notch females. Perfect tans and flawless bodies. I couldn't find one who didn't have her makeup in check. I could tell they were wearing that expensive shit because they each looked like movie stars. I, for one, was impressed with how much class these ladies carried.

One female in particular kept looking our way. She was the baddest chick in there. Beautiful caramel skin, a small waist, C cup breasts and long black hair.

Snake noticed me checking her out. "You like that?"

I was sure not to seem too pressed. "So far she's the baddest chick I've seen in here."

Snake laughed. He shook his head in mock pity. "She's venomous, man." He looked her five-foot-five-inch frame up and down. "That's the infamous Ceazia."

"Damn! That's her? She doesn't look much like a murderer to me."

Ceazia began to put on a show for me and Snake. I tried not to show it, but I was about to drool all over myself. This chick had a spell on me that seemed unbreakable.

I never had a chance to meet Ceazia before, but I'd heard the many tales. The five years I did in juvie down in South Carolina really had me missing out on a lot. Her panther eyes continued to hypnotize me as she walked over.

"Who's this little one, Snake?" She rubbed her hand across my goatee.

"Nobody you gettin' close to, bitch," Snaked snapped at her.

It was never proven that Ceazia was the shooter the day my uncle Vegas, Mickie, and Sonya were killed, but Snake was sure she did it.

"Don't be jealous, daddy. You'll always have my attention." She rubbed Snake's penis.

Snake just looked her coldly in the eyes and knocked her hand away from his manhood.

I couldn't understand how Snake could avoid Ceazia's

spellbinding ways. I was wishing she'd touch me again, especially in the crotch area like she'd just touched Snake, but he wasn't fazed by anything Ceazia did or said.

I constantly watched her throughout the night. The enchantment she had on the men in the club was crazy. I knew she had to be making the most bank in the whole club. Hell, I was ready to give her all the loot I had in my pockets. I guess it was a good thing my uncle Snake was there to keep me from making a fool of myself.

I stared intensely. There wasn't a flaw on Ceazia's body. Her skin was perfect, stomach tight, not a stretch mark in sight, and she had perfect white teeth. She was truly a stunner. No wonder my uncle Vegas was whipped.

Chapter 22

Unknown Man

Fly on the Wall

I'd been watching Ceazia's every move as I sat in a dark corner of the strip club where she worked. That bitch had no idea I was even there. She was so busy flirting and spitting game to niggas, she didn't even notice me nearly breathing down her fucking neck.

All Ceazia saw was the dollar sign. Unless you were frosted from ear to belly button, that's earring to chain, and had on an outfit totaling at least $500, a nigga can forget it. I'd told her time and time again she needed to stay on point. But ever since she got away with shooting Vegas she felt like she was the shit. And these cats constantly blowing her head up didn't make shit no better. This chick truly carried it like she was "the diamond princess." But like I always told her, "Once in the game, you're married to the game." At anytime a nigga could be breathing down her neck, ready for revenge, ready to snatch her off that throne.

I continued to watch as she flirted with Snake and his lil' nigga, Duke. Although I hadn't seen her or even spoken to her in over a month. That girl meant the world to me. I would've given her my last chicken wing just to please her, but the bitch was just never happy. I fell short on niggas' money so many times, because of her. I even had to buck on niggas and rob a couple of them down south just to get back on.

Hell, that damn 745 she was driving was bought on a nigga's money I bucked on. And even with all of that, she still wasn't happy. All she kept hollering 'bout was that nigga, Vegas. I still had to compete against a dead man. But I refused to give up. I still loved her and yearned for her presence.

It seemed like she was working on that nigga Snake now. Even though he knew *C* shot Vegas and had all sorts of hatred toward her, she still got him weak.

I know *C*, and if Snake didn't tighten up he was going to be her next target. And trust me, that bitch had a good aim.

I sat back and watched her get in Snake's brain and send him and his lil' man out the door confused.

Chapter 23

Snake

A Soldier's Struggle

That bitch had me tripping, coming on to me like shit is supposed to be all good. I got every reason in the world to hate her ass, and she knew it. She insisted on trying to play me like a sucker, but I just kept running game to her.

Not only did Ceazia murder my brother, but she also murdered my girlfriend, Mickie. That bitch was lucky to be alive. The only reason she was still walking was because there was a lot of evidence pointing in other directions. But personally I didn't give a fuck. I thought the bitch did it, and as soon as I got it confirmed, she'd be dead.

Duke noticed that I was deep in thought. "What's on your mind, Snake?"

"Nothing, lil' man. Just thinking."

"She got you fucked up, huh, Unc? I can see it in your eyes when you look at her."

"What? You think you so good at reading niggas that you can read me too?"

"Nah, man. That's just how she got me feeling. I mean I

loved Uncle Vegas to death, but at the same time I'm feeling her. It's a struggle, Unc, and I'm fucked up."

Danielle was still up when I arrived home. I knew an argument was in store. Lately she was acting really insecure, and it always led to constant fighting. I hollered at Duke before he left and took that dreaded walk into the crib.

Danielle's face was frowned up as soon as I opened the door. I tried to lighten things up a little. *I would much rather fuck than fight.* "Hey, baby. What you still doing up?"

"What the fuck you think I'm doing up? And don't try that sweet-talking shit with me, Snake. You shoulda brought your ass home before three in the morning!" Danielle turned the TV and lights off and headed up the stairs toward the bedroom.

That was exactly where I wanted her. In the bed. I figured I'll let her vent a while then give her the dick.

I followed her up the stairs with a fake plea. "Come on, baby girl, you know I have to take care of business. How else will you be able to prance around in your Chanel slippers and lingerie? Don't I always come through for you? Baby girl, I try to keep things on the level so you don't have to want for shit. Why can't you understand that all of a sudden?"

I always used the game as an excuse for being out late, even though I didn't do business after ten.

"Why the fuck was your phone off? I paged you five times. You're so fucking inconsiderate when you don't answer my calls. You never know what's wrong, or even if I have something urgent to tell you. If I ever ignored you or turned my phone off, you'd be ready to beat my ass. And you know what, that's what I should do to you right now. There's no way in hell you couldn't have known I tried to reach you. I even hit you up with a two way message blah, blah, blah, blah."

I tuned Danielle out completely. I realized I wasn't getting any ass after all, so I had to resort to plan *B*. I told her I was heading for a cold shower then began to get undressed.

I noticed she was watching my every move. She continued to complain, but her tone lowered with every stitch of clothing I let fall to my feet.

Working out daily to keep my body tight paid off during times like this between me and Danielle. I knew she'd begin to think twice after taking a look at my rock-hard abs, but this wasn't the only part of me that bared stiffness.

Her eyes traveled just a short ways south of my waistline and focused intently.

Once all of my clothes were off, I began stretching as if I was tired. I used this opportunity to flex my muscles.

By then her tone had completely softened.

The ball was now in my court. I gave her a humble look and shook my head. Then I said softly, "You win, baby, you win. I don't want to argue." I walked over to put my arms around her waist. I kissed her gently on her neck.

I knew her pussy would be throbbing in a matter of seconds because such teasing always worked after a fight.

I continued to the bathroom, intentionally leaving the door open for a small tease. I turned the vanity lights over the mirror off, leaving only the dimmed lights over the shower. The setting couldn't have been more perfect for an erotic mood.

I jumped in the shower, opting for steaming hot water. I took my time standing under the massaging shower head. Stress slowly left my body with each drop of water that hit my back and shoulders.

I soon noticed a shadow against the shower door. I could

see that it was the silhouette of Danielle's perfect body. She opened the door and began to kiss me passionately.

I reached to lift her into the shower with me without ever losing the lock between our lips. Water ran down our faces as we kissed. The water soaked Danielle, causing her sheer robe to cling to her wet body. The scene of her soaking wet hair, clothes, and body turned me on.

I quickly disrobed her and lifted her one-hundred-twenty-five-pound frame against the shower wall, fondling her pussy with my fingers. When I inserted my penis into her slippery vagina, she moaned with pleasure.

"Aaaaaaahhhhhh!!!!!!" we both yelled as we came together.

That was all I needed, and it was time for bed.

We climbed into bed together, and then I watched ESPN as I pulled my last few puffs off a blunt. I was trying to quit smoking, but I had to at least start my day off and end the day with a smoke, if nothing else.

Just as I was getting relaxed, my phone began to ring.

"Who the fuck is that calling you this late, Snake? I know you ain't got no hoes calling you at this time of morning while you're laying up next to me."

The caller had awakened the dragon. Her yelling was like her spitting fire at my ass.

I reached over to the nightstand and pressed *end* without even looking at the caller ID and sent the caller to voice-mail.

Danielle looked like she was ready to tag me, but soon she rolled her eyes and laid back down.

Ten minutes later the computerized tunes of "P.I.M.P." by 50 Cent started playing on my phone. "Damn! It's a message on my Sidekick. Who the hell is tripping this late?" I whispered to myself.

I flipped open the phone to check the e-mail. It read: COME SEX ME, and was signed, SWEET SIXTY-NINE. I turned the phone off and laid back down.

I looked to see what Danielle was doing, and she was staring me in my face as soon as my head hit the pillow.

"What, Danielle? What?"

"What you mean, 'What? Who the hell was that?"

I stared Danielle in the eyes with a "C'mon now" look, which bought me some time to think. "It's my lil' soldier, Duke. He just got some ass. You know how he does when he hit," I said convincingly.

At first, Danielle's face seemed as if she didn't want to accept that excuse, but she finally threw her hands up in the air and went back to sleep.

The next morning I went out on the balcony to have my morning smoke and chill before starting my day. The breeze from the river was cool. I decided to check my voice mail to see if the strange caller from last night decided to leave a message. I had one voice mail message and it was the sound of a female masturbating. It sounded so good, it made my dick rise. I had no idea who the woman was, but if she looked as good as she sounded, she wouldn't have to worry about sending e-mails or leaving voice messages any more.

As I listened to the message, I began to feel as though someone was standing over me. I turned around and Danielle was standing at the sliding door, looking through the curtains at me

She was really starting to scare me. I figured I better chill out because I wasn't trying to end up like Vegas.

Chapter 24

Gina

Hot Sex on a Platter

BJ had been my girl since pampers. I was glad I finally had the chance to talk to her about losing my virginity, though. However, I didn't really tell her everything. It was tough talking about that, so I kept things brief.

Ever since I began having sex two years ago at sweet sixteen, I've had the urge to sex men, big, small, short, and tall. I never had sex with guys in my school or my neighborhood, though. That's how I was able to keep my promiscuous ways a secret for so long. Besides, guys don't talk as much as girls, so as long as these boys didn't know each other my fast ways stayed hidden.

Despite the fact that I took all the necessary precautions, I still wasn't able to keep anything from Duke. He was like a bloodhound when it came to sniffing out which females were giving it up.

When he and I finally got together, I was like a bitch in heat. I loved every minute of sexing him.

BJ was around a lot since she got into it with her aunt, so

Duke and I couldn't have sex that often. She was seriously throwing salt in my game. My sex drive was now in fifth gear and I needed some bad.

Fortunately BJ's fine-ass cousin, Ray-Ray, had been around just as much as she, and I began to really feel him a whole lot. There was no resisting this six-foot black stallion. His tiger eyes hypnotized at first glance, and he had muscles as thick as the knots of money in his pockets.

We were all chilling, smoking, and watching movies, when Ray-Ray started to make his move.

"Damn, girl!" he yelled, as I bent my twenty-four-inch waistline over and changed the DVD.

I knew the sight of my soft golden ass would get his attention. I pretended I didn't know what his sudden outburst was about. "Damn, girl, what?"

It was hard to keep from laughing with BJ on the couch. She'd seen me in action before and knew exactly what I was up to.

"You know what the hell I'm talkin' 'bout," Ray-Ray said. "You keep puttin' that shit in my face, and I'm gone do something to yo' ass."

Now it was time to call his bluff. I pulled my terry cloth shorts up in my ass, to resemble a thong, and started to sway back and forth in his face.

He stood up and grabbed me by my butt-cheeks, pulling me close to his body. Then he whispered in my ear, "I'm man enough to see what you tryin'a do, girl. Let's go upstairs."

I looked back at BJ for approval. She shrugged then smiled, so I knew it was cool. I looked at Ray-Ray with a huge grin. "Let's go." I grabbed his hand and led him up the stairs.

When we entered the room Ray–Ray immediately threw me on the bed. He was much rougher than Duke, but I didn't mind. I knew this was going to be excitingly different, so I pulled off my shorts without hesitation.

Knock! Knock! Knock! Knock!

I looked out the window. I tried to ignore the knock, praying that Duke would assume I wasn't home and go away.

Knock! Knock! Knock! Knock! Duke began to bang more forceful.

I grabbed Ray-Ray by the neck and began to kiss him passionately. I wanted him, and by all means I was going to have him.

After the knocking stopped, I turned the stereo on and watched Ray-Ray as he got undressed. His body was nice, his skin was smooth like silk, and his six-pack was well-defined. His body was just as beautiful as Duke's. I figured if the sex was as good, I may have two dicks to screw instead of one.

"Ray-Ray! Ray-Ray!" I couldn't help screaming his name as he sexed me.

He didn't make love to me, he fucked me, and I loved it.

After sex we smoked a blunt to bring down the adrenaline rush. Soon after, Ray-Ray fell asleep.

I went downstairs to check on BJ. She was asleep on the couch in the same place I left her. "BJ." I shook her shoulder.

She opened her eyes slowly. "What's up, girl?"

"Did you answer the door when Duke came over?" I asked her so I could get my lie together.

"Yeah, I did. I told him you were sleeping."

"Okay, that's cool. I'm going to call him now while Ray–Ray is sleeping."

"Damn, girl! You put him to sleep?"

"Yeah, girl! The dick was real good too. You mean to tell me you couldn't hear us up there? I put it on his ass. He really knows how to work it."

Knock! Knock! Knock! Knock!

"BJ, can you get that?" I yelled from the top of the stairs.

She opened the door. "It's Duke," she said. "He says he knows you're here. He heard you yelling for me to get the door."

At first I thought to go and wake Ray-Ray before letting Duke in, but BJ opened the door too soon.

Duke walked toward me and grabbed my arm. "What the fuck is up with you? What type of games you playin', Gina?"

I couldn't think of a lie fast enough, so I just remained silent.

BJ pulled his ego card. "Chill out, Duke. You that damn pussy-whipped you gotta act all crazy and shit?"

He let my arm go with the quickness. "You must be sick in your head, female. I don't get whipped. It's just the principle. I don't like to be disrespected."

"Don't speak too soon. You haven't had *all* the pussy, so you don't know if you could be whipped or not."

Duke eyeballed BJ's voluptuous body and massaged his dick. The other day when he did that I thought maybe I was hallucinating, but this time I was sure.

"What the fuck are you doing, Duke? Why you rubbin' your dick and shit?"

"Come on, Gina, don't trip. You know I always do that shit."

Just then, Ray-Ray came walking down the stairs. "What up, fam?" He dapped Duke up. Then he hugged me. "Aight, Gina." He walked over to BJ and hugged her. "Aight, lil' cuz."

I was in a real fucked-up predicament. I was afraid to even look at Duke. I had no explanation. I didn't answer the door when he came over, and then a nigga comes out my room.

Duke laughed. "You fuckin' that nigga too? I guess word

on the streets is true. You give that ass up quicker than a broke fiend trying to get a fix."

As he headed for the door, I grabbed him trying my best to explain.

"It's all good, shortie. There's no hard feelings. I'll be over some other time to hit that ass." He smacked my butt before pulling out his cell and making a call. As he walked away, he said, "Yo', Veronica, I'm on my way."

Chapter 25

Ceazia

Sleeping with the Enemy

There were so many things to remind me of Vegas. I should have sold the house just like I sold his car, clothes, and jewelry after his death, but I just couldn't give it up. I'd worked too hard and went through too much to just let it go—holding him down during his jail sentence, doing time for a crime I didn't even commit, and harassment from his mistress while doing it. Hell, I deserved everything I had, and Vegas, Mickie, and Sonya deserved what they got too. Anyone else in my shoes would have done the same thing.

Imagine coming home after serving five hard months in jail for a crime you didn't commit and finding *your* man, in *your* house, in *your* Jacuzzi, having a threesome with one of *your* best friends and her lover. That was definitely a death sentence. I had to do it. Luckily, I moved slowly and carefully, and that's why I was still on the streets. Although I didn't regret a thing, I must admit, things hadn't been the same without Vegas.

That little bit of money I made at the strip club just to

hold shit down wasn't even worth the aggravation. I'd done all I could to get back on top, but it just wasn't happening. I was fucking with this nigga from up top, another from the Dirty South, and even that nigga Bear that Vegas used to cop his raw from. And all these niggas combined with me stripping, still couldn't compare to how Vegas was putting out.

It seemed like I had to go for what I knew and keep it in the family. I'd checked out how that bitch Danielle was living, and it looked pretty good to me. I figured if Snake could do for her, then I knew he could do even more for a bitch like me. So as much as I hated to do it, Snake was about to be the next nigga to catch my heart. Hey, desperate times called for desperate measures!

I sat down at the computer to check my e-mail before sending Snake a message. To my surprise there was a return message from him. STOP PLAYING THE GAMES. MAKE YOURSELF KNOWN. THAT MASTURBATION SOUNDS GOOD, BUT I THINK YOU COULD USE MY HELP.

I responded: THE GAME IS OVER. MEET ME AT YOUR REGULAR STRIP SPOT ON THURSDAY AT YOUR REGULAR TIME. I'LL HIT YOU UP WHEN I'M READY.

Thursday came in no time. I headed to the club in a hurry. I wanted to be sure to beat Snake there. I purchased new costumes, got a beautiful golden tan, got my hair, nails, and eyebrows done, and put on my MAC makeup to perfection. I didn't give any dances the entire night. I wanted to be fresh for Snake. I had a new routine choreographed especially for him.

Around midnight he walked in the velvet room and took his usual seat.

That was my cue. I signaled the DJ to play R. Kelly's "Move Your Body Like a Snake," the perfect song, considering my target. I slithered all over the stage, up and down the pole, my eyes fixed on him the entire time. He didn't take his eyes off me either. He licked his lips and looked at me seductively. Just the look on his face was making my juices flow.

After the song ended, I went to the dressing room to freshen up and change costumes. He was still sitting in the same spot when I returned.

I walked up to him, straddled his lap, and whispered in his ear, "This one is on the house." Then I gave him the lap dance of his life.

I started with a slow wind on his lap. I ran my fingers through his hair, moving my vagina in a circular motion on his penis. I loved men with hair. Luckily, Snake had his hair out instead of his usual cornrows. I did every position imaginable for a lap dance.

Once I felt the magic stick, I knew I had him exactly where I wanted him.

I ended the dance, kissed him on the cheek, and returned to the dressing room. "Mission accomplished!" I flopped down on the couch to catch my breath.

I took a shower, put my regular clothes back on, then headed out the club. I went to my car and called Snake's phone.

"Yo," he answered.

"Meet me outside. Just go to your truck."

Five minutes passed, and he still wasn't out. I looked toward his truck to be sure he wasn't already in there waiting. I noticed a strange person dressed in black looking through his truck. I wasn't sure if it was a detective or someone plotting to rob him, but I wasn't getting involved.

I leaned back in my seat so I wouldn't be labeled as a witness.

A few moments later I heard Snake talking to one of the bouncers as he headed to his truck. Once he got in, I walked over.

He looked at me and hesitantly unlocked the door. "So you're sexy sixty-nine?" he said as I climbed in the truck.

"Yep. You disappointed?"

"Do I look disappointed?"

Honestly, I wasn't sure what he was thinking. "Guess not."

"Good. So where we headed?"

I wanted to go back to my place, but I was afraid it might be too much for him to handle. I totally remodeled the bedroom so it didn't resemble the old one. The crime scene was too much for me to handle as well. The old bedroom was a constant reminder of the murders.

I decided to take my chances with the house. "You can go to my crib."

He looked uncertain, but agreed.

A few minutes later, we were at my house. I punched in the code, and we entered the gate. I jumped out the truck and headed to the door.

When I unlocked the door I noticed Snake still sitting in the truck. "Come on in," I yelled.

He just sat there shaking his head no. "I can't do it, ma."

"It's cool. I understand. Let's get a room at the beach."

We pulled out the gate and headed back out.

That was close. I thought that may have ruined the night, so I had to get him back horny. I began to rub his inner thigh, working my way toward his penis. He still seemed to be distracted and unmoved. I was sure Vegas was on his mind, and if I didn't think fast the night would come to an abrupt end. I had no choice. I had to suck his dick.

I popped in a cough drop and unzipped his pants. I gently pulled out his penis and massaged it with my tongue. I was sure to get the dick nice and moist. I didn't want to take the chance of starting a fire, jerking a dry dick.

Giving head wasn't my specialty, but I could get the job done. My goal wasn't to make him cum, but just to get him back in the mood. Snake moaned with pleasure as he rubbed his hand through my hair. Eventually my rhythm was guided by the pressure of his hand forcing my head in an up-and-down motion.

It didn't take long for us to arrive at the hotel. I was relieved when we arrived because my jaws were getting rather tired. We stopped at the front desk and quickly headed to our suite.

Snake's Nextel phone and Sidekick were constantly going off and every time he would press *end*, sending the caller to voicemail. That was the best option Nextel could have ever come up with.

I was eager to get a taste of that loving Mickie had often bragged so much about. I hurried to get the mood right. I turned on the radio, turned off the lights, and cracked the balcony door so we could hear the waves crashing against the shore.

The room came with chilled champagne. I popped open the bottle and poured us both a glass. Drunk sex was always the best sex.

After we finished the last glass of champagne, Snake pulled out a blunt. "I have to hit this before I do anything. It takes the drunken edge off. You wanna hit?"

"Hell nah!"

As soon as Snake finished smoking, he began to undress.

I started to unbutton my shirt.

He grabbed my arm and pinned them to the bed. He got on top of me and began to suck and bite my neck. He snatched my shirt open, popping the buttons off. "You want this dick?"

"Yes, give it to me."

He continued to pull my clothes off, tearing my panties and bra. Then he stopped moving completely. "You don't want it?" He looked at me.

I figured he wanted me beg, so I played along. "Please give it to me, Snake. Fuck this pussy."

That must have given him the drive he needed because he lifted me off the bed, rolled on his back, and sat me across his lap straddled. "Well, show me then." He lifted me by my waist and sat me on his big black handle, which resembled a king-sized Snicker.

Boy, did him and Vegas have a lot in common. We had sex in every position one could think of. By the time we finished, my body was sore and bruised. The sex we had was nothing like the passionate lovemaking experiences Mickie used to talk about. Our sex was quite the opposite. It was rough, hard, and sweaty. Snake didn't caress me, kiss me, or take it slow. In fact, there were times when he would choke me, pull my hair, and even smack me.

"Wow! That was different from the stories I've been told."

He gave me a blank look as he got dressed. "Oh well, new bitch, new tricks I guess." He continued to dress without even looking at me. He pulled out his Sidekick and began to type.

I looked over his shoulders and read: *Got 'em, or she got me, rather.*

He laced his brand-new wheat Tims. "I got to run. How much is a cab going to cost you to get back to the club?"

I couldn't believe this nigga had the audacity to even think I was getting my sexy ass in a cab. "Excuse me? Did you ask about a cab?"

"Yeah. How much you need? I don't have time to take you back to the club. I gotta run."

I laughed to keep from snapping off on him. "Honey, I don't do cabs."

"Okay. I'll have my lil' soldier come scoop you." He opened his cell phone.

"Duke, I need you to come to my spot at the oceanfront, room 112, and pick up this chick for me. She'll be going back to the strip joint. One." He closed the phone and headed for the door.

"Can I pencil you in for next week same time same place?" I asked before he closed the door.

"Yeah, hit me up," he said as he closed the door behind him.

I jumped in the shower to clean myself up. As I dried off I examined myself in the mirror. Snake had been really rough. I had a bruise on my hip, neck, and butt-cheeks.

Knock, knock, knock!

I answered the door in my towel to entice Snake's lil' soldier a little. "Hi, little soldier," I said, admiring his jewelry.

He wore a rose gold soldier charm flooded with diamonds. He reminded me so much of Vegas, it was ridiculous.

"Little?" He looked at me seductively.

"I'm sorry. Did I offend you?" I propped my leg on the bed beside him and began to lotion it.

"Do I look like a little boy to you? Tell me one thing that reminds you of a little boy on me."

"Well, from what I can see there is nothing little boy about you. But there is a lot that I can't see." I looked toward his penis.

"Well, we can solve that now." He stood up to unzip his pants.

I was interested to see what he was packing, so I didn't stop him. In fact I encouraged him.

"If it's pleasing, I'll drop my towel and show you what a big girl looks like."

Without hesitation, Duke unzipped his pants, pulled down his boxers, and pulled out his penis. I had lost the bet. His johnson was the size of a full-grown man, and it wasn't even hard yet. "Drop the towel," he demanded.

I smiled, untucked the towel, and let it drop to the floor.

"Damn, girl!" He licked his lips and massaged his penis.

"Okay, little soldier, you win. Get dressed, I got business to take care of. I'm in a hurry."

Chapter 26

Unknown Man

Still Tailing Them

"Got 'em!" I said to myself as I watched Snake leave his favorite spot on the oceanfront, the Crown Grand Suites. I knew it wouldn't be long before he gave in. Although a nigga tried to prepare for the worst, the shit still hit hard. The thought of him fucking *C* fucked my head up. I had a mind to do some real grimy shit and show them a part of me neither one of them would've liked to see. My wicked thoughts were distracted as Ceazia came within my view.

I'd watched her from the crack of her hotel room curtain. Her naked body was still perfect as she walked in the bathroom for a shower. Just the sight of her sexy frame took me back to the many nights we spent in five-star hotels.

Our last trip was to Las Vegas. I watched as she strutted across the hotel floor, modeling her brand-new La Perla lingerie. She was like a kid on Christmas that day. We'd hit every designer store Las Vegas had to offer.

I focused my attention back on Ceazia's hotel room. Draped in a towel only, she was rushing out the bathroom as she headed toward the door. I wondered who it could be as I waited for her to walk back in view.

"Duke? What the hell is he doing there?" I said aloud.

Through the curtain, I could see freak-ass *C* throwing Duke the seduction game. I watched as she teased and taunted him. I couldn't believe my eyes. Duke pulled down his pants and in a single motion pulled his dick out.

What the fuck! She fuckin' lil' boys and shit now? I jumped out the car, gun in hand, and headed toward the hotel room. I released the safety and cocked the gun back as I positioned myself close to the window for a better aim. *This is it!*

I took one final look into the window and saw Duke pull off Ceazia's towel. I couldn't bare to watch this shit any longer. Sweat began to bead up on my forehead, and the pace of my breathing sped up.

As Duke and *C* exited the hotel room I smiled, relieved that they didn't engage in sex. *I'd hate to have to knock that lil' nigga off.* Although nothing happened this time I knew it wasn't over. Knowing my lil' man, fucking *C* was a personal goal of his and he wasn't going to stop there. I just hoped *C* didn't do anything to cause harm to herself or anyone else.

Once I saw Duke and Ceazia pull off, I returned to my car, turned up Jay Z's "Ninety-nine Problems," and drove off.

Chapter 27

Danielle

Beauty Shop Gossip

It was another damn morning that Snake didn't bring his ass home. Once again his excuse was, "I had to do an all-nighter."

I wasn't even worried about it. I was gonna do Danielle.

To start the day off, I was going to get my hair done. Normally, I did my own hair, but I'd been hearing a lot about this young lady in Norfolk by the name of Dee Dee, who did all the hottest styles. She did big heads, bald heads, knotty heads, chicken heads. It didn't matter.

I pulled up to Creative Styles in the heart of Park Place at nine a.m. sharp. I circled the block twice to be sure I got a parking spot as close to the shop as possible. I needed to be able to look out the window periodically to keep a constant check on my car. Although the location and outer appearance of the shop was terrible, I was relieved to see the inside was really nice.

"Hello, I have a nine o'clock appointment with Dee Dee," I told the receptionist as I walked in.

I took a seat close to the window and took turns watching television and my car until it was my turn. I wasn't there ten full minutes before Snake started calling my phone. I sent him directly to my voicemail. I had no words for his ass and no plans on speaking to him the entire day. *Maybe he'll spend more time at home if I give him a taste of his own medicine.*

The stylist's assistant was a slim girl with huge breasts. Every so often she would stop in the middle of her conversation and yell out numbers to everyone sitting in the waiting area. "Girl in the white, you're number one. Beside her, two. Down the row, three, four, five, and six. Okay, number one, sit in my chair and let me base you. Two, to the bowl. Three, be on standby."

By the looks of things she was running this shop like an assembly line. One slip-up and you were off the line.

"What you gettin' today?" Dee Dee asked number one.

"The works girl, perm, trim, and sew in," she said in her ghetto accent.

"Umph. You must have hit the jackpot last night," Dee Dee suggested.

"Or turned some tricks," her assistant added underneath her breath.

"No, I didn't. My moneymaker came in da club last night and broke me off a little somethin'."

"And what stunts did you have to pull this time?" another one of the girls asked. "Moet bottle up ya ass?"

"Nah, gurl. I got me a new nigga this week. I told y'all I been plottin', but y'all wa'n't tryin'a hear a bitch." She rolled her puny little giraffe neck. "I got dat nigga Snake on my team."

"Snake be breakin' you off like that?" Dee Dee asked in disbelief.

Everybody in there, including myself, had gotten silent

and had puzzled looks on our faces. Out of everybody in the shop, this hoochie says to me, "Is there a reason yo' face all balled up? 'Cuz wa'n't nobody talkin' to yo' ass."

I stood up, grabbed my things, and headed toward the door, saying, "If you must know why I had such an expression on my face, it is because Snake is my man and I can't believe he would spend *our* money on a tramp like *you*."

I darted out the door as fast as I could and headed for my car. "Thank God, I parked close."

Pop! "You talkin' all that shit, bitch. Now back dat shit up!" The hussie hit me in the head with her hooker heels and pulled me by my hair.

"Get the fuck off me!"

People circled us, screaming and yelling, "Fight! Fight!"

I looked around quickly for an escape. As a final hope for survival I opened the Mace on my key chain and emptied the can in her face. "Take that, bitch. That will teach your ass to stay away from my man."

As the stripper ran for cover, I jumped in my car and drove off. I noticed my hair was wet and sticking to my neck. I found that odd because I didn't usually sweat. When I reached back to lift my hair off my neck, my hand was covered in blood.

I rushed to the nearest hospital in a panic. When I got out the car, there was blood all over the headrest. My head began to feel light as I walked in the emergency room.

Two hours and three stitches later, I was all patched up and headed home. To my surprise Snake was home when I arrived. He sat on the couch, his feet propped up on the coffee table, talking on his cell and massaging his penis. He didn't even notice my presence.

"You better stop talking like that, girl, before I come over there and do something to you."

Without saying a word, I walked right up behind him and smacked the taste out his mouth.

He jumped up and reached for his gun.

"Oh, you're gonna shoot me now, Snake?"

My eyes filled with tears. I knew he wasn't going to shoot me, but all the events of the day had taken its toll. I couldn't take it any longer.

He placed his gun on the table and walked toward me. "What the fuck you smack me for, Danielle?"

"I hate you, Snake. I hate you. Look at me. This is all because you can't keep your ass out of the damn strip club."

He examined my head. "What the fuck happened, Danielle? Who did this shit?"

"One of your stripper bitches."

"Who, Danielle? What's her name? What she look like? Where did you see her?"

"Look, I don't know the bitch name. I ran into her at Creative Styles this morning. She's brown-skin, about five-five, small waist, big ass, and long blonde weave. You should know. Evidently you gave her a pretty good amount of money last night. How'd you do that, Snake? You were in two places at once? I thought you were pulling an all-nighter?"

I walked up the stairs to take a shower and wash my hair. I left him standing in the living room yelling alone. I knew Snake was spending time at the strip club. Hell, I had even followed him a couple of times, but I had no idea it was this serious. I tried to convince myself that it didn't matter, as long as he came home to me. Now I was going to have to put my foot down.

As the days passed Snake continued his regular routine. So, again I decided to follow him. I prepared myself for a two-hour wait as he entered the club. This time I decided to stay until he left.

Not even two minutes passed when Snake came back out the club. Following him was a nice-looking female, with a nice body. I knew Snake was responsible for her appearance. Hell, it was almost identical to mine.

They got in his truck and pulled out the parking lot. I was careful not to follow them too closely as they strolled down the interstate.

As they headed toward the oceanfront, I knew there could only be one destination—Crown Grand Suites. I didn't even bother to follow any further. If they were headed to the hotel, there was only one thing they could be doing. Besides if I did catch him, what would I do or say? And I definitely wasn't risking getting my ass whipped again.

I got off the exit and returned home. I decided to call Snake on the way. "What's up, baby girl?"

I wanted to cuss him out and tell him how much I hated him for cheating, but instead I played along. "Nothing, baby. Where are you?"

He laughed. "It's not past my curfew yet, is it?"

"Whatever, Snake. Can you answer my question please?"

"I think you already know."

"Snake, where are you?"

"I'm on my way to this bachelor's party. I had to pick up the stripper for my man. I'll be at the oceanfront."

I had overreacted. I was glad I did turn around, instead of going there and making a scene.

Chapter 28

BJ

A Friend's Deceit

"Aaaahhhhhhh!" I screamed as Duke forced his penis inside of me.

Luckily no one was home to hear my screams, but as loud as I was, I was more concerned with the neighbors hearing me at this point.

"Please take it slow, Duke." I had no idea losing my virginity would hurt so badly.

"Okay, I got you. Just work with me, BJ. Let me get it all the way in first."

I wrapped my arms around him tightly as he slid his hands under my butt-cheeks and pushed me forward giving one big thrush.

"Ooohhhh sssshhhiiiiittttt!!!!!!!!!" I yelled out in pain. It felt like my insides were ripping in half.

Duke began to kiss my neck softly and caress my breast. His gentle touch made things feel a lot better.

I could feel the pain slowly turn into pleasure. I moved my pelvis slowly in tune with his movements. My vagina became moist, making our sex even more enjoyable. I ran my fingers through Duke's hair as he sexed me. I began to moan with pleasure instead of pain.

Duke kissed my neck. "You like that?"

"Yes," I moaned softly.

I couldn't believe I had finally lost my virginity. Too bad I couldn't share it with Gina. I had betrayed my best friend for a guy. We'd always said we wouldn't let a guy ever come between us. I felt like I had just made a huge mistake.

"Duke, what have we done?"

"What chu mean?"

"You're sexing Gina and she's my best friend. I have totally violated."

"Whateva, BJ. You been comin' at me ever since the day you caught me and Gina fuckin'."

"If I'm not mistaken, you were the one eating my coochie in Gina's living room while she was upstairs with Ray-Ray."

"You wanted it, BJ. That's why you ratted her out. But if you feel so guilty, let's just end it here and forget it ever happened." He put out his blunt and threw on his clothes.

I wish we didn't have to end it like that, but I was happy with the decision overall. I didn't want to lose Gina as a friend.

I stopped him as he headed to the door. "Bye, Duke." I looked at him with my best puppy-dog eyes before kissing him on the lips.

He hugged me tight. "I'll see you 'round, shortie."

I knew I was making the right decision, but my heart was broken as I watched him leave through the window.

Ring! Ring!

The caller ID read *Regina Wallace.*

"What's up, girl?" I answered.

"Nothing. I was just calling to see what's up. You comin' over today?"

Normally I would be at Gina's house at least five times a week, but since I had been dealing with Duke I felt too guilty to come around.

"Nah, girl. I'm home alone, so I'm going to chill. But me and Ray-Ray will come over tomorrow," I lied.

As the weeks passed I didn't sex Duke or even speak to him. Gina, on the other hand, was sexing him on the regular. In fact, she was sexing both Ray-Ray and Duke.

Valentine's Day was right around the corner, and I hated the thought of being alone. For once the tables had turned, and *I* was now envious of Gina. Even though I was jealous of all the attention she had been receiving from Ray-Ray and Duke, I still kept my promise and stayed away from Duke. It was hard though. Whenever I saw him, my heart would flutter, but I always kept my distance.

Valentine's Day rolled around sooner than I expected. Gina had all sorts of plans and needed my assistance to make sure everything went accordingly. After Duke and Ray-Ray ran into each other at her house, they both were under the impression that Gina had dropped the other. Gina patched that situation up real quick. Since then things were lovely for her. She had all the newest shoes and clothes times two. Between the gifts from the two of them, Gina stayed laced.

She'd planned to spend the first part of the day with Duke, then go out later in the night with Ray-Ray. It was my job to keep Ray-Ray occupied until then.

She called me about noon. "Hey, girl. I just wanted to make sure we had the plans together."

I was hoping she would have been calling to tell me Duke stood her up, but I wasn't that lucky. "Yeah, I got you. Keep Ray-Ray busy until you call, right? If you don't call, just let him come around seven."

We had gone over the plan a thousand times. I didn't see the need for her to call and give me the rundown for the thousandth time.

I could hear Duke banging on the door in the background.

"Come on, girl. What you doin' in there?"

"Where are you?" I asked, eager to know what Duke had planned for her.

"I'm at the oceanfront at the Crown Grand Hotel. The room is beautiful and the sight is gorgeous. We've been here all day. We plan to watch the sun set on the ocean and everything, girl. My day has been great so far. But I got to go. He's rushing me. Just listen out for my call."

I hung up the phone without saying a word. I cried myself to sleep as I dreamed about being in her shoes.

I woke to the annoying buzz of my alarm clock. It was six-thirty and time for me to call Ray-Ray.

"Yo? What's up, lil' cuz?"

"Come on, it's time to meet up with Gina," I said sleepily.

"I'm on my way."

Ten minutes later he was at my house. I ran downstairs and jumped in the car. We flew down Martin Luther King Boulevard toward Curry Village where Gina lived. We pulled up near her house and headed for the door.

I knocked on the door as Ray-Ray stood beside me with a teddy, flowers, balloons, and all sorts of bags in his hands. He didn't want Gina to see what he had for her, so he stepped aside so she couldn't see him through the peephole.

A few moments later the door opened. "Hey, girl," she said as she opened the door.

I just smiled and stepped aside so Ray–Ray could appear with his surprise.

Ray-Ray walked in and hugged her. "Happy Val—" He stopped in the middle of his sentence and dropped everything.

I stood at the door behind him wondering what was going on. All of a sudden I saw him rush forward and Gina screamed. I walked in the room and Ray-Ray and Duke were locked up together tussling. Gina and I both tried our hardest to pull them apart.

"Please stop it. Please!" I begged and pleaded Ray-Ray.

Eventually we were able to pull them apart.

Ray-Ray headed to his car. "Get my shit from that bitch, BJ."

I grabbed up the bags, leaving the torn flowers, balloons, and teddy behind. I didn't know what to do, so I just did what he asked and decided to call Gina later. I ran out the door and jumped in the car.

Three minutes didn't pass before Gina was calling Ray-Ray's phone. He didn't even bother to answer. He was heated and didn't have anything to say to her. She eventually stop calling, but she did leave a message.

He checked his voicemail as we rode around. Ray-Ray decided to ride and smoke to clear his mind. He handed me the phone after listening to the message. "Call your girl. She trippin', yo."

I called her right away.

The phone rang one time and she picked up. "You sheisty bitch! When I see you I'm going to fuck yo' ass up!" she yelled.

"What are you talking about, Gina? Ray-Ray asked me to get the gifts. I only grabbed them because there was enough tension already. I didn't want to make things worse. Girl, you know I would have brought them right back over there later."

"Bitch, I don't give a fuck about no clothes. I'm talking

about how you set me up. I specifically told you not to bring him if I call. I called a thousand times, and you didn't answer. I even left five messages on your voice mail. We went through this a thousand times. I knew you were going to do some shit. You hate the fact that I'm on top for once and I have all the attention. I've been noticing little shit for the past month. I see how you look at Duke and wear little clothes around him and say slick shit out your mouth. I just chose to trust you because you were my girl. I thought we would never let a guy come between us, but I guess that was bullshit too."

"Gina, I swear on everything I have, I didn't set you up. I was sleeping all day. When my alarm went off, I jumped up and called Ray-Ray. I didn't even check my voicemail."

"Yeah, I figured that's what you would say, but don't worry about it. I owe you, bitch."

Weeks passed and I didn't hear from Gina or see her. I really missed her, but my pride wouldn't let me bow down. I constantly reminded myself I did my part. I tried to resolve the issue, but she wasn't trying to hear it.

Every day at school I was reminded of the situation. There was steady gossip about me setting Gina up. Word was, I was supposed to get jumped by Gina and her crew from out the way. Nevertheless, I still remained me. I went to school every day, sat in the same spot at lunch, and still walked the same halls. Gina knew me better than anyone, and she knew it would definitely take an army to beat me. I'd pick up a weapon, fight dirty, or even avoid a fight if I was outnumbered, but I'd never lose. No one ever had the honor of saying they beat my ass.

I thought the day would never come, but Gina and I finally met face to face. After school one Friday I was leaving the building toward the buses like I did everyday. As I walked to the bus, I noticed Duke. I figured since Gina and

I were no longer friends and now she was all about Ray-Ray, I may as well rekindle my relations with Duke.

"Can I roll with you?" I asked in my most seductive tone.

He paused and examined me from head to toe and squeezed my bottom. "You been keepin' my shit tight?"

"Sure have."

"Well, that's all I need to hear. Come on, I'm parked over here." Duke pointed to a black Lexus GS 400.

He always kept nice cars, but I was really impressed with this one. I got in the car with no hesitation.

Just as Duke began to pull off, a hoop ride steered in front of us, cutting him off. "Damn. What the fuck does this bitch want?"

Gina jumped out the car and headed to my side. Before I knew what was going on, she reached in the window and stole me right in the face.

As a reaction I grabbed her shirt and pulled her toward the inside of the car. I reached in my pocket and with my free hand pulled out my shank, which I always kept for situations such as these. Within seconds my shank was out and Gina had been stabbed three times in the chest area.

Afraid that his car would get damaged, Duke quickly ran over and broke things up.

I looked in the mirror to examine my face as Gina returned to her hoop ride. I wiped the trickle of blood that dripped from my right nostril.

Duke examined my face as well. "You aight?"

"Yeah, I'm fine. Where we headed?" I quickly changed the subject, eager to put the whole thing behind me.

"Wherever you want to go, sweetheart." Duke rubbed my inner thigh. "You missed me?"

I smiled and nodded yes. He looked so damn good driving his Lex with the Clipse banging in the background.

"Those niggas couldn't have said it any better. Virginia's for hustlers."

I wondered how the fuck would he know. He'd been living off his uncle since I'd known him. I questioned him to see if things had changed. "How would you know, Duke? You ain't never sold shit."

"Yeah, that's what you and the rest of these niggas out here think. But that's cool. I like it like that. It keeps my name clear. I ain't gotta prove shit to nobody, ma."

"You got something to prove to me." I untied his do-rag so that I could play in his cornrows.

"Oh yeah? And what's that?"

"That you can't be whipped."

"You got a long way to go, young buck. You can't even say the word *whipped* until you start fuckin' for real."

Chapter 29

Gina

My Baby Daddy

"**S**hit!" I yelled as I slowly pulled the pregnancy test out of the bag. I couldn't believe my eyes. I knew that having unprotected sex could result in an unwanted pregnancy, but I guess I just never thought it could happen to someone like me.

It had been days since the fight with BJ, but the stab wounds I received still hadn't quite healed. The streaking pain I felt with each motion was a constant reminder of the revenge I owed her. I hadn't come up with the perfect plan, but I was definitely going to get her back. Now that I realized she could've made me lose my unborn child, I was furious.

The only real thing that was keeping me off BJ's ass was her cousin. If I didn't love Ray-Ray so much, I would have sent bitches to her house that same day. Even if it took me months to get her, I knew my revenge on BJ was coming. At the moment, I had more important things to worry about, like the fact that my period hadn't come in a month and that I was sitting staring at a colored cotton tip of an exposed pregnancy test.

I was in a sad state of denial, so I reached under the bathroom counter to retrieve the extra test I'd purchased. I slowly removed the wrapper and then sat on the toilet, placing the open end of the test tube under the flow of my urine. Once it was soaked I replaced the cap.

Now the waiting game. I sat the test on the bathroom counter and went to watch a little TV. I hoped David Chappelle's antics would make the time pass, but my stomach constantly ached with fear as I waited the two minutes that seemed to take two hours.

One commercial later the time was up, and I hesitantly returned to the bathroom. I almost hit the floor when I saw that plus sign in bright pink. *Oh, shit then it must be true. I'm pregnant!*

I nearly broke my neck as I rushed through the house, jumping over chairs and running up the stairs to get my phone to call Ray-Ray.

"Happy birthday, baby!" Ray-Ray yelled into the phone as soon as he picked up.

"Fuck a birthday!" I yelled. "You and me got some issues."

"Damn! What's up with you? I guess that's the attitude of a black birthday girl, huh?" Ray-Ray joked.

"Nah, this is the attitude of a black *pregnant* birthday girl. This damn pregnancy test is what's up, nigga."

Since Duke and I were no longer an item, Ray-Ray hadn't been using protection. One night he came over drunk and horny after a long night of gambling and drinking at the bootleggers, we engaged in passionate sex, and he failed to pull out. I knew I was going to end up pregnant the night it happened, but I was hoping otherwise.

"So what you gonna do?"

"What am *I* going to do? Did I get pregnant alone, nigga? What are *you* going to do?"

"Okay, Gina, what are *we* going to do? Ain't no need in all this drama you givin' me now."

"I want an abortion."

"Aight, cool. Just let me know how much it cost. You know I got you."

I sat on my bed sobbing. *How did I get in this situation?*

Normally this would be a time when I would call BJ and ask for her support, but not this time. She had betrayed me and I hated her for it. Duke had betrayed me, and I hated him as well. So had my mother, her boyfriend, and now Ray-Ray too. I had to wonder how one person could be let down so many times. At that moment, it seemed as if I was the only person in the world who had ever been betrayed by just about all the important people in their lives.

How could Ray-Ray so openly agree to an abortion? How could he just hang up on me like that without making sure I was okay? Didn't he understand that I loved him? Didn't he know that this child is a part of us both?

I sat on my bed weeping until I fell asleep, but my afternoon nap was interrupted by the sound of gunshots. I'd heard gunshots nearby before, but for some reason, these shots seemed eerie.

I looked out the window to see where the shots were coming from, but the neighborhood was as peaceful as an April shower. I figured the shots must have been part of a bad dream, and that being suddenly awakened added to the rapid beat of my heart.

Since I was awake, I decided to call Ray-Ray back and tell him that I had wanted to keep my baby. After dialing his cell, I could hear the phone ringing, but he didn't answer.

I called a few more times after that; and some one picked up, but no one said anything. I listened carefully. I heard music in the background and faint breathing. Ray-Ray was listening to our song, "Lovers and Friends" by Lil Jon, Luda, and Usher. For a moment I thought about the countless times we'd made love to that song, but that moment of reminiscing was cut short when I heard the whisper of someone's voice. I listened attentively. I could hear someone trying to force words out, but I wasn't sure exactly what they were saying.

I put my volume up as loud as possible and listened a little harder. And that's when I heard the faint words between gasps of breath, "I love you."

I hung up the phone in disbelief. I began sobbing even more than before. *How could he do this to me? I'm pregnant. And on my birthday!*

My tears quickly turned into anger, the more I thought about Ray-Ray with someone else. I decided to call him back, but this time, the phone went straight to voice mail.

"What's up? This Ray. Leave a message." *Beep!*

"Ray-Ray, this is Gina. I'm sure you're busy at the Celebrity Bash handling your business right now and that's why your phone is off. But what I have to say needs no conversation anyway. I was just calling to tell you that it's over, I'm keeping the baby, and thanks for such a wonderful birthday. And as for as the bitch you're with, I hope she was worth it." *Click!*

I began to think that conniving bitch BJ probably set him up with another chick just to get at me. I jumped up in a panic and threw on my shoes and grabbed my purse. I headed for the door with my mom's car keys in hand. I grabbed the gun Ray-Ray kept at my house for backup protection. Somebody was gonna die, and I didn't plan for it to be me. I jumped in the car and tried starting it up. "Come on, you stupid car!" I yelled hysterically.

I tried and tried turning the ignition, but nothing. The

car wouldn't start. Frustrated and exhausted, I just sat in the car and cried. I lit a blunt as I often did under stress.

After about ten minutes of sobbing and smoking, I actually felt a little better. I got myself together, got out the car, and headed back to the house to my bedroom. I didn't even bother calling Ray-Ray's sorry ass again. Within moments the tension lifted from my body and once again I was sound asleep.

Chapter 30

Snake

Beef on the Streets

Shit was really starting to get hectic around here with these out-of-control stripping bitches. Ceazia's pussy was getting better by the day, my girl was going mad, my little nigga Duke got beef, and I may have picked up a little personal beef of my own.

After that trick at the beauty salon busted my girl in the head I went ballistic. I went up to that shop and threatened to shut the whole shit down unless somebody told me what the fuck happened that day. Of course, it didn't take long for them to start squealing.

I walked in calmly with my gun in hand and locked the door behind me. I stood at the door and asked Dee Dee what was up. She didn't have much to say, so I asked the assistant. She didn't have much to say either. So in order to get the information I needed I had to start making threats. I didn't want to do that because Dee Dee was my man's old lady. But, shit, my girl was involved, and I had to what I had to do. After the threats, those bitches started singing.

I found out it was a trick that went by the name of

Cherry at one of the local strip joints. I paid her a visit that same night. As soon as I hit the door, it was as though an alarm had been hit, 'cause every bitch in there came running from the back.

I dissed one of my regular chicks I would normally holla at. "Naw, baby, I ain't here for that tonight."

It didn't take long for me to spot Cherry in a dark corner. I walked right up behind her tricking ass and grabbed that bitch by her weave.

She squealed as I dragged her from the gentleman she was entertaining and into the men's bathroom. "Aaaahhhh! What the fuck is going on?"

I choked her against the bathroom wall. "Bitch, you lost your muthafuckin' mind?"

"I'm sorry, baby. I ain't know that was your girl."

That grimy bitch already knew she'd fucked up.

"Bitch, don't you ever come near my girl or anybody that got anything to do with me again," I said, smacking her after every few words.

"Okay, okay. Please just don't hit me any more, Snake, please. Whatever you want baby, please."

By this time security was rushing in the bathroom. "Yo, what the fuck is going on?" one security guard yelled.

I turned around, so he could get a look at my face. I figured he didn't know who I was rushing in talking shit.

"Oh, Snake. You aight?" he asked, changing his tone.

"Yeah, I'm straight." I directed my attention back to Cherry. "Bitch, this ain't over." I pushed her in the face.

I straightened my clothes then walked out the men's restroom calmly. I stopped at the bar, drank a shot of Patrón then exited the club.

As I rode home, I was confident that the next time Cherry saw Danielle her attitude would be a lot better. Now that the situation was dealt with, I began to think about my lil' soldier, Duke. It seemed like he'd caught beef behind some little hot-ass female. It was getting harder and harder to school that lil' nigga these days.

My brain jumped from one issue to another. As if my issue with Cherry and Duke wasn't enough, now Danielle was tripping too. She'd been following me, checking my text messages and phone, and even searching through my pockets. I didn't make a fuss though. I just played along and watched my steps.

She was starting to scare me. I wasn't trying to end up like my brother Vegas.

The other night I went to the strip club to pick up Ceazia and Danielle was following me. I didn't realize she was following me until I was on the interstate and almost to the oceanfront. Now the average nigga would have panicked, but instead I started to plot. I knew Danielle didn't know what Ceazia looked like, so that wasn't a worry. She knew I would be headed to one place, the Crown Grand Hotel.

Five minutes to the destination I received a phone call from her. I played it cool, and the lies just rolled off my tongue. I came off on top. Danielle's whole attitude switched. Instead of me being the bad one, she felt guilty for accusing me.

Now Ceazia, that bitch was venomous. I knew it before I even fucked her, but she was so irresistible. It was taking all I could to stay away, but she kept reeling me in.

Ring, ring!

"Yo!"

"What's up, baby? Are we meeting up tonight at the usual spot?" she asked in her sexy voice.

"Yeah. I'll hit you up around ten. Keep your phone on."

"Okay."

"Aight, sweetheart. I'll talk to you later."

I hung up and headed out the way to holla at Duke. We had a full weekend ahead of us. It was the Annual Seven Cities Celebrity Weekend Bash. All the hottest entertainers, athletes, and ballers were sure to attend. Everyone looked forward to this event each year. It was the time for us to shine.

"What up, unc?" Duke said as he hopped in the truck.

"What's up with you, nigga? Word on the street is you got beef. Care to fill me in on that shit?"

"Oh really? 'Cause word on the street is you're in that same boat."

"I can handle my shit, young buck. Can you say the same?" I punched him in the chest, as a reminder that I was still the boss.

He buckled as he tried to explain. "Man, that ain't no beef for real. That nigga Ray-Ray is just a little upset about a tussle we had at Gina's crib on Valentine's Day. That's old."

"Ray-Ray? Ain't you knocking his little cousin off?"

"Man, I'm good. I got this shit together."

"Aight, lil' soldier, handle your handle," I said as we pulled up to the Quick Shop on the corner.

I ran in the store to buy a box of blunts. I could see the chickens flocking around the truck, trying to holla at Duke. *I gotta teach that nigga to have a low profile.* I was sure we had already been over that shit, but I guess it didn't sink in.

By the time I arrived back to the truck, Duke was standing outside the door hugging on some hoodrat chick.

"Yo, Duke, come on, nigga."

"Aight, mommy." Duke smacked the chick's ass before hopping in the truck.

"Aight, young fuck," she said with a wink.

"Duke, what the fuck you doin', man. You just can't be

knocking any old bitch off. You gotta make it a privilege to fuck. Otherwise the top-notch bitches not goin' to be tryin' to fuck."

"Man, that's an old head. How many niggas my age hittin' old heads? Why you think she call me *young fuck*? I don't give a damn about these young chicks no more, man. I got some shit in store. I'm 'bout to knock off a couple of real bomb-ass top-notch bitches."

Thirty minutes later we were at the Hampton Coliseum. We pulled up and parked front and center. I knew niggas wouldn't be ready for my truck. It was events like these I looked forward to. Niggas were dizzy by the spin of the twenty-four-inch stop and go's on the Range. I copped it especially for this event.

Me and Duke hopped out the truck to holla at a few people.

Martinez, an odd look on his face, was the first to greet me. "What up, Snake?"

"What's good, man?"

"Not too much, man. It's a lot of envy out here today. As matter of fact, I've heard whispers of your name."

I knew something was up. I knew that nigga Martinez like the back of my hand. "Oh yeah? What they talkin'?"

"It's that nigga, Joker. Talkin' about he gotta straighten you out 'bout runnin' up in his girl's spot."

"That's it, man? That's what got you worried, nigga? Where dat nigga at?"

"That ain't it, man. I know you can handle yours. It's more to it."

Now this nigga was really starting to piss me off. "What is it, nigga?"

"It's Duke, man. Niggas talkin' about gettin' that nigga."

I understood why Martinez hesitated with that statement. When it came to my little soldier, I didn't fuck around. "Oh yeah? Who the fuck is talking?"

"It's that nigga, Ray-Ray."

"Duke." *Do I coach him on defense or do I just send him home?*

Duke was a hothead, and I was afraid how he may react. I didn't want anything to happen to him, and I didn't want him to do anything he would regret. I had to make a decision and fast.

"What's the deal, unc? You fuckin' with my game right now."

"Duke, on some real shit, I gotta holla at you."

We headed back to the truck and jumped in. I looked him in the eyes. "Tell me what's up with you and this nigga Ray-Ray."

Duke responded with an explosive laugh. "Unc, please tell me you ain't got me in here about that nigga."

Just like I figured, this nigga had no idea. I started the truck.

"What you doin', Snake? We just got here, man. I know you ain't gon' let this fool punk us."

I had nothing to prove to Duke, so I didn't respond. I just put the truck in reverse.

"Stop the muthafuckin' truck, man!"

"Who the fuck you hollerin' at, nigga?"

Duke stared at me with a killer grit.

"Fix yo face." I grabbed him by the collar, trying to instill the fear that seemed no longer present in his heart.

"Fuck you! I ain't no damn child no more, Snake!" He pushed me in the chest.

My first instinct was to punch this lil' nigga in his face and break his fuckin' jaw, but instead I chose to let him learn the hard way.

Ssssskkkkuuuuurrrrrrrttttttttt!

I slammed on the brakes, almost giving the both of us

whiplash. "You think you hard, nigga? Then get the fuck out. Hold ya own." I handed him the nine from my waist.

Duke jumped out the truck with no hesitation. "I got my *own* to handle my own." He handed me the gun back and pulled out a chrome nine of his own and cocked it back before replacing it on his waist.

As quick as he jumped out, I pulled off. Just as I was headed out the parking lot, I ran into Ceazia. She was looking fly as shit too.

I pulled up behind her BMW 745. She was the only female at the Coliseum killing the scene with the gunmetal gray 745 LI with the chromed factories, newborn wit' the paper tags and "straight glasshouse, no tent." She was definitely doing the damn thang.

"What's up, baby girl?"

She grinned and looked at me seductively with those panther eyes. "You." She lightly kissed my lips.

I could feel my nature rising. I didn't know what it was about that chick, but she had me in a deadly trance.

"I see you killin' them with the Range and spinners. How can I get down? You got some spinners for me?"

I laughed. She and I both knew exactly what it would take for her to get down. "You know what it takes. What's good for tonight?"

"I don't know," she said. "You got something?"

Bang! Bang! Bang! Bang! Our conversation was interrupted by gunshots.

"Get in the truck!" I yelled.

Ceazia jumped in the back seat behind me. I pulled off immediately, glancing in my rearview mirror. Shit was chaotic, people running in every direction.

Bang! Bang! Bang! Bang!

I pulled off immediately and glanced in my rearview mirror again. *Sssssssssskkkkkkkkkuuuuuurrrrrrrrrttttttttttttt!* I slammed on brakes then busted a U-turn in the middle of the parking lot and headed back to the scene.

Once there, I jumped out the truck. It was as though none of these things existed as I ran closer to the center of the action, where I could hear Ceazia screaming in the background.

"Snake, noooooo!"

I could feel Martinez pulling my arm as I grabbed my nine from my waist, but his grip wasn't strong enough to hold me back. As I took my final steps, my body froze with disbelief. It was my lil' soldier, dying on the battle field, but still holding his gun at attention. I was so taken by the scene before me, I didn't realize Ray-Ray was standing in front of me with his gun pointing at Duke.

My brain raced as we looked each other in the eye, never saying a word. *Do I get him before he get me? Will he get Duke if I threaten to get him?*

I decided to take my chances. I quickly aimed my gun, but Ray-Ray beat me to the punch.

Click, click, click!

Saved by the bell! That bitch nigga was out of bullets. Left with no other choice, he jumped in his car in a desperate attempt to escape.

I took my time aiming at him, confident he wouldn't get far.

Bang! Bang! Bang! Bang! Shots rang out for the final time.

I was puzzled by the shots I heard as Ray-Ray's body bounced with every shot as if he was having convulsions. When the firing ceased, his body lay slumped over into the passenger's seat of his car.

I glanced around quickly as I grabbed Duke and put him in the truck. We rode in silence as I sped through every red light on the way.

I glanced down and noticed my blood-filled sleeve. I'd

been hit in my right arm. I tried to figure out where the shots came from. *Maybe those finals shots were meant for me. The shots were fired before I even had a chance to pull the trigger on my gun.*

I was just glad me and Duke were still here because I'd fucked up. This shit would have never gone down if I'd gone with my first instinct and just left the Coliseum.

Chapter 31

Unknown Man

Watch Your Back

Always lurking, again I was on the scene. I'd heard of the beef Duke and Snake both carried on the streets, and I knew shit would go down. That's why I made sure to be there. There was no way I was going to let them niggas die at the hands of anyone else. This was my revenge and I had to be the one to lay them to rest. I had a team of young cats by my side trained to kill, and all I had to do was give them the word.

Today was a small test of just how quick one of my lil' dudes can be on the trigga. I would pay a million dollars to have an instant replay of the look on Snake's face when he heard the shots ring out. He looked as though his life had flashed before his eyes. I had to take that lil' nigga Ray-Ray down.

Funny how life works, huh. Snake and Duke was two niggas I wanted dead and because of me they still alive.

Snake was caught slipping again. He should have never

left Duke at that celebrity event alone. Duke had better be thankful that gold digging bitch, *C*, was there to keep Snake around for a little while longer. If not, he would have been nowhere in sight when Duke got hit.

Chapter 32

Ceazia

Chaotic Crisis

Snake's phone rang continuously on the route to the hospital. Everyone was anxious to know what was going on. I noticed that out of all the hundred and one calls he'd received, he ignored them all except one. From the way the conversation went, I was sure he was speaking with his girl.

"Baby, shit is crazy. I'm on my way to the hospital. I'm aight, but Duke was shot. I'm leaving Hampton and on my way to Norfolk General," Snake ranted into the phone, answering question after question, as though he was being interrogated.

I rolled my eyes out of jealousy then quickly focused my attention back on Duke. I held him tightly as blood drained from his nose and mouth. "Hold on, lil' soldier. You're gonna make it, baby."

All I could vision was Vegas laying in the Jacuzzi filled with his own blood, and the two women lying doubled over in the Jacuzzi, dead along with him. The thought was clear as if it was just the day before when I unloaded my gun on them.

It seemed like only moments had passed once we got to the hospital because it wasn't long before we pulled up to the emergency entrance. Snake rushed to the back and pulled Duke out the back door. Others rushed over to help him. It didn't take long to get Duke in the hospital and the emergency team to come and roll him off to the trauma unit.

Family members and friends arrived shortly after we did. Every one was hysterical, asking Snake, "Who did this? Where was he shot? Is he going to make it? How is he?"

I could see the frustration and tension in Snake's face. He didn't respond to anyone. He just stood in the middle of the floor motionless. I'd never seen him speechless and so full of anguish over anything. I knew he was going to explode at any moment.

"Why don't we go outside and get some air?" I suggested while taking his hand, leading him toward the exit door.

Surprisingly, he followed along without argument. Once outside he sat on the bench rubbing his head. Stress was written all over his face. Duke was his lil' soldier, and they were extremely close. I could understand why he was so upset about his lil' homey being shot.

Snake finally spoke. "I shouldn't have left him there alone. I could have prevented this shit," he said, as tears rolled from his eyes.

I never thought I would see him shed a tear. I placed my arm around his shoulder. "It's not your fault, Snake. There is nothing you could have done. He's going to be fine."

He tensed up when I touched him. I pulled back and looked him over. His sleeve was red in color.

"It's my arm. I'm hit," he said calmly. "I've been so distraught over my lil' soldier that I didn't realize I'd been hit too."

I asked him to remain where he was until I came back with a nurse.

He grabbed my arm, preventing me from moving. "Please, I don't want any help right now. I just need a minute to think."

"Okay, Snake, but you're going to eventually need to get that looked at."

I agreed to give him a few moments before getting him medical attention. Drops of blood began hitting the ground, but he still refused to get help at the moment.

We didn't say any words to each other. We just sat in the cool night air embracing one another, watching people constantly walking in and out of the emergency room waiting area.

I noticed a nice-looking young lady walking briskly toward us. She had a perfect frame and flawless skin. Her designer attire was definitely an outfit that would fit perfectly into the closet of a diva as me.

As she walked closer, she examined me closely, eventually pausing directly before me. "My name is Danielle. I'm Snake's girlfriend. And you are?" She extended her hand.

I felt embarrassed as I extended my bloody hand and my hair was a mess. "Hi. I'm—"

"You're a stripper."

Out of respect for Snake I didn't respond. That bitch had no idea who I was. Normally I would have whipped her ass just for walking up on me the way she did.

"Danielle, now is not the time for this shit," Snake told her.

She looked me up and down, examining every inch of my body. "From the looks of things you were around when all this took place. And what exactly were you doing with my man, if I may ask?"

"Look, Danielle, I am Vega—"

"You don't have to explain" Snake quickly stopped me in my tracks, like my identity was some sort of secret.

"You're right. She doesn't need to explain—you do." Danielle stepped a little closer to Snake and me, her arms folded. "So what were you doing there with this stripper?"

I stood up and balled up my fist ready to attack. I had to show this female that she might've needed to take a second thought on making the wrong move. She stepped back and stood a little closer to Snake, as if he would provide some sort of protection if I decided to beat her ass. I realized this little scary chick wasn't any threat at all. Her bark was surely more vicious than her bite.

"I'll take it from here, thanks." Danielle rolled her eyes then squeezed between Snake and me.

The little bitch only wanted some attention, and it almost cost her an ass-beating. Once I saw that she posed no real threat, I didn't resist. I got up silently and walked to another bench at the end of the corner. I watched as the both of them entered the hospital and disappeared behind the emergency room door. There were quite a few people at the bench smoking cigarettes.

As stressed as I was, I figured I would try one myself. "Excuse me, may I have a cigarette please?" I asked an attractive young girl.

"Help yourself." She handed me the entire pack never even looking up. Every so often she would open her cell phone, begin to dial a number then hang up.

I wondered what worries such a young girl like her could have. The curiosity was killing me. "Looks like you're having a hard time making that phone call."

The young girl finally looked up. She too examined me from head to toe. "Looks like you're having an even worse time than me. You're covered in blood. What happened?"

I didn't expect her to come so direct. "You're right,

sweetie. I've had a hell of a day. Now why don't you tell me about your day? Why are you so sad?"

"Look, lady, maybe you should just mind your business," she said as she burst into tears.

I rubbed her on her shoulder. She obviously wasn't as tough as she portrayed. Another one whose bark was much more vicious than her bite. I was beginning to wonder if it was contagious and I was a carrier.

"It's okay, honey. I know exactly how you feel. Just let it all out."

She finally told her story. "There were only three people in my life who loved me as much as I loved them. I've already lost one and I may lose the other two today. And even worse it may be my fault," she continued to explain. "My boyfriend, Duke, and my cousin, Ray-Ray, had a shootout at the Coliseum today and maybe I could have prevented it. But I didn't ease the bad blood between them and this is what it led to. I've even lost my best friend because of this. She dates my cousin, and I don't even have the courage to call her and tell her the bad news."

I consoled her, ultimately giving her the courage she needed to call her friend. I assured her she wasn't alone and that there was always someone worse off than she.

As we spoke, I didn't bother telling her I knew Duke or was present at the shooting. I knew she would want details of the event and I didn't think that was in her best interest.

I finished my cigarette and called one of my girls from the club to take me to my car.

My girl Storm answered the phone in her usual snappy tone. "Yeah, bitch!"

"Hey, I need you to come pick me up from the hospital."

"Girl, why? What happened? Oh shit! You was at the Coliseum! Don't tell me you were in the middle of that shit. Girl, you aight!"

"We'll talk as soon as you get here."

I knew that would guarantee my ride to the Coliseum. *The shit a nosy bitch would do for news.*

Once I ended my conversation with Storm, I picked up my conversation with the young lady where we left off. "I feel like I have a certain connection with you. You remind me so much of myself. I know you don't know me from Eve, so let me introduce myself. I'm Ceazia." I extended my hand.

"I'm BJ. Nice to meet you, Ceazia."

"If you ever need anyone to talk to, please feel free to call me." I gave her my number.

I headed back toward the emergency room entrance. I wanted to say a few words to Snake before leaving and check on Duke. When I entered, Snake and several other family members and friends were in the conference room speaking with the doctor.

"Duke has several gunshot wounds to his upper body. We're prepping him for the operating room now. We expect the surgery to last approximately eight hours. There is a waiting room on the 6th floor. The immediate family can wait there for counsel with the surgeon after the surgery is over."

The questions began to overflow as soon as the doctor ended his sentence.

Snake was still silent just as before.

I wanted so badly to comfort him, but his lady friend stood close by. Rather than disturb the peace, I left the emergency room unnoticed and waited outside for my girlfriend.

Chapter 33

Gina

Bad News

Ring, ring, ring! Ring, ring, ring!
I was awakened by the constant ringing of the phone. I looked at the caller ID *Jasmine Smith*

"Hel-lo!" I yelled into the phone. I didn't understand why this bitch would be calling me.

"I'm not calling you about, Gina—" BJ began to say before I cut her off.

"I know you're not. You ain't that damn brave. You got me once, but believe me, bitch, it ain't over. The next time I see you, that's your ass!"

"Well, maybe you can beat my ass at Norfolk General Hospital. I thought you might want to know Ray-Ray has been shot. He's here at the hospital, and he's in critical condition."

This can't be true. I just spoke to him. He's fine. This is a game. She's trying to get back at me. But what if she's telling the truth? Who would do such a thing? Maybe she had Duke set him up. But I know she wouldn't do that to her own cousin. What the hell is going on?

My thinking was interrupted by BJ's cry. "He's, he's, he's not going to make it, Gina. He's not going to make it."

I could feel the pain in BJ's voice. I hung up the phone immediately. I ran around the house frantic as I grabbed my clothes and purse. I knew exactly where I last placed my mom's keys, so I grabbed them and headed to her car.

"God, please let this car start. God, please let this car start."

A few pumps on the gas, a few bangs on the steering wheel, and a few profanities later I was on my way to the hospital.

I ran through the emergency room doors and spotted BJ along with her aunt and other family members. After noticing the saddened faces of Ray-Ray's family, reality set in.

"Nnnnnnnooooooooooo!" I screamed as BJ's words echoed in my head. *He's not going to make it, he's not going to make it, he's not going to make it.*

BJ rushed over and grabbed me as the strength left my body and I collapsed to the floor.

"Please tell me he's fine, BJ. Tell me he's fine."

I looked at her for a response, but she didn't answer.

I grabbed her by her shirt and began to shake her. "Do you hear me? I know you hear me, you bitch! Tell me he's fine. Tell me he's fine!" I yelled at the top of my lungs.

Again she didn't respond. She just stood motionless as tears rolled down her face.

"This is all your fault, you bitch! You started this beef!"

"How could you say that, Gina? Their beef was behind you and your cheating ways. You're to blame, bitch! I'm losing a cousin and a boyfriend! What the fuck are you losing?"

"I'm losing a baby father. You're the reason my child is not going to have a father, BJ!"

"You're pregnant?" BJ said in a soft whisper.

"Yes, I am. And thanks to you, I will be a single mom."

Deep inside I knew BJ was not at fault, but I had no one else to blame. My life was destroyed. Ray-Ray was the only person left in my life that I trusted.

The emergency room lobby became silent as BJ and I argued back and forth. I looked to my right and noticed Duke's brother and other family members standing silently as spectators. I quickly made them my next target.

"And that's the family of the murderer! Maybe you should stand over there, BJ!" I pointed at Duke's family.

Immediately people from both families stood up. The tension quickly thickened in the room. No one said a word, but suddenly a huge fight broke out. Chairs were flying, people were screaming, and many of us were crying beyond control. The hospital security was almost worthless, but good thing the police detectives were handy in calling for backup.

In the meantime, the detectives were in the middle of the chaos, breaking things up in no time. They managed to separate the families with threats of handcuffs and jail time. Soon more police arrived on the scene forcing those who weren't members of the immediate family to go home.

Once home I thought about the last time Ray-Ray and I spoke. It was breaking my heart as I reflected back to my phone call to him earlier in the day.

I cried from the paralyzing pain of the day's events. The thought of living another day without him was unbearable. I never knew such a terrible day would come. Nothing could've ever prepared me for this trauma.

I wanted so badly to go into my mother's room and crawl in the bed with her, but I knew better than to expect her to understand my hurt. After coming home to tell her about my pregnancy, Ray-Ray's death, and the drama at the hospital, all she was concerned about was her car and the fact that I'd taken it without her permission.

She said to me, "You mess with all the wrong guys anyway, Gina! That boy didn't mean you no good. Whatcha want me to say? And now you done got yourself pregnant, and he ain't gon' be around to help you. You shoulda seen it comin', Gina, 'cause that boy wasn't nothin' but a no-good hustler. You made your bed hard, now you gon' have to lay in it. Give me my damn keys, and it better not be a scratch on my car."

My first mind was to disrespect my momma by cussing her out and throwing up her bad choices in men too. Bubba was far from being a saint, and deep down Momma knew he was guilty of raping me.

Every time I tried to forget about how much betrayal I'd experienced in my young life, something else would happen to keep me on the path of mistrust. I wanted to hate my mother for not being there for me in all my times of need, but my heart wouldn't let me.

I stayed in my room the rest of the day unable to sleep. I was weak from crying and not eating. I cried so much my brain began to pound.

Chapter 34

Unknown Man

The Crossroads

It's always sad to lose a young soldier, but that's life on the streets. I felt sorrier for those two little girls more than anything. It was sad BJ had to lose a cousin and a best friend. And then that chick Gina lost her child's father. It was fucked up they had to be out there like that.

Ray-Ray's funeral was huge. They really laced the lil' nigga. He had Benz stretch limos, a gold-trimmed casket, and was buried in one of the nicest cemeteries in Virginia Beach. His line of cars leaving the church to the gravesite was at least three miles long. He was really doing it for a young buck. His shit was better than some of the OGs from the hood.

I guess you never know how many people really love you until you're gone or on your death bed. I had no idea that lil' nigga had so much love on the streets.

Of course, there were at least five chicks there claiming to be his girl. His family knew Gina was the main chick, so she was treated as such. She rode in the limo, sat on the front pew, and did all that first-lady shit.

I was amazed to see her and BJ consoling each other during the funeral. I thought that after the hospital drama they would be at each other's throats even more than before.

I had no idea so many niggas that was supposed to be on Snake's team was friends with Ray-Ray too. I saw a lot of cats at his funeral that wasn't supposed to be there. I realized I had to keep my eye on a few niggas who seemed to be playing both sides of the fence.

Chapter 35

BJ

Water under the Bridge

It'd been two years since Ray-Ray's death, and things between Gina and I hadn't progressed very much. I mean, there was no beef, but we just didn't have that bond like we used to. The only time I saw her was when she brought the baby over on the weekend, and on birthdays and holidays. She looked terrible and always seemed depressed. From what I heard, since Ray's death she hadn't even dated anyone. It broke my heart to see her in that condition, and that's why I planned on making it my personal duty to repair our friendship.

Ding dong!

When the doorbell of grandmother's house rang, I knew it could only be Gina. She brought the baby over each Friday like clockwork. I was excited to see my little kinfolk.

"Hey, RJ," I said, giving Ray Junior a kiss on the cheek.

"He's been a little cranky today, so he may be sick. I packed some meds for him, two sets of outfits for each day, and—"

"Gina, I know the spiel. You've been bringing him over

here saying the same thing for quite some time now," I said, cutting her off.

Gina looked at me and didn't say a word.

I wondered what could be going through her mind, but I was used to her not having much to say. She was just so different than she was before Ray-Ray's death. I wanted the old Gina back. I tried to hold a conversation with her in an effort to get her to open up like she did back in the day.

I took RJ from her arms. "So what have you got planned for this weekend?"

"Nothing. Just going to clean the house and get caught up on some things," she stated, avoiding eye contact.

"Well, I've been invited to a little gathering tonight, and you could come if you like."

"No. I don't have any money or anything to wear."

"No problem. I'll pay your way, and you can borrow something of mine to wear."

I had plenty of things she could wear. The past couple of years had been lovely for me, since Duke had stepped his game up. I even had shit that still had the tags on them. I'd shop for nothing but the best. I owned gear ranging from Gucci to Versace to Luis Vuitton and Chanel. All of my handbags were namebrand too.

As a matter of fact, I was sure she'd like this new Donna Karan outfit I'd never worn. I described the set to her.

Her face brightened up. "Oh, I don't know, BJ." She sighed.

"I just would really like to spend some time with you, Gina. I miss you." I gave her a small hug.

Amazingly the hug was all it took to finally put somewhat of a smile on Gina's face. When I let her go, her face was more relaxed, and she had a pleasant gleam that accompanied her smile.

She agreed to hang out with me, so we set plans for me

to meet her at home around eleven. I offered to drive, since Duke had recently bought me a brand new Acura TL.

I ran in the house to call Ceazia. I'd been in touch with her since the day I'd met her at the hospital. Since BJ and I were no longer best friends, Ceazia had become the big sister and best friend I never had. We talked every day and sometimes two or three times a day. I told her everything I was going through, and she told me everything there was to know about living the life as a gangster's girl.

"Hey, lil' momma," she said just after picking up.

"Hey, *C.* Just called to tell you I will be at the party tonight, and I'm bringing Gina with me."

"Oh so you were able to convince her to come, huh? How'd that happen?"

"I guess it was timing. I was just as shocked as you are now."

"You know what, lil' momma, I'm glad to hear this about you and Gina."

We finished up our conversation and agreed to see each other later.

Next I called Duke. I was eager to tell him the good news too. I could never reach Duke on the first try, so I tried calling again. And again. And again.

I dialed up his business phone.

"BJ, this betta be a fuckin' emergency! You know I don't want you hitting me up on this line."

"No, it's not an emergency, but this is the only way I can contact your ass. I've told you over and over again if you don't answer your phone when I call, it scares me. I have no choice but to think you're dead or in jail," I said, leaving out my real thought of him cheating.

"Yeah, and I told you if I don't answer, then I'm obviously busy."

"Well, with the line of business you're in I just can't assume you're okay. Just learn to answer the phone please," I begged.

"Yeah, okay. What is it, baby? I'm in the middle of some business right now," he calmly said.

I liked when my man softened up just after begging him for something. I got goose bumps when he called me *baby*.

"Well, I just wanted you to know that I'm going out tonight with Ceazia and Gina."

"What? What the fuck I tell you about that bitch Ceazia? And when the hell did you start fuckin' with Gina again? I know you didn't call me thinking I'd be happy about hearing this shit."

I asked over and over again why he disliked Ceazia so much, and all he could tell me was, "She's trouble. She can't be trusted."

"Duke, I'm going out with both of my friends tonight. And I started back fuckin' with Gina as of today."

I knew me hanging up the phone on him was grounds for more argument, but at least it would have to wait because he mentioned he was taking care of business when I called.

I opened my closet doors and sat on the bed. I'd arranged my closet so that I could see it from the edge of my bed. I had my shoes in plastic boxes with pictures, my belts were hanging from tie racks, and my clothes were sorted by item. All the jeans were together, short-sleeved shirts, cargo pants, long-sleeved shirts, and dresses. It took me no time to find the perfect outfit for myself. Then it was time for Gina.

After Gina had the baby, we were around the same size. I chose stretch jeans for her, rather than the Donna Karan outfit I originally had in mind. She finally had an ass, and I wanted her to flaunt it. But she also had a small bulge in the front that we needed to hide. Stretch jeans were perfect for that, because it gripped the ass just right but squeezed the tummy. Then I found her a baby doll top, cupping her breasts, but flowing at the bottom like a shirt dress.

I called her up.

"Hello," she answered on the first ring.

"Hey, girl. I found the perfect outfit for you, but I just need to know if you have some white sandals and a bag to match?"

"Yeah, I think so. I haven't been anywhere in so long, I'm not sure what I have anymore."

"Okay, cool. Well, take a look, and if not, just let me know what you do have. Maybe we can work with that."

"All right, girl. I'm going to take a quick nap. Just call me before you come."

Chapter 36

Gina

Forever Haunted

I looked in my closet to see what shoes and bag I could wear. At least a year had passed since I went through that stuff. I'd been wearing sweatpants, T-shirts, and sneakers on a regular basis.

I searched through my closet as though I was looking for a pot of gold, throwing old shoes and clothes in every direction. I came across things that I hadn't seen in years. I smiled as I picked up one of RJ's newborn Tees. Staring at that T made me remember how small and precious RJ was as a newborn. He was, and always has been, everything I could imagine my child to be. I hugged the picture of my son, admiring how much RJ resembled his dad at birth and even more so now.

I soon came across a picture of me and BJ. I was surprised to see how much she and I had changed in our appearances.

"Wow, was I small back then!" I stated as I took a moment to exam my small frame.

I continued to search, finding everything except a nice

pair of sandals and a bag. I was deep inside my closet near the final corner. Just as I was about to give up, I came across a Bloomingdale's shopping bag. I wondered where it could have come from as I pulled it out. I was sure I never purchased anything there. Hell, Norfolk doesn't even have a Bloomingdale's and I hadn't been outside the Seven Cities my entire life.

Maybe it's something that belongs to my mom.

I opened the bag. There were two large wrapped gifts, a smaller gift, and a card. I opened the bag with caution, starting with the card. It was a birthday card signed from Ray-Ray.

Tears began to well up in my eyes as I opened the gifts. There were sandals with a matching bag and a necklace with a diamond locket. I opened the locket to find a picture of Ray-Ray and me inside.

I sat on the floor thinking. It was my birthday gift from Ray-Ray and it had been sitting in my closet since his death. He must have hid it from me in the closet, but he never got to tell me because he was killed. This was a pleasant surprise, but I still couldn't believe it.

I called BJ to tell her the news. She was just as stunned as I was about the revelation.

"Gina, you've got to be kidding me? Really? After all this time, you're just now finding your birthday surprise?"

"Yes, and I know it sounds strange, but I just had no idea Ray-Ray had hidden these things so far back in the closet. Had you not asked me to go out, I still wouldn't have found the bag."

"So how do you feel? Are you happy?"

"Yes, but I also feel guilty, BJ."

"Why, Gina? You are my girl, and I wish for things to be the way they used to be between us. You can still talk to me."

I sighed. "Ray-Ray pissed me off after I gave him the news of my pregnancy. After thinking long and hard about how upset he made me, I tried to call him to set things straight. Once I reached him, I could hear faint sounds of what sounded like him and another woman having sex. I later realized he wasn't betraying me after all. What I heard was his last dying words to me." I began to cry.

"Gina, everything is going to be okay. Talk it out. What did Ray-Ray say to you?"

I continued to sob and could barely speak, my voice trembling.

"I understand that accepting Ray-Ray's death is a bit hard, but I also know that he still lives."

"Huh? What are you talking about, BJ?"

"Don't you feel him? Don't you see him, Gina? When you hold the beautiful son you birthed, don't you feel close to Ray-Ray?"

"Yes. I know what you mean because I do see Ray-Ray when I look into my baby's eyes."

"I know you do, because I can see him too. Please try to be strong, Gina. RJ needs you."

After our conversation, I couldn't help but reflect back to the day Ray-Ray was killed. I remembered the dreadful phone call I received from BJ.

I looked at the picture of me and Ray-Ray in the locket, then thought of our son RJ. I know Ray would have been a wonderful father. We would have been a perfect little family.

All the events in the past hour had become overwhelming, so I took a generous amount of my prescription medications in an attempt to take a little nap before our night out.

It had become routine for me to take sleeping pills and Prozac on a daily basis, sometimes two or three times. After Ray-Ray's death I couldn't function properly. I wasn't eating like I should, and a good night's sleep was almost impossible due to nightmares. After months of counseling, I was finally able to live a regular life with the help of plenty of daily medications. Little did people know that my sleeping pill, in great doses, was how I managed to cope with things.

"Dear God, please take this pain away from me," I repeated over and over as I tried to fall asleep. This too had become a daily routine. It'd nearly been two years, and I still said these words repeatedly in my head each night until I fell asleep.

The nightmares kept the memory of Ray-Ray's death fresh. The continuous pain of losing him was like no other pain I had ever felt before. It was a pain so deep, no amount of medication or level of sedation could ease it, so I steadily increased the amounts of meds, hoping to find the needed dosage.

Tears rolled down my eyes every time I thought of Ray-Ray. I called his phone every day, sometimes twice a day, hoping there'd be an answer. I never disconnected his phone just so that I could hear his sweet voice.

Ring, ring!

I jumped at the sound of the telephone with hopes of seeing the words, *wireless caller,* across the screen of the caller ID. No such luck. *It isn't him, and it never will be him. God, please take this pain away from me. God, please take this pain away from me. GOD, PLEASE TAKE THIS PAIN AWAY FROM ME.*

Chapter 37

BJ

Girls Gone Wild

Ring, ring! Ring, ring!

I called Gina's house for the twentieth time. Every time I called, her voicemail came on. I knew things were too good to be true. All she had to do was tell me she no longer wanted to go out. I didn't even bother leaving her a message. I just got dressed and headed straight to the club. I was determined to have a good night, with or without her.

As soon as I pulled up to the club I noticed *C* standing out front. "Hey, girlie!" I yelled. I parked the car and headed toward her.

"Hey, lil' momma." She gave me a tight hug and a long kiss on the cheek as though she hadn't seen me in years.

C always seemed to be so touchy feely. She had to be the most affectionate female I knew. She introduced me to all of her friends, who were all pretty and dressed very nice. I felt privileged to even be welcomed around such a high-class clique.

Once in the club, guys began to flock from every direction. I'd never seen anything like it before. I felt like a celebrity. Not once did we even go to the bar. Guys were sending drinks to our table left and right. We had everything, Hpnotiq, Absolut, and Moet, sent to our table. I was loving it.

It wasn't long before the combination of alcohol and reggae had everyone headed to the dance floor. I followed directly behind them. I observed *C*'s sexy moves as she danced seductively to the reggae riddims. I was intrigued with how precise she moved her hips. It seemed so natural. I studied every move, making a mental note.

As she danced I noticed one of her girlfriends come behind her and dance along. Then I looked at the other girls to see if they noticed, but to my surprise they were doing the same. Unsure how to react, I left the dance floor in a hurry. I immediately went to the bar to order a bottle of water. I figured maybe I was a little too drunk and needed to sober up a bit. Maybe things weren't how they seemed. I could have been overreacting. I sipped my water slowly as I stood at the bar alone.

"Wa gwan?" a sexy baritone voice said to me in patois.

"Hi," I said, timidly examining the fine dark Jamaican man that stood before me.

His skin was as dark as rich chocolate, and his smile was as white as snow. His broad six-foot frame towered over me as he spoke.

"So yuh down like di gal dem yuh roll wit'?"

"No, I don't get down like that," I said sternly.

"Yeh, mi would like fi give yuh mi number."

"Hey, Judah." Storm, one of Ceazia's friends, pinched him on his side, interrupting our conversation.

"Wappen, Storm? Wappen, Cinnamon?"

I noticed he greeted *C* by her stage name, which could only mean one thing. He knew her from the strip club.

"Wa yuh name?" he asked.

Storm put her arm around my neck as though she was protecting me from some sort of beast. "Her name is BJ, and she is too young for you."

"Wa mek yuh so sure?"

" 'Cause she's Cinnamon's *little* sister. Besides you need someone in the major leagues for the games you like to play." Storm gave him a seductive look.

By this time the whole entourage was off the dance floor and surrounding us. They all seemed to know Judah very well. Although he didn't seem too interested in any of them, he purchased each one of them a drink.

Tired of all the commotion from the night, I decided it was time to go home. I said goodbye to everyone and headed to my car.

Once in my car I pulled out my cell phone and called Duke, and like every other time I called, he didn't answer.

Knock, knock!

A knock at my window nearly scared the hell out of me. I cracked it just enough to talk. "What's up, Judah?"

"Yuh nuh have mi number."

Since I already had my phone out, I took his number and promised to call. Before leaving, he told me I could find him at this club every Thursday through Saturday and to give him a call and he'll let me in free. I was flattered by his kindness.

When he left, I pulled off and tried calling Duke's phone over and over again. The entire ride to my house I called him, but there was no answer. This time I didn't even bother calling his business phone.

When I got in the house I took a bath and tried calling Gina to tell her how much fun she missed out on. Again, I only got her voice mail. Then I made another hopeless attempt to contact Duke.

I tried to force myself to sleep as I thought about the

events of the night. I reminisced about how it felt to be on top of the world and to have all eyes on me in the club. I played *C*'s dance moves over and over in my head, mimicking them while I lay on the bed. Then I thought about Judah and how sexy he was as he spoke to me in his baritone voice. I figured he was involved with the club some how. He seemed to be pretty popular among the club goers and quite generous with the patrons as well.

I tried calling Duke one last time. But this time his phone was off and went straight to voicemail every time. That was the last straw. I only had one option left—go by his house. I hopped up and threw on a sweat suit and headed out the door. I was at his house within ten minutes.

I circled the neighborhood twice for surveillance before pulling into his court. I couldn't believe my eyes as I pulled up. "Please don't let this be as it seems," I said to myself as I parked my car a couple of houses down and walked toward Duke's home.

The closer I got to his house, the clearer things became. There was a white 745LI, with chrome factories, and paper tags. The only one like it in the area.

"*C*, you sheisty bitch!" I walked toward her car, getting angrier with every step.

Now it all made sense. That's why Duke pretended to hate her so much. That's why he didn't want me around her. That's why *C*'s first advice to me was to leave him whenever I talked to her about our problems.

I pulled out my shank and stabbed each one of *C*'s tires as I walked around her car contemplating my next move. My first thought was to go off on a rampage and bust her windows, kick dents in her car, spray paint all over it, then go in the house and whip her conniving stripping ass. But then I thought things through. If I was to do those things it would probably be Duke to fix them and then they would be right back where they left off. I walked to Duke's car and slit his tires too.

I returned to my car unnoticed and thought long and hard as I went back to my house. I was so hurt, I couldn't cry. I had too much anger.

When I got home I couldn't sleep. The thought of Duke and my so-called big sister fucking haunted my mind. I began to think maybe this was what I deserved for the fucked-up shit I'd done to Gina years ago. I fucked Duke when he was with her, and now *C* was returning the favor. Now I knew how it felt.

Gina had no idea I'd fucked Duke behind her back. I felt it was time to come clean. I tried calling her house again, this time from my grandmother's line. I knew if she saw that number she would definitely answer, thinking that something might be wrong with RJ. To my surprise she still didn't answer. Now that certainly wasn't like Gina. Something had to be wrong.

I put on my sweat suit back on and headed out, this time going to Gina's house. I knew she was home because her car was out front. I banged on the door repeatedly, but there was no answer.

After no response, I retrieved the spare key she always kept under the welcome mat at the back door. I grabbed the key and quickly unlocked the door. I knew she might be mad, but this was a risk I was willing to take.

I yelled from the back door. "Gina!"

When there was no response I immediately headed to her bedroom while continuously calling her name.

I walked in the room to see Gina sound asleep. She was okay. I sighed in relief. I didn't understand how someone could sleep so hard, but I was relieved just to see that she was okay. As I walked toward her bed I noticed a bottle of prescription medication on the nightstand. I figured she'd taken her meds, and that's why she was sleeping so soundly.

I grabbed her blanket and pulled it over her. As I pulled the blanket up I noticed her body felt stiff and cold. "Gina!" I yelled in a panic, shaking her.

She wasn't waking up, so I grabbed the phone and dialed 911.

The emergency technicians arrived in no time. They quickly came in the room, forcing me out as they attempted to revive Gina.

The paramedic walked from the bedroom and took off his gloves. "Miss Smith?"

"Yes."

"I'm sorry. She didn't make it."

My body froze in disbelief. *Flop!* I was out like a light, passed out on the floor.

The past few weeks have been a living hell. I hadn't gone out the house not once, not even for Gina's funeral. I hadn't seen sunlight or smelled the rain.

I hadn't even talked with Duke or *C*, although the pain of their deceit had really set in by now. They still had no idea I knew their secret, and I had no plans on revealing it. They just figured my isolation was due to Gina's death.

As I got up to bathe I examined myself in the mirror. My hair was knotty and stood on top of my head. That beautiful young natural glow was gone and replaced with an elderly ash. I couldn't stand the sight before me. I had to do something. In an attempt to make myself feel better, I filled the tub with hot water and aroma therapy bath beads, turned off the lights, lit candles all around the bathtub, and soaked to the relaxing tunes of Usher.

Thirty minutes later I felt revived.

I grabbed my phone and began to dial Duke's number, but hung up before I hit the final digit. I still wasn't prepared to speak to him. Yet I desired the companionship of someone. My lover was gone, my big sister was gone, and now the only friend I ever had was gone. There was no one to turn to.

As I sat on the bed nearly back to the point of depression, I thought about Judah. What better time than now to call him. I dialed his number slowly, hoping he would still remember me.

"Hello?"

"Hi, Judah. It's BJ. I met you at The Mango Tree a few weeks ago." I really didn't have the energy to play the let-me-refresh-your-memory game. Hell, if he didn't remember me, then that would be an indication that he gave his number out a little too often for me.

"Wa gwan, BJ? I'm glad to hear from you."

"I'm sorry it took so long for me to call, but I had to do a thorough background check on you before I called. I had to make sure you weren't some sort of psycho or rapist or terrorist or something." I didn't want to let him in on all the drama I had in my life the past few weeks.

"Mi tek it mi clear? Background check came back okay?"

"Sure did. Are you going to be at The Mango Tree tonight?"

Since Duke and I hadn't been talking, my money was looking kind of funny. I really needed to make some moves just for financial stability, if nothing else.

"Every Thursday through Sunday. You comin' out tonight?"

"Sure. Why not? I have nothing else to do. So what exactly do you do there?"

"I play music and throw different parties. We refer to it

as a sound. The name of my sound is Macten Sound. We're based here, New York, Florida, Atlanta, and Jamaica."

"Sounds interesting. I guess that's why you're so popular," I stated, trying to inquire about his dealings with *C* and her girls without being too obvious.

"Popular wid who? Your girls from the other night?"

"No, not just them. I meant in general, but since you mentioned them, how do you know them anyway? They seemed really interested in you."

"I know them from the strip club. Dem nah really interested in me. It's just that I'm pretty generous with dem and I hire a couple of them on a regular basis. It's their job to get money, so they always on the grind. So just how close are you and Cinnamon?"

Not wanting to let him in on the grime of that little bitch, I pretended that things were still good between us. "Oh, *C*? She's my girl. The way we met was wild, but we've been friends for the past couple of years. She's like a big sister to me."

Chapter 38

Unknown Man

Hear No Evil, Speak No Evil

You wouldn't believe the shit you see when you're lurking in the night. Seemed like *C* was making more and more enemies by the day. I knew it wouldn't be long before the young girl caught on. It'd been nearly two years, and she was still at it.

I had plenty of opportunities to do her in, but just when I was about to, she started calling again, popping shit about how much she miss a nigga. For a minute I almost believed her, but as much as I wanted to trust the bitch, I knew she was still doing dirt. It was all game with *C*. I guess she hadn't gotten Snake where she wanted him, so she still needed me by her side.

Sure I was going to still holla at her and hit that, but at the same time I was still lurking. It was fucked up that she was messing with Duke, but I guess the bitch was so desperate to get at Snake, she was willing to try anything.

For some reason Snake backed off of her. I wasn't really sure, but I figured it had something to do with that stalking wifey of his, Danielle.

Little did C know that four muthafuckas were hot on her trail—me, Snake, Danielle, and now that lil' chick, BJ.

Chapter 39

Snake

Family Feud

Duke just didn't get it. I was tired of talking to this lil' nigga. I tried to warn him about Ceazia, but he wasn't hearing me. Now I heard he was fucking her. It was all over town that one of those project chicks he'd been fucking caught *C* at his crib one night and slit their tires.

I fucked up one time by letting him move on his own, but I refused to do it again. I called him.

Ring, ring! Ring, ring!

"You have reached the voicemail box of 757—"

I didn't even bother leaving a message. I just hung up and called him on his business line.

"What up, unc?" Duke answered on the first ring.

"Yo, nigga, I need to holla at you. Come by the crib."

"Aight, give me like an hour. I'm in the middle of something right now."

"Nah, nigga, now," I demanded, putting him in his place.

I was prepared for the usual power struggle argument, but surprisingly Duke agreed to come right away.

Duke greeted Danielle as he walked through the door. "What up, sexy?"

I walked in the living room to see him lounging on the couch, and flipping through the channels, but his attention seemed to be elsewhere. I turned my head in the direction he was looking. I realized exactly what he was admiring.

"Danielle, go to the back. Me and Duke need to talk business."

As she headed into the bedroom, I whispered in her ear, "And why don't you put some clothes on while you at it."

She gave me an awkward look. From her expression, I knew she knew exactly what I was insinuating.

My words interrupted Duke's fantasy. His constant massaging of his dick as he licked his lips, was a definite window into his thoughts. That lil' nigga was getting off on my girl.

"What up, lil' nigga?" I flopped down on the sofa next to him and snatched the remote out of his hand. "You don't need this. You ain't paying much attention to the TV," I said, just to let him know I saw him peeping out Danielle.

"Aw, come on, unc. It ain't shit for me to look at Danielle. I been checkin' her out for the past couple of years. Don't tell me you getting all sensitive 'bout that shit now."

"Naw, man, that's the least of my worries. I'm more concerned about the shit I hear about you and *C* fuckin'. So what's up with that? You knockin' her off or what?"

"I ain't even gon' lie to you. Since she stopped fuckin' you, she been comin' at me strong. And you know me, I ain't the one to turn down no good pussy."

"Duke, I only fucked the broad once. You ever wondered why I didn't continue fucking her after that one time?"

"Nope, not once. That ain't my concern, unc. Evidently she wanted something different. From the looks of things she was feeling me from the first time we met at the strip joint. The only reason she probably ain't holla is 'cause you was throwin' salt in the game, hatin' on a nigga and shit."

It was obvious his dick was getting a little too big for his Superman briefs.

"Duke, she's out of your league, man. The bitch has a hidden agenda. And just so you know, she didn't stop fucking me, I stopped fucking her. And you notice she ain't even holla at you until I dissed her trifling ass. In fact, you ain't the only nigga she started fucking after I dissed her. Word is, she back fuckin' with that nigga Bear. So you think that's cool? That's probably why that nigga been givin' us such a problem with business and shit lately. Look, man, the bitch is bad news and bad for business. And most importantly I'm almost certain she killed Vegas. She on her way to a death sentence. All I need is one solid piece of evidence and she's gone, Duke. I'm putting her to rest. So, if for nothing else, at least drop the bitch for your uncle and my brother," I said, putting all my cards on the table.

"Look, unc, I hear everything you sayin', but ain't shit poppin'. Vegas is dead. Let that man rest in peace. *C* is feeling me, and I'm feeling her, so ain't shit gon' change. And as for that nigga Bear, fuck him. He's just one man on the team. One monkey don't stop no show. As for you, all I can say is do you, unc, 'cause I'm gon' do me without a doubt." Duke stood up and put on his NY cap, tilting it to the side as an indication he was leaving. "Gone." He then closed the front door behind him.

I knew talking to him was like talking to a brick wall. I didn't even bother to go after him or force him to hear me.

Danielle walked toward the living room, now fully clothed. "What's going on?"

"Nothing. Let's go to bed," I said, annoyed at her eavesdropping.

"Duke is having sex with Ceazia?"

"Danielle, stop asking me about this shit. Everything good. Now let's go to bed." I grabbed her by the arm and led her toward the bedroom.

Of course Danielle wasn't letting shit go that easily. Lately she'd become very unruly. I wasn't really sure why, but it was going to cause me to smack her ass one good time to let her know who was boss.

When we got to the bedroom, I dropped her arm and walked around her and headed to the bathroom while she stood in the middle of the floor yelling.

"I don't want to hear this shit, Danielle," I yelled, closing the bathroom door.

It wasn't long before she was quiet.

I stepped out of the bathroom and back into the bedroom. I noticed Danielle was no longer in the room, but that was cool with me. Relieved that the dragon was at rest, I rolled a blunt and watched a little TV before I prepared for bed.

Once I finished smoking, I glanced at the time. It was twelve midnight, and Danielle still hadn't come to bed. I walked toward the living room to see what she was doing. It was completely dark. Not even the television was on. I wondered what the fuck she was doing in the dark.

I could faintly hear her speaking to someone. I walked a little closer then realized she was on the back porch. I could hear her talking, but there was no response. I figured she was on the phone. I walked closer then stood at the door and listened.

"I don't know what's up with him," she said, "but he really needs to start treating me better before someone else steps up to the plate." She laughed. "Boy, you are so crazy."

Boy? Who the fuck this bitch talkin' to? I backed away and headed to the bedroom to avoid busting through those

French doors and choking the shit out her sneaky ass. I turned off the TV in the bedroom then hit speaker on the cordless phone. That bitch had no idea I was listening.

"Damn, baby, I don't know why that nigga trippin'. You holdin' shit down at home, I mean you know, in the bedroom and shit?" I heard a familiar voice say.

"I guess. I mean he doesn't complain."

"You don't sound confident. You deep-throatin', takin' it from the back, and ridin' that thang too?"

"Yeah, I do all of that."

This conversation was definitely out of line. I wanted to see just how far the two of these muthafuckas would go.

"Anybody can do those things. The question is, are you doing it right? Are you throwing that ass back when you getting hit from the back? Are you moaning with each stroke? Are you bouncing up and down on that dick, taking each inch?"

"Mmmmmm, yyeessssss." Danielle moaned as though her pussy was dripping at the thought.

"Sounds like you feelin' that type of talk."

"*Feeling* it is not the word."

"Well, I may as well finish it up. I need you to follow my every instruction. Put your hands in your panties for me and rub that clit. Get it nice and wet for me. Once it's wet, put your fingers in your mouth, and lick the juice off. Let me hear you lick those juices, baby."

"Mmmmmm, it tastes so good."

I threw on my clothes, grabbed my keys, and headed out the door. Before I left, I stopped by the back porch to pay Danielle a little surprise visit. I opened the door to see her with one hand on the phone, the other in her panties, and her legs cropped open on the patio table. I didn't say a word. I just looked at her.

She turned around and noticed my presence, yet she didn't seem startled. "What?" she said. "Isn't this the same position you were in the day I walked in the house after getting my ass whipped by one of your bitches?" She turned back around and continued her conversation. "Now where were we, baby?"

Smack! I smacked Danielle so hard, she dropped the phone and fell out the chair.

She immediately burst into tears as though I had practically killed her.

Showing no emotion, I walked off and closed the door behind me, locking her outside. *Maybe that nigga can help her get into the house.* I headed out the front door and locked it as well.

It was a Sunday night, so there wasn't many places to go other than the strip club and the reggae joint. Trying to avoid *C*, I hadn't been hitting the strip joint lately, so I chose the reggae club. The Mango Tree.

The club was off the hook as usual. Although I wasn't a reggae fan, I loved to watch the ladies move to that shit. I grabbed a table in the corner near an exit, then I hit the waitress off decent so she could look out.

As I got relaxed and sipped on my Remy, I noticed *C* walk in. She didn't even notice me. She seemed to be on another trick mission because as soon as she came in, she headed straight to this nigga from around the way. I didn't really know him, but like any nigga that's getting money, I knew of other niggas getting it too. Plus he happened to be one of those niggas. From what I heard, he was a Jamaican cat down with Macten Sound that wasn't only getting it in the streets, but was killing niggas in gambling too.

C and dude didn't talk very long. They had a few words and he bought her a drink. It seemed like after all her seductive tactics, she still wasn't able to get him to trick. After her drink, *C* disappeared into a dark corner. I figured she'd posted up there to try her luck with the next nigga.

I continued to enjoy my drinks and observe the goings-on around me.

An hour had passed, and C still hadn't come out of her corner. I started to get the feeling she was trying to be inconspicuous herself. That began to make me feel a little uneasy. After I finished my drink I had planned to leave.

Just when I was ready to go, I noticed Duke's lil' shortie stroll in the club, looking all Hollywood and shit. "Damn! She sure ain't no lil' girl no more," I said to myself.

BJ was never really built like a little girl, but she had a lot of those lil' girl qualities, like the long blonde weaves, the long acrylic nails, the sneakers, and the lil' girl wardrobe.

Hell, if I didn't know who she was, she would definitely be mistress material. She was young and tender, no one knew her, and I could easily shape and mold her into whatever I wanted. *Fuck Duke! He needs to see the flip side of the game. He wants to play hardball, well I'm 'bout to pitch.*

I swallowed the rest of my drink in a hurry, but before I could move, she was already headed toward the same Jamaican cat that *C* was trying to get at earlier. *This nigga must really be doing it!*

I watched him and BJ chat away. I knew my lil' soldier was putting down for shortie, so she wasn't hurting for no money. I thought shortie was head over heels for my lil' man. Guess she heard about that lil' incident with C after all. I watched as she laughed and drank with the dude.

She seemed to really be enjoying herself, so I decided to lay off her. What the fuck was I thinking? Hell, I know exactly what I was thinking. I was thinking that nigga keep testing me.

"Hey, Snake?" an excited voice said, interrupting my thoughts.

"Oh damn! What's up, lil' shortie? You lookin' real good tonight." I eyeballed BJ from head to toe.

"Thank you."

She still had that young girl innocence, and it was turning me on.

"Would you like a drink?" I watched her dance to the reggae music.

"No thanks, I've had enough. This is my song."

She moved just like that conniving bitch Ceazia. Oddly instead of turning me off, it turned me on even more. She was way too innocent to accept a proposition, so I knew I had to come at her in another direction.

"Yo, I'm 'bout to get out of here. You need anything? You all right?"

"Yeah, I'm fine."

"Well, take down my number, just in case something arises. You in the family since you fuck with my lil' soldier, so I gotta make sure you well taken care of."

She screwed her face at the mention of Duke. She popped her cell phone open and took the number.

"Aight, lil' shortie," I said before walking off.

I patted myself on the back as I headed home. It felt good to know my game was still on point. BJ fell right into the trap and gave me all the right signs that she wasn't feeling Duke.

I pulled up to the house reluctant to even walk in. I didn't want to be nowhere near Danielle's stupid ass. I was liable to smack the shit out of her at any moment of a flashback.

As I walked to the bedroom, I saw her sleeping soundly in the bed. *How the fuck she got in the house?*

I didn't even bother waking her. I just jumped in the

shower, threw on some boxers, and headed to the kitchen for my nightly ritual. That's when I realized exactly how she got in. That ignorant bitch threw the patio chair through the French doors. I simply shook my head in disbelief. I poured a shot of Hennessy then took a Goody's Powder to help me sleep.

Since I was shot, dreams had been haunting me every night. I didn't know who the shooter was at the Coliseum that day, and it still got me shook. At times, I wanted to just rule it out and say all the bullets were meant for Ray-Ray and I just got in the crossfire. But I couldn't even think of anyone that wanted that lil' nigga dead, besides Duke.

I'd run every possible nigga through my head, but still no one fit. Just like with Vegas's death, until that shit was figured out, I wasn't going to rest.

Chapter 40

Ceazia

A Stab in the Back

It had been several days since I'd last talked to my lil sis, BJ. But after seeing her out last night, it was apparent that she was doing just fine. Besides, I needed to know just how close she and Judah were, as well as she and Snake. I wasted no time calling her up.

"Hello?" BJ answered the phone in a flat tone.

"Hey, lil' momma. How are you?"

"I'm good. Feeling a lot better."

"I know. That's why I called. I heard you went out to The Mango Tree last night. So how was it?"

"It was nice. I needed to get out of the house, so I decided to go see Judah."

"So what you think about him? Are y'all, like, talking or something?"

"Well, we talk on the phone, but nothing really major. He seems like a really nice guy. I'm feeling him, and it looks like he's feeling me the same."

"Oh okay. But what about Duke?" I threw out Duke's name in an effort to get BJ to change her feelings about

Judah. Judah was my fish, and there was no way I would let her come in and steal my catch.

"What about him? Aren't you the one who always told me I deserve better?"

I did tell her that on a regular basis, but that was when I was trying to steal Duke from underneath her nose. "Yeah, you're right. I just don't want you rushing into anything too soon. I mean, do you even know anything about Judah?"

"Well, we've rapped quite a bit, and I know enough to know that he is potentially a good catch."

"Well, did Judah tell you what he does for a living?"

"Yes, he did. He explained to me that he plays music. He has a sound in several places, and he travels to different spots to play music at clubs or for different events."

"Oh really. I guess he left out the fact that his sound is just a cover-up for what he really does."

"What do you mean, 'what he really does'?"

"He runs a huge drug ring, BJ, and those areas where he has a sound are places where he has shop set up. I know you haven't been able to tell, but Judah's a very dangerous man. Haven't you noticed how much respect he gets in the club?" I didn't give her time to respond. "That's because he's a rude boy, a bad man. It's not safe to be around him. Who knows when someone is going to get the balls to step up to him and take him out? And I know you don't want to relive another death by shooting." I hated to have to pull the death card on her, but I felt I had to come strong and hit home to convince her.

BJ sat silent for a while. "I had no idea about any of this. You're right. He does get lots of respect. I noticed that from the first day we met. And, no, I don't want to relive another death. I don't think I could. Maybe I'll ask him about it. He seems to be very honest. Maybe he doesn't know me well enough to tell me such things just yet."

I quickly came to realize that this little girl wasn't as naive as I'd thought. I decided to take another shot at deceiving her. "Oh and another thing I think I should point out, did you notice me and *all* my girls knew him? And did you notice he referred to me as Cinnamon?"

"He already told me he knows you all from the strip club. I have no problem with that. He's even invited me to come with him. In fact, I just may take him up on that offer and go tonight. You gon' dance tonight?"

"Yeah, he does know us from the strip club, but it goes a little farther than that. He's a big gambler, and he has these card parties where he invites strippers over. Me and my girls."

"Oh really? So what exactly goes on at those parties, just stripping or a little more than that?"

"At those parties anything goes. Unlike the strip club, there are no rules at a private party. If you got money to pay, then we play."

"Wow! That just really doesn't seem like Judah. I'm not going to give up on him just yet, though. I still would like to get to know him a little better."

I was beginning to get upset with this bitch's consistency, so I had to go for the gusto. "Look, BJ, I didn't want to come right out and tell you this, but he's fucking my girl Storm for three years now. He keeps her laced, and she's pregnant with his child as we speak."

Again the phone became silent. I was certain I got the better of BJ.

"I'm sorry, BJ. I hope you're not hurt. I tried to change your mind about him without saying that, but you just wasn't trying to hear me," I said with a phony sincerity.

"That's okay, C. Thanks for telling me. Niggas will be niggas, I guess. Well, with that news, I guess I'll call it a night and head to bed."

"Mission accomplished!" I said aloud after hanging up the phone.

I'd spent so much time convincing BJ to leave Judah, I didn't have time to question her about Snake, but I didn't sweat it because I knew there was going to be plenty of time for that.

I sat gloating over the fact that I was knocking them out one by one.

Speaking of Snake, I sure could use some Jackson dick right about now. Of course I'll have to settle for Duke, since Snake is on some shit right now. But it won't be long before I have him back where I want him.

Beep! Beep! I hit Duke on the Nextel alert.

"What's up, *C?*"

"I want to see you," I said in my most seductive tone.

"Aight, you can come through. I'll be home in about thirty minutes."

"See you then."

It was always simple to get whatever I wanted from Duke. The sex was pretty good for a young buck, so I didn't mind fucking him at all. Besides, every time I went over, he hit me off with some money.

An hour later I was at Duke's crib. I could smell the stench of Hennessy and Hpnotiq on Duke's breath as he walked near me.

"Want a drink?" The words slurred from his mouth.

"Yeah, just give me a shot of Hennessy."

I figured I'd better have something in my system or I would be leaving soon. I definitely needed a drink to tolerate his drunken ass.

Duke brought me the Hennessy, and I threw the drink back, taking it all in one gulp. I exhaled as the liquor burned, leaving a flaming path down my chest.

He walked toward me, grabbed the back of my head with one hand and my ass cheek with the other and stuck his warm tongue in my mouth, kissing me softly, which was much different from the "wham-bam-thank-you-ma'am" sex I was accustomed to.

My body actually shivered with excitement as he kissed me passionately. Before I knew it, I was completely submissive and taken by his obsession.

Duke began to rip my clothes off piece by piece, as we stumbled up the stairs toward his bedroom. We busted through his bedroom door and landed on the dresser. He bent my naked body over and squeezed my hips tight as he inserted his penis forcefully.

My body ached as Duke pounded me from the back, my ass shaking and breasts bouncing with every thrust.

"You like that?"

"Yes."

He grabbed me by my hair and forced my head back. "Whose pussy is this?"

I looked at his reflection in the mirror. I didn't know what Duke put in that shot of Hennessy, but it really had me bugging. The image in the mirror just wasn't what I thought I should be seeing. When I looked in the mirror, the reflection I originally saw was Duke, who then changed to Snake, then to Vegas.

I put my head down and closed my eyes, hoping the hallucination would disappear.

"Whose pussy is this?" Duke asked again, pulling my hair and forcing me to look in the mirror once again.

"It's yours, Duke, it's yours."

"Open your eyes and look in the mirror. Watch me fuck my pussy then, bitch!"

I slowly opened my eyes and looked at the mirror, this time focusing on my reflection. That's when the truth settled. I realized everything I really wanted at that moment. The touch I'd felt was the hands of Vegas, the kiss I'd felt was the lips of Vegas, and the passion I'd felt was the hunger of Vegas. This took me back to the memorable moments of the sweet love Vegas and I shared.

The memory of our anniversary night on the cruise was vivid. I could almost feel the cool air around me as I thought of Vegas secretly sexing me from behind in the night air. Then there was the spontaneous moment we'd shared together on the weight bench in our home.

"Whose pussy is this?"

My brain was now on Snake. The familiar words, "You like that? Whose pussy is this?" were the words of Snake. I thought of the rough sex we'd shared at the hotel. As I thought back to the multitude of bruises I had the next day.

As I looked in the mirror and stared into the eyes of the young Duke, it was apparent that these three men shared something a little more powerful than a last name. It was an uncontrollable attraction that brewed a combined lust I had for each of them.

Chapter 41

Duke

Have My Cake and Eat It Too

Who the fuck said you can't have your cake and eat it too? Well, somebody needed to pass the word to that muthafucka that Duke from Norfolk, Virginia made history! Not only did I have the cake and eat it, but I did it while everyone was watching. I'm just that sweet! Just to boost my ego I think I'll give that shit a try right now. I'd already had *C* and ran her ass. Now Danielle was going to be my next piece of booty.

I picked up the phone and pressed *star 67* before dialing her cell number.

"What's up, Duke?"

"And how did you know it was me, sexy?"

"No one else blocks their number when calling except you."

My manhood rose at the sound of her voice. "So how you doin'?"

"Not too good, Duke, not too good."

"What's wrong, baby girl?"

"It's Snake. He just won't treat me right. I know I was

wrong for that little escapade that you and I had, but compared to the things he's done that's nothing. I've never cheated or even looked at another guy. That conversation between us wasn't even supposed to happen. He won't forgive me. I don't know what to do. Do you think you could talk to him?"

"To be honest, Danielle, Snake is not even feeling me right now. Me and that nigga ain't really getting along."

"What do you mean? Is it because he caught us on the phone that night?"

"Nah, actually I haven't even spoken to him about that. He was pissed off at me before that. He was mad from when I left your house earlier that night."

"So what happened? I heard you all speaking about Ceazia. Does it have anything to do with her?"

"Yeah, it did, but I'd rather not go into it," I said, trying to draw more curiosity.

"Duke, please tell me what's going on. It must be something really bad to tear you guys apart. I mean, you all were like father and son."

"Danielle, even though Snake and I have our differences, he's still my uncle. But at the same I got much love for you. So I'm just going to leave it at this. You're a good girl, and you deserve a good man. Any nigga would love to have a woman like you, so you don't have to settle. You see all the signs. I don't have to point shit out to you. I know you've heard the saying, if it looks like a duck and quacks like a duck, then it is a duck. Well, in this case, let's just say, if it looks like a stripper, and acts like a gold digging ho, then it's Ceazia."

"I know exactly what you're saying, Duke. You don't have to say anything more. On that note I think I'll say goodnight."

"Good night, sweetie. And if you need to talk, don't hesitate to call. I'll hop out the best pussy to talk to you."

Two down, one to go. I wanted to taste a piece of BJ's cake now. Since her girl died, she'd been real fucked up. But I think she had enough time to heal. I was starting to miss that tight poonanny. I broke her virginity, so I owned the pussy and planned to keep it that way.

Ring, ring! Ring, ring!

The automated voicemail came on. That was odd, because it was late and I knew BJ wasn't out anywhere. I decided to try calling again.

"Hello?"

"Why the fuck you ain't answer the phone when I just called?" I yelled. "How many times do I have to call to get an answer?"

"Why the fuck is you callin' me with this bullshit?" She hung the phone up in my ear.

That shit really fucked me up. *Where the fuck did she get balls from to talk to me like that and hang up on me?* I dialed her number again. I figured that death shit must really have her tripping.

"Hel-lo?" she answered in an annoyed tone.

This time I tried a different approach. "What's up, baby? How you feel?"

"I'm good, Duke. What do you want?"

"Wha chu mean? I'm calling to talk to my girl. You are my girl, aren't you?"

"The last I checked, although you don't act like it. A real boyfriend would have sent flowers, dropped by for a surprise visit, called constantly. You, on the other hand, just dropped off the face of the earth."

She was right. During the time BJ was mourning I was using it as an opportunity to fuck *C*, and any other broad willing to give up some ass. But I still had to come up with something.

"I'm sorry, baby. I've never had to console someone during a loss, so I don't know how to act. Please forgive me. As a matter of fact, why don't you let me make it up to you?" I said, running game.

"Make it up to me, huh? And just how do you plan to do that?"

"How about this? Just throw on some clothes and come over right now."

"No, Duke, I don't think that's a good idea."

"Why not, baby? I miss you. I miss seeing that sexy body, I miss your pretty smile, I miss holding you at night. And I miss you farting in your sleep."

"Ha, ha, ha, ha, ha!"

"See, I bet you haven't laughed that hard in days. Who else besides me can do such a thing?"

"You're right, Duke. I think I'll take you up on that offer. You better make it worth my while too, nigga."

I rushed and filled the bathtub with hot water. I added BJ's favorite bath beads from BATH & BODY WORKS and lit candles all around the tub. Then I ran to the kitchen and grabbed some strawberries, cherries, and grapes. As a final touch I ran to the corner store and grabbed a single rose and a cheesy little card that simply read, "I love you."

The killer would be the message I wrote inside. A woman would better appreciate a blank card with a hand-written message from the heart, than a Hallmark card with a beautiful poem. I reached into my box of cards, letters, pictures and many items I'd collected from women over the past years. I grabbed a letter from my ex-girlfriend, Kim Todd. Her poems always said the right things. I figured I'd change a few words to make it fit and put that same poem in my card to BJ.

I ran to the bed and placed the rose and card on the bed and some vanilla massage oil on the nightstand. Then I grabbed my *Love and Basketball* DVD, her favorite movie, and put in the DVD player.

A good twenty minutes hadn't passed before my doorbell rang. I was sure to turn all phones off, house and cell, before opening the door. I wasn't taking no chances in fucking this up.

"Hey, baby." I kissed BJ on the cheek.

She greeted me with a tight hug, and I was really feeling it.

I stepped back and looked at her. I quickly guided her to the bathroom. "I have a hot bath waiting for you with your favorite bath beads. Why don't you get in, and I'll bathe you."

"This is nice, Duke. I didn't know you had it in you."

"Anything, my baby." I smiled and licked my lips.

I grabbed the net sponge and filled it with body wash. I started with her toes and washed each one gently then slowly moved up, washing each part of her body and giving it a gentle kiss.

After her bath, I led her to the bed and directed her to lie down. I poured the massage oil all over her body and gave her the massage of a lifetime. When I was done she was so relaxed.

As she laid on her back, I pressed play to begin the movie then fed her fruit continuously as we watched.

When the movie was done, she looked at me. "Duke, what has come over you? What more could a woman ask for?"

"Just one more thingI handed her the rose and card."

She read it aloud:

"My love, my heart
I have loved you from the start.

Please forgive my doggish ways
For it is with you I want to stay.
I can't live without you. No I shall not.
Please come back home, I love you a lot.
                              Love always,
                              Duke"

When she was done, she gave me a passionate kiss and stroked my erect penis.

Thanks, Kim! I thought. I grabbed her hand. "No, baby. Tonight is all about you," I said softly in her ear. Then I laid her on her back and kissed each part of her body before resting my head in her lap and sending her into ecstasy.

Chapter 42

BJ

Revenge Tastes Like Chocolate

Damn! You really put it on me. I stared at a peacefully sleeping Duke. Although I knew about the dirt he'd done, I still desired to be with him. We'd been through so much together, I couldn't just walk away. I'd never made love to anyone besides him. I didn't even know if I was capable of making love to anyone else.

"I love you, Duke," I whispered softly then kissed his cheeks. I rubbed my hand across his scarred chest.

Tears came to my eyes as I thought back to the day of the shooting. I almost lost him to war and now I was losing him to lust. After all I'd sacrificed, he repays me by sleeping with somebody I considered a big sister. *That's it. I've made up my mind. I should have never come here in the first place.*

I hopped out the bed and began putting my clothes on in a hurry. If he woke up, it would've been even harder for me to walk away.

Before leaving, I stopped in the kitchen and wrote a small message on a notepad:

> *Sorry but I can no longer do this. It's over, Duke.*
> > *Love always,*
> > *BJ*

The ride home was long, even though I only lived ten minutes away. I wondered if I'd made the right choice. My heart was telling me no, but my mind was telling me yes.

Once I got home the thoughts of Duke began to haunt me once again. In a desperate attempt to get him out of my thoughts, I called Judah.

"Yo."

"Hey, Judah. How are you?"

"I'm good. How are you?"

"I'm okay, I guess. Just got a lot on my mind."

"Oh yeah? Like what?"

"Nothing big. I spoke to Ceazia the other day and—"

"Ceazia? Please don't tell me that bitch feedin' you bullshit."

"Well, she told me some things that I just want to ask you about. Do you engage in sex with any of the strippers there?"

"No, I don't. Those parties are mostly about gambling. I just invite the girls to lure in more guys. I watch the table all night, baby."

"Well, what about other than the parties? Did you ever have sex with any of them?"

"Look, BJ, from the day you've met me I've been nothing but honest to you and that's not going to change. So if you ask me a question just be sure you want to know the answer." He stated as though he was preparing me for bad news.

"I want to know, Judah. I don't want to come into this relationship blind. Let me know what I may have to face in the future."

"Okay, look, I did have sex with one of the girls on a regular basis. It was nothing serious, just something to pass time. The girl always wanted to include Cinnamon. I was never really feeling her. I would watch them, but I only had sex with her friend. After a while I stopped dealin' with the chick, and she start actin' all crazy and shit. Now she claims she's pregnant. When we were together I would look out for her and even look out for Cinnamon too. So now that I'm gone, the money is gone. They see I'm feeling you and they just want to fuck shit up. So it's up to you, baby girl."

"Don't worry, Judah. I believe everything you're saying. Trust me, I know how Ceazia gets down. I got your back as long as you got mine, baby."

"Good to go?"

"Excuse me?"

He laughed. "So everything straight?"

"Oh yeah, everything good to go."

"Lata."

"Bye."

It felt so refreshing to talk with Judah. It was like he was my sunshine during the storm.

As I prepared a hot bath and got my clothes out for the day, I thought of that bitch *C.* I owed her big time. It had to be something to make that bitch think twice the next time she thought about doing some fucked up shit.

I figured I'd have to start hanging out with her more, to find out her deepest secrets, then use them to destroy her. When I got out the tub I was ready to begin my journey to the sweetest revenge.

I called her up. "Hey, big sis," I said, faking enthusiasm.

"What's up, lil' momma? You sound much better!" She responded in a tone that I am sure was just as fake as my own.

"Nothing. Just ready to get out the house and do some things, you know, girl stuff."

"Okay. You know I'm always down for a girl's day out, so

why don't I come by and scoop you and we can go out together."

"Okay. Come by in an hour."

I grabbed my purse to see just how much money I had. I realized I didn't have any money for a girl's day out. *Let me think, let me think. Judah . . . nah, I can't call him for money already. Duke . . . nah, just left him a Dear John letter.* Then it hit me—*Snake!*

I wasted no time calling him up.

"Hello?"

"Hi, Snake. This is BJ."

"Oh shit! What up, lil' shortie?"

"Well, I called because you said to call if I needed anything. Well, I'm sorta in a bind. Do you think you could help me out?"

"No problem. Just come check me. I'm in the area right now. Meet me at the barbershop on Granby."

"Okay, I'm on my way."

I grabbed my purse and headed out the door. "Thank God for that nigga."

The barbershop was only around the corner, so it took me no time to get there. I parked my car right in front and took my time strutting up to the door. All eyes were on me as I pranced inside to the barber chair.

"Damn! Lil' shortie, that was fast," Snake said.

"Oh, I was already on my way out when I called," I lied, trying not to seem desperate.

"Right, right." He dug in his pocket and handed me a wad of money.

I didn't bother to count it. I thought that would be quite tacky. "Thank you. I really appreciate it." I gave him a tight hug and a flirtatious look.

"Anytime, sweetie."

I rushed back to the crib to wait for C.

Honk! Honk!

Like always, she was right on time. I put on my phony face, grabbed my Marc Jacob bag, and ran out the front door.

"Hey, girl!"

"What's up, lil momma?"

"So what's on the agenda for today?" I plopped down on the new tan leather seat and struggled to put on my seat belt.

"Well, we can start by grabbing lunch, then we'll head to the spa, then to the mall. How does that sound?"

"Sounds good."

Ceazia picked my favorite spot, The Cheesecake Factory.

So that I didn't seem too obvious, I started the conversation by talking about my problems. I knew that was all it would take to get that girl talking. From previous conversation, I'd learned that stories about men mistreating women really burned her up. I began by telling her how depressed I'd been the past couple of weeks because of Gina's death and because of issues with Duke.

Of course she was more concerned with the issues I had with Duke and encouraged me to elaborate.

With tears in my eyes I spoke, "I feel like Duke doesn't appreciate me. He treats me like shit. I've been nothing but good to this guy, *C.* Why can't he treat me right?"

"BJ, like I told you many times before, the answer is simple—you are too good for him."

"I understand what you're saying, *C,* but it's not that simple. I just can't tell myself I'm too good and walk away. I've given so much to keep this guy happy. All I ask in return is that he does the same."

"Well, what is he doing exactly? Whatever it is, it must not be that bad because it's not enough to make you leave him."

"Well, I found out that he's cheating on me. I'm not really sure with who, but I know for a fact he is. I really don't want to get into it because it makes me so mad. I mean to the point like if I find out who it is I may just do something crazy!"

"Umph! I know what you mean, girl. Niggas will make you snap and lose your mind. It seems like Duke just can't help himself, lil' momma. It's in his blood. All those damn Jackson men are alike."

"Why you say that? From what I hear on the streets, you had the good life with Vegas."

"Yeah, I did, but things aren't always as they seem. You see, a guy can do and say anything, but the true test is what goes on when you're not watching. Trust me, honey, everything between me and Vegas wasn't always peaches and cream. As a matter of fact, just like you, I made a hell of a lot of sacrifices for that man. You'd be surprised at the things I did for him." She put her head down.

I'd never seen the fuck-niggas-and-get-money Ceazia so distressed. I kept the conversation going so she'd tell me more. "So what did he do that was so bad?"

"The ultimate, BJ, the ultimate."

"Well, like you told me, it must have not been that bad, because you didn't leave him."

Ceazia responded in an angry tone, "And how would you know?"

"Well, because you all were together until his death. If you had left him, y'all would not have been together when he died."

Ring, ring! My cell phone rang, interrupting our conversation.

I glanced down at the caller ID. I wondered what Snake wanted. I hit the *end* button and sent him to voicemail. "Sorry about that. Now where were we?"

"We were at the part where you assumed that I didn't have the strength to leave Vegas after he'd deceived me."

"Oh yeah. So what did he do?"

"I really don't want to get into it, lil' momma, but just know that I handled mine. Now you need to get the strength to handle yours."

"*C*, I hope you don't get upset when I say this, but it seems to me that you have some sort of vendetta against any and every Jackson man."

"Vendetta? That would be too nice of a word. I despise those muthafuckas."

"Well, maybe if you explained things to me it will give me strength. I'm sorry, but right now I just can't sympathize with you. You have to explain to me why you're so angry."

Ceazia took a deep breath and slowly exhaled. She scooted over closer to me in the booth then grabbed my hand and looked me in the eyes. "BJ, what I'm about to tell you, I have never shared with anyone. I consider you my little sister, so I'd trust you with my life. And that's the only reason I'm telling you this."

"I understand, *C*. Your secret is safe with me."

"Okay. After serving time in jail for a crime involving Vegas, I was released and came home unannounced to surprise him. Well, I ended up being the one surprised. I walked in on him, my best friend, and another female in the Jacuzzi getting high and making out." Ceazia wiped the tears that were streaming down her cheeks. "BJ, I was numb with hurt when I saw that. I literally blanked out. It was as though I was in a trance as I shot continuously into the tub killing all three of them."

My mouth dropped with disbelief. I grabbed her and hugged her. "I'm sorry, *C*. I had no idea. I am really sorry,"

I said sincerely. *How could I ever deceive this girl?* I thought to myself as I consoled her. I had a total change of heart.

As we finished eating *C* continued to tell me about the relationship she and Vegas had. As we enjoyed our day at the spa and shopped she continued to share.

By the time I reached home that night Ceazia had nearly shared her entire life story with me. I was much more appreciative for my life. My heart really went out to her. She had been from extreme highs to extreme lows. The poor girl just wanted the life she'd always dreamed of.

Chapter 43

Danielle

A Woman's Intuition

It was midnight, and Snake's ass wasn't home. Duke was right—I was too good for his cheating ass. It was sad that a young kid like Duke could recognize a good woman before a grown-ass man. But that was okay. I was going to feed into every little pass his little soldier made at me.

Ring, ring!

"Hello?"

"What up?" he asked, as though it was six in the evening and not after midnight.

"Nothing is up, Snake. What do you want?"

"Look, Danielle, I'm really upset right now. I was actually calling because I feel real fucked up and I needed someone to talk to, but I see you're not that person." *Click!*

I didn't know how to react, not because he hung up in my ear, but because I was baffled by his tone. Snake really did seem upset. Everything began to run through my mind.

I got myself together then struggled to call Snake back. His phone went straight to voicemail. I dialed the number over and over again. Before I knew it, I'd dialed his number over twenty times and it was still going to voicemail.

I tried text messaging him. Still no response.

I called Duke, figuring he would know if there was a problem before anyone.

"Duke!"

"What's up, Danielle? What's wrong, baby?" he asked concerned.

"It's Snake. Where is he? He called and he was really upset. Now his phone is off. I think something is wrong. Have you talked to him?"

"Slow down, momma, slow down. I'm sure Snake is aight. He would've called if some shit went down. Just chill out. I'm gonna check on shit for you and let you know what's up."

"Okay."

After an hour had passed and still no return call, I began to dial Snake's number again. And just as before, it went straight to voicemail. I could no longer wait for Duke to call me back. An hour was long enough.

I grabbed the cordless phone and dialed his number.

"Yeah, Danielle."

"Did you hear from him?"

"Nah, but I checked shit out, and everybody that saw him out the way said he's been fine all day. So everything cool. Just try to get some rest. I'm sure he'll be home soon."

"Okay, Duke."

Again I found myself pacing the floor. I had to do something to get some rest, so I took a couple of sleeping pills and lay down.

I tossed and turned for another hour. It wasn't happening. I couldn't think about anything except Snake. That was it. I'd made my mind up. *If Duke won't look for Snake, then I will.* I hopped out of bed and got dressed. I called Snake's phone one final time, and just as all the times before, it went straight to his voicemail.

I grabbed my purse, dropped in the gun Snake had given me for emergencies, and headed out the door. My first stop was Park Place in Norfolk, where Snake spent most of his time. I drove by the barbershop, and it was closed. Not a person in sight, not even one person on the block. Then I rode past his family's house a few blocks away, and there was no signs of him there.

There was only one other place to check, the strip club, which was where I found him. I was sitting in my car, thinking of a master plan, when my phone rang. It was Duke.

I guess he is a man of his word. "Hello?"

"I was calling to check on you."

"Oh, I'm fine."

"Aight. Well, hit me if you need anything."

"Well, have you heard from Snake?"

"Nah, but trust me, he aight."

"Okay. Well, I'm going to bed," I lied then hung up.

I waited for Duke to enter the club then I threw my car in drive and sped out of the parking lot. The entire drive home my mind raced. I couldn't believe both Duke and Snake would attempt to pull wool over my eyes. But little do they both know I will get to the bottom of this shit. I pulled into the driveway of my house and raced inside. The first place I headed was the bedroom. I've never been one to look for trouble because I was always taught if you look you shall find, but this time Snake has pushed me there. I began my search in his nightstand drawer. There I found several napkins with females' names and numbers on them. From the sound of the names it wouldn't take a genius to figure out these were numbers he'd collected from the damn strip club. As I searched further I came across a piece of paper with the name Ceazia and several phone numbers and an address written in Snake's handwriting.

"Ceazia," I said to myself. The name seemed familiar to me, but I just couldn't put my finger on it.

I went to his closet and began to look around. Snake and I had separate closets, so other than hanging up his clothes from the dry cleaners, I never had reason to look inside. I knew he kept his personal weed stash in there and a box where he threw dollar bills and coins.

I started with the weed stash and found nothing. Then I searched the money box and came across a nude photo. It was actually set up as a model's comp card. There was a large photo on one side in black and white, then several smaller photos on the other side in color. The name *Cinnamon* was on the top with contact numbers listed underneath. The bitch was obviously a stripper.

I examined the card thoroughly, looking at each picture. As I looked at the photos, the chick still seemed familiar to me, but again I couldn't really put my finger on it. I grabbed the photo and paper with the information on it and headed to my office in the house to make a quick copy. As I made the copies, things began to come together. The girl on the photo was that bitch from the hospital. I knew she was a stripper from the time I met her. *So Cinnamon is her name, huh.* Then I went on to make a copy of the paper with the name Ceazia and the phone numbers. That's when I noticed the number on the paper matched the number on the photo.

"Well, I be damned!" I said out loud.

The bitch from the hospital was Ceazia, Vegas's ex-girlfriend. No wonder Snake had stopped her as she began to explain who she was. I'd heard the stories about her, I'd just never seen her.

I couldn't believe Snake would stoop so low as to fuck with his deceased brother's girlfriend. *That muthafucka!*

Chapter 44

Snake

Smiling Deceit

"What up, sexy boy?" Ceazia said as she hopped off the stage.

"What up, sexy girl?" I looked her up and down.

Ceazia came to an abrupt halt. "Excuse me? You're actually responding to me?"

"Yeah. Is something wrong with that?"

"Lately you've been giving me a serious cold shoulder, so I thought we were on some beef shit."

"Nah, I just been having some problems at home, and a lot of shit goin' on in the streets. Nothing directed toward you personally, though," I lied.

Just like that, *C* began her flirt routine. As she chatted with me and rubbed her hands across my face and through my hair, I noticed Duke staring from across the club. I began to tune her out as I read Duke's actions. He was obviously upset about the conversation that *C* and I were having.

After a few more minutes, Duke came up to me. "What up, Snake?" he said, calling me by my name instead of the usual *unc.*

"What up, lil' soldier?"

"I'm surprised to see you talking to *C*. From our last conversation, I thought you weren't feeling her at all," Duke said, attempting to call me out in front of Ceazia.

"Me and *C* already had that convo. Right, baby girl?" I stroked Ceazia's back.

"Yep!" She quickly responded, full of smiles.

Duke grabbed C by the arm and pulled her away. "I need to talk to you." Like a rag doll he jerked her around while yelling profanity.

That whole scene was pretty comical to me. It was amazing the power a cat could have over a chick, just because he was feeding her a few dollars every now and then.

After he finished scolding her as though she was a young child, it was my turn. I walked up to him and said in his ear, "Yo, we need to talk."

Duke followed me as I walked out the club and headed to the truck. Before I could say anything he began to speak. "What up with you and *C*, man?"

"Ain't shit, Duke. Like I told you, once it's confirmed that she killed Vegas, I'm taking her out."

"Man, I wish you would get off that shit. If homicide investigators can't pin her to the murder, what makes you think you can?"

"Look, Duke, I have all the evidence I need. You either down with me, or you're not." I couldn't tell Duke how I'd gotten the evidence because I didn't want to put nobody, including myself, in the hot seat.

"Whateva, man. Like I said before, do you and I'm gon' do me. Enough talking." Duke hopped out the truck.

I just couldn't tell Duke all the details. I wasn't trying to incriminate his lil shortie, BJ.

Hell, on the real, I didn't even think BJ realized she was the leak. Earlier today I'd called her to make sure she was straight with the little change I'd given her to handle some things. She must have mistakenly pressed the speaker button, allowing me to hear the entire conversation between her and Ceazia.

After hearing her confession I was ready to kill her at first sight, but I knew I had to remain calm. So after a few shots of Hennessy and a blunt filled with purple haze, I was relaxed enough to devise the perfect plan. I'd already taken the first steps at the club. Now I just needed to secure my position.

I called Ceazia from my truck.

"Hey, sexy," she sang into the phone.

"What up. I need some companionship. I can't think of anyone I'd rather be with right now other than you. What you gon' do about that?"

"Whatever you want, baby. You already know how I feel. I'm always down for being with a real one like you. What? Your girl not turning the tricks I turn?"

"Nah, she holdin' shit down, but I just want something different. If you think you can fit the bill, then I need you to come roll with me."

"Fit the bill? I can be all you need and then some. I just feel sorry for your girl 'cause after tonight, I'll be all the woman you can ever think of."

Shit! She actually began to turn me on. The truth was I hadn't had sex with Danielle in over a week, so I needed some bitch to turn some tricks . . . not necessarily Ceazia, though.

"Yeah, sexy, you soundin' just like the something different I've been waiting on."

"Well, yeah, I'm that something different, but I have to be totally honest. I need some motivation for being your everythang."

"What type of motivation you lookin' for? Monetary?"

"Money talks and bullshit walks. But since you're a real baller, I got confidence that you gon' pay what my shit weighs. And, just so you know, my shit is heavier than a muthafucka."

"Oh yeah? Well, my money is long since we're talking American dollars here. And, you're right about one thing, *C.*"

"What's that, baby?"

"I *am* a real one, and don't you forget it."

"I won't. So tell me, how we gon' do this?"

"Well, how about this, you give me the four one one on my brother's murder, and I'll pay you tremendously for it."

"What makes you think I've got information?"

"C'mon, *C*, you know I must've figured the cops were hot on you for something. Even though you didn't kill Vegas an' 'em, I know you got some word on who did it, right?"

"Well, I got some idea, but I ain't blabbing for free. Telling you the least little thing puts my life at risk."

"Naw, sexy. See, that's where you're wrong. Just let me cover you. You don't have to worry about trouble following you, and that's *my* word."

"That's a deal, but it's going to cost you at least a hundred grand."

I readily agreed, knowing that she would never live to get the loot anyway. "Not a problem. Any amount of money is worth it when it comes to my brother."

"Okay, baby, just let me know when and where."

I smiled to myself. I knew within a matter of minutes, my penis would be wet, and my plan complete.

Chapter 45

Unknown Man

Can't Turn a Ho into a Housewife

Just earlier today at lunch, Ceazia was coming at me like she was ready to give up on this lifestyle as long as I was willing to hold her down. Of course I agreed to that. She told me everything I wanted to hear, but I was still on my shit. I told her I wasn't for no games and she knew it too.

She didn't even know I'd been sitting in the cut watching her every move tonight. I made it a point to follow her to see where her head was at. It looked like she was trying to fuck Snake again, and from the looks of things she had him and his lil' soldier on some beef shit.

But I'd gotten hip to her game. I knew she'd tell a nigga whatever he wanted to hear just to get a few bucks out of him.

Right now she was just so fucked up, she couldn't even see it. She thought that nigga Snake and his lil' soldier Duke was the best she could get, next to Vegas.

If it wasn't for them, she'd be mine and be the housewife that I knew she could be. So what does that mean? Only one muthafuckin' thing—those niggas had to go!

Chapter 46

Ceazia

Just What the Doctor Ordered

That hundred grand was going to put me right back on top. Thank goodness for the gold between my legs and the hustle I got along with it. I knew Snake could only hold out so long anyway. I mean who else was going to put it on him like me? Deep-throat his big black dick, take it in the ass, and then allow him to drench me in a golden shower?

And that's exactly why he decided to come back. This time I promised not to let him go, but first things first. I had to get my ex-boyfriend off my back. This nigga was starting to act like he was losing his mind.

I'll admit that I would hit him up with some sex for loot every now and then, but now I couldn't get his ass off my back. He thought he fucking owned me. I'd seen him following me and shit. Now he was even threatening to kill my ass if I fucked him over, as if I had his ring on my finger or something.

Now that I had Snake in the palm of my hand, I didn't need this nigga running up on the scene, fucking shit up. I called him to keep things in order.

"What up, *C?*" he answered.

"Nothing, baby. Just checking in. I thought you might want to know that I'm going out tonight," I lied, so he wouldn't be checking up on me while I was out with Snake.

"With who, Ceazia?"

"I got a money scheme. I'm planning to hit Snake up for some money. Like a hundred grand."

"And just how do you plan to do that? Snake ain't as dumb as he looks, Ceazia."

"It's simple. I told him I have some info on his brother's death, and he's willing to pay me for it. I'm going to give him some bullshit story and then buck."

"Sounds kinda dangerous, if you ask me."

"No, it's cool. He wants this information bad, and he's going to pay up."

"Damn! I see your mind is made up."

"Yeah, but baby just think about how cool things gon' be between us once I get my hands on this money. You've had my back, and now I can do something nice for you. Me and you can even bounce out of here when I'm done."

"Aight, *C.* I just want you to be careful. Call me when you're done."

Ding-dong! Ding-dong! Ding-dong!

I rushed to the door to see who the hell was constantly ringing my doorbell. I looked out the peephole and saw Duke with an evil look on his face. I took a deep breath and slowly cracked the door open.

"Why the fuck you ain't answerin' your phone?" He pushed his way through the door.

"I didn't hear my phone ring," I said, confused at his aggression.

"Bitch, I've been calling you since I left the club. Your

freak ass probably was on the phone with Snake. Where the fuck your phone at?"

"I am not giving you my phone." I looked at him like he was crazy then walked away. "You are seriously trippin', Duke."

He was up on me before I could see him coming. He grabbed my throat. "What the fuck you say?"

I grabbed his wrist in an attempt to loosen his grip. My eyes began to bulge as I gasped for air.

When I was damn-near death, Duke made the mistake of letting my throat go.

As soon as he freed me, I ran to my purse and pulled out my chrome nine-millimeter and pointed it right at him. "I'm sure we both know that I know how to use this. And I never miss my target."

Duke smiled, licked his lips, then calmly walked toward me. He was going to force me to do or die.

I put one in the head as he came closer.

"What you gon' do, *C?* You gon' kill me? You gon' shoot me? Huh?"

I stepped back, and then lowered the gun.

Duke exhaled and gave a small victorious grin.

That was the wrong thing to do to an angry bitch like me. I raised my nine and pressed it hard against his temple. "You know I'll do it. Please don't make me," I said in a stern whisper.

"So that neither of us get hurt, I'm going to leave and give you some time to think about what you just did," Duke said softly. He turned his back toward me as a sign there was no fear then walked out the door.

Whew! I exhaled then sat on the bed with trembling hands.

A real bitch would have shot his ass, I thought to myself as I came down off my adrenaline rush. I figured I just didn't have it in me any more. One thing for sure, I wasn't ready to commit another murder.

Good thing Duke made the right move by leaving. He was right. I could have gotten one of us hurt or killed. *What if he would've turned and pulled his gun on me?*

Chapter 47

Duke

A Woman Scorned

After *C* pulled that stunt, my head was real fucked up. I couldn't even drive. I only made it to the corner. I had to stop and take a smoke after that shit. I guess that bitch just may have been a killer after all. Pulling out on a gamer in a normal scenario would mean somebody, if not all people involved, would end up dead.

I ain't never had a bitch to come at me like that. All sorts of shit ran through my mind, but I had to play it cool just to let that bitch know I ain't the one to be fucked with.

Dealing with a crazy bitch like *C made* me miss BJ. I decided to give her a shout.

Ring, ring!

She answered the phone as though I was bothering her. "Yeah, Duke."

"What up?"

"Nothing. I'm with my boyfriend."

"Boyfriend?" I said, surprised that she even had the balls to say that shit to me.

"Yeah, my boyfriend. I am seriously involved now, and

we're planning to move to Atlanta together. So please do me a favor and forget my number."

"Aw, naw, you got the game all wrong, shorty. You gon' always be mine. I suggest you tell ol' boy that he needs to wrap his shit up and be outta there when I get there."

"Nigga, please. You ain't got no pull here no more. Don't come around here trying to go for bad, because you gon' mess around and get served if you do. My man ain't having no shit!" And just like that BJ hung up in my ear.

Still sitting in my car, not far from Ceazia's crib, I continued to pull on my blunt. Soon I began to feel much more relaxed. I popped in a CD and prepared to pull off.

Just when I thought I couldn't take any more surprises, I saw Snake drive past. There was only one place he could be headed. I figured it may be interesting to see just what was about to go down. I sat in the cut and watched as he entered the gate to Ceazia's home.

A few minutes later she came out and hopped in her car, Snake pulled off, and she followed directly behind him. I then fell in line behind her. I was sure to keep my distance as I followed because I knew Snake would constantly be in his rearview.

I continued to follow them as they hopped on the interstate and headed toward the oceanfront. I already knew where they were headed. Snake could only be taking her one place, his favorite hotel at the beach. I thought this nigga would be smarter than that.

I watched them park then head to the room. All sorts of things ran through my mind. *Should I call Danielle and blow his spot up? Nah, that would be a bitch move. Should I just run up in there and blow his spot up? Nah, that would be a psycho move. Or maybe I should just call him and act like there is some sort of emergency.*

Every option that ran through my mind seemed wack.

There was no real cool way to handle this shit. I continued to sit and contemplate.

With nothing to lose, I decided to call Danielle.

She answered the phone with a serious attitude. "What Duke?"

"Damn, ma! What's all the attitude about? Somebody would think we ain't cool."

"It's about cheatin'-ass niggas that call themselves boy-friends and their lyin'-ass nephews. I know the game, nigga. Now what?"

I had no idea what Danielle was talking about, but for some reason I felt like it had something to do with lying for Snake about the strip club. "What's going on, Danielle? Talk to me, baby."

"Look, Duke, I've gone through Snake's shit, and I know he's fucking with that trifling bitch Ceazia. And I know you know all about it because she was there when you got shot."

"What you mean, Danielle? Where is all this coming from? You got shit twisted, baby girl," I stated, to get more information out of her.

"Duke, I saw her number and address written on a piece of paper in Snake's handwriting, then I found a card that had a picture of her with the same numbers that were writ-ten on the paper. I also saw her at the hospital with Snake the day y'all got shot. It really doesn't take a genius to put two and two together here, Duke. Now you either can tell me the truth, or we can end this conversation now!"

"Sweetie, I've been giving you hints for the longest. I told you the night we were going to the strip club, that you were too good for him. It's only so much a nigga can do without just coming out and telling you directly."

"How could he do this to me, Duke?" Danielle began a hysterical cry. "Look at the time. It's three in the morning

and he's not even home. He's probably at the hotel with
that whore now. As a matter of fact I'm going down there."
Danielle slammed the phone down in my ear. *Click!*

That was easier than I thought. Now all I had to do was
just wait for her to come and blow up the spot.

Chapter 48

Unknown Man

Final Straw

C said she was meeting up with Snake on some scheming shit. I took it upon myself to follow her.

It was like déjà vu, as I sat outside the same hotel looking through a crack in the curtain at Ceazia and Snake. I watched as she went into the bathroom and Snake sat on the bed playing with his gun nervously. I saw the suitcase sitting in the corner and assumed that was *C*'s hundred grand. Maybe she wasn't lying this time.

After ten minutes had passed, Ceazia came out of the bathroom draped in a towel only. As soon as she got within arm's reach, Snake grabbed her and pulled her on the bed. Although they were no longer completely in sight, I could tell some sort of sexual act was going on. I didn't know if this was part of her plan to buck or what, but I wasn't feeling that shit at all.

Ceazia just had to try my patience. Now she was going to get a nigga killed and herself hurt. *Some bitches just don't get it.* I realized I had to bang her head in a few times to knock some sense in her ass. I never had the need to beat a chick, but now I saw why niggas did it.

I took the safety off my gun, cocked it back, put one in the head, and headed for their room.

Chapter 49

Snake

Resting Day

This is it, I thought to myself as I opened the room door to let C in. I sat the suitcase in the corner and laid on the bed. I ran scenario after scenario through my head as I waited for her to finish showering.

I should just go in there and put one in her head right now. Nah, too messy.

The little bitch must've been anxious to hook up with me because before I could think of another option, the shower turned off. I had to return my gun to my hip quickly because she headed out of the bathroom, draped in only a towel, and still dripping from head to toe.

C pranced over to me and let her towel drop to the floor. "Oh, it looks like someone misses me," she said. She continued to touch, tease and caress me in the most seductive ways.

I threw her wet body down and dove into her already-moistened kitten, ready to kill it first.

Ceazia screamed out in pained as I drove every inch of my manhood inside her.

I covered her face with the pillow, as she pierced my back with her nails. The more she flinched with pain, the harder I fucked her, forcing the pillow in her face to fade out her screams.

Suddenly, I had thoughts of suffocating her with the pillow, so I began to forcefully press the pillow in her face to the point where she physically began to struggle for air.

Ceazia dug and clawed my arms and back, but I maintained my focus. Like a crazed man, I never quit pounding her pussy as I continued to smother her. I was extremely turned on at the thought of her dying this way.

Boom!

A loud noise interrupted my tortuous sex just as I was about to reach my climax. We both jumped up startled by the loud noise. We turned around to see the room door kicked in and a figure standing before us with a gun aimed.

"What the fuck is going on? Bitch, you trying to play me? I told you what you had coming if you fucked me over!" he yelled.

"Oh, thank God, you're here, Bear. The money is in that suitcase in the corner. He was trying to rape me. I was screaming for help." Ceazia rushed to put her clothes on.

I couldn't believe this chick. She was putting on an Oscar-winning act and this punk-ass nigga was buying it.

"Get the fuck up, Snake," he demanded.

I slowly stood to my feet, scanning the room for a possible weapon or escape. As I stood up, he pressed the cold barrel of his Glock into my back. I took a deep breath, realizing this may be the end. There was no need for negotiating. This nigga came here exactly for this. I thought I had gotten *C*, but it looks like she'd gotten me. I didn't know she had enough sense to even attempt to set me up.

Ceazia and my brother Vegas hit Bear for a hundred grand, and now the tables had turned. How funny was that?

Now Bear and Ceazia were hitting me for the exact same amount.

"You set me up, *C?* I shoulda just killed your ass while you were in the shower like I started to do. You think you're gonna get away with this, bitch?"

"Shut the fuck up, punk. Ain't nobody set yo' bitch-ass up. I have been after you for a while. I've been watching *C* and you for a while now. I could have done you in at the Coliseum, but that was too easy. I rather see you suffer. You and your brother have done enough. Now it's my turn to reign.

"*C*, grab the money. I'm gon' do this nigga, then you're coming home with me."

Ceazia quickly jumped up and did exactly what he said. I watched her throw on her clothes and grab my bag. Once she was fully dressed, I knew my time had run out. I closed my eyes and reflected back on my life, then said a silent prayer.

Bang!

I jumped to the floor and grabbed my gun once I realized I wasn't hit. I looked up to see Duke at the door and Bear slouched in the chair. This was one time I was extremely glad to see my little soldier. Duke had put one into Bear's chest, and Bear lay in the chair, bleeding from his mouth.

Ceazia stood in the corner motionless, and Duke stared at the both of us. No one spoke a word, but if I had to guess, Ceazia knew for sure her time had run out. I knew I'd come here for one reason, and I wasn't leaving until it was done. So as planned, I grabbed my gun to complete my mission.

"Get the fuck on the floor, *C*," I said, gun pointed directly at her.

"Please, Snake. I-I-I didn't know Bear was coming here. He's been stalking me and shit, and I know he's crazy, so I was just scared when I told him you tried to rape me. I know I shoulda told you about him stalking me, but I thought I had put a stop to him doing that."

"Yeah, bitch, so you put my life on the line instead of yours, right?"

"Snake, I was scared. Don't you want to know who killed Vegas? I thought that's what we were here for. Keep the money, just let me go." She threw the bag my way.

"Naw, bitch. I came to get my dick wet and to kill yo ass. I've known for a long time you was guilty. I was just waiting on the right moment to send you to see your maker."

"Please, Snake. That's some bullshit. Who told you I'm guilty? You know you can't be listening to what people on the streets say."

"You're good, but not that damn good. And I don't believe that fake-ass story about how Bear got here either. Your time was out whether that pussy-ass nigga showed up or not. Get the fuck on the floor like I told you, trick!"

"Nah, nigga. *You* get on the ground." Duke pointed his gun at me.

"How you gon' pull out on me, lil' soldier? Fuck you, Duke. *C*, get the fuck on the floor!"

Bang!

Another shot rang out. This time I was hit. I could feel my knees give out, then I began to fall in what seemed like slow motion.

Bang! Bang! I shot back as I fell to the floor.

I looked over at Duke lying near me. He huffed and puffed as he tried strenuously to catch a breath. "How you gon' shoot me, unc?" he said, taking his final breath.

That's when I looked over at Bear, who was still alive.

Duke didn't shoot me. It was Bear. I'd shot my lil' soldier. I'd killed my nephew.

That was it. I refused to fight any longer. I was ready to die. What more did I have to live for? I laid silently and closed my eyes preparing for eternal rest.

Chapter 50

Ceazia

Quick Getaway

In a crazy frenzy I walked over to Snake and grabbed the gun from his hand. I fired one final shot to make certain he wouldn't live. I stepped over his body and took a look at Duke. There was no need in wasting a bullet on him. He didn't even have a fighting chance after Snake's shot hit him.

I looked over at Bear who was struggling to speak. I stood over him silently, watching the blood trickling down his chin as he gripped his chest. The more he tried to talk, the more it ached me to see him struggle that way. I thought about how much control over my life he had lately and quickly took him out of his misery.

Bang! I put a final shot to Bear's head. I needed to be free from his grip, and this was the perfect opportunity. Besides, it was never in my plans to share any of the loot with him anyway.

I grabbed the suitcase and rushed out the room, making sure to leave no traces. There was no way I could be involved with another murder. And this time it was three on the scene.

I didn't even bother to run through their pockets or take any jewelry. I just fled as quickly as possible. I rushed to my car and hopped in. I sped out the parking lot so fast, I nearly ran into someone head on.

Bbbbbbeeeeeppppppp! Bbbbbbbbeeeeeeppppppp! The crazy bitch laid on the horn.

I looked up as I surveyed the place. "Oh shit!" I said aloud as I locked eyes with Snake's girlfriend, Danielle. *What the fuck is she doing here?*

I contemplated killing her too, but I didn't have enough time. I could already hear the sirens from a distance. The police were on their way, and I needed to be no place in sight.

I sped home and grabbed my dog, Prissy, grabbed all my money, filled up a few bags of clothes and hit the road, leaving all else behind. I had to get the fuck out of dodge, and this time, I was going far, far away.

Chapter 51

Ceazia

Since I'd moved to Atlanta, I'd come in contact with a new breed of niggas. I even managed to cop myself, an entertainer. It wouldn't be worth speaking on, if I wasn't indulging in all the benefits that came along with it. Not even Vegas, God rest his soul, could set me up like this dude with the long-overdue extravagance a true diva like me deserved.

The hundred grand I bucked Snake for was well worth it. He should have slept with both eyes open because thanks to that money, I was able to get the clothes, crib, and attitude necessary to pull a true Atlanta baller.

It didn't take long for me to peep out the competition and catch on to the game chicks ran in the *A*. Off the top, I knew I had to come at the fellas from a different angle, so I took it back to the basics.

No one in Atlanta knew my past, or anything about me for that matter, so I could easily portray whatever image I wanted. I decided it was time to challenge myself by taking on a role that wasn't anything near the real me. I decided to be a good girl. What guy doesn't love the girl next door? I found that innocence that I had hidden deep inside when I was lost and brought it back to life. Now it was Miss Prissy, bitches.

In all honesty, I don't know if I actually hunted down my prey or if he carelessly just stumbled into my trap. Nonetheless, I ran into one of the hottest rappers on the charts, Parlay. His real name was Jason Williams.

It was barely even a month after I had settled down in my nice little condo in the Peachtree area that I met Parlay. It was the night of his album release party at Visions Night Club.

One would have thought that I was the guest of honor, the way heads turned when I arrived at the event. Folks automatically pegged me as Parlay's girl, just assuming that someone of his caliber wouldn't be caught dead with anything but the shiniest trophy on the shelf. It didn't take a rocket scientist to figure out where the man of the hour was parlaying, no pun intended. All I had to do was follow the trail of hair weave, silicon, and clear stiletto shoes. I positioned myself where I didn't necessarily have a clear view of him, but that wasn't what was important.

With my back toward him and his entourage, I ordered a drink from the bar. After receiving my drink, I slowly turned around on my stool. Looking down at my drink, I innocently, yet seductively, took a sip from straw. I then slowly looked up, and just like I knew he would be, his eyes were fixated on me.

Upon first glance, I knew I had him. It was something about the way he looked at me with those deep-set brown eyes that let me know what was up in a matter of seconds. So what if he did have his woman on his arm, and a few groupies to boot?

Once I hypnotized him with these panther eyes of mine, it was game over. I knew at that moment Parlay would be mine to keep.

I took the long strapped, black evening bag off my shoulder and pulled out Parlay's latest CD that I had picked up at the record store after getting my hair done. I took one more sip of my drink, then sat it back down on the bar before heading his way. With my signature strut, the crowd seemed to disperse for me until I was situated in front of his table.

"Excuse me, Mr. Parlay." I batted my eyes. "Could you autograph my CD for me please?" I slid him the CD and pulled out a black Sharpie from my purse.

Without saying a word, his eyes said, "For you, baby, anything," and he stuck his hand out and accepted the pen that I offered.

"Thank you," I said to him as he handed me my CD.

"Anytime."

I turned to walk away. *Hell, that's all he could say.* My ass had a tendency to make niggas speechless.

"Hey," I heard him call, as I had made my way through the crowd.

I turned to look back at him.

"You forgot your pen," he said to me, holding up my Sharpie.

He reminded me of an old boyfriend who was all too thrilled when he found that the chick that just dropped his ass left something of hers in his apartment.

"That's all right," I said. "You keep it. You never know who else might want your autograph too." I winked and then stepped.

As I exited the club I looked down at the CD Parlay had signed. I had to pat myself on the back for that one. In record time I had done what all those hoes would spend all night trying to do. I had gotten him to personalize my CD with both his autograph and cell phone number.

I guess the shortage of straight men and ample strip clubs had turned all the girls bisexual. Luckily, I was a freak in the bed and willing to explore just about anything for the love of money. I learned that many men in Atlanta assumed bisexuality was just simply a part of life. The ones I came across seemed quite disappointed to hear that I didn't get down like that, but when it came to Parlay, I took no chances.

When he expressed his fantasy of having another chick join us in bed, I quickly delivered. His birthday, June 15th, was right around the corner, and I couldn't think of a more perfect gift. Of course, I lied and I told him that it would be a first for me, but I assured him he wouldn't be disappointed. I was banking on the one experience I had in Cancun, along with instructions from a wide collection of lesbian porn to make me a pro.

I scouted Atlanta for the hottest chicks the city had to offer, from The Gentlemen's Club to Magic City, and I must say, I was pretty impressed when I finally found Diamond. Not only was she attractive on the outside, but she was just as beautiful inside. She stood five-feet, eight inches, with a small waist. Her skin was a cocoa-brown with red undertones. I loved her jet-black hair, which had deep waves all the way down her back. Plus it didn't hurt that she had a perfect white smile to add to her sex appeal.

Diamond, like most of the perspective candidates I had in mind, was a dancer too, but not the same type of dancer as the other girls. A creative arts graduate from Georgia State University, she spent her days working at her very own dance school created for the city youth. To top it all off, she was a Scorpio just like me, sharing the same sexual appetite along with many other things.

I was on one of my weekly shopping sprees at my favorite store, Neiman Marcus, in Lenox Mall. As I sat trying on a pair of snakeskin Versace sandals, I noticed a young lady staring from afar. At first, I thought to myself, *what the fuck is this chick staring at?*

She came over. "Those shoes really look nice on you."

"Thanks."

"Wow! That heel is high. I don't think I could even walk in those."

"Oh, it's not hard at all. It's only a three-and-a-half inch heel." I slid it off my foot. "Here. Why don't you try it?" I handed her the sandals.

She sat down in the chair next to me and placed the shoes on her feet. "Perfect fit," she said. She stood up and took a couple of steps before she stumbled and fell directly into my lap.

"Told ya!" She laughed hysterically. While still sitting on my lap, she continued to chat. "My name is Diamond, and you are?" She extended her hand.

"I'm Ceazia. It's nice to meet you, Diamond." I gave her a small shove to get off my lap.

"Oh, I was so comfortable here." She stood up and removed the shoes from her feet. "I almost forgot we were in a department store." Diamond gave a seductive stare as she handed me the shoes.

I watched the shoes dangle in front of me before I took them from her hand and placed them back in the box. "Well, Diamond, it was nice chatting with you," I said, gathering the shoes I wanted to purchase. I then walked away.

"You all set, ma'am?" the salesman asked.

I nodded and proceeded to follow the salesman. Just as I

made it to the register, Diamond handed me a business card.

"Can't wait to hear from you," she said with confidence.

Like a dude, I found myself watching her hips sway back and forth, butt bouncing with every step. I shook my head and proceeded to check out at the register, knowing damn well that she had every reason to be as confident as she was because I had every intention on ringing her phone.

"May I speak to Diamond?" I spoke through the phone receiver.

"Speaking."

"Hi, Diamond, this is Ce—"

"Yes, Ceazia," she said, cutting me off.

I was impressed, but didn't lead on. "How are you today?"

"Better now," she replied.

I could hear her smile over the phone.

"Same here. So, Diamond, I have a little bit of running around I have to do today and I was just wondering—"

"I'd love to. Is two o'clock fine?"

I took the phone away from my ear and just stared at it. *Can you believe this bitch?* I chuckled and put the phone back to my ear.

I arrived at the restaurant at two o'clock sharp to find an even more prompt Diamond already seated and sipping on an Iced Tea. Upon joining her, and after our pleasantries, I quizzed her on a few things just to see where her head was. I wasn't trying to bring just any old chick into my man's home.

After a few more meetings with Diamond, I was convinced that she was the one. Even though she was only twenty-one, she seemed to have a lot going for her. Whether it was lunch, a movie, dinner or just hanging out at her place, I was more and more impressed at each of our meetings.

Finally, as we sat on the couch in my condo, the time came for me to proposition her. Telling from the photo albums I had flipped through, I had seen her hugged up with a guy or two, so I figured she wasn't a stranger to the dick. To my surprise, her response to my proposition was just the opposite of what I had expected.

Diamond placed her hand on top of mine. "Look, Ceazia, I really like you, and I love a girl who is into pleasing her mate, but the thing is, I *really* like you. I'm sure Parlay is a really nice lay, and it's not that I'm trying to be with you on the side or anything, but if I am going to be with you, I don't want any added interruptions." She stroked my hair and leaned in closer, going for the kiss.

Fuck! I had to think quick on my feet, as not to allow her to flip the script on something that was my production.

As her soft lips touched mine, I sat there waiting for her next move.

When her tongue separated my lips, I pulled back shyly. "Diamond," I whispered.

"You okay?"

"Yes, it's just that . . ."

"Shhh." She placed her index finger on my lips. "You don't have to say it. I can see it in your eyes. You've never been with a woman before Ceazia, have you?"

I didn't mind allowing her to feel like the elder in the relationship, as long as in the end I got what I wanted. I slowly lowered my head, as if embarrassed by my lack of experience. "I'm sorry if I led you on to believe that—it's just that when I saw you I was so intrigued by you. I had never felt that way before about a . . ."

"A girl."

"No, a woman. I guess me asking you to be with me and

my boyfriend is because I was just scared to be with you alone. I figured if I froze up or anything, I could use Parlay to run interference."

"I hear what you're saying, but I really want it to be all about you. Just me and you."

"I really want to be with you too, but I would feel much more comfortable if we did a threesome. I know I'm being selfish, but at the same time, I wouldn't feel as though I'm cheating on Parlay."

Diamond sighed. "I want you to be comfortable. I guess we could look at this as sort of a tester. We each get to sample before we sit down to a full-course meal with each other."

"But what if you don't like the sample and I never get a full taste of you?" I licked my lips.

"Don't worry," Diamond said. "That's not going to happen. I just want to make you happy."

"Well, I'm glad you're into making me happy, but what would really be pleasing to me is seeing Parlay sex you from behind, while your head is buried in my lap."

"That's exactly what I wanted to hear, baby. You won't be disappointed."

Chapter 52

Danielle

Playing the Game My Way

Another day, another dick, I thought to myself, as I brushed my teeth and watched Dario through the bathroom mirror. He lay on the bed like a bump on a log. Sex with him was never a thrill, but it kept my position as next candidate for partnership with the law firm secure. For each day I had to relive this tortuous act with him, I added another kick to Ceazia's ass. She was the reason why I was in this predicament in the first place. And little did she know, the day I got the chance, I was gonna make sure she relived every miserable moment I had to deal with since Snake died.

After Snake's death, a life of hell would have been a step up for me. But knowing that everything happens for a reason, I'd endured the series of set backs that was supposed to land me in the town I was in today, leaving crab-ass Virginia behind.

Once relocating to the ATL, I landed a job with one of Atlanta's biggest law firms, Johnson, Smith, Davis and Williams. After getting this job by all means, and I do mean *all*—I needed to be the next partner. The one way to secure that position was to lock one of the senior partners, Dario Duncan, between my legs.

Fat, black and ashy, and topped off with a small penis, Dario had nothing to give me not even the slightest thrill. One thing I'd learned from the drama with Snake was that sex could secure any woman's needs, as long as it was with the right person.

Not quite Mr. Right, but definitely Mr. Right Person. Shit, I would've much rather masturbated while viewing a DVD from my extensive porno collection, than had sex with him.

I walked into the luxurious master bathroom, which Dario had decorated in an earth tone and stone décor. I untied the belt, opened my robe and let it slide down my shoulders and onto the floor. I took three steps into the completely tiled two-head shower.

"DDDDaaaaaaarrrrriiiiiooooo", I sang from the bathroom shower.

I imagined him grunting, as he rolled his fat ass over, pulling the covers over his face as he did each morning after we had one of those sickening rendezvous. My stomach turned, as I thought about the sex we had the previous night. *An hour of foreplay for a minute of play. The things you gotta do to stay on top.*

"Big daddddyyyyyy!" I called him again, using my sex kitten appeal to lure him from a deep sleep into my gauntlet.

I figured the sooner he woke up, the sooner he could get his Jenny Craig-dropout ass up and dressed, so I could be on my merry way.

After calling out to him again, Dario finally raised his naked body from the dead. With nothing but rolls of fat, he entered the bathroom looking like a yawning hippo as he wobbled toward the shower.

"Hey, sweetheart."

"Hey to you," I replied.

"What's up?"

"Nothing, baby." I stepped back into the shower. "I'm just taking a shower so I can get dressed and get ready to go, but I didn't want to leave without saying goodbye."

He hopped in the shower and quickly found my body that was buried in the steam. I tried to wash up as quickly as possible because I didn't want to take the chance of him getting a hard-on and wanting more sex. I didn't feel that my stomach could bare another episode.

As I turned around to rinse my face, I felt a brush across my back. At first I ignored it, hoping it was just his fat stomach brushing against me, but it didn't take long for me to realize it was his hand.

"No, Dario, you don't have a condom, baby," I said in my best baby girl voice.

"You can't leave me like this, Danielle."

I didn't have the time or patience to go back and forth with him, so I closed my eyes and did what I had to do. I got down on my knees and gave him the blowjob of a lifetime. I never gave them lazy-ass blowjobs that sometimes defeated the purpose of not fucking a nigga in the first place. If you didn't give it your all, he might not come and you'd end up having to spread them legs anyway just so he could hurry up and get off. Then you'd end up sucking his dick *and* fucking him. So if I was gonna do that shit, then I was gonna do it right.

I took Dario by his hard limb and placed it in my mouth. I paused and allowed it to lie on my tongue, my lips wrapped around it, allowing the warmth of my mouth alone to stimulate him. Slowly, I began going back and forth on him.

"Deep-throat this big dick, baby," he mumbled between groans. "That's right, choke on this big dick."

* * *

I quickly washed up and jumped out the shower. In ten minutes flat, I was dressed and out the door. I wasn't wasting any more time. I had to get the hell away from him before I found myself having to let him hit it from the back after all.

Once I was in my car, a nice little fully-loaded Eclipse, I headed straight to the interstate. After getting a couple of miles away from his ass, I pulled out my cell phone and called up, Richard, my fiancé. "Hi, baby!"

"What's up, baby?" he responded.

I'd met Richard shortly after my move to Atlanta. His lawyer just happened to be one of the senior partners of the firm I worked for. One day, as I headed out for lunch, he was on his way in to speak with his attorney. Our eyes locked at first glance. Once I realized that I was staring at him and that he had caught me staring, I put my head down in complete embarrassment. Then I thought to myself, *hell, he's staring at me too.*

"Hey, sexy," he asked with a nod, "what kind of trouble could a sweet-looking girl like you possibly be in, where you need the services of this place?"

I smiled. "I'm not in any trouble. I usually am trouble."

"I see. Well, Trouble—"

"*Danielle.*"

"Excuse me?"

"The name is Danielle, not *Trouble.*"

"Ummm, Danielle"—he extended his hand—"I'm Richard, Danielle, but like I was saying, if you ever want to get into some trouble with me," he handed me a card from his wallet, "just holler at me."

I took the card and headed out to lunch. Needless to say, once I got off work, went home, took me a shower and got relaxed, I called his ass quick, fast, and in a hurry. From that day forth that six-foot-six, two-hundred-pound caramel frame was mine to keep.

Richard was my baby, and I loved him to death, but he was always on the road. Since he played for the NBA, he spent nearly six months out of the year away from home, and the other six months was split fifty-fifty between time with me and hangout time with his boys. I hated being apart from him, but I knew as an NBA wife, I had to learn to live with him not being home as well as deal with the boys, groupies, whores, and even the down-low athletes that I'd heard so much about.

"When am I going to see you?" I asked.

"Hopefully I can come through one day this week, baby. You miss me?"

"Yes, I do, and I want my man home with me."

"Man, don't start that shit, Danny," he said. "You already know how it is. Like I've told you before, as my wife, this is the shit you're going to have to deal with. This is my life, so speak now or forever hold your peace. And don't hold that shit in until the preacher asks you at the altar."

Damn! I guess he told me. "I'm sorry, baby. Just know that I miss you. Have a good game tonight. I love you."

"Love you, too."

I flipped the phone closed and placed it down in my purse.

Five minutes hadn't passed before my phone rang again.

I fumbled through my Marc Jacob bag, trying to get it. I looked down at the caller ID, and to my surprise it was Jonathan, a young man I'd met one day while sipping a frappachino at Starbucks. He was sort of the metrosexual type. Not really my style, but I figured his position as a buyer for Chanel would have great benefits. So, without hesitation, I put him on my team.

"Hello," I said in a sing-song voice.

"Hello, beautiful. How's your day going?"

"It's going okay. I just spoke to Richard. He upset me a little, but I'm fine now."

I was always open with any guy on my team that was part of the starting line-up. I made sure to let each one of them know up front about the star player that I was on the side-line cheering for. That way each one was aware of his position and could play it accordingly; even if it meant he had to be benched momentarily. Jonathan was especially understanding, and he and I had a perfect arrangement. He was married to his wife, and I was married to the game. He understood the rules perfectly. No feelings, no questions, just physical pleasure for him, and financial and material pleasures for me.

"How about brunch?" Jonathan offered.

"Sure. Where would you like to meet?"

We decided to meet at a delicatessen in the Buckhead area of Atlanta.

I had arrived at the restaurant a few minutes earlier than Jonathan and decided to take a seat and check my home voice mail.

You have three new messages, the automated recording said.

"Hmm, three calls," I said to myself, anxious to know who had called me. My eagerness soon turned to dismay after the first two messages, only bill collectors. When I reached the third message, my finger was already set to delete the message, but when I heard the familiar raspy voice of Shawn, I nearly dropped the phone.

"What up, sexy?" he said on the message as his words climbed out of the receiver and right into my ear, sending a chill down my spine. "This is Shawn. You know you ain't have to buck on me like that. I'm home and can't wait to reclaim my money and my kitty cat. Holla at a nigga 917-222— he said, reciting his number.

My body froze in a panic as my brain raced.

What the hell is Shawn doing home? I thought he would never get out. What about Richard? What if he finds out I set him up? What if he already knows and is setting me up? What am I going to do?

Shawn was Snake's New York drug connection. After Snake died, Shawn and I had an arrangement. Basically, he kept me on the status that I was accustomed to, and in exchange, I kept him happy sexually.

In the beginning, I felt extreme guilt and planned to renege on the little agreement, but Shawn had plans of his own. It was only a matter of weeks when Shawn became possessive and abusive, totally violating all the rules of the arrangement. With no way out and tired of the obligation, the beatings, and being dependent on him, I made a vow to get him, as well as Ceazia.

A few phone calls and a few months later, I was successful in setting him up. I'd finally gotten him off my back. He was served with ten indictments, which resulted in a sentence of twenty years federal time. He went straight to jail, did not pass go and did not collect two hundred dollars. With no get-out-of-jail-free card in sight, my job was finally done.

Free from Shawn, I set out for a new beginning. It was time to put my law degree and parents' high-class status to work. I'd moved out of Virginia and into Atlanta, leaving no trail. I just had no idea that fool would get out and track me down.

"Sorry to keep you waiting," Jonathan said softly in my ear.

"Oh shit!" I screamed while holding my chest, scared half to death..

"I'm sorry. Did I startle you?"

"No, it's okay. I was just deep in thought and didn't even notice you coming behind me."

During the entire time at lunch, I found myself in a daze. That message from Shawn really had my head screwed up. I mean, I swear on everything, I could hear that nigga's voice as if he was right over my shoulder.

"Danielle. Danielle. Danielle," Jonathan called out to me.

By the time I answered him, I could tell he was pretty annoyed at my inattentiveness. "I'm sorry. Baby, I have a lot on my mind, you know, with the big case coming up and all. One mess-up and it could ruin my chances for partner," I lied.

I had to be careful never to get Jonathan upset. Unlike the others, I knew he would leave my ass at any time if I got out of line. I definitely wasn't trying to take the risk of losing his top-notch dick.

"I can tell there is something bothering you, sweetheart. If you like, I will excuse you from lunch early."

I accepted, and agreed to make it up to him later.

He paid the waiter, walked me to my car, and kissed me goodbye.

His kiss alone made my body steam with lust.

"Why don't you come over to the condo and let me give you a nice massage?" He opened the car door for me, allowing me to slide into the driver's seat.

"Okay, baby, but no sex."

"No sex." He winked and then headed over to his white Jaguar .

* * *

Twenty minutes later, we arrived at his Alpharetta condo. It wasn't where he lived, it was where we played. Jonathan rented a condo just for our secret rendezvous. Since we each had a significant other, we both had a lot to lose and couldn't risk the chance of getting caught red-handed at some hotel. From the jump, we both agreed to never jeopardize losing our mates by getting caught having sex in either of our homes. Our lovers' pad was more than a worthy investment.

We wasted no time getting down to business. One glass of champagne and one body massage later, I found myself engaged in passionate sex. Jonathan made love to me like a chef preparing a delicacy for the queen.

After forty-five long minutes and several multiple orgasms for me, he finally reached his peak. "I love you, Danielle," he moaned as he thrust himself deep inside me, forcing out the words through clenched teeth.

Again, I found my body in a state of panic. I grabbed my chest and tried to pace my breathing without looking too obvious.

Luckily, Jonathan's phone rang, allowing him to direct his attention elsewhere. "Hello." He reached over and grabbed his phone off the end table. "Just a minute, sweetie," he said to me before getting up out of the bed and walking his naked body into another room for privacy.

That was my indication that it was his wife on the phone. Getting a little jealous, I quickly got dressed and began to gather my things. I headed toward the door, clearing my throat just loud enough for him to hear. I then walked past him in an attempt to get his attention and rush him off the phone.

Evidently it worked, because a few moments later, he walked behind me and grabbed me around the waist. "You're so cute when you're jealous," he whispered in my ear and then kissed my neck.

"Who's jealous?" I headed out the door.

Jonathan rushed to throw on his boxers and the rest of his clothes.

Once I reached the car, he gave me a small peck.

I hopped in and drove off, admiring his sexy frame from a distance. Sure, I allowed his wife to win this time, but hearing those three special words was a definite sign that my position would soon be changing to first string.

Chapter 53

Angel

Caught in the Act

One thing I hated was a nigga trying to play me. I knew it wouldn't be long before I caught John's cheating ass. I'd been tracking his cell phone calls for the past two months and following him for the past two weeks. It took nothing for me to trap his careless ass. After only a quick glance at his phone bill, it was obvious who the other woman was. There was only one other number that appeared on his bill as often as mine and as long as mine.

I decided to follow his little sneaky ass and like the dummy he was, he led me right to her. Only a man would be so damn stupid. I watched as John and his tall, slim, label ho walked into a small condo in a quiet and secluded part of town. I could only wonder if he'd purchased this secret spot for this exact purpose. I measured my time perfectly, aiming to call his phone right in the middle of the act.

"Hello," John answered promptly.

He'd passed the first test. He answered the phone right away and as relaxed as a sleeping baby.

"Hi, baby," I said, trying to sound excited to hear his voice.

"Hey, sweetie. What's up?"

"Nothing at all. I just was thinking about you and wanted to hear your voice. How's work?" I continued with small talk just to see how long he would chat. I figured it was only a matter of time before Miss Thing would cough, or clear her throat or something loud enough for me to hear to make her presence known.

"Work is fine, baby. Actually I'm with a client right now."

"Oh, I'm sorry. You should have said that in the beginning. Normally you don't even answer when you're in the middle of a meeting."

"Well, this is sort of a casual client. He understands how it is when the wifey calls," he said with a little giggle.

"Oh, okay. Well go ahead, baby. Handle your business. I'll call you later."

"All right, baby."

"Love you."

"I love you too, Angel."

I was surprised how easy our conversation went. It made me wonder how many times I'd called before when he was with her.

Five minutes after I hung up, John's little friend came prancing out the front door, and he came rushing behind her with nothing on but a pair of boxers.

I could have very easily stepped out of my "her" Jag that matched Jonathan's "his," with my four-inch stiletto pumps and matching bag that housed my nine, and let both the female and the man whore take one in the dome.

John grabbed her from behind, placing his arms around her waist as they walked together to her car. It took all I had not to run my car right into the both of them as they sat at her car kissing.

I decided to follow her. My first instinct was to get out of the car at the next red light to confront her trifling ass, but I didn't want to make any rash decisions that I'd regret later. The longer I drove behind her, the more it set in. *My husband of ten years, Jonathan Powell, is having an affair. The same man that had nothing more than a high-school diploma and four years in the service under his belt when we first met. I practically made him. I gave him style, I gave him charm, I pointed him in the right direction, and now that he finally has a ground to stand on, he wants to be the king of the hill and send me tumbling down the side like a worthless little Jill.*

My anger soon turned into pain. Tears began to blur my vision as I drove. Just as I was about to turn off and head home, the ho turned into a parking garage designated for Atlantic Station Lofts, which wasn't the address attached to her name when I did my detective work. This had to be where she lived. *Jackpot!*

Just as this little hussy had come into my life and torn it to pieces, I planned to do the same to her. Once I was done with her, everything she touched was going to turn to shit.

I rushed home. I figured, or at least hoped, he had to take a shower and wash any traces of the other women off of him. Once inside, I changed clothes then pulled out the cleaning supplies. I cleaned the house from top to bottom then began to cook his favorite meal of steamed fish and vegetables, with my homemade jerk lemon and ginger sauce.

I dimmed all the lights, lit the fireplace, turned on the new Kem CD, and filled the Jacuzzi with hot water.

Five minutes later, John walked through the front door. "Wow! It smells great in here. What did I do to deserve this?" He walked into my arms and hugged me tight.

"Nothing at all, honey. It's just a small token of my appreciation for you being such a great husband." I took his coat and led him to the Jacuzzi.

He looked around at the spa-like atmosphere, "Baby, you appreciate me that much?"

I just nodded and smiled.

As John took his clothes off and relaxed in the Jacuzzi, I set the candlelit table. After adding a few final touches, the table was perfect. The food had a fresh steam, and there was just enough lighting to create a romantic ambiance. I poured us a glass of Pinot to top things off. I then went and met John at the Jacuzzi, where I stood with only a towel in one hand and his silk pajama pants in the other.

"Here you are, sweetie," I said, handing him the towel.

I admired his body as he stepped out of the Jacuzzi. I took a deep breath as the thought of that scandalous bitch caressing his perfect body flashed before me. I had to keep cool.

"Let's eat, honey." I handed him his pajama pants. "I cooked your favorite."

I pulled his chair out for him as we approached the dining table.

"Umm, umm, umm! Steamed fish. This truly is royal treatment. If I didn't know any better, I'd think this was our anniversary."

After I prepared his plate, I sat down next to him without preparing a plate for myself. I picked up his fork and cut a piece of fish from his plate. I then placed it in front of his lying lips. He smiled and slowly opened his mouth and took it all in.

"I hope you didn't get too full," I said, taking the napkin and wiping his mouth after feeding him the last bite on his plate. "You haven't had dessert yet."

"Oh, baby." John leaned back and rubbed his stomach. "Later for dessert. I know I can't eat another bite."

I threw the napkin down on the table, stood up, and grabbed him by the hand. "Good, because this dessert doesn't consist of you eating another bite." I pulled him up out of the chair and led him into the bedroom. I walked him over to the bed and pushed him down gently by the shoulders into a sitting position.

I untied his robe and slid it off of his shoulders. "How about a massage, baby?"

"Wow, honey, you're really spoiling me. This is really freaky, almost scary." He softly patted me on the behind as I stood in front of him. "Almost like one of those 'Stepford Wives.' Is there something I should know? Did you wreck your Jag? Or did you quit your job to pursue an exotic dancing career? What is it, Angel?" John let out a nervous giggle.

I slowly moved my hands down his torso, ending at his midsection. He seemed to get hard instantly, as I massaged his shaft. I quickly moved from a hand massage to a tongue massage. John's intense moans were an indication that I had sent him to another world.

Grabbing my head, John guided my motions in tune with the thrust of his pelvis.

My mind began to drift as I thought about his little mistress. I wondered if he had grabbed her the same way, if he'd moaned with each stroke just like he was doing now.

Just as I thought about biting his dick instead of sucking it, my mouth filled with the warm bitter taste of his ejaculation. I sucked every drop of cum from his penis. John shivered with pleasure as my tongue reached the head and I licked the final drop, tilting my head back and swallowing as though I was taking a shot of Patrón.

"Damn, Angel. I don't think you've ever given me head like that before."

"That's just the beginning, baby. I think we should explore other areas of our sex life."

"What? I thought you were happy with our sex life."

"Oh, I am, baby. It's not me. It's you I'm worried about."

"Me? Angel, what's going on? Where is this coming from?"

"Well, the ladies and I were having a really interesting conversation today at the spa. Basically, we were discussing how you must please your man in the bed because there is always another woman willing to do what you won't do. So it made me think of areas that maybe I was a little close-minded on, like oral sex, anal sex, and threesomes. So far I've crossed one bridge. Now it's time to cross the others." I spoke in a serious tone. "Let's maximize our sexual experience. What do you say?"

"Is this some type of trick, Angel?"

"Sweetie, no. Some of the ladies have experienced all of the things I've mentioned, and they gave me some wonderful tips."

Jonathan just shook his head. "I don't know, Angel. All of this has kind of taken me by surprise."

"I won't take no for an answer," I said sternly, as if it was something he had to do for me. This way he would be more apt to go for it. "I want us to have a threesome, and I'm leaving it up to you to choose the woman."

"Baby, I don't know anyone. I don't even know how to approach a woman with such a request."

"John, it's really simple. We live in Atlanta, honey. Forty percent of the women here are bisexual. I'm sure there's got to be a woman or two from your job that are hot for you. I'll give you a week. Let me know when you have someone." I pulled the covers back and snuggled up under them. "Now let's go to sleep. It's getting late. I love you," I said, then kissed him.

Chapter 54

Jonathan

Indecent Proposal

*D*amn! *That was some million-dollar head,* I thought as I massaged my dick. Angel had never given me head like that before. It's like she'd taken Blowjob 101. I used to complain about the money she spent at the spa, but that shit finally paid off. I have to admit, it was rather scary that she chose the day and time I'd just left Danielle to give me the royal treatment.

As Angel lay next to me sound asleep after making me cum and making her demand, I had to pinch myself to see if I was dreaming. *Looks like I'm gonna have my cake and eat it too.*

Every man's fantasy was about to be my reality. The only trick was to get Danielle to agree to a threesome. I figured she would resist in the beginning, but I had a week to work on her.

I kissed Angel gently on her cheek. I slowly pulled the sheets back and crawled out the bed trying not to wake her. I crept into the living room to give Danielle a call before I went to sleep. Not only did I need to oil her up to pop the big question, but we also needed to discuss my little out-burst I had during sex earlier.

As I dialed her phone number, I decided that I may or may not pop the big question, depending on how the conversation flowed.

"Hi, Jonathan," her sweet voice sang as she answered the phone.

"What's up, gorgeous? Sorry for calling so late. I just wanted to call and wish you luck on your case tomorrow."

"Oh, thank you. That's what I love about you, Jonathan. You are so thoughtful."

"This is the big case at the circuit court, right?" I asked just to let her know I knew all the specifics.

"Yes, it is. Glad to know you are really interested in my career."

I'd scored a few brownie points. Step one to getting her to agree to a threesome with Angel and me.

"You know my wife and I had the strangest conversation tonight," I casually mentioned.

"Oh really? What did you all talk about?"

"Well, it seems like her day at the spa had a huge impact on her today. Evidently she and some of the young ladies there had a little please-your-man chat."

"Please-your-man chat?"

"Yeah. She came home catering to me in every way, dinner, massage, sex, then she began to go on about how we should maximize every sexual experience."

"Oh really? And just how does she suggest you all do that?"

"Well, as you know from previous conversations, Angel was never really a winner in the bed. Hell, you practically turned me on to every exotic sexual experience there is. Well, now she's trying to step up to the plate, even though there isn't much she can offer me at this point because you and I have just about done it all. But when she voiced one suggestion in particular, my mouth nearly dropped to the floor in disbelief."

"She wants to please her man and step up to the plate now, huh? Well, I guess that leaves little room for a mistress now, doesn't it?"

"You know, Danielle, you're absolutely right," I said, trying to upset her.

"So I guess this is goodbye then?"

"In a way."

"What do you mean, in a way, Jonathan?" she asked, her frustration obvious.

"Well, you see, it will be 'Goodbye, mistress,' and 'Hello, mutual sex partner'." I hinted at the subject the best way I could without just coming out and saying it.

"Mutual sex partner? Okay, Jonathan, enough of the games. Just let me know what the deal is."

"Okay, Danielle, you asked for it straight, so here it is." I took a deep breath. "Angel wants to have a threesome."

"Excuse me? I don't think I heard you correctly. Angel wants to have a threesome?"

"Yes, baby, she does. She even wants me to pick the woman. When she asked, you were the only one that came to mind. I know this may seem sort of strange, but think about it. We'll no longer have to hide and what a convenience this would be!" I tried my best to convince Danielle that this was an opportunity that not every man and his mistress were fortunate enough to be presented with.

"I don't know, Jonathan. I mean, I've never done anything like this before."

"Well, it's just an option, baby," I said in an attempt to downplay the entire idea. "Like I told you earlier, I love you, Danielle, and I can't think of anyone else I would rather share this experience with. I don't want you to feel forced.

Just sleep on it. We'll talk about it more in the morning if you like."

She sighed. "Okay, Jonathan, but I'm not going to lie, this is a bit much to swallow. I will sleep on it and maybe we can do a late lunch tomorrow and discuss things further. Besides, I owe you a makeup lunch anyway."

We both chuckled.

"Well, I gotta go. Big case in the morning. Goodnight, Jonathan."

"Goodnight," I responded before hanging up.

"Yes," I said, balling a fist and lifting my knee as I headed back to the bedroom and slid back in bed. I kissed Angel's beautiful face. *Thank God for beauty shop gossip.*

Chapter 55

Ceazia

Girls Gone Wild

"What the fuck was I thinking?" I said to myself while washing my tears away in the beads of water that fell on my face. Parlay's big day had finally come and things had surely gone wrong, wrong, wrong. I couldn't believe the shit that had just gone down tonight. I wasn't ready for that shit at all.

The so-called threesome didn't happen anything like my threesome with Vegas on our Cancun vacation. I know I ain't no ménage a trois queen, but I had seen enough pornographic videos to know a little something-something.

It was like Parlay had just lost his damn mind or something. Everything was going as planned in the beginning. Dinner was perfect, his party at the strip club was a ball, and when he saw his dessert, he was delighted. But it was at the after-party that pushed me to the limit.

Our night started off lovely with a quiet dinner on the deck of his house. I'd hired our own personal chef to come out and cook for us hibachi style. We sat overlooking the river from Parlay's deck. The night was beautiful, the bonfire and candles blending perfectly with the full moon above.

The musicians were awesome. They started off by playing classical music, then flipped it by playing some of Parlay's rhythm and soul favorites.

"Happy birthday, baby," I said over an instrumental of one of Alicia Keys's songs. "I hope you've enjoyed everything." I massaged my man's perfectly manicured hands.

"Baby, just sitting here with you alone is much more than a nigga could expect. You know most cats can't even appreciate shit like this. Hell, most of these hood rats out here wouldn't even be able to put some shit like this together for their man."

"I'm glad you're happy. I have to admit, though, at first I had no idea where to begin."

"Well, you did a damn good job, shortie. Ain't no chick ever done nothin' like dis for a nigga befo'," Parlay said in a country accent.

I had no problem doing whatever it took to secure this nigga. I knew he was my meal ticket. You see, with guys of Parlay's caliber, you had to come at them from a different angle. They expected chicks to want them for their money and fame. So when a chick comes along paying for shit, never asking for anything, declining trips, and doing thoughtful things, she stands out.

Once the chef had delivered us the final course of his meal, I tipped him and the musicians and sent them on their way. It was time for Parlay and me to head to his favorite strip club, Bottoms Up, where I'd reserved the VIP section for him and ten of his boys.

I scanned the club quickly as we entered. It was as though an alarm had gone off as soon as we pulled up to the valet, like in the movie *The Players Club*. When we hit the door, dancers were already heading toward the empty VIP area.

We followed the bouncers closely as we maneuvered our way through the packed club to the area that was reserved for us.

The waitress met us there almost simultaneously.

"Let me get five bottles of Rose," my baby ordered, "and the sweet honey and white chocolate-flavored Cristal."

"Okay that will be—"

I whipped out my American Express and handed it to her. "Start a tab, sweetie."

"Okay. Will you need anything else with that?"

"Yes. I need change for five thousand, all twenties, and send over Juicy, please."

"Juicy, doesn't do private—"

"Just tell her it's Parlay's birthday, and he is requesting her presence," I told her.

I already knew the spiel. I'd heard it over and over from my man. Juicy was the hottest stripper in Atlanta. Renowned for her all-female parties, she'd been in every uncut video on BET, and was envied by every dancer to hit a stage. The bitch was hot without a doubt, but things had gone to her head. Now she was on some superstar shit.

Juicy had a bunch of high-class rules and shit, one of them being that she didn't allow one man to halt the money of several men by doing private dances. She strolled in the club at whatever time she chose and hit the stage within an hour of her arrival. Once on stage, if the DJ didn't have the selection of reggae she requested to dance to, she refused to dance. Until she got at least a hundred dollars thrown to her feet on stage, she wouldn't even as much as clap her ass cheeks.

Tonight I had stacks to spend and was ready to pop rubber bands for that bitch.

Five minutes later the waitress came out alone.

"So what's the deal?" I asked, prepared for the worst.

"She said she will stop by after she comes off stage."

"All right." I handed the waitress twenty dollars for her effort. I already knew the deal. Juicy wanted to see how we tipped while she was on stage before she even considered coming over.

"And now the moment you all have been waiting for," the DJ yelled over the tunes of the theme music to Rocky.

All eyes were on Juicy as she stepped on stage covered by her white cotton boxing robe that had her name embroidered on the back and a picture of her face airbrushed underneath it. Once Juicy was positioned on stage with her legs spread and hands on her hips, the DJ cut the music off.

"Okay, fellas, come wit' it! Y'all niggas know the routine," the DJ said into the mic.

That was my cue. I quickly grabbed a thousand-dollar stack of twenties and headed to the stage. I stood there looking Juicy eye to eye as I peeled off the twenties and tossed them to the stage floor as though I was dealing a deck of cards. That was surely gonna get that ass moving.

"Gotdamn, shortie!" the DJ yelled. "Now all y'all niggas should be embarrassed up in this bitch, letting a broad outspend ya'll broke asses." He laughed then threw on "We Be Burning" by Sean Paul.

Juicy dropped the robe and displayed the baddest body I had ever seen on any female. Her honey-bronze skin was like a custom paint job. Every curve and cut seemed to have been hand-carved by God Himself. Her long, slicked-back, "I-Dream-of-Jeannie" ponytail slithered around her neck like a snake.

In all honesty, she wasn't the best of dancers. As a matter of fact, she didn't really dance at all. Just swaying her hips back and forth seemed to be enough for the men.

I dropped a couple more twenties and when I turned around, I landed right into Parlay's arms.

"Oh shit!" the DJ yelled when he spotted Parlay up at the stage. "Shut the club down! Niggas step ya game up." He stopped the music. "We got muthafuckin' Parlay in this bitch tonight!"

After Juicy's set was over, she left the stage and rushed toward the dressing room.

I know this bitch ain't trying to play me.

About twenty minutes and one shot of Patrón later, Juicy came prancing over fully dressed in a Juicy sweat suit. "What's up, sexy?" she said, staring dead at me. "You wanted to see me?"

"Well, actually, I was requesting your presence for my boyfriend. It's his birthday."

"Oh, it's his birthday." She turned her attention to Parlay and headed in his direction. "Birthday bbbbboooooyyyyy," she sang out, getting his attention.

The look on his face was priceless. He looked up at Juicy and then over at me.

I smiled and nodded my head as an indication that Juicy's presence was all my doing. Now that I had delivered, although not to my satisfaction since the bitch was fully dressed, I figured I could at least take a potty break. I must admit, I felt like I was the shit.

When I got back to the table, Parlay was enjoying his gift. I sat off to the side sipping on a bottle of water as I watched him and his boys wild out.

My moment of joy was interrupted by the skinny little waitress that had served us the entire night. "Excuse me."

"Yes," I responded full of attitude.

"The owner would like to speak with you," she stated nervously.

"The owner? For what?"

"She didn't say, but if you could follow me—"

"No, ma'am. If the owner would like to speak to me, then she needs to come over here. Can't you see it's my man's birthday and I've paid good money for the cake?"

The waitress walked away without saying another word, and I focused my attention back on Parlay and Juicy.

I felt a tap on my shoulders. "Excuse me."

"Yes," I said, ready to blast whoever it was.

When I turned around, I froze with astonishment. I didn't know if I should jump on this bitch or hug her. I hadn't talked to her in years.

"What's up, Chastity?" I said, deciding to break the ice.

"What's up, *C?* How have you been?"

Still unsure of her vibe, I kept it short. "I'm good." I looked her up and down. "So what's up?"

"Oh, I was just coming over to thank you all for your business and to offer you a picture on our wall of fame. I had no idea—"

"Yeah, I know. You had no idea it was me. I'll get Parlay and the fellas together so you can get your picture. Send Picture Man over."

"All right. Will do." Chastity walked away. "Oh and, *C,*" she said as she stopped and turned around, "Glad to see you again."

I shook my head and smiled to myself. *Like hell you are.* My high was now fully blown. I had no idea what to really think about Miss Chastity.

I walked over to the table where Parlay and the fellas were. "Excuse me, baby." I tapped Parlay on the shoulder. "The club owner wants a picture for her wall of fame."

"Cool," Parlay said, never taking his eyes off of Juicy.

I then gave all his boys word too.

Chastity returned with the cameraman at her side. "You all ready?"

"Let's do it," Parlay stated, oblivious to everything going on.

All his boys gathered around him, and I made my way by Parlay's side. We all smiled for the camera as the picture man took a couple of shots. Then they all went right back to partying as before.

Chastity lingered around for a moment. "So what brings you here?" she asked.

"Just celebrating my boyfriend's birthday."

"I see." She shook her head.

After a few more seconds of watching Parlay and his friends celebrate, she said, "Well, I guess I better get back to work. Here's my card. Give me a call some time." She gave me a hug before leaving.

I wasn't sure what to make of that. Chastity and I were friends from a long time ago, but after Vegas and Meikel's death, she, along with several other chicks I thought were my friends, all disappeared. I assumed they had disassociated themselves from me because they figured I was responsible for Meikel's death. This was the first time I'd seen anyone from my old crew since the murders.

I placed her card in my purse and glanced at the time, One a.m. *Time for the fat lady to do her thing.*

After a performance of a lifetime, five thousand dollars worth of tips, and a matching tab, the party was finally over. Now it was on to the after-party.

I called Diamond to give her a heads-up that we were on our way. I ran down the blue print one last time. It was simple, Diamond was to be his love slave, nothing more, nothing less. Whatever Parlay wanted, she was to deliver.

When we arrived home, Parlay had no idea that the party was actually just beginning. As we entered the house, he thanked me for the special evening I had arranged for him.

With a huge mischievous grin on my face, I didn't reply. I just took him by the hand and led him to the bedroom. As we made it to the doorway, I released his hand and allowed him to enter ahead of me.

The room's set-up was beautiful. I had Diamond sprinkle rose petals all over the floor, there was soft instrumental music, over fifty tea-light candles, and last, but not least, Diamond was spread across the bed like a duvet.

"What the fuck?" Parlay stared at Diamond. "Baby, this is just too much. This shit is crazy!" Parlay was like a kid watching a magic show. He couldn't figure out the trick. Dick hard, he just stood there with a Kool-Aid smile.

It must have been obvious that I was going to need some help snapping him out of his trance, because Diamond got up and led him and me both to the bed by the hand.

Once there, she turned around and faced each of us. She looked at me, then kissed me on the lips. She looked at Parlay and kissed him on the lips. Slowly, she unbuttoned his shirt and slipped it off his shoulders.

"Raise your arms," she said softly to me. After sliding my shirt over my head, she placed her arms around me and unsnapped my bra as she French-kissed me. Once the bra met my shirt on the floor, Diamond made her way back over to Parlay and began unbuckling his belt.

The next thing I know, his pants dropped to his ankles, and her tongue was down his throat.

Diamond pulled me by the hand down onto the bed. "Lay down," she whispered. She pushed me back and kneeled before me, her lips kissing my things. Not long after, her tongue was flicking at my clit.

Once Diamond realized how into it I was, she got up abruptly and had me scoot up to the head of the bed. She then laid me back down on my back and placed my legs on her shoulders, as she licked me from nipple to clit, then back up again.

Lying directly on top of me as though she had a penetration stick of her own, Diamond spread my legs and pressed her vagina directly on top of mine, sending my body into ecstasy.

"Aaaahhhhh, Diamond!" I screamed with pleasure. I couldn't believe a bitch had me calling out her name.

Parlay stood over us watching, stroking his dick up and down.

"I told you you wouldn't be disappointed," Diamond whispered between small nibbles on my ear.

Diamond laid him down between us, and we took turns sucking his penis and his nipples.

Parlay pulled me on top of him so that I was riding him backwards. Diamond sat in front of me with her legs around my waist and began sucking my breasts and massaging my clit, as I slowly bounced up and down on Parlay.

"Oh shit," he moaned.

Not wanting him to reach his peak, I lifted up and handed him a condom as an indication that it was time for him to sex up Diamond. After securing the condom on his dick, he bent Diamond over and entered her from the back.

Wanting her to work that magic tongue of hers again, I crawled up underneath her and spread my legs wide.

She smiled taking the hint and buried her pretty little head between my legs. Like a snake, her tongue slithered up into my pussy and sent a feeling through me that I'd never felt before. In and out, her tongue plugged me up like a dick making cum run out of me like a faucet.

Diamond sat up and smiled a smile of victory. She got up and started throwing her ass back at Parlay.

I sat up on my elbows and glanced up at them. Her eyes were closed, and her hand was between her legs stuffing Parlay's dick inside of her.

My heart skipped a beat when he passionately kissed Diamond's neck and whispered in her ear, "Give me that wet pussy, baby. Give me that good, wet pussy."

I lay motionless, my blood boiling. Not wanting to ruin the mood, but definitely needing to stop the madness, I gently pulled Diamond toward me, leaving Parlay on his knees with a hard, wet dick. I turned Diamond over onto her back and began kissing her passionately.

Parlay then grabbed my waist to bang me from the back.

I grabbed his penis to remove the condom, and again my heart nearly dropped out. There was no condom. *Where the fuck was the condom? I know he didn't remove it during the switch.*

I continued to kiss Diamond while Parlay fucked me from behind. At that point, I wanted him to just cum and get this over with, for my vibe totally ruined. "Cum for me, baby. Cum in this wet pussy," I begged, hoping to speed along the process.

"No, baby, not yet. Come suck my dick. I want to cum in your mouth."

I happily agreed. Hell, anything just to get that shit over with. I sucked away as Parlay began to finger Diamond.

I closed my eyes, hoping that when I opened them I would wake up and this would all be just a bad dream, but when I opened them, I saw him tonguing her down like he was a marine who'd been out to sea for six months.

My first instinct was to just get up and walk out, but there was no way I was leaving them alone together. Hell, at the rate they were going, they might've fucked around and made a baby. I just closed my eyes again and prayed for the escapade to be over.

A few minutes later, Parlay was splashing my throat with warm liquids.

I opened my eyes to what I thought would be relief but instead, it was hell before me. Parlay's face was covered by Diamond's pussy. She had rested her foot on his shoulder for him to eat her out.

She sat moaning in ecstasy, as he squeezed her ass like he was sucking the juice from an orange. It took all I had to keep from kicking that bitch in the back of the head and choking the shit out of Parlay.

Diamond began to quiver, and Parlay didn't hesitate to swallow every ounce of her cum.

"Well, I guess the party is over," I said, not wanting to give Diamond the chance to try to lay on the bed and recuperate.

She must have gotten the drift. A few minutes later, she was dressed, and I was escorting her to the door.

"Bye, baby," she said, attempting to give me a goodbye kiss.

"Bye." I quickly stepped aside and closed the door, meaning, "No thanks, and get the fuck out!"

Chapter 56

Danielle

In the Heat of the Night

Ring, ring! Ring, ring! I woke to the sound of a ringing phone.

"Hello?" I answered without even looking at the caller ID, assuming it was Jonathan calling me back.

"What up, beautiful?" Shawn's raspy voice said from the other end of the phone.

I rubbed my eyes and looked at the clock on the nightstand. *What the fuck does Shawn want at three fifty-eight?*

"Yo!" he yelled into the phone again.

"Yes, Shawn."

"Open the door."

Please tell me this is not happening. I struggled to get out of my bed and put on my robe. I briskly tiptoed to the front door.

"Danielle!"

"I'm still here." I looked through the peephole and was relieved to see there was no one in sight.

"So what's taking so long? Open the damn door, girl!"

"Shawn, shut the fuck up! It's four in the morning. I

don't have time for your damn games." Knowing that he wasn't really outside my house, I felt comfortable popping off at the mouth. I untied my robe as I headed back toward my bedroom.

"What?"

"You heard me, nigga."

Spsh! Spsh! Spsh! Boom!

My journey was interrupted by the sound of gunshots. I screamed as I fell to the floor in the hallway, dropping the cell phone. I lay on the floor motionless, unsure what to do. I heard steps coming in my direction.

"I didn't want to get ignorant, boo-boo, but you made me," I could hear the voice around me, and through the cell phone in front of me.

Shawn stood before me, gun still in hand and smoke rising from the silencer as I struggled to my feet. "Why couldn't you just open the door, baby girl?"

"I went to the front door, and I didn't see you out there."

"Come on, Danielle, you should know me better than that. I was at the back door. You actually think I would stand at the front and cause a commotion with all these whities around? Shit, bad boys would be here in no time."

Still a little shaken up, I walked into my bedroom, and Shawn followed right behind me.

"So what do you want, Shawn?" I asked, hoping this was an easy fix. I prayed it was his money and not pussy.

"Come on, you know what I want."

All of a sudden I regretted entering the bedroom in the first place. "Please, Shawn, it's late. I don't have time for the games. What's up?"

"Well, it's a couple of things." Shawn began rubbing his hands together. "For starters, you can come off my cash. Now I ain't no crazy nigga, so I know you done dug into it a little, so I'm gonna give you break. All I need is one hundred fifty grand. We'll write off the rest. I'll charge that spending to the game." He looked at me for approval.

Shawn wasn't a dumb nigga by far, but he had to be stupid to think I still had one hundred and fifty thousand dollars for him. Hell, it was more like fifty grand, but I refused to tell him that, especially with that gun still in his hand. "Okay, Shawn, I'll give you your money." I folded my arms and flopped down on the edge of the bed. "And once I do that, will you leave me alone?"

"Maybe." He smirked.

I rolled my eyes. *And just what the fuck is that stupid-ass grin across your face for?* "Whatever. Shawn, I'm getting married soon, and I'm up next for partner with one of the best law firms in Atlanta. This is too much to lose from fooling around with some convicted felon. So, I beg you, please leave me alone. Give me a week and you will have your money. After that, I beg you disappear."

"What?" Shawn yelled at the top of his lungs, causing me to nearly jump out of my skin.

My mind flashed back to one of the many beatings I'd received from him. "Nothing, Shawn. I'm just really tired and kind of frustrated. The thought of me losing everything I've worked so hard for just crossed my mind. I'm sorry. I will give you your money, I promise. But please, please don't mess things up for me."

His phone began to ring. "Hello?" he said.

"Yo! Wa you a deal wit'?" I heard a deep Jamaican voice on the other end. He was loud, enabling me to hear every word.

Shawn walked out the bedroom and out into the hallway. "I got you, man. I'm handling some business right now. Give me a week."

Unfortunately, I couldn't hear a word he was saying as he walked farther away and into the kitchen.

Just as I was getting up to move a little closer to the door, he came back down the hall. "Aight, ma," he said as he entered the bedroom. "One week."

"Yes, one week."

He paused for a minute and then said, "All right then, one week. I'll holla at you in a few days." He headed toward the back door he'd shot through earlier, which was now hanging from the hinges.

"I'll deduct the money for my door from your money that I owe you," I shouted as he walked away.

I looked up at the ceiling. "Thank you, Lord." I then took a deep breath, got up from the bed, and went to the back door. As if shooting the door off the hinges wasn't enough, this fool went as far as to kick it in too. Luckily I had a fenced-in back yard and a storm door that I could lock until I got the back door repaired.

I locked the storm door and headed back to bed. Once in my room, I prepared to get at least a couple hours of sleep before my day began. I laid down and glanced at the clock one last time. I snuggled my pillow and pulled the cover over my head and reflected on the events of the night.

Chapter 57

Angel

Unfulfilled Destiny

"What a wonderful day today will be." I reached over and turned off the beeping alarm clock and then kissed my cheating, sleeping husband on the lips.

He yawned and stretched. "Oh, are will still on the cater-to-your-man tip?" He rubbed his morning hard-on.

No we are not, dumb ass. I gave him a pleasant smile.

I got up out of the bed and headed to the bathroom to shower.

Jonathan had no idea I was up listening to him on the phone last night. He and his little mistress were both falling right into my trap. This was almost too easy.

I showered quickly and threw on some clothes.

"What's on the agenda today, honey?" he asked, as I stood in the bedroom mirror, brushing my hair into a ponytail.

"Just heading to the gym right now. I'm not sure about later. We'll see what the day brings."

"Wow! That's the luxury of owning your own business,

huh? Maybe I should quit my job so I could be more like you." He laughed.

"Honey, I'm going to drive your car today. Could you get mine detailed for me? It's a mess."

The truth was, I needed his keys to make a copy of the key to his little secret love palace.

"Sure, baby, no problem." He kissed me on the forehead and then headed toward the bathroom. "Drive safely."

I grabbed his key and jumped in his car and headed to the store. I made it my first priority to get a copy of the key. There were a couple of keys I wasn't sure about, so I made copies of them too. *One had to work.*

Once that was done, I called John to see exactly where he was. He'd mentioned something about a meeting this morning, and I'd heard from his conversation with Danielle that she had a huge case this morning as well. This would leave their secret love cave open for my inspection, but one could never be too sure.

"Hello?"

"Hey, honey," I said. "Just calling to make sure you were up and getting dressed. I don't want you to be late for your big meeting this morning."

"Thanks, sweetie. I'll be heading out the door in about another thirty minutes."

"Okay. Have a good day."

"Thanks, sweetie."

"Jonathan."

"Yeah?"

"I love you," I said softly.

"I love you too. Bye."

I put the pedal to the metal and sped across town. I parked a few spots from the condo to avoid chat from any nosy neighbors in the area. I knew this was going to be a great day when the door opened on the first try.

The place was nicely decorated, almost too nice for a man. Granted, John had plenty of style, but the detail and accessories had the fingerprints of a woman's touch all over it.

My stomach turned as I looked at the crumbled lavender sheets. I thought I was gonna be sick. I ran to the bathroom and hugged the sink. I took deep breaths, hoping to make the nausea go away. Once I gathered myself, I sat on the toilet to take a few last breaths before leaving the condo. I had seen enough.

I noticed the garbage can to my left, next to the commode. I rummaged through it. To my dismay, there was no condom. He didn't even have the decency to protect me from any number of the diseases that tramp could be towing around.

I struggled to get out the house as fast as I could, my eyes swelling with tears. As I made my way out of the bathroom and back through the bedroom, I noticed a small object glistening from the corner. I headed over to get a closer look. I bent down and picked it up off the floor and checked it out. "A diamond earring," I said. "And two carats at that." I tossed the earring in my purse and headed out the door.

Now it was on to my next stop, Atlantic Station.

I drove to the loft apartments I had followed Danielle to yesterday. I pulled into the parking garage and walked to the lobby area. I looked around for any piece of information that would lead to her apartment number, but there was no clue.

As I returned to my car, a guy in a black Bentley coupe pulled up behind me.

"Yo!" he shouted from his car window.

I looked over each of my shoulders. "Are you talking to me?"

"Yeah. You parked in my spot, shortie."

I checked out his ride and the jewelry he was bound to catch a cold from. It was just far too much ice.

"Oh, I'm sorry. I had no idea. I'm leaving now anyway." I pulled out my keys and went to put my hand on the door handle to open it up.

"A few seconds longer and your shit would have been fucked up," he joked.

"And that would have been a charge—destruction of property."

"I ain't worried about that. My fiancée is an attorney for one of the biggest law firms in the A."

His bragging was music to my ears. He could only be talking about the one and only Danielle, my little home-wrecking friend. "Well, good for you." I began digging in my purse. "Well, let me give you my card," I said as I approached his car. "My name is Angel Powell, and I'm a wedding planner."

I didn't notice how fine this man was until I got closer. *Damn! I would trade John's tired ass for this man any day! What the hell is wrong with that bitch?*

"Okay, Angel, that's a bet." He took the business card and placed it in her pocket.

"Not to be rude, but just how far do you think that card will get in that pocket? You'll forget about it, and it will end up at the dry cleaners." I pulled out another card. "Why don't you try putting this one in your wallet?"

"Wow! Feisty lil' thang."

"I look forward to hearing from you." I headed back toward my car. Just then I stopped and turned back toward him. "Oh, what is your name?"

"I'm sorry. We didn't properly meet." He placed his car in park and stepped out. "Let's try this again. How you doin'? My name is Richard Anderson."

"Nice to meet you, Richard." I shook his hand, hoping that he couldn't see how mesmerized I was by his features.

"I'll be giving you a call, shortie."

"Looking forward to that, Richard." I smiled and headed back to my car and threw it in reverse for Richard to back up and allow me to pull out. I put the car in drive and pulled off. I watched as he whipped his car into the parking spot I had just occupied. The Houston Rockets license plate read *LOYAL 1*.

I headed to the city's Circuit Court, where Danielle's case was being heard. That was something else I had overheard Jonathan mention during his phone conversation with her. *What are the chances of me bumping into her fiancé like that? I've really got this bitch in the palm of my hands now. There are so many ways I could take things at this point. Maybe I could do her the same way she's been doing me and screw her man. I would love to do that. Or maybe I could just spill the beans. No, that's too simple, and why would he believe me anyway? It would be too easy for her to get out of that one without solid proof. I definitely have some sorting to do.*

I parked in the courthouse garage and headed to the court lobby. There I read the docket, located Danielle's courtroom, slid past security, and sat down in the back of the courtroom.

I scanned every bench so that I was fully aware of my surroundings. I didn't even get to the third bench before I saw John's stupid ass. *Supporting his woman, I see.* Any closer and I would haven mistaken him for the defendant in the trial.

I shook my head in disbelief as I continued to scope out the area. That was enough for me. I had to leave. I quietly tiptoed out of the courtroom and headed toward the elevators. I wasn't more than ten feet away when I heard the door open. I looked over my shoulder and saw John coming out. He was saying something to the guard and wasn't looking in my direction.

I immediately turned back around and made a beeline to the stairwell. I headed out the courthouse and to my car. When I entered the garage, I noticed a young man comfortably leaning against my car.

"Is there a reason why you are leaning against my car like you make the payment each month?" I asked.

"Damn, you gotta lot of heart for such a lil' woman," the man responded with a deep New York accent.

"Can I help you with something, or should I just scream for help?"

"No need for that, ma. I'm here to help you."

"Help me? I doubt there is anything you can help me with, sweetie. Now if you will excuse me, I would like to get in my car." I grabbed my car's door handle.

"I know you're following Danielle because she is sleeping with your husband," he said.

I got into the driver's seat, trying to seem uninterested. I put the car in reverse and backed out. I grabbed the parking ticket from my armrest and headed toward the parking attendant. I passed the young man on the way. I watched his every move as I waited in the line to pay and exit.

Just who the fuck is he, and how does he know all of my business? I could no longer bare it. I put my car in reverse and drove back to the area where he stood.

"I knew you would come back."

"Okay, what's up? How the hell do you know this stuff?"

"Baby girl, I'm from the streets. I've been following you just as long as you've been following Danielle. Looks like we're out to grab the same fish," he said.

"Oh yeah? And why are you after Danielle?"

"It's a long story, ma. Let's just say she has something that belongs to me, so if you're willing to work with me, we can do the damn thing together."

"I need to know exactly what's going on between you all before I commit."

"Nah, boo, it's not even on that level. She's my ex. I'm just trying to put a lil' heat to her to make her come off the goods, that's all."

"Okay. We can put our heads together. You scratch my back, and I'll scratch yours." I looked him up and down. "So what's your name?"

"Shawn. And yours?"

"Angel." I dug out a business card. "Give me a call later. Maybe we can meet some place and talk about things."

Chapter 58

Danielle

Three's Company

I was surprised when I looked across the courtroom and saw all three of my men. Believe it or not, I wasn't the least bit nervous about all of them being there. If anything, I was excited by the level of support being shown to me.

Jonathan sat back dressed in an Armani suit as though he was a prosecuting attorney. Not too far from him sat my husband-to-be, Richard. I was most excited about his presence. Something like this was huge for him. Hell, he was hardly ever in town, and when he was, he was always so busy that I only got a small portion of his time. So for him to take time out of his schedule to come see me do my thing, was more than just amazing to me. I looked over at him from across the courtroom and blew him a small indiscrete kiss. He gave me a tease of that amazing smile of his and a wink of the eye. *God I love that man!* I thought as my lace Vicki's instantly became soaked.

Last but not least, right in front sat Dario. He hadn't actually gained the title of my man, but until my position of partner was secure, he could've called himself whatever he pleased. I'd worked long and hard to prove myself at the firm, and screwed just as long, to make sure my work didn't go unnoticed.

I took a deep breath as I reviewed my notes for the case. This was a done deal. There was no way I could lose the case, but I always liked to be extra prepared.

"Defense, your opening statement," the judge said.

I struggled to my feet. My chest balled up with pain. Everything around me began to spin. Within seconds everything was black.

"Oh my goodness! Someone get help," I heard a voice shout. "Stand back and give her some air."

"Danielle, baby, it's me. Open your eyes, sweetie."

I opened my eyes slowly and focused in on the owner of the voice. "Richard?" I said as I attempted to get up.

"Yes, baby. Don't move. We're gonna get you some help."

"What happened?" I touched the huge lump on my head.

"You passed out, honey. Everything is okay though. Just relax."

All I could think about was how I'd ruined everything. What the hell had just happened? This was my big case, and I couldn't even get past the opening statement. I could only imagine what the firm partners were thinking.

Once I was able to get steady on my feet, I picked up my file.

"Don't even think about it." Richard took the file out of my hands and placed it on the table.

"I have to, Richard. They're counting on me. I'm just a little exhausted, that's all. I'll be fine."

Before Richard could respond, the paramedics arrived and sat me down to check my vitals.

"I'm fine," I said.

"Everything seems normal," one paramedic mumbled to his co-worker.

Eventually the paramedics gave me a clean bill of health for the time being, but instructed me to go see my family doctor. The judge decided to adjourn the case until the next morning.

Damn it! I thought to myself. I felt defeated before the game even started. I stuck my file into my briefcase and walked from the courtroom into Richard's arms. We got all the way to his car by the time I realized that we weren't anywhere near the parking level or side of the garage where I had parked.

"My car?" I questioned Richard, rubbing my head.

"I'll drive. Baby, we should leave your car here. I don't want you driving home. We can come back up here and pick it up tomorrow."

Although I didn't feel like driving, I really needed some time alone. My cell phone had been vibrating off the hook, and I needed to talk to Dario to make sure things at the firm were still in my favor.

"It's okay, sweetie. I feel fine to drive. Just follow behind me."

He rubbed my face. "You sure?"

"I'm fine. I promise."

"All right then. If you start feeling funny again, just pull over immediately."

"I will." I gave Richard a kiss on the cheek and hopped out of the car to get into my own.

I pulled out my cell phone and looked down at it. I had five voice messages and seven missed calls. I returned the calls first, beginning with Dario.

"Danielle, are you okay, sweetie?" he asked, first thing.

"Yeah, I'm fine. I think it was just nerves, but what are the partners saying?"

"Oh, don't worry about that. Just don't let it happen twice. Otherwise, they're gonna say you aren't well enough to work the case, and we both know you really need this one."

"I'm so lucky to have you on my side." I sighed. "What would I do without you?" All those times being on my back was truly paying off.

"No. What would I do without *you?*" Dario said sincerely. "You know, Danielle, when you passed out, it scared me to death thinking that I might lose you. I thought about—"

"Dario, please . . . I can't have this conversation right now."

Next I called Jonathan.

"Hey, Jonathan."

"Well, hello there. You had me a little worried. I had to catch myself from running to the front of the courtroom when you collapsed."

"I'm sorry. I've been having these episodes a lot lately, but it's never been this bad."

"Baby, you really should get that checked out. It sounds like anxiety or panic attacks."

"I will call my doctor as soon as I get home."

"You do that, honey and I'll check up on you later. Take care," he said and then disconnected the call, and just in the nick of time too.

I pulled into the garage of Richard's loft apartments and whipped into the reserved parking spot. Richard pulled in right behind me and rushed to the car to help me out. Had I known this was all I had to do to get a little attention from him, I'd have fallen out flat on my face months ago.

"Let me help you," he said as I stepped out of the car."

I was perfectly capable of walking alone, but I let him help me every inch of the way.

Once we were in the apartment, he laid me on the bed and brought me some water and the cordless phone to call the doctor.

"I think you should call your doctor, baby. Maybe you're pregnant."

"Richard," I said, as if he was being foolish.

I knew he wasn't going to let up, so I called right away.

When the doctor came to the phone, I explained everything that had happened. He suggested that I make an appointment with the psychologist and come in for an evaluation. I wasn't too fond of the thought of seeing a head doctor, but if this was going to put my position as partner at risk, I was unquestionably going.

"I'll see you then, Doctor Obetz," I said after confirming the time and date of my appointment.

"So what did the doctor say, Danielle?"

"Honey, I'm not pregnant. The doctor believes that I'm having panic attacks."

"Panic attacks?" Richard said with a puzzled look on his face. "So what's causing them? Do you think that's why you can't get pregnant?"

"Richard, honey, listen to me. Panic attacks are a result of stress. It has no direct effect on pregnancy."

"I'm sorry, sweetie. Just relax." He fluffed my pillow and began to undress me.

I could already predict what was going to happen next, as Richard began to massage my body. When he finished, I felt his hands lift from my body and his lips replace them. There was no way he was going to let the day pass without having sex with me. Knowing him, he probably marked his calendar and followed my menstrual cycle so he would know when I was ovulating. Which means what? That's right, my chances of getting pregnant were at its greatest.

I didn't bother putting up a fight.

Chapter 59

Richard

Bun in the Oven

At times I think she really doesn't want to have a baby and that she's probably still sneaking and taking the pill or something. But I can't understand why. Hell, she's dating just about the most eligible bachelor in the NBA. There were women who would love to trick a nigga into bearing his seed. So, I admit, Danielle had me somewhat baffled.

I stepped out of the shower.

"Richard!"

"What's up, baby?" I wrapped a towel around my waist and entered the bedroom.

Danielle was standing in the middle of the floor, holding my jeans in one hand and a business card in the other. "What are you doing with this card?" She walked over to me and shoved the card in my face.

"Babe, if you read the card, you'll see she's a wedding planner. I thought you would be thrilled to know that I'm actually taking some initiative to get things rolling with the wedding."

She looked down at the card again. "Oh." She sighed. "Well, it's just not like you to have some chick's card in your pocket."

I took the card from her hands and laid it on the dresser. "Why are you up snooping around anyway? You need to lie down and get some rest. Quit stressing yourself out. That can't help with us trying to get pregnant."

"I'd love to get some rest, believe you me." Danielle gave me an apologetic kiss on the lips. "I have to go to the office for a little while."

"What? Is that all you think about?"

"No, of course work is not all I think about, but making partner is the most important thing in my life right now."

"Danielle, are you serious? Your job is the most important thing in your life right now? Your fucking job?" I slipped on my pants and walked over to sit down on the bed. "You know what, I wasn't trying to go there, but because this job is so important to you, you don't want to have a baby. You're afraid a baby will ruin your little law career. Just admit it, Danielle. Be a woman about your shit."

She walked over to me. "Maybe to a conceited eligible NBA star, my career is mediocre, but it's mine and I am not jeopardizing it for anyone. Not even you!" she yelled back.

"Thanks for confirming things, Danielle. Go make partner, since that's most important. Just remember, if you don't take care of home, someone else will." I got in bed, pulled the covers over me, and turned my back to her.

"Fuck you, Richard!" She stormed out of the room and slammed the door behind her.

What the fuck did I just do? I sat up in bed and contemplated going after her.

I got up and headed to the kitchen to get something to drink. I grabbed a bottled water from the fridge then headed back to my bedroom. As I passed the dresser, I stopped and picked up Angel's card. I took a sip of water and contemplated for a moment.

After taking another sip, I decided to give her a call. I figured Danielle would be impressed if I was able to show her some wedding invitations or location ideas or colors or something. I got the phone, sat down on the bed and dialed the number on the business card.

"This is Angel," a female voice sang from the other end of the phone.

"Hey, Angel. This is Richard."

"Oh, yes. Hello, Richard."

"I didn't expect to call so soon, but I figured I'd surprise the wifey and get things rolling a bit."

"Okay. Well, when and where would you like to meet to discuss things?"

"How about the Atlanta Fish House."

"Perfect. Let's say tomorrow at noon."

"See you then."

When I pulled up to the restaurant, I got out and handed my keys to the valet. As I headed toward the doors, I saw Angel standing there waiting for me.

She looked down at her watch. "On time. Impressive."

"I handle my business." I held the door open for her.

After ordering our drinks and appetizers, Angel immediately jumped right into business. "So lets start with the basics," she began.

I couldn't help being distracted by the sight of her perfect breasts. I nodded, forcing my eyes to stay focused on her face.

"Richard, what colors is your wife interested in?"

"Look, Angel, I'm gonna be honest with you. I have no idea what my fiancée wants. I was hoping to get things started to impress her. I fucked up with her last night, so I'm trying to win her heart back."

"Awwww, how sweet." She sipped her tea. "Okay, let me help you out here. I'm going to start by asking you a few questions to get a feel of her personality, and we can go from there."

Angel asked a hundred and one questions, from Danielle's work to her leisure. By the time she finished with all those questions I thought she should be able to plan the entire damn wedding with no assistance form Danielle or me.

An entrée and dessert later, our discussion was done. With the one piece of information I was able to provide— the actual wedding date—Angel was able to give me plenty of starting points. She had already chosen a few possible locations. She even brought some color swatches and samples of invitations. I must say, the girl knew her stuff.

"Thank you so much. I'm sure my wife would be pleased," I said as I paid the bill.

"You know what would be even more pleasing?" She grabbed her purse and stood up.

"What's that?"

"It would be great if you planned the entire wedding alone. I mean it's not every day that I'm going over color swatches with the groom-to-be," she said as we headed toward the exit. "I think your effort is to be commended. Usually it's the bride-to-be who always has the stress of wedding planning. Why don't you take on that responsibility? I mean, it will be a first, but I'll walk with you each step of the way."

"Bet!" I yelled back as I walked over to my Range Rover.

Things went pretty well. I can't wait to share this with Danielle, I thought as I headed to Run And Shoot to ball with the fellas. I dialed Danielle as I headed toward the gym. The phone rang continuously, but she didn't answer. I left her a message, informing her that I had a surprise for her.

"If this doesn't get me a baby, I don't know what will." I said to myself.

Chapter 60

Ceazia

Give Them an Inch . . .

"Ungrateful little fucka," I mumbled to myself as I straightened the small mess left from my ecstasy nightmare last night. I was hoping Parlay would at least spend his entire birthday weekend with me. At times I swore he had some other chick out there on the side. Even though I offered him every sexual fantasy imaginable, he only wanted to sex me fifty percent of the time I wanted to sex him. So who was getting the other fifty? I wouldn't have been surprised if he was fucking Juicy on the low, or if he started fucking Diamond.

I noticed his luggage neatly sitting in the corner of the bedroom while he was downstairs waiting on his car to pick him up and take him to the airport. I tiptoed to the door and peeped out to make sure he wasn't anywhere in sight. I then made my way back over to the luggage and stared at it, no longer able to resist the urge to search through it.

I wasn't sure what I was looking for, but I needed some sort of sign to give me an idea of what was going on. I'd changed so many aspects of my life for him and I refused to get played.

As I rambled through his things, I came across condoms. That was strike one. What the hell did he need condoms for? I continued to search but found nothing else suspect. I did, however, come across his itinerary. Luckily, the flight was for him and his manager only. Once again I tiptoed over to the door and peeked out.

Seeing the coast was clear, I rushed to the office and made a quick copy and returned it back to its rightful place.

"*C.*"

"Yeah, baby."

"The car is here. I'm out. I'll be back in a couple of days." He kissed me on the lips and headed out the door.

I walked over to the bedroom window that faced the driveway, separated the blinds with my hands, and watched as he jumped in the black Escalade. I turned around and leaned against the blinds. I couldn't help but wonder if his trip was a legit business trip or just some secret rendezvous.

I decided to go downstairs to make myself a bite to eat. My eyes brightened up as I noticed his cell phone on the nightstand. "Seems like Mr. Parlay was in such a hurry he forgot all about his little cell phone," I said to myself. "Looks like I'm about to get all my questions answered."

I picked up the phone and sat down on the edge of the bed. "Oh, we have a call from Juicy. Strike two!"

I had no idea they'd even exchanged phone numbers. I'd been so focused on Diamond, that I hadn't really paid much attention to Juicy. I should have known as soon as he had the chance that he would get at her. Thanks to one birthday treat from me, I'd hooked up a deadly situation.

I continued to scroll through his numbers, but nothing else came up suspicious. Next, I searched through his cell phone address book. No suspicious females listed there.

Before ending my cell phone investigation, I noticed there were numerous saved numbers with no names. I grabbed a sheet of paper and wrote down every number in his phone that had no name attached, then I continued a couple last searches through his phone. I checked his pictures and finally I his text messages. Still nothing. Now satisfied with my findings, I placed his phone back in its original spot. I wondered how long it would take him to realize that he'd left it, and even more curious to find out if he would come back for it.

I had to know what was up with Parlay and Juicy. I couldn't call her though, that would be too obvious and not my style at all. I'd never been a fan of the "insecure girlfriend" phone calls, so that option was out. That's when it hit me. *Chastity! Why not call Chastity.*

I called her up.

"This is Chastity," she answered the phone in her most professional voice.

"Hey, girl. This is *C.*"

"Hey, Ceazia. I wasn't expecting you to call."

"Well, I wasn't expecting to call either."

"So what made you?"

"Well, I was calling to ask you about one of your girls."

"Juicy?"

"How'd you know that?"

"Well, I can see from last night that you had an added interest in her."

"Yeah, I guess you could say that. Is she on the schedule for the next few days?"

"Yeah, she is. Thursdays through Sundays are her busiest nights."

"Okay, great."

"So you comin' out? Maybe we can play catch up. You know there's a lot of things I want to chat with you about."

"Well, I'll give you a call, and maybe we can chat over lunch," I lied.

"Okay, cool. Is this a good number for you?"

"Yeah," I said, even though I really wanted to say no.

After speaking with Chastity, I decided to call Diamond.

"Hi, sexy."

"What's up?" I replied.

"So you calling for more?" Diamond asked.

I wish I would let your trifling ass fuck my man again. I would have to kill your ass, bitch. "Uuuuummmmm, maybe."

"So what's up?"

"Nothing much. Just sitting here bored and alone. What do you have planned for the weekend?"

"I was planning to spend some time at the dance studio, but other than that, nothing really. Unless you had something in mind."

"Well, why don't we spend the weekend together. That will give us some time to really get to know each other. Parlay's out of town for a couple of days, so it will just be me and you."

"Really? You really want to spend the weekend with me? When should I come over?" Diamond eagerly asked.

"How about now."

We ended the call with her promise of being at my doorstep within the next hour.

Now that I had all the prime suspects covered, I was in the clear to call Parlay. At first, I accidentally called his cell phone that he had left, but then I decided to call his other one. After just one ring, it went straight to voicemail. I knew he wasn't on the plane already, so there was no reason for his phone to be off.

To ensure that I was not getting played by Parlay, I decided it was time for a true private investigator to do a little detective work. While waiting for Diamond's arrival, I grabbed my laptop and did a quick Internet search for Atlanta's top private investigators. After checking out the profile of a few, it didn't take long for me to find one I felt would be able to handle my job. I wrote down all of their information and then called the office. I needed background information on every muthafucka I was dealing with.

I felt as though the investigator had been hired to investigate me, with all the questions he was asking. I told them exactly what I needed and who I needed it on.

By the time our forty-minute conversation was over, I had equipped the investigator with a shitload of information. I provided Diamond's full name and phone number, as well as the information off of her modeling card. I gave them Juicy's place of employment and phone number, and I faxed them a copy of Parlay's itinerary.

Ding-dong!

I logged off the computer and opened the door, having no idea what the weekend had in store for me. Although the little session we had the night before was good, I wasn't up for a bunch of clit-licking and coochie-grinding all weekend. I just needed her here to make sure she wasn't with my man.

Chapter 61

Angel

Bring Out the Gangster in Me

When I started out this morning I had no idea I was going to get this close to that trifling bitch, Danielle. After lunch with her fiancé, Richard, I practically had all the information I needed to ruin her life. But why stop there? I was interested to know what her little friend, Shawn, had up his sleeve. I searched through my purse to grab my cell phone. I figured I may as well give him a call since I was on such a roll.

"Yo!"

"Hey, this is Angel. I met you earlier. You wanted to talk to me about Danielle."

"Oh yeah. What's up?"

"I wanted to know if you wanted to get together today and talk. I just left her fiancé, and I was able to get a lot of information from him. I figured we could combine what we have and maybe come up with something."

"That's cool. Let's meet somewhere near the West End,"

"No can do," I quickly replied. That was definitely not my type of area to be hanging out at.

"What? You afraid to come on this side? Scared of your own people?" Shawn chuckled.

"Not at all, but I am not coming over there. We can meet in the city."

"That's cool. How about Justin's?"

"See you there in about thirty minutes."

In no time, I was at the restaurant. I parked my car and had a few minutes to spare, so I returned a phone call from one of my clients who was trying to change her color scheme only one month before the wedding.

The sweet sound of Mary J. Blige chimed through my cell phone as my indication that John was calling.

"Hi, John," I answered, not too enthused.

"Hello, honey. How's your day?"

"My day is just wonderful," I said, rolling my eyes.

"Well, that's good. I was just checking on you."

"Baby," I said, "did you think about what we discussed last night? Still no one in mind?" I asked, hoping to put the pressure on him. "I want to do this while it's fresh and I'm feeling a little risqué. I'm afraid if we procrastinate, I may change my mind, and it will never happen."

"Okay, Danielle," he said, sounding as if he was trying to end the call. "I'll see what's up and let you know."

"Tonight, John. Let me know what's up tonight," I demanded.

"Okay, all right, Angel," Jonathan replied and disconnected the call.

I had to continue to play my cards right, which is why I let him get away with calling me by that bitch's name. Now I had to get in Shawn's head and see where he was coming from and soon things would be lined up perfectly.

"Angel," I heard someone say as I felt a tap on my shoulder.

I turned around to find Shawn standing there. "Shawn?"

He confirmed with a nod.

"Let's grab a table," I said as I walked from the bar toward the hostess. "Excuse me, miss, we're ready to be seated at a table now."

She quickly sat us down, provided us with a menu and took our drink orders.

Once she walked away, I jumped right into things. "So, Shawn, tell me your story. What's your beef with Danielle?"

"A woman who wastes little time."

"Time is money."

"Then we're on the same page already. I already told you, ma. My beef with Danielle is that she owes me a little something."

"Look, Shawn, I understand that you may have to abide by your little street code and can only tell so much of whatever it is that's going on between you and little Miss Danielle, but I'm not from the streets, honey. You're dealing with a professional woman who knows how to handle her business. I'm not going to be sloppy with anything I do. You can trust me on that. So, if we're going to be working together, I need to know everything there is to know, so that I know what I am dealing with and what I can expect, feel me?"

"Ha-ha-ha! Yeah, ma, I feel ya."

"Okay, great. So what's your story?"

"Listen carefully because I'm only going to tell this story once." He cleared his throat. "I know Danielle from years back. She lived in Virginia and dated this dude that used to cop from me."

"Excuse me?" I interrupted Shawn. "I need you to use English, honey. I'm not familiar with all this street slang."

He shook his head and sighed. "Okay, her man, Snake, was a dude that used to buy drugs from me. Well, he ended up getting murdered, leaving Danielle on her own. Of course she wasn't able to take care of herself and live the life she was accustomed to." He allowed his mind to wander off and reminisce for a moment. He shook his head. "Hell, she couldn't live at all. And you know me, like any man where I'm from would do, I took advantage of her situation. I snatched her up during her most vulnerable time, and we kicked it.

"I basically kept up that lifestyle she was used to, and she kept me pleased. Then after a while she began to trip, being unruly and shit. So every now and then I had to discipline her. Things began to get worse and worse. It got to the point where I had to sleep with one eye open. Then out of nowhere the narcs were on my ass, and I ended up in jail. A month later, Danielle was nowhere to be found. It didn't take a genius to put all the shit together of how all of sudden the narcs were on my ass. Bitch sold everything I owned and dipped, taking the money in my stash with her.

"I figured all along that Danielle had been setting me up," Shawn said, twisting his lips and nodding his head, "but when she disappeared like that, it confirmed things even more. Feds threw decades at a nigga, so that bitch thought she was home safe. I ended up getting out a lot sooner than anyone expected though. As soon as I hit the pavement, I did my homework and found out that she was living here in Atlanta, at some big law firm, screwing her way to the top." He leaned back in his chair and sipped on his drink that the waitress had just sat down in front of him.

"I've already paid her a visit to make my presence in the ATL known. Everything in me wanted to ring that bitch's neck, but I just let her know that all I need from her is my money. All that other shit between us is squashed. I don't even care that she set me up. The fact is, I didn't let her know that I know she's the one that set me up." He leaned forward and stared into my eyes. "But, like I said, I ain't even on that shit. My main mission, ma, is to get my loot and get the hell on." He leaned back in his chair and took another sip of his drink. "Ahhh!" He crossed his arms. "So what's your deal?"

"What do you mean, screwing her way to the top?"

"Come on, now." Shawn sucked his teeth. "You may not be from the streets, but I know you know what the hell I mean by that. Think about it—she's engaged to an NBA star, Richard Anderson, and she's basically secured her position as partner with the biggest law firm in Atlanta by fucking the shit out of one of the senior partners. Some cat named Dario."

Tears began to fill my eyes. This bitch had everything. Was her life not good enough that she had to steal my little joy too?

"Come on, boo, I thought you was a soldier," Shawn said. "You gotta be gangsta for this shit. You can't get on a mission to seek revenge and be crying and shit. I can't risk you crackin' under pressure."

I picked up a napkin and wiped my eyes. Just then the waitress came over to the table. She was prepared to take our orders, but when she saw that I was emotional she looked over to Shawn, who held his hand up signaling to her to come back.

"So what's it gonna be?" he said to me. "Turn that hurt into hate, ma."

"All I want to know, Shawn, is if Danielle is a woman who sounds as though she has everything, what does she need my man for?"

"It's simple. Danielle longs for attention and praise," Shawn explained as though he was Dr. Phil himself. "That was the only missing element from her perfect little life and that's where your husband steps in. He has nothing more but that needed compassion."

"Okay, well, basically I suspected that John was cheating. Not to provide you with too much information, but I knew this when our sex life changed. He would often beg me to be a little more adventurous when it came to us having sex. That just wasn't me though, you know, so I would always decline. That didn't stop him from trying to persuade me. I mean every night he had a DVD or new toy or some sort of gel or cream for me to try, but I just wasn't into it. Then one day everything just stopped. No more nagging or begging about trying things. Hell, he barely even asked for sex, period. I knew then that the reason he wasn't nagging and begging anymore was because he didn't have to. Someone else was giving it to him willingly without a fuss. I was bound and determined to find out just who she was.

"So I started by tracking his cellular bill," I continued. "That was my starting point. From there I was able to obtain a name and the rest is history, leading up to the present." I gave Shawn a serious look. "Leading up to the future."

"Are you ready to order now?" the waitress asked.

"Oh, I'm sorry. Yes, we are." I quickly scanned the menu and ordered.

Shawn did the same.

"I'll be right back out with your orders," she said as she took our menus and walked away.

"I used every connection I had to get any available public information I could on Danielle," I informed him. "Probably just like you did. But then I figured that if she was the one my husband was fucking, then sooner or later he'd lead me to her and that's exactly what he did."

"Just like a man," Shawn snickered. "I don't know what the fuck we be thinking. Guess we just be hypnotized by the scent of pussy and can't think straight."

"Anyway, one day I followed John, and he led me to a

condo that they used as their little love nest. I saw the two of them enter together like they were husband and wife. That was the final straw."

I waved down the waitress and asked for a glass of water because a bitch was on fire now.

"I followed Danielle to the Atlantic Station Lofts," I told Shawn. "I checked out the place, but it was negative according to the information I had dug up on her. My conclusions were uneventful, but as I was going to my car getting ready to leave, I ran into Mr. NBA, her husband-to-be."

"No shit?"

"No shit, diarrhea, or piss," I said, popping off a little ghetto slang of my own. "He was agitated because I was parked in his reserved spot. We had a couple of words, and that's when I found out that he was Danielle's fiancé."

"He just told you that shit?"

"Not just right out. The name 'Danielle' happened to come up. I knew the odds that he was speaking of the same Danielle I was looking for were damn good. Anyway, I gave him my business card since I just happened to be a wedding planner."

"What about when he mentions your name to her?"

"I do business under my maiden name, so she'll never put it together. And, yep, he did call. We even had lunch together. I was able to gather a whole lot of information from him about our little marked woman."

"Yeah, ma, I think you gon' hold up just fine." He cracked a smile. "So now that we got why we want this bitch so bad out of the way, let's talk about what we're going to do to get her. You seem to have all the brains. So what's our plan? They say a man can never go wrong with a combination of street smarts and books smarts."

"You want your money, and I want her whole world to

cave in. In order to do that, I have to get close to her. The closer I am, the easier it is to destroy her. She definitely doesn't need to know that you and I know each other, so don't even mention John's name to her. Definitely keep that quiet. Meanwhile, just keep putting the pressure on her about your money. Pretty soon, I should be able to give you a little something to help persuade her a little more."

"Damn! I fuck with you, ma. You are gangsta in a high-class kinda way." Shawn laughed. "So once you get close to her, then what? Tell me, Angel, what's the end that's going to justify your means?"

A wicked smile spread across my lips as I proceeded to tell Shawn the details of what I had in mind as the ultimate plot for revenge. Danielle thought her world might have crumbled before, but this time she'll be lucky to even have a life.

Chapter 62

Jonathan

Three's a Party

Angel was really pressuring me about this threesome thing, almost to the point that I was starting to feel uncomfortable. I mean, she was starting to act like me. I couldn't understand it. I had tried to mention a threesome before and she stormed off into the bathroom and cut me off from sex for almost a week. Now all of a sudden she had this thing about pleasing her man. Maybe it was more of a fantasy for her than a moment of pleasure for me. Nonetheless, I was going to at least put forth the effort of making it happen. After all, what does a man have to lose when it comes to a threesome with his wife and his mistress?

I picked up the phone and dialed Danielle's number.

"Hello?"

"Hello, Danielle. How do you feel?" I asked, hoping she would say horny.

"Better. Much better. You know I called the doctor, and you were exactly right. It was panic attacks. Evidently I'm stressing too much. I made an appointment to see a psychologist later in the week."

"Well, that's good. You've gotta take care of yourself. A beautiful woman like you shouldn't be so worried," I said, laying it on thick. "Where are you now?"

"At the office."

"Baby, give yourself a break. Why don't we do dinner?" I figured after a few martinis that would be the perfect opportunity to pop the threesome question.

"I'll have to check. Richard is in town, and he may have something planned for us." She paused. "On second thought, fuck Richard. What time?"

"Let's say seven."

"Perfect. See you then."

I hung up the phone curious as to what old Richard boy had done this time.

"This may be Angel's lucky night after all," I said as I picked up the phone and dialed her number.

"Baby, I have a candidate," I said as soon as she picked up the phone, not even allowing her the opportunity to say hello.

"That fast, huh?"

"Huh? Baby, earlier you were saying I had to hurry and not procrastinate. Is this some sort of trick?"

"No, honey, not at all. I'm just surprised." She paused for a minute. "So who is it? Is it any of the ladies I've met?"

"No. Actually, it's one of my clients. I thought it would be awkward to have a threesome with someone in the office and have to see them every day," I lied.

"Oh, okay. So when will you know for certain whether she's game or not?"

"Well, that's what I was calling you about. I am taking her out to dinner tonight. I've already thrown the idea out there for her to think about. She didn't say no, which means she may be interested. She's never done anything like this before, so she wanted to talk to me about it a little more. I need you to be available around seven just in case she wants you to meet us at dinner, or if she decides to be down with it afterwards."

"Sounds like a plan," she replied. "I'll await your call."

"You do that," I said.

Seven o'clock rolled around in no time at all. I finished up a few things at the office, then called Danielle and confirmed our meeting location. Of course I allowed her to pick the place and she chose Houston's.

When I arrived at the restaurant, Danielle was already there. I walked up behind her and began to massage her shoulders. "We're going to release all that tension tonight." I kissed her on the neck.

"Ahhhh," she moaned. "That feels so good." She turned around and gave me a small kiss on the lips.

Danielle had already signed in our names, and a few moments later, we were led to our table. Once seated, Danielle began to look over the menu.

"So is everything okay with you and Richard? I'm only asking because you seemed a little irritated with him earlier."

"No, everything is not okay. We had a huge fight, and I haven't spoken to him since."

"Hey, hey, hey! None of that. You heard what I said when I came in. We are releasing tension, not stressing. Now what would you like to drink? And I'm not talking about soda or tea."

"How about a shot of Patrón?" Danielle was quick to say.

I looked over my own menu. "What are you eating?"

Just then the waitress walked over to our table. "Are you both ready to order?"

"You ready, honey?" I asked Danielle.

"Sure."

We ordered a couple of appetizers before ordering our main course. Then we ordered more drinks, an apple martini for her and a Heineken for me. I didn't mind her being fucked up, but I needed to be fully aware of all that was going on.

Danielle flagged down the waitress. "Excuse me, could the gentleman and I have another shot of Patrón?"

Three shots of Patrón and three Heinekens later, I was a bit tipsy myself. I made sure the waitress kept my glass full of water, though, to flush out the alcohol.

In between bites of our entrée, Danielle and I found ourselves talking and laughing constantly, but about what, I had no idea.

I looked at my watch. It was already nine o'clock. Time had slipped away. I excused myself and took a trip to the restroom. On my way back to the table, I thought to check my cell phone because I had turned the volume down before going in the restaurant to meet Danielle.

I had five missed calls from Angel. "Damn!" I said to myself under my breath. I made a U-turn and headed back to the restroom to give her a call. Her phone rang, but there was no answer. I waited a few seconds and tried her again, but it went to voicemail.

After a third strike, I headed back to the table to join Danielle and noticed another young lady speaking to her, chatting like old friends. As I got closer my drunken eyes cleared. "Shit! What the fuck!" I said out loud.

They both turned their heads in my direction.

"Oh, you're back. I thought you had fallen in."

"Hi, honey." Angel walked over to me and gave me a hug. "I'll take it from here," she whispered in my ear. She then pulled her head back, winked at me, and kissed me on the lips.

My heart raced as I sat at the table with my wife and my mistress. *God, don't let Danielle say the wrong thing.* The last thing I needed was for Angel to find out that I'd been sleeping with Danielle. And with Danielle in her drunken state, Lord only knew what could happen.

"So, Danielle, I'm sure my husband mentioned our little fantasy to you." Angel sat down in the chair next to Danielle.

"Yeah, he did, but I don't know just how I feel about all that yet," Danielle said in a slur. "I've never done anything like that before. You know, it's not every day a girl gets an invitation to join a husband and wife in a threesome. Then again, in this day and age—"Danielle giggled alone.

Angel scooted her chair closer to Danielle's. "Oh, that's a disappointment." She began to rub Danielle's thigh. "I was really looking forward to it, Danielle. And now that I've seen you, I'm starting to look forward to it even more."

My mouth was hanging open. I couldn't believe this was my wife sitting in front of me. I couldn't help but wonder if Angel had had a few herself before arriving. I'd never seen her with this much courage before.

Angel wasn't the same "I-don't-suck-dick, don't-go-near-my-ass, no-that's-gross" woman. Just seeing her in action made my dick rise. I discreetly slid my hand under the table and began to massage my erect penis, as Angel worked her magic on Danielle.

"I've never done anything like a threesome either," Angel said. "You can ask my husband. I haven't done much of anything, but all that is about to change."

Danielle raised her eyebrows. "You sound as though you have a few tricks up your sleeve."

"I just might." Angel lifted her hand from Danielle's thigh. "And you look like you could probably teach me some new ones." Angel took her index finger and thumb and picked the cherry off the toothpick that Danielle had taken out of one of her drinks. She dangled it in Danielle's face. "What tricks can you do with this?"

"Mmmmm . . . I think I could think of a few things."

"Let's see."

Danielle stuck out her tongue and began to slowly lick all over the cherry, flicking and teasing it with the tip of her tongue.

Angel began rubbing Danielle's thigh again.

This shit is crazy.

Danielle used her entire mouth to inhale the cherry, making sure she sucked on the tips of Angel's fingers in the process. Once the cherry and stem were completely hidden inside Danielle's mouth, she smiled a seductive smile at Angel.

She took her index finger and thumb, and removed the cherry from her mouth. "Now it's your turn," she said, swinging the cherry in front of Angel.

"I don't think I can compete with you, but I'll let you be the judge of that." Angel slowly licked the bottom of the cherry back and forth.

Out of nowhere, Angel bit into the cherry, and some juice squirted onto Danielle's hand. Angel gently took her hand and licked it off.

That was it. I'd seen enough. It was time to take this to the crib. My dick couldn't stand to be teased any longer. "Okay, ladies, let's wrap this up." I signaled for the waitress to come over to our table, paid the bill, and left her a healthy tip.

We all stood up and headed out the door. I felt as though everyone around us knew that we were going home to have a threesome. As silly and as arrogant as it may sound, I felt proud. I straightened my back and walked a little taller than usual. I grabbed each of their hands, one on each side of me, and guided them through the door.

Once outside, each of us began to scramble for car keys. There was no way I could break up this party by allowing each of us to go our separate ways. In addition to that, there was no way I could let Danielle drive. Not only was she in no condition to drive, but I was afraid that if she parted from us, she'd have time to realize what she was about to do and change her mind.

"Hold on, Danielle. I know you don't actually think you are driving. Hand over the keys." I grabbed the keys from her hand. "You can roll with me."

I noticed a dart from Angel. Clearly she was notifying me of her disapproval.

"On second thought, why don't you ride with Angel, and I'll follow behind you ladies?"

Angel took her by the hand. "Yes, Danielle, why don't you ride me—I'm sorry—with me."

Damn! I suddenly thought. *What if the two of them decide to finger each other or something play with each other's clits and cum? Then where will that leave me?*

I packed up my selfish thoughts and headed for my car. Angel had a closer spot than me, so she and Danielle hopped in her car. I finally reached my car and hopped in. Once I started it up, naturally I wanted to head straight to the condo I had rented for me and Danielle's secret rendezvous, but how would I explain that one? I knew that everything was pretty much engraved in stone to go down tonight, but I still didn't feel comfortable enough to bring Danielle to my home. Hard dick or not, something just didn't sit well with me on that one.

I took out my cell phone and dialed Angel's cell phone.

"Yes, John."

"Babe, I was thinking we should get a hotel room."

"For what?"

"I don't know. Forget it. Go ahead to the house." I hung up.

After about a ten-minute drive, I was pulling into the driveway behind Angel. *There's no turning back now.* I stepped out of my car and followed the ladies into my home.

As soon as the women were inside, they began tonguing each other, passionately and rubbing their hands in each other's hair. There went my dick again, damn near busting out of the zipper of my pants.

Angel looked over at me and then at Danielle and signaled us to follow her with the nod of her head. "Come on, let's go, you two."

Up the steps and into our master bedroom, Angel led us like she was the mother goose and we were the goslings. Once in the bedroom, she went to the attached master bath and turned on the water in the Jacuzzi.

"You wanna come stick your hand in it to make sure it's warm enough?"

Danielle made her way over to the Jacuzzi.

"Aren't you afraid getting in the Jacuzzi will sober her up?" I whispered into Angel's ear.

"John, she's pissy drunk. I don't want a damn date rape charge. Plus, the bitch is one step away from being partner at Atlanta's biggest law firm. We would be underneath the jail."

"Feels real good," Danielle said. "I can't wait to get all up in it."

"Good." Angel walked over to me and placed her hands on my chest. "Why don't you make yourself useful and set the bedroom up? Make it a little romantic."

I turned on some music, lit some candles, and brought

out all the toys, lotions, oils and sex games I'd unsuccessfully tried to get Angel to use. Hell, I figured tonight may be the only opportunity I'd get to use them.

Just as I finished setting up things in the bedroom, Danielle and Angel walked in. Angel was wearing the long burgundy and black satin, oriental-looking robe that she always looked so delicious in. Danielle looked pretty edible herself in one of Angel's other robes, an all-black poly and cotton number that fell to her lower thighs.

"Wow! You ladies are beautiful."

Any other time I would have pounced on them like a kangaroo, but of all the moments in the world, of all the situations I've ever found myself in, I picked this one to freeze up. I sat on the bed with a stupid grin on my face. *What the fuck are you doing, John? Get yourself together. This is the best fucking night of your life.* I tried giving myself a little pep talk.

Danielle placed her hand on my crotch. "John?"

"Yeah?"

Angel began to rub my back. "You okay, honey?"

Before I could answer, Danielle was undoing my pants.

"I'm fine. Are you ladies okay?"

"Oh, that's what you're worried about." Danielle directed me to stand up while she pulled my pants down.

I kicked my shoes off and stepped out of the pants.

"John, it's okay. I'm comfortable with it." Danielle gently pushed me back down on the bed.

Angel then proceeded to take off my shirt.

"Angel told me all about you being worried that I may feel as though you are taking advantage of me because I might've had one too many. That was so thoughtful of you."

Danielle caught the look I shot at Angel, but I don't think she realized what it was for. "Give me some paper," she said.

"Huh?" I asked.

"Give me a pen and a piece of paper."

"Right there," I pointed, "in the side table drawer."

Danielle pulled out a pen and a piece of paper from the tablet that was inside the drawer and proceeded to write. I looked up at Angel, who had a puzzled look on her face.

"Here you go." Danielle dropped the pen on the side table and handed me the piece of paper. "Go ahead, read it out loud."

"I, Danielle, willfully agree to engage in a ménage a trois, also known as a threesome, with Mr. and Mrs. Jonathan Powell on this night, April 19, 2006. Signed and dated by Danielle—"

"Now, how's that?" Danielle said as she took the note from my hands and laid it on top of the pen.

"Well, now that we're past that stage, let's have some fun. We can start by playing sexual dice," I suggested, determined to put each one of my pleasure toys that I had spent an obscene amount of money on, into action.

I pulled out the pair of dice. One read *kiss, blow, suck, lick,* and *touch,* the other, *nipple, butt, lips, dick,* and *clit.* I shook the dice and blew on them. "Who's first?"

"I'll go first," Danielle offered. She rolled the dice. *Lick nipple.* "So whose nipple do I lick?"

"The both of ours," Angel was quick to say. "John, get naked." She pointed to my boxers and socks.

Danielle removed Angel's robe and then gently pushed her onto the bed. She began to slowly lick her nipples one by one. When she looked up and noticed that I was completely undressed, she used her index finger to signal me to come join them. As soon as I sat down, she pushed me back and started licking my nipples.

Next it was Angel's turn to roll. She picked up the dice and rolled *kiss lips.*

"Awww, that's way too simple!" Danielle yelled.

Angel grabbed Danielle by the face and tongued her down. She then turned to me and gave me a small seductive kiss.

Finally it was my turn at the dice—*blow clit.*

Danielle screamed, "Whew!!!!! Big money!"

I looked at both ladies. "So where do I start?"

"Here." Angel slid the robe off of Danielle and pushed her on her back.

Danielle pulled her neatly shaved lips apart and gave her pussy a few gentle pats. "Yeah, right here, baby."

I dived in, tongue first.

"Wait!" Danielle grabbed my head and pushed me away. "Pull out the video recorder."

Without hesitation, I pulled out our two-in-one digital camera and set it up. I then went back over to the bed where Danielle had been keeping her pussy warm by rubbing on it.

"Now let's get down to business." Danielle forced my head back to the position I was in before.

I licked her vagina cautiously, trying to please Danielle and provide a little action for the camera, but at the same time, avoid angering Angel.

For the next few minutes, I licked her pussy like I was a dog and she was my feeding bowl. I sucked on her clit, licked it, and plunged my tongue in and out of her pussy until she was fucking my face.

Meanwhile, Angel was making sure her tongue gave each nipple an equal amount of attention.

When that part of the session was over, Angel poured us each a glass of wine. We drank the wine from each other's glasses and tongues until finally, it was time to fuck.

Angel laid me down in the middle of the bed. Danielle began kissing me as Angel massaged my dick, nut sack and all.

I cupped each of their asses and squeezed, not doing any more to Danielle than to Angel. The last thing I wanted was for the needle to get pulled off the record and the party to be over. I then allowed my fingers to travel to their pussies and enter them. Simultaneously, they moaned and flexed their pussies around my fingers.

It didn't take long for both women to want my finger replaced by my dick.

Of course, Angel was quicker to the draw. She hopped on me and slid down my dick like a porno star, and began popping her pussy.

"Ummm." Danielle took her finger and began fondling Angel's clit.

Before long, Angel collapsed on my chest.

Danielle couldn't wait to get hers. With Angel still laying on me, she scooted her up by the ass so that my dick was accessible. She then stuffed my dick inside of her and began fucking me like crazy, banging into Angel.

Angel flinched and closed her eyes. "Oh shit!"

"You like this, baby?" I asked her.

"Yes," she replied and began kissing me.

I grabbed her by the head and shoved my tongue down her throat, while Danielle fucked me so hard that the bed was banging into the wall.

"I'm about to cum," Danielle screamed.

Danielle got up and poured us each another glass of wine. "Just what I need to take the edge off," she said. She sipped. "Ahhh."

"We've gotta get you to your car," I reminded Danielle.

"Yeah, you're right," she said. "I'll call a cab."

"Oh no, you won't," Angel said. "I'll take you."

"Well, thank you." Danielle gazed at Angel. "Angel, you are a beautiful person. I've never met anyone so sweet. Are you sure it's not a problem? It's awfully late."

"I won't have it any other way."

Feeling obligated, I offered to ride along, but Angel refused saying it was girls' time.

I couldn't argue with that one. I saw them off, then headed to the bathroom. I took a hot shower, changed the sheets on the bed, and in a matter of seconds, was off to sleep.

I was startled when I felt a small shake on my shoulder.

"John, wake up."

"Yeah, baby. What is it?" I said with a stretch and a yawn.

"I really like her. She's a nice woman. I thought you said she was one of your clients?"

"No. I met her through one of my clients," I lied.

"Oh, okay," she said as if she was buying it. "She offered me a job, you know."

"Job?" I turned over to face her.

"Yeah. She said once she gets her position as partner, she'd love to have me as a paralegal."

"But, Angel, you know nothing about that line of work. And what about your wedding planning?"

"She said she would train me. I really think this is something I can do along with my planning. It's extra income."

"I don't think it's a good idea, Angel. We're not trying to make this woman a permanent part of our lives. That's just too close for comfort."

"I disagree, but we'll talk more about it tomorrow. Good night." Angel kissed me on the cheek and then fell fast asleep.

The thought of Angel and Danielle working together kept me awake. I tossed and turned for the rest of the night. I started to call Danielle to ask her what the hell was on her biscuit. What type of dumb move was that to offer my wife a job? There was no way this was going to work.

I turned on the television to clear my brain, so that I could finally get some sleep. An hour later, the TV was watching me. Hopefully when I woke up, I would find that my conversation with Angel was nothing more than a nightmare.

Chapter 63

Danielle

Steps away from the Finish Line

My head was pounding as I struggled to put the keys in my front door. When I finally got the door open, I rushed to the bathroom, dropping my clothes on the way, and prayed to the porcelain god. I vomited so much, I had to have thrown up everything I'd eaten for the past two days.

I drug myself from the toilet over to the bathtub and flopped myself inside. I turned on the water and filled it as high as I could without it overflowing and then turned on the jets. I lay my head on my bath pillow and relaxed. As I enjoyed my moment of relaxation, I reminisced over the events of the night.

My thoughts moved to Angel. What a sweet woman. I had no idea she would be so likeable. She was totally opposite from what I expected. The way Jonathan had spoke, you would've thought she was just some boring homebody that liked to nag and gossip.

I wondered what would make Jonathan cheat with me on someone as sweet as her. I knew I could be a stone-cold bitch sometimes, but Angel didn't seem to have a mean bone in her body.

On the ride from the restaurant to her house, she really opened up to me, telling me how she and Jonathan had been dating since she was eighteen and that she was a virgin when they met. She thought her husband resented her because of her lack of sexual experience, which is one reason why she wanted to give him a threesome. She also went on to say how her husband didn't feel her wedding planning business was bringing in enough revenue.

Something in me just had to offer her the position as my paralegal after hearing her story. I guess I saw it as my way to repent for what I had been doing with her husband behind her back. I'd never really had any female friends, but Angel was all right by me.

The more I thought about Angel, the more guilt I began to feel for having a relationship with Jonathan. How could I ruin such a happy marriage? Angel didn't deserve this. Jonathan was loving sweet and thoughtful. She deserved to have her man to herself.

Tears began to well up in my eyes. I stepped from the tub and prepared for bed. Before I got in, I got on my knees and prayed. "God, I know I'm not the spiritual person, but this is one time I need You. I realize what I have done is wrong, Lord, and I need to correct it. I beg for Your strength and guidance with this situation. In Jesus name I pray. Amen."

Bang! Bang! Bang! There was a huge knock on my front door.

Not again. I was sure it was Shawn here to torment me again. I took my time walking to the door. This time I headed to my newly installed back door first. No one was there.

Bang! Bang! Bang!

"I'm coming," I yelled as I headed to the front door. I peeped out the hole and was shocked to see Richard. I opened the door right away.

"Why the fuck you ain't been answerin' yo' phone, Danielle?" He yelled as he forced his way through the door.

"Richard, I don't even know where my phone is. And why are you here banging on my door in the middle of the night?" I asked calmly.

"I've been fuckin' callin' you all day!"

"Don't talk to me like that, Richard. I am not a child." I walked back into my bedroom and closed the door behind me. I had a long night and was too tired for the bullshit.

I was wakened by the bright sun shining through the bedroom blinds. The clock read eight a.m. I got up and walked into the living room, expecting to see Richard on the sofa.

I returned to the bedroom, but there was no sign that Richard was even home. I opened the door and saw a note on the bed.

I already have a demanding career and it seems that you've become more and more involved in yours. This is slowly causing an enormous strain on our relationship. Although it was supposed to be a surprise, I've taken the liberty of planning our wedding. This should give you the time needed to concentrate on your career. Once your new position is obtained, and you are all settled in, I hope you are able to put more time into perfecting our relationship. Until then, I'm stepping away. Maybe this will relieve some of the stress that you are under. Eventually, the time will come when you will have to decide on your career or a family. Hopefully you will make the right decision. Take care.

I was blown by his letter. I wasn't sure if he was leaving me or just giving me the space necessary for my success. Sad to say, but I was glad he left this letter. I loved Richard and wanted to get married, but right now my only priority was my career. With him out the way, I could finally focus on that and not have to worry about planning the wedding or having a child.

As days passed I heard nothing from Shawn, less and less of Richard and Jonathan, and more of Angel and Dario.

After taking on that big case and winning it, I finally received my promotion as partner. I'd also stopped having the panic attacks. I now had no constant pressure from Richard to have a baby, and I was finally at a point in my career where I could tell Dario to kiss my ass.

Richard had finally given me a break, but Dario had stepped in and became an even bigger headache than Richard ever was. Our little fling had obviously gotten the best of him, and he was on some shit now, I mean completely whipped.

Just when I cut Richard off, he decided that he was in love with me and wanted to have a relationship.

"Dario, sweetie," I said, caressing his big fat face as we sat on the couch in his house. I knew this would be the last time I'd ever have to touch this man again. "You've known from the beginning about Richard, and our wedding date is coming up soon."

"I know, but that was then. This is now. I had no idea my feelings for you were going to develop into what they are now."

"Dario, please don't make this any harder for me than it is now." I lowered my head for effect. "I really can't handle this. You know how much making partner means to me.

I'm already having a hard time balancing things out. Please don't add onto it, not now. I have to stay focused."

He looked so fucking pitiful sitting there, eating up every last bit of my lies.

"Who knows what the future holds? Let me get comfortable in my position and marriage. Things could change."

He put his hand on top of mine and looked into my eyes. "Danny, I care about you so much, and I'm gonna respect your feelings. The last thing I want to do is pressure you."

I thought I saw a tear in his eye. *I swear to God if this big, black nigga cries, I'm gonna smack him across his fat face.* This shit was becoming comical.

"Just knowing that the future may hold something for the two of us is enough to keep me going." He leaned in and stuck his disgusting tongue in my mouth.

I quickly pulled away and stood up. I looked down at my watch. "Well, I gotta go now. I have a late appointment with a client."

He stood up to walk me to the door. "I'm gonna miss you, Danielle."

"Dario, we work together every day." I chuckled.

"You know what I mean. Making love to you."

"I'm gonna miss making love to you too," I lied.

As I started toward the door, Dario stood up and followed. "You sure you don't have five minutes to spare?" he asked.

I turned around and squeezed his cheek. "Not even two minutes." I then made my way out of the door. I turned and waved at Dario. I smiled the entire time I walked to my car. I unlocked the door, gave him a wink, got in, and pulled off.

* * *

After I stood up to Dario and told him we could have nothing more, there were several occasions at the office when he tried to be an asshole, but I still remained cordial with him. He wasn't doing anything serious, just small things like increasing my workload and giving me the extra shit that no one wanted. Since I'd hired Angel as my assistant, all the extra shit he piled on me, I gave to her.

Now a co-worker and friend, Angel and I became nearly inseparable, and the guilt about Jonathan began to bother me even more than before.

I'd made up my mind. It was time to cut off any further sexual relations with him. Since the night of our threesome, I had been avoiding Jonathan and distancing myself from him, but I had never really taken the time to just really cut things off. I realized now that he had to go. I needed to tell Angel the truth. I was hoping that she could find it somewhere in her heart to forgive me.

Chapter 64

Ceazia

Gangster for Life

It was time to meet with the private investigator and find out just what the fuck Parlay had been up to. I had gone on as normal, never giving him the slightest clue that I thought he was messing around on me. I still loved him, so the sensitive side of me didn't have any trouble pampering him as I'd done before. After all, it hadn't been proven, so I still gave him the benefit of the doubt.

I watched the clock as the time counted down to my ten o'clock meeting with the investigator. All sorts of things ran through my mind as I drove to my destination. I thought about who it was or if it was more than one chick. I even played out in my head how I would react if I was to find out that he was kicking it with Diamond.

Diamond and I had become rather close over the past few weeks, almost to the point where I would rule her out, but I didn't put nothing past no bitch.

Of course, I arrived at my destination a little early. I took a seat at a table by the window and watched for the investigator to show up, tapping my foot and twirling my thumbs. I was too antsy to even order anything.

"Whew. Thank God," I said to myself as I noticed the investigator walking up. I stood up and flagged him down as he entered Barnes and Noble. "I thought you would never get here," I said as he approached the table. I extended my hand to greet the old, shabby-looking white man.

"Good morning, Ms. Devereaux." He grabbed a seat.

"So what have we got?"

"Well, before we get into the details of my findings, let me explain a few things." He pulled a folder out of his briefcase and placed it on the table. "First, I don't normally like to do the cheating investigating because it's so intense. I've had quite a few bad experiences, so to protect myself as well as others, I give the requested information, but it is also limited."

His last line went in one ear and right out the other. Unless he was going to limit his fee, he was going to tell me every damn thing he had uncovered.

"Now, let me give you the details of my investigation." He unfolded his arms and opened up the folder. "As I noted when you originally hired me, I like to have at least thirty days to do a complete investigation to confirm that the information I've collected is accurate. In your case, we've had a little less than the usual thirty days, because this is only a situation where you wanted proof that your mate is having an affair and nothing more." He began going through the folder, laying out photos. "I followed Mr. Parlay to several entertainment celebrity events, business meetings, and several nights out with the boys. All of Parlay's trips were legit. There were no secret rendezvous, no orgy after-parties, and no groupies waiting outside of his hotel room."

"Mr. Featherworth, I understand that it's policy to give a brief overview, but do you have pictures or video or something to show me of Parlay in the act of cheating on me or something?"

He paused for a moment as if irritated. "Yes, I do." He went to the back of the folder and pulled out a stack of pictures. "These photos were—"

"Just let me have them." I grabbed the stack of pictures from his hand. "I'll ask the questions after I take a look."

The first picture, a side shot, was of Parlay's naked tattooed body. He was grabbing the waist of a firm body that he was pounding from the back. Picture number two was a picture of a pair of hands grabbing Parlay's buttocks tight as he was in the midst of receiving intense brain. The pictures went on and on, shot after shot. I was fuming with anger as I placed the pictures down on the table.

The investigator gave me a moment to gather myself before speaking. "Now, would you like to know where each of the photos were taken?" Mr. Featherworth asked.

"Yes, please," I responded, unsure if I really wanted to know.

"If you look on the back of each photo there is a number. Here is a sheet that corresponds with each number." He handed me a sheet of paper. "The location, time, and date is noted on each." He then pulled out another piece of paper from the file and handed it to me. "Now if I can just get your signature here." He placed an *X* in front of a blank line. "All it states is that I've explained all liability information and my policy in total." He handed me a pen to sign with.

I grabbed the pen and signed my name. As far as I knew, I could have been signing my life away. In a daze, and without saying a word to him, I pulled the envelope that held his final payment out of my purse and laid it on the table in front of him. I got up from the table and headed to my car.

As I drove, things began to set in. *What the fuck made me think I could give it all up for a man?* One thing I'd learned from Vegas was that when you find something you're good at, do it and do it well. If I'd have stuck by that, I wouldn't have been in this predicament. Parlay had definitely pulled one on me, and now he had to pay.

I began to put a plan in action. I could tell from the pictures that I could rule out Diamond and Juicy as suspects. I knew it had to be someone from his camp. The investigator said that all his trips were legit, so that left his personal assistant, the company secretary, or some new female artist on the label or something. Whoever it was, the bitch better beware, because old *C* was back!

Chapter 65

Angel

Time for Some Action

What more could a woman scorned ask for? In pursuit of revenge against my cheating husband, everything had fallen into place just as planned. As I sat at my desk logging off my computer and preparing to end my work day, I couldn't help but think about how close Danielle and I had become. I think she'd even considered me a friend.

One thing I'd noticed about Danielle was that she was out for self. Her priority in life was to do whatever it took to make sure she was set for life. She may have a beer every now and then, but she definitely had a champagne budget. Even though she had a very successful basketball star as her fiancé, she wasn't sitting back and waiting on the goods. The last thing she probably ever wanted to do was to be solely dependent upon a man.

After spending only a few times in the same room with both Dario and Danielle, it was clear to see how she'd used poor little Dario as a stepping stone to get her position as partner in the firm.

Poor Dario was nothing more than tar on the bottom of

her shoe, and if he'd found out how she'd used him, I was sure he would've found a way to get the other partners to vote for discharging her of her position.

Richard and I had become quite a team. I slowly changed my style and appearance to his liking, adding long tracks to my hair and wearing the designer labels that he was so used to buying for his women.

With each outfit, I was sure to wear a plunging neckline emphasizing my breasts, which Richard tried his best not to admire during each of our meetings. But he couldn't help from keeping his eyes from traveling down to my pretty tits. He noticed when I noticed, and I always blushed, letting him know that his wandering eyes were okay by me.

He started to confide in me, asking for advice on his and Danielle's relationship. Always giving the worst advice, I suggested that he do things to occupy himself and give her space. I suggested that he do all the things she hated, like hanging out with his friends and spending time out of town. I told him that she'd end up missing him so much that she'd come to her senses real quick. I convinced him that right now Danielle's career and health were most important and that he shouldn't give her any extra stress or hindrance.

Shawn had been patiently waiting for me to get things rolling so that he could make his move.

I told him, "Tell her that you are going to tell Richard about the debt she owes and her past involvement in the game."

"I don't see that making her sweat none," Shawn said into the phone.

"Then threaten to tell Richard about the details of her little dinner with me and John." I paused. "On second thought, that might be too much ammo. Threaten to let her little affair with Jonathan come to the light, then threaten to tell me about her affair with my husband." I figured that would be enough to get her a little nervous.

"All right," Shawn agreed. "But I ain't no man of idle threats, so we need to come with the real. Fuck all this fore-play."

"Oh, don't you worry, Shawn. The best is yet to come," I said before ending the call.

As I left the office, I went to go tell Danielle to have a good evening, but she was still in depositions, so I headed out of the office and drove home.

After arriving home, I walked up to the front door. I took a deep breath and then exhaled. I put the key in the lock and went inside. Closing the door behind me, I headed straight to the living room, where I knew John would be sitting, watching the evening news.

"We need to talk," I said right away.

"What's up, honey?" John stood up from his chair to make his way over to greet me with a kiss.

I put up my hand to stop him in his tracks. "It's over."

"Excuse me?"

"It's over Jonathan. I'm not happy in this relationship. You don't treat me the way you should. I deserve better. I'm just settling by being with you."

"Angel, where is all of this coming from? Listen to your-self. Do you know what you are saying? This is crazy." He headed toward me.

"I know exactly what I am saying, and I mean every word. I want you out now."

"Don't do this."

"It's over, John, it's over." I walked away.

"Angel, don't walk away from me," he called from be-hind me. "Don't make me do this, Angel." He grabbed me by my shoulder.

I jerked around, pulling my shoulder away from his hand, only to find it around my throat.

"Damn it, Angel, listen to me!"

"Get off of me. Let me go," I yelled as I hit him, begging for mercy.

"You are not going anywhere. We've been together too long. I won't let you go." He threw me to the floor.

In all our years of marriage, he'd never laid a hand on me.

Scrambling to get away from the raging bull now coming toward me, I crawled into the guest bathroom. When John tried to grab me, I kicked at him and got up and ran into the guest bath. "Go away. Just leave me alone. It's over. Just leave, John," I shouted through the bathroom door as tears flooded my eyes.

"Open the door." John kicked the door. "Open the fucking door, Angel." He kicked it again, and for a moment there was complete silence.

Boom! The bathroom door came crashing off its hinges, with John standing there looking like a mad man.

Smack, smack, smack! He hit me repeatedly in my face.

I struggled to my feet and ran to the kitchen and grabbed the cordless phone off its base. Even with him yanking at me and hitting me, I was still able to dial 9-1-1.

"Help me, please. My husband is trying to kill me," I screamed into the receiver, pretending to talk to the police. I had dialed 9-1-1 but I pushed the flash button to hang up the phone before the operator could answer.

"No need to call the police," John said, releasing me. "I'll be gone before they get here." He walked over to the utility closet and grabbed a garbage bag from it. He then headed to the bedroom. "You ain't even gotta tell me what the fuck is going on," he yelled. "I knew it was pussy you loved. All that bullshit you spoke about making me happy. I knew from the day you mentioned a threesome it was all for you," he continued to rant as I heard things slamming and crashing. "So what? You love the pussy that much that you're leaving me for Danielle? Well, guess what, Angel? I've been fucking Danielle for months now. That little threesome wasn't a first for me to be all up in that. Didn't you see how perfectly my dick fit inside her? So how do you like that? Fuck you, Angel! Fuck you and Danielle!" He walked out of the living room and to the front door with a garbage bag full of clothes and shoes.

Once I heard the front door slam, I exhaled and hung the phone back on the receiver. I ran to the front door and peeped out to make sure John had driven off. I opened the door and locked the security storm door, the big door, and placed the chain on it. I turned around and slid down the door.

I knew all along about him and Danielle, but to hear it come from the horse's mouth just brought on a new pain. He said those words to me like I wasn't shit, like I'd meant nothing to him all along.

I sobbed hysterically as the reality set in. After what seemed like hours of crying, I gathered myself and went to the master bathroom to take a hot shower. I took off all my clothes and walked over to the mirror to examine my bruised body and swollen face. My hair stood on top of my head in every direction, and my eyes were red and swollen from crying. I wondered if there was any hope after this. Spirits low and unsure of what to do next, I was ready to give up on my plot of revenge. I had no more energy or fight in me. I was tired, hurt, and drained.

After getting out of the shower, much calmer and relaxed, I began to straighten up the mess made from me and John's struggle. I still couldn't figure out why he was in such a rage. Hell, even if I did want to fuck Danielle instead of him, it wasn't like he himself hadn't been fucking her all along anyway.

As I cleaned up the house, I tried to think things through. I decided that it was best to put all this behind me. I had to let it go and move on.

I went into the bedroom and gathered any memories or connections I had to Danielle. I gathered the pornographic home DVD we'd made the night of our threesome, the copy of the condo key, and the the ménage a trois contract she'd written. I placed all these things in a bag and got in my car. Unsure where I was headed, I began to drive. I drove around looking for the perfect place to toss the items.

I ended up near Jonathan and Danielle's secret love nest. I drove cautiously as I entered the neighborhood. Since I had kicked John out, I was sure this was where he had gone. What I didn't expect to see was Danielle's car parked in the driveway behind his.

All the aggression from before hit me like a ton of bricks. I sat and focused on pacing my breathing so that I didn't do anything stupid.

Instead of running up in there and going crazy, I drove away. I drove as fast as I could to get out of the area. I knew if I'd stayed any longer, I may have done something I'd regret. In what seemed like five minutes flat, I was home.

I drug myself into the house and made my way into the kitchen. I poured myself a glass of wine and turned on the TV. Sure I had decided to leave John, but I refused to let that bitch Danielle win. The game was back on and poppin'. There was no turning back now. I took the final sip of my wine and laid down to sleep. I had a big day ahead of me.

* * *

The next morning I woke up before the alarm clock even went off. I took my time getting dressed, had a hearty breakfast, and headed in to work.

I walked in and sat right down at my desk. "Good morning, Danielle."

"Hey, girl!" she said all perky, as if John hadn't told her about our altercation and the little secret he'd shared with me about their affair. "I'm glad you're a little early. I have this big meeting this afternoon. Of course, Dario failed to tell me until last minute, and I need to prepare for it."

"Oh, you know I got your back."

"I know. Which reminds me, we really need to talk."

"What's up?" I asked.

"Well, I was hoping we could chat over lunch or something."

"Girl, you know it's gonna eat me up if you don't talk to me now."

"Okay, but we gotta make this quick," she said. "Step into my office."

I followed Danielle into her office.

"Well, this is quite awkward for me, but it's been on my conscience for some time now." She sat down on the corner of her desk as I stood by the door. "I really would have preferred for us to have this conversation outside of the workplace, where we'd have time and privacy." She took a deep breath and then walked over to the window and stared out of it for a moment. She turned her attention back toward me. "Well, we've grown very close in such a short period of time, and I feel like I've known you for years. You're like the best friend that I never had and it's only right if I come out and tell you the truth." Danielle sighed and grabbed my hands.

I wasn't sure if this was to keep me from hitting her, or if it was to console me, but either way I was prepared for the worst.

"Angel, Jonathan and I had relations prior to our ménage a trois, and I'll understand if you no longer—"

"Shhhhh! Say no more, Danielle. I know all about it. Last night I realized that John and I could no longer be together. I told him I was leaving him and in the middle of our argument, he told me all about the relations you all had." I put my head down momentarily and then looked back up at Danielle. "Now I have a confession—I'm in love with you. I am willing to put all this behind us and start new, just you and me."

Danielle was speechless as she looked up at me.

"Last night John and I had a huge fight, and he beat me. He actually put his hands on me, Danielle." I started to cry. "He had an anger I'd never seen before. I mean you should have seen the look in his eyes. He shouted things about me loving the sexual experience you and I had, and he was right. I did enjoy it, and I want to continue to have it."

"I don't know what to say. This is all just too much, too fast." She began to pace.

If I could have captured the confused look on her face, I would have bottled it up. It was priceless.

Knock, knock!

"Come in."

I wiped my tears away.

Dario walked into the office, probably jealous that Danielle was spending time alone with someone other than him.

"Look, Danielle, I'll talk to you later."

At my desk, I prepared the files Danielle needed for her meeting. I intentionally left out important information and only compiled notes that were basically useless. Pretending to be busy, I buzzed Danielle, who was still in the office with

Dario. It wouldn't have surprised me if she was sucking him off every now and then, just to keep him quiet.

"Yes, Angel."

I could tell she was on the speaker phone. "I was just wondering if I should clear your schedule from lunch through the end of the day, since you have this big meeting."

"Oh, yes please. Thank you."

I waited for her to disconnect the call. Danielle had a bad habit of not releasing the call when she was on speaker phone. I listened as she and Dario chatted.

As usual, Dario was complaining. He wanted more between them, he missed her and he was starting to feel as though she had used him, blah, blah, blah.

After a while I was bored listening to him complain and beg. Just as I was about to disconnect the call, it dawned on me that I could use this to my advantage. I pressed the conference call button and called my extension, which of course went straight to voicemail, to record the entire conversation.

As Danielle darted out of her office and headed toward the conference room, I handed her the file I had put together and sent her into her meeting poorly equipped. She was headed to a gun fight with a knife.

I couldn't wait for that meeting to end. I didn't even go to lunch. I wasn't going to take the chance of putting on my best performance. She came storming out of the meeting at around three o'clock, signaling with a nod for me to come into her office.

"What happened here, Angel?" She tossed the file on her desk.

"What do you mean?"

"This file is missing so much of the information I needed to present a complete overview. There was stuff in here that wasn't even relevant to this file at all. I found myself rambling on and on."

"I'm sorry, Danielle. My mind has really been gone this morning. I've just been through so much. I'm torn between my feelings for you and the hurt I feel. I mean the fight with John last night was a bit much, and then the thought of you all being together is really starting to get to me," I said, fishing for pity.

"I understand." Danielle sighed. "What more could I expect?" She flopped down in her chair. "Look, I know the guys are going to be calling me any minute now to discuss what happened today in that meeting. I probably won't be needing you anymore today anyhow, so why don't you take the rest of the day off to get yourself together? Take a couple of days off if need be."

I walked over to Danielle and hugged her compassionately. I rubbed her back then brought my hands up to her breasts and massaged them.

As she dropped her head back in pleasure, I gently grabbed her by the neck and placed my tongue in her mouth, kissing her passionately.

"I'm sorry about the mess-up today," I told her. "I know what you really want to do is let me go permanently and I understand, but I'd rather have you than this job. So to make this a lot easier for you, for the both of us, I won't be returning."

Her lack of eagerness to try to change my mind let me know that everything in her really did want to fire me, but she felt so guilty that she couldn't.

"Think about everything I've said to you today about how I feel. You might be letting me walk away from this job, but I hope you decide not to walk away from me and give us a chance." I gave her one last peck on the lips and walked over to the door. "Please make the right decision."

I returned to my desk and started cleaning things out completely. I had already gotten a box to put my things in.

Once I was all packed up, I retrieved the previously recorded message from my voice mail and forwarded it to the other two senior partners, but not before recording an introductory message of my own first. "This is a conversation that I overheard," I said into the phone. "Wishing to stay anonymous, I will just forward this for you all to review. Taking the company policies and guidelines into consideration, I am sure this is a matter that you would like to be aware of."

I picked up my box and headed out to my car. I called Shawn on my way out.

"What's up, Angel?"

"Nothing much. I've started to put things in action. Now it's your turn," I said.

"Dat's what's up. Where do I need to step in?"

"Well, I have a few things that you could definitely use to your advantage."

"Oh yeah?"

"Yep. I have these pictures that you won't believe and a letter to go with it. You call up miss home-wrecker and tell her that you have these things, and trust me, she'll give you whatever you want."

"Nuff talk. Where you want to meet?"

I made arrangements to meet Shawn and give him the letter and a copy of the pictures I'd edited perfectly from the DVD, making sure my face was cropped out of each photo.

I then called Richard and confirmed our weekend meeting to go over some final stages of the wedding planning. Pleased with the little destruction I'd already caused by popping off a couple of firecrackers, I headed home, looking forward to the big boom.

Chapter 66

Jonathan

True Colors

Bang, bang, bang, bang!
I woke to the sound of someone banging on the door. I rubbed my eyes and headed to the front door. I opened it to find a crying Danielle.

"I have to end this. We can no longer deal with each other. It's karma. Bad things are happening because of the affair you and I had," she cried hysterically and shoved a number of papers in my face.

I looked at the paper and read the title that appeared on her company letterhead, "Discharge of Commitment of Duties." No explanation was needed there. Danielle had been fired.

"What happened, Danielle? You can't honestly think you got fired because you had an affair with me?" I laughed at the thought.

"This is not a joke!"

"Danielle, what you are saying is crazy. I know you're upset because you lost your job, but I'm sure there is a logical reason."

"We never should've had an affair. We never should have had a threesome. This is all your fault!"

"Maybe you lost your job because you were screwing the partner. Did you ever think of that?"

"Stop! Just shut up!" Danielle screamed.

"The truth hurts, huh?"

"This is my life, Jonathan. I've worked hard for this."

"You're not the only one who's lost something, Danielle. Have you forgotten that I've lost my wife?"

"I'm sorry, but partner with the biggest law firm in Atlanta doesn't come a dime a dozen."

"Well, I guess you should have thought about that before you convinced my wife to leave me."

Danielle put her hands on her hips. "Excuse me?"

"Come on, Danielle, I'm not stupid. You think I didn't notice how things changed? First, we had a threesome, and you turned my wife out. Then you offered her a job. Then you two started spending more and more time together, and I started hearing less and less from you. Next, out of nowhere, my wife decides to leave me. I'm sure that's because she loved your pussy more than she loved my dick." I laughed and walked out the room.

"Are you serious?" Danielle followed behind me and kept going on and on.

"What did you expect to gain from Angel? I know you, Danielle. You don't deal with anyone unless you can get something out of them. So what is it? What does Angel have to offer?"

"I can't believe what you are saying? You really surprise me. First, you're hitting women, and now this."

"Okay, Danielle, you are obviously in denial, so here it is, straight and forward. Let's start with Richard. Poor Richard has no idea that you are only interested in him because he's a husband that can provide a more than stable income for you. He's nothing but a security blanket that you can't wait to spread out and get all wrapped up in. He's a perfect kickstand for times like this. Then poor Dario was nothing more than a crutch to get your position as partner. Me? I couldn't provide you with any thing material other than a few pieces of clothing. But you needed me for that attention, affection, and a listening ear that no one else provided. Now Angel, I can't figure out for the life of me what you needed from her. Was it pussy? What was it, Danielle. Help—"

Smack! I was interrupted mid-sentence by a slap to the face.

I grabbed Danielle by the wrist. "I think it's time you leave," I said through clenched teeth.

Danielle snatched her wrist from my grip, grabbed her things, and stomped out the door, slamming it behind her.

Chapter 67

Danielle

The Walls Are Crumbling

I could have sworn someone had cast an evil voodoo spell on me. First, I get caught up in a crazy love triangle between Jonathan and his wife, causing me to lose a friend and assistant, then I lose my job, and now I was on the verge of losing my man.

Every time my phone rang I damn-near jumped out of my skin because Shawn had been calling my phone, constantly making all sorts of threats about how he was going to ruin my life. He claimed that he knew about me cheating with Jonathan and Dario, and said that he planned to tell Richard.

I didn't think he'd really take it that far, but I was in no position to take any chances. Right now Richard and a healthy savings account were all I had left. Unsure if Shawn had really gone through with things, I decided to give Richard a call to feel him out.

"Hi, honey."

"What's up?" he said with little emotion.

"Nothing much, just thinking about you. How are things

going with the wedding planning? Now that I'm no longer working, I have a little time on my hands. Maybe I can help out."

"Nah, baby, that's quite all right. I'm doing a pretty good job handling this on my own. All I need you to do is rest up for these last couple of weeks," he said.

"Okay. Well, good luck on your game tonight. Will you be coming home this weekend?" I asked, hoping to see my man.

"Yeah, I'll be there. I have a couple of last-minute things to wrap up with the wedding planner."

Lately all I'd heard from Richard was, "Wedding planner this, wedding planner that," but I guess I should've been happy. Not many women can say their fiancé planned the entire wedding.

My phone began to beep, so I quickly wrapped up my conversation with him. "All right, sweetie. Well, call me when you get into town."

"Will do," he said as he hung up.

I clicked over to my other line. "Hello," I said in my most annoyed tone, aware that it was Shawn on the other end.

"Time is ticking, Danielle. Maybe you think this is a game. I've given you one too many chances. This is it, shortie. Either come up off my loot, or you're gonna be very sorry."

"Okay, Shawn, let's make a deal. I'll give you ten thousand now and give you a little more in a couple of weeks. As I'm sure you know, I am not working right now and I have a wedding coming up, so my money is kind of tight."

Shawn remained for a bit. Then he said, "Cool."

I made arrangements to meet Shawn and gave him the money as promised. I figured that would hold him at least until the wedding.

If I could just have until then, that would be long enough to keep him at bay. Once Richard and I said, "I do," everything would fall into place. Once I was Mrs. Richard Anderson, I planned to move from Atlanta to Houston, where my future husband spent most of his time. Hopefully this time I could pull a disappearing act. Satisfied with my preliminary plans, I decided to watch a little television.

As I sat on the couch and flipped through the channels of the plasma TV, Angel came across my mind. Ever since she'd resigned a few days ago, I hadn't spoken to her. I picked up my cell phone and gave her a call.

"Hello?" she said in a sleepy voice.

"Hi, Angel. It's Danielle," I said softly. "If this is a bad time—"

"No, no, it's fine."

"I just wanted to give you a call since we hadn't spoken in a few days. How is everything?"

"I'm making it. I haven't spoken to John, but I've been working on a big wedding and it's kept me pretty occupied."

"Great! I'm glad things are working out for you. Things haven't been as rosy for me, though. I lost my job at the firm."

"Oh my God! What happened? I'm so sorry to hear that, Danielle."

"Somehow the senior partners found out about a little relationship I was having on the side with one of the partners. The funny thing is, they only fired me and not him. Deep inside, I feel like he had something to do with it. I mean, it just so happens that as soon as he and I had a deep conversation about us not having a committed relationship, things went downhill."

"I'm truly sorry. I know how hard you worked for that position and how much it meant to you. You must be devastated. Is there anything I can do to help?"

What a sweet girl! I thought. I'd never run into such a nice girl. The more I talked to her, the more guilt I felt. Even though I had completely cut John off, I still felt like I owed her something.

"Why don't you come over? I'll call over the masseuse and chef, and we'll have a day of pampering. I'm sure we could both use it."

Angel happily agreed and headed right over.

Chapter 68

Ceazia

Regretful Affair

With Diamond on my side, we rode through the streets of Atlanta on Parlay's tail like Thelma and Louise. The pictures were just what I needed to confirm my suspicions that Parlay had a bitch on the side. Now I planned to do a little detective work of my own and catch him in the act. I was on him like white on rice.

Dressed in all black and loaded with a camcorder and gun, I was better prepared than a crazy paparazzi.

We pulled up to a nightclub in the downtown area of Atlanta. I had never been to it before and wasn't the least bit familiar with it. It looked like a strip club, and the crowd of people in line seemed sort of odd. The people just didn't look like the type of crowd typical for clubs Parlay frequented. The people were dressed as though they could care less what celebrity popped up on the scene.

Parlay drove straight to the valet and I fell back, parking in the main lot. I watched as he chit-chatted with a couple of folks and then walked right through the front door without a problem.

"All right, girl. You ready?" Diamond rested her hand on mine for support.

"Let's do it."

We got out of the car and headed to the back of the line. After about a fifteen-minute wait, Diamond and I were in.

Once inside, I looked around the club. It had a weird vibe to it, like they were in a world of their own.

The club was split into two areas, a downstairs and an upstairs floor. We went into the first side of the club. There, we saw a number of female strippers on the bar, on stage, and a few giving table dances. Unlike most of the predominantly black strip clubs in the area, this club had all races of women dancing.

When Diamond and I had searched the area well enough to convince ourselves that Parlay wasn't around, we moved to the next room. This room was full of male strippers. Surely Parlay wasn't in there, so I walked right back out and headed to the upstairs room.

At the bottom of the stairs a bouncer asked if our name was on the list, saying that area was reserved for a private party.

"Oh, I'm with Parlay's group," I said, sure his name was on the VIP list.

The bouncer scanned the list quickly. "No Parlay here, ma'am."

Hoping I could use some of my sex appeal, I flirted a little, then took a peep at the list. "Well, maybe it's just under my name."

"What's your name?"

"My name is Tina," I said, choosing a name I saw listed on the paper.

"Okay, let's see." He scanned the list again. "There you are, Tina plus one," he said, checking me off the list

"I'm Tina, and here's my plus one." I grabbed Diamond

by one hand, as she gave the bouncer a flirtatious wave with the other.

We headed up the stairs to VIP, where things began to get stranger and stranger. All the women seemed to be oversized, overdressed, and wore too much makeup. Everybody was so flamboyant, it was definitely over the top.

I walked to the bar to get a drink, continuing to scan the crowd.

"Whatcha havin', sweetheart?" a deep voice said.

I turned around to see a RuPaul lookalike like no other. That's when it hit me. We obviously had strolled into a party for drag queens. No wonder Parlay's name wasn't on the list.

Diamond and I both looked at each other at the same time and did everything we could to keep from laughing. Never mind the drink, I grabbed Diamond, and we exited the room just as quickly as we had entered. That little scene was enough for me.

We left the club and headed to the car. We pulled out of the parking lot into a line of cars that were all waiting to exit the lot. Horns were blowing, and people were yelling at the one car holding up the line.

I pulled around to take a look at the car. To my surprise, it was Parlay. I pulled back into a parking spot to be sure he couldn't see me, then I called his phone.

"What up?" he answered.

"Hey, honey. What are you doing?"

"Nothing. Chillin'. Leavin' the club."

"You on your way home?"

"Nah, so you probably should stay at your crib tonight. I'ma bring some of the fellas over. We got a new artist we tryin' to break in, you know, sort of like an initiation."

"Oh, okay."

I rushed to Parlay's house. I knew him and his entourage wouldn't come in until late, giving me just enough time to go to the house and set some things up before he arrived. Using the "Private I" equipment I had gathered, I set up a hidden recording device in his bedroom, as well as the two guest bedrooms. If any action was going down, I would definitely catch it on camera.

Satisfied with my surveillance set-up, I left, and Diamond and I went to my crib for the night.

The next morning I woke up eager to find out just what had gone down at Parlay's house the night before. I jumped out of bed and took a quick wash-up. I got dressed and dropped Diamond off at home, certain I could handle the rest by myself.

"If you need me," Diamond said as she exited the car, "you know I'm just a phone call away." She winked and walked away.

I smiled, finding comfort in the fact that for the first time in a long time, I just might have met someone who actually did have my back.

After watching Diamond walk up her walkway and get into the house safely, I headed straight to Parlay's place. I pulled up to the house and saw that both his and his manager's cars were in the driveway.

No matter what was going on, Parlay's manager, Hakim, was always at his side. I wouldn't be surprised if he was the one who had arranged every booty call Parlay had ever had, handpicking the women to Parlay's preference and shit.

"Good morning," I sang as I entered the house.

The alarm system sounded. "Front door ajar," the automated voice stated as an indication that I had entered the front door.

After disengaging the alarm, I began to look around the

silent house. Surprisingly, for a bunch of fellas to have occupied it the night before, it was pretty clean.

"Don't look like much of a party went on here," I mumbled. I walked to Parlay's bedroom and put my ear up against the closed door and heard nothing.

Next I slowly opened it, only to see Parlay's head sticking out from the covers that wrapped his body. He was sound asleep.

I tiptoed over to the window.

"Rise and shine, sweetie." I opened the curtains, allowing the sunlight to shine right into Parlay's crusted eyes.

"Uuuummmmm . . . close the blinds, *C*," he grunted.

"Get up, baby. I have the cleaning service coming in today," I lied.

"Damn, Ceazia!" He threw back the covers and sat up in the bed.

"Come on, sleepyhead, get it moving." I clapped my hands to hurry him on.

Parlay stood up and stretched. "Damn, girl!" He rolled his eyes at me as he climbed out of bed and headed for the bathroom.

I stood there listening as he closed the door behind him. After he peed and flushed the toilet, I heard him turn the shower on.

Bingo! I ran and gathered up all the surveillance equipment. I started with his room, and headed to the first guest room. Afterwards I went to the second guest room. When I entered through the door, I was met by Hakim. *Shit, I forgot about his ass.*

"Damn! You could have at least warned a nigga," he yelled, walking out of the room ass-naked, brushing by me, and nudging me on the shoulder.

I figured he was still drunk. "Sorry."

It didn't take Parlay any time to get dressed and head

out the door. Like every Sunday morning, he was headed to the gym.

As soon as he left, I began reviewing the video, and as expected Parlay was up to no good. I almost threw up at the events I was witnessing. "Nooooooooooooo, God, noooooooo, anything but this." I ran through the house. I had no idea where I was running to, I just ran and ran to get away from that haunting image. I ran up the stairs, stumbling near the top. There I just lay and sobbed. "Why, God, why?"

Ring, ring!

"Hello," I said, still sobbing.

"Oh, baby, you don't have to tell me. The video wasn't good?"

I spent the next hour telling Diamond about the video. She provided well-needed support and, because of her, I was able to get myself together and come up with a plan of revenge.

Before long, the hurt and great disappointment I'd felt had turned into a great anger. From this point on, it was straight gangster. I started with the media. I called the radio stations and started the rumor. Remaining anonymous, I told them what I'd discovered and told them I had proof. Then I hit the Internet, starting with myspace.com, BET, MTV, and any other message board I could get to. I even posted pictures and put a snippet of the DVD on sale through Internet purchase. By the end of the night I'd spread my discovery all over the United States.

I packed up all my things and cleaned out Parlay's safe. Then I headed back to my condo, where Diamond met me. I knew it wouldn't be long before Parlay would be contacting me, and it would be war. I made arrangements to have my things packed up, and headed out.

Amazingly, leaving Diamond was the hardest part. We'd grown closer than I had ever expected over the past month.

Not willing to let me go, Diamond decided to roll with me, and off to Virginia the two of us headed.

Once in VA, it was back to the old stomping grounds. I had a new outlook on life and a new attitude. With that in mind, I headed straight to Dee Dee for a new hairstyle to go with my new attitude.

Surprised to see me, I received service as soon as I walked in. It was great to be back in the old neighborhood. The shop hadn't changed one bit.

"What chu havin', lil' *durty*?" the assistant mocked the slight Southern accent I had picked up during my short stay in Atlanta.

"Cut it all off," I said, shocking everyone. "Not just a trim, not just split ends. It all must go."

The entire shop got quiet.

Dee Dee said, "What?"

"Cut it all off."

"Are you sure? Because once it's gone—"

"I'm sure." I shot her back a look as if to say, "What are you waiting for?"

Dee Dee grabbed a wad of my hair and chopped it off. "Well, there is no turning back now." She laughed.

"That's cool. Give me a Mohawk," I said.

A couple of hours and a new hairdo later, I was out of the beauty shop and on my way to the tattoo shop.

I went out on a limb due to my new transformation. I walked in the shop and chose a tribal tattoo. "I'll take this from the beginning of my ass crack all the way up my spine and to my neck," I said, again shocking everybody in the shop.

"That's gonna be painful," the artist stated. "Is this your first tattoo?"

"Yes, it is."

"You sure—"

"Yes, I am."

"Okay, let's do it."

Chapter 69

Richard

Party Over

"What a fucking night!" I mumbled as I grabbed my bags and headed out the locker room after the game.

"Anderson! Anderson!" I heard a fan shout as I exited the door.

I turned to see a thugged-out fella standing in the cut. Unsure if this nigga wanted to rob me or beef, I kept walking.

"Yo, son, I think you may want to hear this," he continued to yell and walk toward me.

I really wasn't for the bullshit, so again I tried to ignore him and kept walking.

"I'm trying to holla at you about your wifey, Danielle," he shouted.

I had to stop at that point. "What's up, man?" I dropped my bag on the floor, just in case I had to go toe to toe with this nigga.

"Yo, kid, I ain't got no beef. I'm just trying to hand you these. It's just a little something you may want to look at be-

fore you get married next week." He handed me an envelope and walked off.

Now safe in my car, I decided to take a look. I wondered
what was so important that this nigga went through so
much to get it to me. Everything, from anthrax to hate
mail, ran through my head as I opened the envelope.

"Pictures?" I said to myself, as I pulled out the photos
backwards.

I wasn't ready for the surprise before me as I flipped
them over. My wife-to-be was giving some nigga head. I continued to flip through the photos and saw my wife in every
position imaginable, doing tricks I had never seen. Then to
put the icing on the cake, she was doing these things with a
woman.

*I should call this bitch and check her trifling ass. Better yet, I
shouldn't even go home. I should just get with one of these groupies
and bring her to the crib then kick Danielle's ho ass out.*

I wasted no time calling Angel.

"Hello?" Angel answered in a sleepy tone, making me
aware of the time.

I was so wrapped up in the moment, I didn't even realize
it was after eleven p.m. on the West Coast, which meant it
was after two a.m. in Atlanta. "I'm so sorry for calling so
late, Angel. No disrespect."

"It's okay. What's wrong?"

"Damn! It's that bad, huh? This bitch really got me
fucked up."

"What happened, Richard?"

"The wedding's off, Angel."

"No, Richard, we can work this out. The wedding is next
week."

"Nah, shortie, it's a wrap."

"Are you still coming here tomorrow?" she asked.

"I dunno."

"Please still come. We can have lunch and talk about things. Maybe it's not as bad as it seems. Sleep on it, and we'll talk tomorrow."

Still not really in the mood, but wanting to have someone to discuss Danielle's deceit with, I agreed to meet with Angel the next day.

Normally I never participated in the after-game gatherings, but tonight I refused to return to a lonely hotel room and wallow in pity. I couldn't believe that bitch could be so dirty.

I called up my homeboy to see where niggas was hanging for the night. Not many people were out, but a few of the fellas was at one of the local strip clubs. As crazy as it may seem, I'd never gone to a strip club before, so I had no idea what to expect. I pulled up to the valet, took a deep breath and headed inside. I spotted my boys right away.

Excited to see me out, they called over every top-notch chick in the place. I had lap dance after lap dance and bottled water after bottled water.

What seemed like a gallon of water and a hundred chicks later, I was ready to roll. I hollered at my boys and headed to the hotel.

I checked my phone on the way. I had five missed calls and three messages all from Danielle, which was odd. Danielle was never the type to blow a nigga up. It was as though she knew what was up or something. Refusing to call her back, but interested in what she had to say, I listened to the messages.

First message. "Hey, baby. Great game tonight. Give me a call."

Second message. "Richard, I've called you several times and you won't answer. I hope everything is okay. Give me a call."

Third message. "Okay, this is ridiculous and not like you. What's going on? I'm going to sleep. I'll see you tomorrow. I hope you have a good excuse."

I laughed at the thought of this bitch actually having an attitude with me while I was holding pictures of her fucking some dude and a chick.

The next morning I woke up refreshed and eager to get back to Atlanta. Sleeping the whole flight through, I woke to the voice of the captain, "Flight attendants, prepare for arrival."

Angel had offered to pick me up from the airport. Normally this was something Danielle would do, but there was no way in hell I was calling that bitch.

"Hi, Richard," she sang as I walked up to the car.

"What up, Angel? Thanks for picking me up, *and* you were on the time."

"When have I ever let you down?"

Sad to say, she'd been there more than my own fucking girl. Just thinking about that made me remember the pictures.

"Did I say something wrong?" Angel asked.

"Just a lot on my mind. Where we headed?"

"This little Thai restaurant just outside the city. I figured we needed a small secluded spot."

"Perfect."

When we arrived at the restaurant and seated ourselves, Angel got right to business. "Okay," she said, "what's the deal? Are we having a wedding or not?"

"Damn! You right to it, huh?"

"No need to sugarcoat. You're a grown-ass man."

I loved her feistiness. She'd been that way since day one and I loved it. I laughed. "What? You want to fight?"

She smiled. "You'll lose."

My mind drifted as I gazed into her smile. I'd never noticed just how pretty her smile was until now.

"Hhhheeeellllloooooo, earth to Richard."

"What up?" I asked like I wasn't daydreaming.

"So what's the deal, Richard? We don't have much time."

"Aight, Angel, I'm just gonna put it out there. Danielle cheated on me. She had a more than freaky threesome, and I've got the pictures to prove it. There's no way out. The wedding is off."

Angel shook her head as I spoke.

"What is it, Angel?"

"Nothing."

I was sure by her expression that something was wrong. "Angel, talk to me."

"I wanted to tell you. I swear, I did."

"Tell me what, Angel? Come on, baby girl, you can talk to me."

"It's just that I feel so bad. I should've told you. I was being so selfish."

"Angel, listen to me." I grabbed her hands. "Whatever it is, you can tell me."

"I have to leave. The wedding is off. I'll send you your termination papers." She got up from the table and walked away.

I threw twenty dollars on the table and rushed behind her.

"Angel, wait up." I met her at the car.

She unlocked the door, and I got in.

I didn't say anything. I just rode with her as she drove to nowhere.

Fifteen minutes later, I finally spoke. "Turn there." I pointed to the Grand Hyatt on Peachtree.

After she pulled in, I ran in and got a hotel room and called her in.

We walked to the room in silence.

I opened the door and signaled for her to enter. "Make yourself comfortable. I come here all the time when I feel like I just need to get away from everything."

"Thank you. I feel so bad, Richard. Could you ever forgive me?"

"Forgive you for what? What is it, Angel?" I sat beside her on the bed and placed my arm around her neck, begging her to tell me.

"I knew she was cheating on you, but instead of telling you, I encouraged you to give her space. I gave you all the wrong advice. I've done this long enough to know when someone is cheating. I'm sorry." Angel began to cry, but her tears seemed to carry more pain than just this situation.

"Angel, it's okay. I know you're not telling me everything. I can see you have more pain inside. You want to talk about it?"

She forced out a grin. "You got all night?"

"Yes, I do." I smiled then pinched her cheek.

Angel went on to tell me how she'd been married for so many years and put her all into her husband who just turned his back on her one day and began to cheat. She felt even more guilt because she knew what it was like to be cheated on and yet did nothing when she knew Danielle was cheating on me.

"Angel, it's okay. I don't hold you responsible. I'm just sorry you had such a terrible experience. Your husband had to be crazy to leave such a wonderful woman like you." I hugged her.

"Thank you, Richard." She lay her head on my chest and sobbed.

Exhausted from all the events, I lay back on the pillows and pulled Angel beside me. I pulled her hair back and kissed her on her forehead. "Why couldn't you be my angel?"

To my surprise, Angel lifted her head and kissed me gently on the lips. Then she kissed me again, and again, and again.

I knew exactly what was about to happen, and I wanted it bad. I had no regrets as I removed her clothes piece by piece.

The next morning Angel and I ordered room service and had breakfast in bed. After breakfast, we showered together. Neither of us had any regrets as the day went on. Noon rolled around in the blink of an eye, and we had to depart. We'd decided not to call the wedding off. It would definitely be one to remember!

Chapter 70

Danielle

Here Comes the Bride

"What a beautiful bride," I said to myself, as I twirled in front of the mirror in my ten-thousand-dollar dress. I made it look worth every penny. The beaded hand-sewn pearls, pure as if they had been removed directly from the oyster and applied to my dress, covered the entire top, including the back of the bodice. The sheer sleeves had pearls sewn in the seams, going down my arm and around my wrists as well as the neck of the dress. The six-foot removable train was now gathered and clasped to the back of the dress, but it was the veil that really set things off. It was something I had seen on the cover of *Soap Opera Digest* while I was standing in line at the grocery store. The base was nothing but pearls, with layers of sheer made out of the exact material as the sheer on my dress. The designer made it and the veil an exact replica. I felt as though I was a star about to take a photo shoot for the cover of a magazine.

Richard had really outdone himself. I could just kiss the wedding planner he'd hired to put it all together. I couldn't have done a better job myself.

"It's time," a voice yelled from the other side of the door before it cracked open.

"Angel! What a surprise!" I exclaimed when I saw her walk through the door. I was beyond excited. "I didn't think you'd make it."

"Oh, I had to be here for this." She hugged me gently. She then held both of my hands in hers. "You look sooo beautiful. This will be the wedding of all weddings. I took a peek around the church before coming up, and the set-up is gorgeous."

I smiled. "You know I always aim for the best. You should see the layout of the reception. Girl, I'm talking ice sculptures, and we have an awesome dance troupe performing. Are you going to make the reception?"

"If you make it that far." Angel rolled her eyes.

"Excuse me?" I asked, confused by her sudden change in demeanor.

"I said, 'If you make it that far.' I'm sorry, I guess I'm still a little bitter about my divorce from John. Forgive me. This is your day. Enjoy, sweetie." She gave me a hug and made a quick exit, but not before turning to look at me over her shoulder and smile.

I turned and faced the mirror. Just then I heard the music begin to play. "All right, baby girl, it's show time."

I rushed to the ballroom door to make my grand entrance. Smiling and walking with my head high, I felt like a queen, as I walked down the aisle covered with rose petals. Richard stood there smiling as if this were an arranged marriage and it was his first time seeing his chosen bride.

Once at the altar, I placed my hands into Richards's.

The preacher proceeded with a few words. He then asked the question, "If there's anyone who objects to the marriage."

I felt as though one of those damn pearls from my gown

was stuck in my throat when I heard Richard begin to speak.

"I would like to make a statement before we go any further," he said, scaring the fuck out of me.

I whispered, "What the fuck are you doing?" I smiled to the gathering, trying not to seem too rattled. I silently repented for using foul language in a church.

Richard turned his head and nodded to his best man. His best man returned the nod, and exited the door to his left.

Everyone began whispering and chit-chatting, while the word *embarrassment* wasn't enough to describe my emotion.

A few seconds later, the best man rolled in a film projector. He then nodded to one of the ushers who was standing at the church doors. The next thing I knew, the lights dimmed, and a screen to my left and a screen to my right came on.

What the hell! My chest tightened and my heart began to race. The panic attacks were back. I was still trying to be a beautiful bride and a very little part of me was hoping for the best. I stood up straight and closed my eyes briefly to try to meditate on something positive in order to keep from falling over in a sweat.

All of a sudden, the guests roared with comments and gasps.

When I opened my eyes, I couldn't believe the sight before me.

"Oh my God!" I heard someone say.

"This is crazy!" another voice shouted from the back.

An older woman gasped. "I have never!"

I was just as shocked as the guests at what appeared on the screens—pictures from my threesome with Jonathan and Angel. I looked over at Richard, who was just standing there, shaking his head in disgust.

"Richard, please. That isn't me. Someone is trying to ruin our wedding day."

Richard, his eyes focused on the screen, didn't budge. It was as though I was talking to a brick wall.

People began to get up and leave, while the nosier ones stayed to see what would happen next.

"I guess the best still wasn't' good enough for you, Danielle." Richard gave me a look of disgust before walking off and leaving me standing there alone at the altar.

"Richard!" I yelled out one last time as the tears rolled from my eyes.

He turned around and looked at me.

"I'm pregnant. I'm having your baby." I knew if anything could make him reconsider, that would be it. I knew how important having a child was to him.

He shook his head and walked out the door.

The next few weeks were hell for me. I thought I had lived through hell before, but this time, the flames were even hotter. I'd fallen into a deep depression and all I wanted was to just die. The child growing inside my belly was the only thing that kept me alive. Otherwise, I would have committed suicide a long time ago. I might as well have been dead though. I had nothing more to look forward to.

I turned the phones off, cutting off all communication with the world. I had no desire to be a part of it and hadn't seen outdoors for days.

A knock at the door interrupted my daily swim in pity. I drug myself from the bed and opened the door without even looking through the peephole. Hell, at this point I could only hope for a crazed murderer to be standing outside my door.

"Come on, ma, you can do better than dis." Shawn stood on my doorstep and looked me over from head to toe.

"Fuck you! If you're here for money, I don't have none. I have no money, no job, no friends, no hope, and no one who even cares!" I said, trying to hide my tears.

"I care, baby girl. That's why I'm here."

"No, you don't. Fuck you, Shawn. This is all your fault anyway. You did this to me. You gave him those pictures. I know it was you, and don't you dare try to deny it. You ruined my life!" I began hitting him repeatedly in the chest. "You ruined my life, you bastard!"

He let me get a few licks off before he grabbed me by my wrist. He pushed me back as he kicked the door closed behind him with his foot. "Sit down and shut the fuck up." He pushed me down onto the couch and examined himself for bruises or scratches. "Now calm your happy ass down," he said, breathing heavily. "You did this to yo' gotdamn self. Look, Danielle, I just came to the *A* to get my loot, but when I got here I saw that I wasn't the only one out for you."

"What do you mean?" I asked.

"Dat bitch, Angel, is the one who set you up. She been plotting on you for the longest, and your dumb ass, fell right into her trap. Now I admit, I approached ol' girl just to see where her head was at and shit. I needed to let her know that my vendetta was bigger than hers and that she needed to fall back. But then she got to talking about how you ruined her life and shit, so I decided to let her get hers off too, you know, for closure. All that other shit was her idea. She gave me all that stuff, the pictures and everything, and paid me to give it to yo' man. I really wasn't down wit' dat, but I needed my loot so bad, I was down for whatever.

"I hoped dat ten grand would be able to hold shit down for a while, but I owe niggas and they are tired of excuses. I was desperate, ma. What it all boils down to is that it's either me or you. I could easily tell them you robbed them and put you under the fire, but I promised to handle things, ya feel me?"

I couldn't believe what Shawn was telling me. I respected him for telling me the truth, but I still knew that I had to keep him at arm's length.

"Damn! I had no idea." I got up from the couch and paced. "And just to think that I offered her ass a job, that I actually felt sorry for her. Well, ain't this a bitch?" I laughed.

"So what's the deal, Danielle? I still need the loot."

"Okay, Shawn. You want your money, you help me get Ceazia Devereaux, and I will get you every dime, I promise."

"Ceazia? *C.* Wifey of the late Vegas? You still after that bitch?" Shawn laughed, as if to say it was an impossible task.

Now I knew it wasn't an easy feat or I'd have long had her ass by now. "Yeah. Is that a problem?"

"Man, you should have been got that bitch. She was right here in the *A* with you. Dat bitch just moved back to VA."

That was all I needed to hear. I had to get out of Atlanta anyway and now I had motivation. "Okay, so let's do it, since it's so simple."

"You ain't said nothing but a word." Shawn grinned mischievously and extended his hand. "I hope you ready to ride or die, because this shit is 'bout to get real gangsta!"

I extended my hand, with a promise to keep it real as we set out on our mission to get Ceazia.